# MAMELUKE BATH

Andrew Asibong

*For Frank*

"Crawling at your feet," said the Gnat (Alice drew her feet back in some alarm), "you may observe a Bread-and-Butterfly. Its wings are thin slices of bread-and-butter, its body is a crust, and its head is a lump of sugar."

"And what does it live on?"

"Weak tea with cream in it."

A new difficulty came into Alice's head. "Supposing it couldn't find any?" she suggested.

"Then it would die, of course."

"But that must happen very often," Alice remarked thoughtfully.

"It always happens," said the Gnat.

—Lewis Carroll, *Through the Looking-Glass*
*(And What Alice Found There)*

# PART ONE
# ST. PAULY

# 1

My mother went to Iceland on New Year's morning. I tried to stop her from leaving, but she faced me off, lifting her skirts and baring her teeth.

"Don't stand in my way, Christie," she howled, blank eyes streaming cold grey tears. "I'm fifty-nine years old. It's my last stab at the real thing. And a northern wind is calling me."

Three months earlier she'd met a hulking Icelander named Jón, on an Internet site named NOR-DIKK. This was a social forum of sorts, aimed at *white-hot Scandinavians and their steamy Northern mates*. Furious, I'd protested: Iceland wasn't even a real part of Scandinavia! But my mother didn't care. She'd never been one to let details get in the way of a good ethnic fantasy. And besides, this was a question of roots.

Her own father was purportedly descended from Ulrik Christian Gyldenløve, an eighteenth-century Count of Samsø. Never having been lucky enough to meet this vaguely royal daddy, my mother had spent an entire lonely childhood dreaming of his fairytale Danish forebears. Her little-girl fancies were all the more heartbreaking for having played themselves out against the tawdry backdrop of crumbling, poverty-stricken Marseilles, where her own mother Leda, a deranged Alsatian waitress, had eventually settled. To her lifelong chagrin, my mother wasn't just depressingly proletarian, she was also garishly, unspeakably Gallic.

She'd fled north across the Channel on her eighteenth birthday, and had been drifting in and around England's East Midlands (and, briefly, its Peak District) ever since the early 1970s. It wasn't exactly the court of Christiania; but at least it wasn't France. It would do; at least until something better came along. For in her stubborn, frosted daydreams, my mother glowed with all the chilly radiance of Greta Garbo in blonde-face. And once my beastly father—himself as remote from Nordicity as it was possible for a human being to be—had at last abandoned us, I began to hear the ancestral snow-cry mumbling in her veins, stirring from its brief decade of zombified slumber. The mumbles turned into shrieks, each decade louder and more frenzied than the last, demanding what my mother's heart had always longed for more than life itself: the coming of an ice-man.

Jón had been living in St Pauly, the largest city in the East Midlands, just short of a year, dabbling as a DJ and recording artist in garage and dancehall. His ultimate goal was to bring what he called "a certain Viking rigour" to the dying days of the English grime scene. On his NOR-DIKK profile, he described his artistic vision as a fusion of Dizzee Rascal and Strindberg's *Ghost Sonata*. But by August he'd given up all hopes of transfiguring St Pauly's urban sounds, and was heading back to his native Iceland, to take over his aged father's fishing business in Höfn. About to turn forty (and having exhausted much of his volcanic island's eligible female population in punkish youth and young manhood), Jón was keen to go back home with a foreign bride in tow. If he and the woman could start a family together, so much the better. If not, they'd adopt three babies from Greenland.

Closer than ever to madness after forty English summers, my mother was ready to kill for a new life. She wanted renaissance and she wanted it now: the endless, wintry dreamtime that would allow her—at last!—to explore her mysterious septentronial heritage. She signed up to NOR-DIKK one Friday evening in September, after the wine-bar rhapsodising of one of the nameless office slatterns. The giggling secretary had shown my mother a picture of Freddy Ljungberg's Swedish cock in Calvins. After that, there was no stopping her. The next morning, quivering with excitement in front of our moribund iMac, she typed an obscene phrase into NOR-DIKK's search engine. There was no point being coy, after all, chuckled the webmasters. NOR-DIKKERS looking for an instantaneous match should state their preferences without shame! My mother might just as well have rubbed the genie's magic lamp. Jón's sexy 'Peer_Gyddy' profile popped up at once, a virtual frog prince in our own front room!

It was an abracadabra moment. My mother screamed with joy, drinking in the wonder of her own erotic conjuration. And so it was that Jón and Hélène found each other. It was like a slice of electronic hoodoo, or an ancient Norse saga. They concurred at the end of November that it was a love-match. But instead of grime boys or dancehall queens, a choir of snow-white Nordic voices were chosen to croon over the advent. They streamed nightly from Hélène's massive Sennheiser headphones (Jón's predictable first gift), an icy affliction, an endless procession of exclusively Scandinavian minstrels. Stina Nordenstam and Håkan Hellström, Marit Bergman and Lykke Li: these were the new hearth gods of our modest English home, a mocking, blond brood of pugnacious elves, musical progeny of the real Jón, an essentially conservative North Man, whose loquacious odes to blackness seemed to have vanished clean into cyberspace as suddenly and irrevocably as he himself had burst forth into the real world.

The soulless troupe of snow-pixies enjoyed a more intimate kinship with my mother than I could ever have dreamed. Throughout December, Hélène rolled madly on our sofa, clasping the silver headphones to her head, positively orgasmic in the ecstasy of her sudden Scandinavian belonging. These were her people. They'd finally come. And no matter how desperately I longed to join them, I was eventually forced to admit that, when all was said and sung, these musical Vikings would never, ever be mine. As for the whole "Afro-Nordic scene" which my mother, forever quoting Jón, had so breathlessly evoked at the start of the courtship in an attempt to reassure me, it was just so much nonsensical hot air, a multicultural fantasy dreamed up by the Vanilla Icelander in a vain attempt to sound post modern and hybrid and cool.

"Jón *gets* me, Christie," wailed my mother now, crumpled in a lachrymose heap at the kitchen door, her two Sugarcubes-themed suitcases quite exploded around her, and her skirt still hitched up at her waist. "He's my Zeus, my swan-god, my Venus as a boy. You can't give me what he does. It's just not in your genes."

And at that Hélène rose, smoothed her velvet skirt back over still shapely white legs and knee-high black boots, re-locked the two exploded suitcases, and walked out of our house forever. I didn't try to stop her. I didn't cry. My heart was broken, but there would be no second Troy.

I ambled, bogle-like, towards the kitchen, where broken pieces of crockery and handfuls of Hélène's dyed yellow hair still littered the blue-tiled floor. I boiled the kettle, oblivious to these alarming indices of my recent distress. Whatever had happened, she'd deserved it. All I needed to calm my nerves now was a strong, sweet cup of Tetleys. Luckily, a mug had survived the ice storm. I sat down at the table, gulping my tea, trying to ignore the family of white, hippo-like troll-creatures that danced around the mug (for it was one of my mother's beloved Finnish *Moomins* collection).

I had to think.

Fragments of china jagged into my feet and elbows, starting off moderate rivers of blood. I didn't care. I pondered one question, and one question only: not how I would find money to eat (spaghetti was still cheap, and I'd never been much interested in any food besides pasta) but rather how I would pay for the final year of my crippling studies. After all, these were austere times, as people never stopped repeating, fish-eyed and unreflective. I didn't give a damn. Austerity or no austerity, I had unspeakable things to say in this doctoral opus of mine. And my mother's fresh acts of betrayal had made me all the more determined to say them. Thatcher was nine months dead, but no revolutionary baby had slipped from her corpse as we watched the old witch burn. It was up to me. When the New Year snows began to melt, I started seeing Judd, twice a week, for *attachment therapy and counsel*, at his rooms in Mameluke Bath. I know I had no money. I know. But something had changed. My life had finally become unliveable. I needed some warmth and I needed some truth and I was prepared to die for just a moment to snap at the heels of either one of those hard-to-get bitches.

On a sunny Friday afternoon in late September, exactly a month after my thirty-ninth birthday, I arrived at the Master's office on the first floor of the North Wing at St Pauly University campus. I'd been summoned to discuss that most delicate of questions: the long-delayed payment of my tuition fees. Someone must have been briefing the Master on how to crush a louse humanely, for just seconds into our interview I noticed that his gaze—usually so cutting and aloof—today seeped a distaste that was almost moving in its restraint. As I read the requested one-page abstract that outlined my area of research, he peeped coyly over me, a look of mild confusion inflecting his botoxed visage. I glared back at him, trembling: let him dare accuse me of irrelevance.

"Talking animals," the Master repeated softly.

He beamed with compassion. I wanted to box his ears. Instead, I clutched my sweaty, scribbled abstract ever more tightly against my chest. To me, it was a grimoire.

The Master swallowed a snigger.

"What?" he coughed. "Like Danger Mouse? Garfield?"

"No," I muttered, already terribly weary. This interview was senseless. "As I've just explained to you, and as I've stated in my abstract, I intend to analyse the articulate animal in literature."

The stifled snigger became a smirk. Was this a sign for me to go on? I had less than nothing to lose.

"There are many, and they tell us something crucial. I want to find out what it is."

"I see."

He rocked back on his executive swivel chair, designer glasses pushed up on liver-spotted slap-head, skeletal fingers pressed together in vacant non-reflection. God, I hated him. What a slimy kaw-kaw, this grey-skinned, wraith-like provost! Even before floating, scum-like, to the top of St Pauly's bath water, he'd been a meat-headed cunt. And now he'd spied my fissure, smelt my guilt, slipped right in, and made himself at home. He grinned and slobbered inside me, his defenceless host, with all the sleazy cheer of a liberal democrat.

He still hadn't asked me to sit down. My throat and neck burned. And now the Master—Professor Brian Ferry, O.B.E.—began to lecture me about *the state we're in*.

"Forgive me, Christie. I don't mean to poke fun. But we must be sensible! You have every right to investigate the chatter of cartoon beasts. For that matter, you could train as—oh, I don't know!—as a voodoo specialist if you wanted to. But you don't have the right to ask taxpayers to fund such self-indulgence. Not in a time of austerity. You have to take personal responsibility for that kind of thing."

I remained silent.

"Your mother left you enough money to last you until when? The spring?"

I would not engage with such insulting abuse.

"And are you supplementing those funds with extra work?"

I would explain nothing to this hideous, Etonian bugulnoz.

"Are you considering all the job options? You can't afford to be picky."

I waited for him to hang himself with his own rope of neo-liberal moronism. It was too late for me now, anyway. All my ships had sailed.

"How much rent are you paying in town? Was that a wise move? It can't be cheap near Opoponax Gardens."

It was all I could do to stop myself from screaming out loud at his arrogance. Where the fuck did *he* live? A ghetto hovel?

"Christie, you've toed the line since Hélène moved to Iceland. Yes, you've been *truly humble*. You were always such an uppity little girl."

I flushed, brushing my sleeve across suddenly prickling eyes. The Master paid no attention.

"You've worked hard for St Pauly: the telephone fundraiser in February; those subjunctive tutorials over the summer; the admin work, the cleaning... Believe me, it's all been noted. It's all been noted."

"Thank you," I growled.

"Which is precisely why you've come this far. On loans, political correctness, large dollops of goodwill. But Christie: enough is enough! You've been working on this interminable thesis for three years now. And before that you did two M.A.s!"

"I'll take out another loan."

"You've taken out all the loans, Christie! There are no more loans."

"I'll do the subjunctive tutorials for free."

"Nobody wants the subjunctive tutorials, Christie! Nobody needs them."

I took a deep breath. I knew what I was doing.

"I'll feed the lice."

At this the Master raised his eyebrows and nodded approvingly.

A spontaneous game of rounders had broken out among undergraduates in the late September sun. Shouts of clear, upper-class enjoyment rose to office level, pouring cleanly through the open windows. The Master wiped his mouth and swivelled his chair around to gaze out at the sporting students. He seemed bewitched by their simple cries of fun.

And then—diminutive animated animal that I am—I let out a groan so forlorn that the Master jumped, and rolled back from the window with a little bleat of dismay. He looked at me and sighed as I approached the enormous desk, grasping each side of it with dripping hands. I was ready to play the only card I had left.

"When my mother left, Master," I began, trying in vain to connect with fleeing, unfocussed eyes, "you promised her I'd be taken care of. You told her I'd be safe till submission. Well, I'll submit this spring! And then I'll be gone! I'll get a post in America, at N.Y.U., at U.C.L.A.! They're crying out for people like me there. I'll be out of your hair; I'll leave St Pauly forev—"

The Master waved me silent.

"Your mother cared for you a great deal, Christie. I'm not sure you realise the sacrifices she made for your education."

Nine months after Hélène's traitorous New Year's Day flight (with not a peep from her since), I was beginning to lose patience with the ceaseless stream of St Pauly boggarts who never tired of telling me what a wonderful woman my mother had been. And if the Master was now going to pretend that she'd been fucking him all those years in his office on *my* account, well, he could just—

"The nicest secretary I've ever seen at St Pauly," he gasped. "In any department. It's hard...you don't..."

The old grey nuli's enthusiasm faltered momentarily for the building blocks of language. And then at last it came. The system-king's ultimate accolade:

"She was the most extraordinarily efficient administrator."

The Master shook his head and loosened his tie, splashing me indiscriminately with the sudden seepage of horny nostalgia. I dug my fingernails into my palm, hoping against hope that, no matter how unjustified my mother's saint-like legend, her former lover might perhaps now find himself so violently felled by the moment of erotic recollection that he would be moved to perform one last act of generosity.

But instead all he said was:

"It's remarkable how unlike Hélène you are. It's no surprise, of course, given the way your father was. I've seen the photos."

I unclenched my fists, and prepared to dissolve. It was all over for me now.

But wait: maybe something *had* changed. The Master seemed to have softened. He rose from his chair and stood in front of his desk, pink-shirted arms lightly folded. He smiled. I backed away, clasping my abstract even more religiously to my ever-tightening chest. The Master took a deep breath, removed his glasses and shut his eyes tightly in fervent concentration, as though about to recite a terrible prayer.

Then he spilled it:

"You are the daughter of the only woman I've ever loved, Christie, no matter how ashamed I am to admit that. And, no matter how little you resemble her, Hélène cared about you. She told me that time and again, in this office, lying naked on this desk, my seed trickling down her creamy thighs."

He absent-mindedly stroked the desk behind him, as if it were a favoured magical cat. And then he suddenly opened his pale eyes very wide onto my appalled and reddening face.

"Oh, how sweet! So you *do* change colour when you're moved! I'd always wondered. Listen, Christie: I'm going to give you one more chance. One more chance to prove your activities useful."

I squeaked with relief, launching into a torrent of heartfelt gratitude. But the Master held up his hand again.

"Not so fast, Christie! You're getting ahead of yourself! You always do."

What did this sinister moloch *want* from me?

I tried to imagine what it would feel like if he suddenly stuck two of his cold white fingers down into my bra, or lifted one of those tiny black leather feet up and into the crack of my skirt. I would deal with it! I would simply pretend that he wasn't a real person, that this was a dead man molesting me: a ghost. Hadn't I always known that some greasy-haired demon with dirty fingernails would sail in at the end of my thirties to defile me forever?

"Now don't worry, Christie," he chortled reassuringly. "It's nothing nasty. I just want to ask you two very important questions. The questions relate, in a sense, to the important issue of research ethics."

"Whatever," I said, wrong-footed.

"My first question is this. Are you listening carefully?"

"*Yes.*"

"Right then, here goes. What exactly do you give back to this society? To the community of St Pauly?"

"That's easy!" I all but sang. "I'm a responsible citizen! I write regular film reviews for the *St Pauly Piper*. I've volunteered at Crisis every Christmas for the past five years..." (I flushed with excitement as I prepared to deal him my ethical trump card, my *pièce de rèsistance*, the cherry of charitable goodness on top of the whole Big Society cake) "...and next Tuesday I shall take a taxi out beyond the Elysian Fields Estates to begin volunteer work as a Mentor to one of the new batch of asylum seekers!"

I beamed, waiting for the Master's cry of congratulation: after The Doctorate and Analysis with Judd, this was my Third Leap Forward.

But instead he looked quite shocked.

"Asylum seekers? Mentoring? Why on earth would you waste your time on such an asinine scheme? It's a wonder St Pauly Council's still got the funds for such bleeding-heart bunk."

I sighed. Of course I should never have hoped to convey the divine enthusiasm I'd conceived for the mentoring project. Not to this business-like ghoul. Already he looked as if he might be preparing to throw me out, all patience curdled, those misty-eyed memories of acrylic afternoons spent fucking my mother exhausted for today.

"Master, please! Your second question?"

"What?"

For the first time in our meeting he sounded irate.

I blundered on regardless.

"You had a second question for me. On research ethics? I'm sure I can give you the right answer, I'm sure I can!"

"Oh, you are, are you?"

He'd put his amused look back on again.

"All right, then, Miss Smithkin, riddle me this: of all your bestiary of 'literary' talking animals, which is your favourite?"

"Oh, that's easy!" I cried, delighted at such unexpected engagement. "It's Berganza!"

"And who, or what, pray tell, is Berganza?"

"Berganza is one of the two talking dogs in Cervantes' 'Colloquy of Dogs'," I explained breathlessly. "He wanders around seventeenth-century Spain, observing ordinary people: how they talk, how they live. Sometimes he intervenes: barks, bites. His mother was a witch, and *she* was the one who turned him from a boy into a dog. So in fact he's half-human (or fully human, really), but he's still a dog. A dog that can talk! He ends up working in the Hospital of the Resurrection, and that's where he tells his life story to another dog, Scipio. Scipio might be his long-lost brother, or he might just be his friend. A soldier who's dying of syphilis overhears the whole doggy dialogue and writes it all down."

"How completely bizarre!" cried the Master, clapping his hands in delight.

"Isn't it?" I replied, shoots of gratitude suddenly blooming in my heart.

The Master had just engaged with me. He'd asked me a serious question about something I genuinely felt to be real.

"And does this dog Berganza speak in English?" he went on, still palpably intrigued.

"Well, no. As I say, the story is by Cervantes, so the characters speak in Spanish."

"And can you speak Spanish, Christie?"

"Yes, I can! I got an 'A' at A-Level."

"*¡Muy bien!* And can you bark like a dog, Christie?"

"I'm sorry?"

"A simple question: Can you bark like a dog? Like your hero Berganza barked? When he wasn't busy chattering out his life-story in Spanish, presumably..."

"I didn't say he was my hero, I just happen to find his observ—"

"Answer the question, Christie."

"I already told you I'd feed the lice..."

The Master smiled.

"Perhaps, in due course, we shall ask you to make good on that generous offer. But, for now, I'd simply like you to bark like Berganza. If it's good enough to spend precious money researching, then it's good enough to put into practice. Or are you admitting now that your research is impractical?"

He was insane.

My mother had been fucking a complete lunatic since 2002. This same lunatic was one of the most influential men in the country. And he was commanding me to bark. If I wanted to have even a cat's chance in hell of being allowed to pursue my precious research, of finally becoming a doctor of philosophy, I would have to bark for a madman.

I barked.

Like no dog on earth, like no wolf, no quoll, I barked.

I howled and growled and woofed and whined.

Absent was the shame, the embarrassment, and the sheer vicarious cringe at how *weird* the Master's desire was. There was no point puzzling over it. When people try to reduce you to the level of beast, they invariably do so from a place of deep and inexplicable depravity.

Nor did I have time to wonder how I was going to explain my bestial acquiescence to my kind but judgmental head-doctor, Judd, the following week in Mameluke Bath. I'd figure that one out over the weekend.

So, I barked.

I don't know for how long.

And, as I began to drool great gobs of canine saliva I never even knew I had in me, all the way down my new burgundy H & M blouse, and even as far down as my Oxfam denim skirt, I could dimly make out the Master's gigantic, twitching shape. He nodded maniacally against the yellow haze, arms still tightly folded, as he danced and rocked on the massive wooden desk. For one brief moment I thought I saw him rub the area where his wrinkled penis must have lurked inside his trousers.

And then it was over.

The Master clambered down from the desk and returned to the executive swivel chair, its back now turned toward us, bored by our spectacle of humiliating intimacy. Looking out the window instead of sitting, he now seemed more interested in the game of rounders taking place outside on the lawn.

"All right, Christie," he snapped without facing me. "That's enough. You can have one more semester. I give you until February to submit your final thoughts on the ethics and aesthetics of Danger Mouse."

He sat down again and casually poured himself a glass of sparkling Mameluke Bath. The sight of that stuff has always made me want to heave. I noticed now that dozens of empty M.B. bottles littered the office: their ridiculous µlogo glowed fluorescent-green in every plush corner of the room. The Master turned his back on my involuntary retches: he was lost again in the game of rounders, and in the noisy slurping of gratuitously expensive Peak District spring water.

I picked up my briefcase and left the office without a word, clutching tightly at the abstract in my other hand. It was crumpled now, and predictably sweat-sodden, but it was intact. I bent down outside the door to slip it into my briefcase. Snapping the case shut I felt strangely victorious. The long queue of student-debtors that lined the corridor outside the Master's office (and stretched all the way down the interminable staircase leading to North Wing's exit) stared at me as one, incredulous, cow-like.

I strode proudly past them, my head held high in a cloud of triumph. What did they know about anything? They weren't as special as me. They weren't going to leave that building alive like me. And was even one of these pretentious wretches fortunate enough to have been granted a rendezvous, beyond the Elysian Fields Estates, that coming Tuesday with a desperate asylum-seeker by the name of Mukelenge Mambackou?

*I* decided to go to the Ethics department in East Wing to photocopy my library copy of *Femmes-félins et zoomorphes transculturels*. If I really was re-enrolled now, then I had the right to use the departmental photocopiers again. And I determined to put that hard-won right to use.

But as I scuttled past the administrators' half-closed

door (alas, Ethics still shared a floor with French, as well as two temperamental photocopiers), I fell straight into it: the inevitable woodland trap. Julie One's ratty, whining voice was shrieking out my name. It rang around the empty corridor, a solid prick of sonic vulgarity. And as I swung round to face them both, I sighed once again. Sliding my tongue down the filthy throat of the naked old witch from Room 237 would have been a less rancid, less *sickening* experience than starting a conversation with...

*(GROAN)*

...The Secretaries.

"Christie, love! So you're back among us."

The two Julies leaned out of the doorway, blue eyes open wide, identical half-smiles playing around painted pink lips as they cocked middle-aged blonde-and-grey heads—a bobbing pair of idiot cousins. I felt my face grow hot, and my palms begin their inevitable drip-drip-drip. They wouldn't ask me to shake hands with them. I could dispense with that particular worry.

But still the fluid ran. It didn't matter. The sheer idea of skin-contact still makes my hand-water come gushing out in streams. I gripped my briefcase more tightly still (all the while praying that the rivulets wouldn't actually spill from the soaking handle and onto the floor), and edged along the polished wood towards the two well-meaning women.

"Yes. They're letting me stay enrolled for writing-up. It's settled. They've agreed."

"Oh, that's *fantastic!*" said Julie One.

"You were writing something really good, Professor Thomson said," added Julie Two.

"Well, I still am writing it," I replied, a little haughtily. "And it's going to be paradigm-shifting."

"Paradigm-shifting?" repeated Julie One, as though seriously expecting me, an intellectual, to enter into a conversation about the ethico-political implications of my doctoral thesis with her: an aging slut *sans diplôme*.

"And what's your mum have to say about it?" Julie Two

butted in. "She was so pleased when you finally saw sense and came here to do the first M.A. To *her* French Department. Pleased as punch, she was. Like you was finally joining her family, she always said."

I decided to ignore this last remark. If my mother had seriously considered my doing an M.A. in the department where she had worked as a lowly secretary for the past twenty-five years as a final confirmation of our (at the best of times) disgusting and nebulous kinship, well, that said a lot about her fucked-up way of seeing things.

And anyway, I'd left French for Ethics a long time ago.

"I haven't heard from Hélène for a while," I said briskly. "She's—"

"I'll bet Hel's having a fab time. I mean: Iceland, for fuck's sake! Volcanoes! Black beaches! Lagoons! Beats St Pauly any day of the week."

The Julies beamed.

"Lucky cow. Is she staying much longer? What does he do, her young Viking?"

"He raps," I said impatiently, and turned around sharply, away from foolish forked tongues.

I pictured their outraged, low-caste faces in my mind's eye, and smirked.

*Well, of all the...!*

*Get her!*

*Who does she...?*

I continued my corridor-journey, still smirking, superior. I didn't creak. I didn't drip. I didn't look back once.

My supervisor, Professor Emmeline Thomson, was gliding serenely down the corridor towards me. A tiny old woman whose short, grey hair, mean expression and sagging face I didn't recognise accompanied her. The face exuded power, though: I knew that kind of face. The old woman clung onto Emmeline's arm like an angry, tyrannical child.

"Emmeline!" I cried down the hallway, unable to

contain myself.

(I really was excited.)

"It's all right! They're letting me stay on to write up! I've just cleared it with the Master!"

"Oh, Christie, I *am* glad!" called Emmeline to me.

(And she really did seem so.)

The two women eventually arrived at the spot where I had stopped to wait for them. The old woman tugged at Emmeline's arm, visibly annoyed at being detained in this way. I peered at her, before giving a little jump backwards. So this was—

"Christie, I'd like to introduce you to our new visiting professor: Madame Marianne Kollek," gasped Emmeline, redness seeping out in frightened streaks from her middle-class, academic face and dashing down nervously into her flabby, white neck.

Emmeline Thomson is my thesis supervisor, and I am grateful to her for a certain touching concern over the years. She even agreed to keep me on after my move from French to Ethics. But the truth is that she is a bland and cowardly woman. Rumour has it that she is in fact the first cousin of national treasure Dame Emma Thompson (she dropped the 'p' in 1996 in a laughable gesture of false humility), but that is surely the only interesting thing about her. I gazed in pity at her pink, shapeless, terrified form. So different from the dark, lean, truthful shadow I myself cut. I'd often wondered what she thought of me, really. She must have first seen me tiptoeing along this spooky corridor when I was all of nine years old, thirty years earlier, ten paces behind Hélène on her first day at work. A little brown shadow and a head of hard, black plaits.

"Of course," I said, with hypocritical respect. *"Enchantée, Madame."*

But Marianne Kollek didn't appear to have registered that I was even there, engaged in a conversation of equals with her bumbling academic guide.

"We're terribly lucky to be hosting a star like

Marianne," Emmeline went on, more embarrassed now than ever. "This could mean the difference between staying open or shutting down for the School of Humanities. In the long run, I mean."

I nodded politely. I had just enough self-possession to refrain from observing that if it was still buying Marianne Kollek's shit-for-brains, vulva-based 'water-feminism' today, forty years after the strange fad's brief hour in the early 1970s Left Bank sun, then perhaps the School of Humanities didn't actually deserve to be saved. I wondered if Kollek had brought her brigade of Swiss 'water-women' with her. It was said that they followed her from institution to increasingly obscure institution, her sisters in aqueous-feminine nomadism. And while I could understand the allure of Stanford or Berkeley, the idea that these wretched liquid-acolytes would up stakes and move to St Pauly, England for three years, just to follow this intellectually impoverished, anachronistic charlatan—well it was just too silly for words.

"Christie is one of my many doctoral students," explained Emmeline to a visibly uninterested Marianne Kollek. "She's working on something very promising. I think you actually met Christie's mother on your brief visit last year, Marianne. Do you remember the French administrator? Hélène Larsen? One of the finest secretaries our department has ever been lucky enough to have at its disposal."

And on she burbled and blustered and ran, enthusing and exclaiming about my animal-project and my charming, loyal mother, amid an unending stream of creamy middle-class platitudes. But Marianne Kollek, who was busy inspecting a mark on one of her ugly black pumps, finally snapped, straightened up, and gave a violent yank at Emmeline's sleeve.

"*Cette négresse m'ennuie!*" she yelled.

As the two women scurried past me down the corridor towards whatever moist meetings and dewy discoveries they had planned on campus for this crucial pre-term Friday, I saw Emmeline's head twist back briefly in my direction. For an instant it shuddered in its socket, mortified, apologetic.

# II

*I* shuffled, depressed, through the Damascus Shopping Centre's huge automatic doors, like one of George A. Romero's living-dead ghouls, or one of those dancing Harlem zombies from *Thriller*. I wasn't moon-walking; just shuffling.

The crowded lakeside banks of the university campus hadn't been the best place to try to calm down. A coterie of blonde, South African exchange students and an *awful* tanned, Home Counties chicken-youth wouldn't stop squawking no matter the daggers I gave them. Why on earth did they want to study in the East Midlands anyway? I'd had to gather my things together and clear the hell out of there, on the first bus bound for St Pauly city centre.

I couldn't go home; it was still too early. The sun was still out.

So I wound up in the Damascus Shopping Centre.

That's where I wound up, generally, when I felt this wretched. I liked to keep watch just outside the toilets on the third floor. The men who accumulated around the 'gents' just looked so desperate, so *sad*. It made me feel saner. Compared to these half-crazed, sexually maladjusted monsters, I felt as if I actually had some control over my life.

On this particular late Friday afternoon in September, however, there seemed to be surprisingly little toilet traffic. I sat down on the bench between the two genders and waited.

I had time.

I began to go through the contents of my bag, extracting each of the day's acquisitions, one by one, for desperately hopeful inspection. And, at last, right at the very bottom, I found the brown envelope that St Pauly Council had finally sent me that morning: the envelope containing the details of Mukelenge Mambackou.

I'd heard about the asylum seeker mentoring scheme from Emmeline Thomson, of all people. Her facetious ginger brother-in-law had begun "helping out" a young woman from Mali, and was apparently finding the whole experience "really deep, Emmie". And although I'd laughed long and loud to myself at the idea of Emmeline's pompous cunt of a kinsman trying his impotent luck on a poor young African maiden fleeing persecution, that night I was visited by a terrifyingly earnest vision. In the vision I saw *myself* in the city centre, on a bustling Saturday morning, keeping a brunch-time rendezvous in Muriel's Tearoom with that very same African maiden! *I* was the one showing young Salimata (or Angélique, or Mathilde) the sights and sounds of St Pauly, not Emmeline's cretinous brother-in-law! *I* was the one helpfully explaining contemporary East Midlands life in all its banal and gory detail! How sublime that vision was, and how it made me shiver with the sensation of an authoritative, indisputable Englishness! And as I'd skim-read the details of the new asylum bill, I'd become aware of the series of tiny "tsks!" escaping my pursed and privileged lips, each one accompanied by the same predictable gasp of "disgusting!"

So they were letting only five hundred a year past customs now.

The poor wretches who made it to Stage II were penned indefinitely in centres on the coast, like so many cattle.

The Mentoring Scheme was for the lucky few who made it to Stage III: they were allowed to enter cities, and to move with supervised freedom, provided they kept the bright grey 'A' badge pinned to their person at all times.

And the only way of guaranteeing consideration of their asylum application in the first place, no matter what their circumstances, was to sign a form consenting to a six-month period of concentrated lice feeding.

My sympathy was boundless. I would find meaning in protecting these tragic people. Protecting them as I myself had never been protected.

But now, five months later, as I sat outside the Damascus Centre loos, clutching St Pauly council's big, brown envelope, the prospect of my upcoming Tuesday meeting with the Category III asylum seeker Mukelenge Mambackou at the much-discussed Lionheart Complex seemed only to intensify the anxiety that had so obviously set in for this late September weekend. Gone for good, those April flights of philanthropic fancy. I wasn't going to be able to help this 'Mukelenge' character. I couldn't even help myself! Did I honestly think I could cure my own cancer of the soul by befriending a just-arrived wretch who had the misfortune to be even more of an alien than me? Could friendship with a faceless African really cure me of my own ironic negrophobia? I was pathetic.

Judd would laugh—and he'd be right to. His mocking, up and down, pseudo-Caribbean gaiety always rattled around my brain the moment I opened my eyes.

"These quasi-ethical...*schemes*, Christie...These Caulfield-esque *positions*...they are truly...*quixotic*! You'll do anything to scramble from your feelings, to preserve—and at any cost!—that appalling..." (he'd hover for nine beats before descending, jaws wide open, on the perfect psycho-therapeutic putdown) "...that *futile* MOCK-DIGNITY."

Sometimes I wondered why I carried on seeing Judd. Sometimes I listened to his tired stream of Freudian mumbo-jumbo, and wanted to laugh in his face. What platitudinous bullshit he was capable of spouting! I hated having to get the train to Mameluke Bath for our sessions each week, even though Judd always insisted that the old associations of my past would intensify the treatment. But it was too expensive, too upsetting, and full of the same scary bikers of my childhood. And the bottom line was simple: *it wasn't helping*. Maybe I only put myself through it because Judd was...well...what he was. Maybe I was just sucking on his psychoanalytic joint in the hope of some swarthy paternal approbation. And all for what? I blew no smoke for New Dark Daddy.

No.

No.

Mukelenge Mambackou would be my last chance for renaissance.

The original benevolent doll-uncle, I could cultivate him, plant-like, in my spare time, and for free. He would be my own private golem, raised from mud and summoned, by conjuration, to provide a design for life and a reason for living. I smiled, elated. I was going to rescue old Uncle Mukelenge. And old Uncle Mukelenge was going to rescue me.

I felt the salty, tingling sensation pricking into my nasal passages and under my eyes, and then, immediately, the tears began to spill out, more of them than I could possibly have prepared for, a veritable flood. Before I knew it, they were dripping onto my jaw. I began to wipe fiercely at my face with my sleeve, getting ready to carry out a furtive scan in case anyone from the university might have seen me.

And that was when I crashed violently to my knees on the filthy mall floor. Someone (something?) had literally *flown* past me out of the men's toilets, pushing me off my bench and onto the ground. I hadn't had a chance to catch even a glimpse of the entity, which had vanished into thin air by the time I was able to rise, groaning and exclaiming, from the litter-strewn mire. How was I going to explain this one to Judd? It was turning into a day of unspeakable non-sequiturs.

I didn't have the energy to get back onto my bench straightaway. Instead I sank onto the floor in front of the toilet door, my photocopies strewn before me, adrift in a welter of chaos and biting resentment. My black tights (so it really *had* happened, I exclaimed with a cry of disgust, as I removed them that night in my bedroom) were laddered in three different places.

I sprang up at last and pushed my way angrily into the toilet. At least I could wash off the worst of the floor grime there. I don't think it had occurred to me that—this being the right-hand door, clearly emblazoned with the universal symbol of masculinity—I, as a mere female, was technically denied entry. That sort of prohibition has never really cut it with me.

A panic-stricken man-boy stood at the automatic hand dryer, half-bent, his little bottom jutting out behind him slightly, utterly absorbed in the ritual act of hot air cleansing. He didn't appear to see me (no one ever did!). He seemed concerned only with drying (or simply heating?) his face, and clung onto the machine's knob as if it were a life-giving nipple. The air streamed up to his grateful, bobbing head (I could almost see the infra-red glow), making a crowd of lovely dark strands stand up in a shock of cartoonish pleasure. I wished my own hair would rise like that when the wind or warm air blew on it. It always just hung, ironed and stiff, like a doll's. But this man-boy, this creature who hovered before me now at the automatic hand dryer, was so *good* looking, his freckles so alluring, the flames that seemed to spring off his electric crown so real, so innocent, so pure, that he made me want to curl up and die. My cheeks flushed dark with envy and grief.

"Excuse me," I began.

He turned to face me now, green eyes open wide in a kind of childish terror, as he watched me struggling to find my words. I couldn't find them, of course, I couldn't, because staring now at this pretty revenant was filling me with an oceanic fear, a sensation as overwhelming as the north wind itself. His trendy garments clung to him like holy armour: dark blue baggy Levi jeans (out of which poked the white beginnings of a pair of Calvin boxers), tight red 'Mr Happy' t-shirt (from which an inhuman yellow 'happy-face' grinned one-dimensionally at me, empty eyes turned upward to heaven), and emerald-green Adidas tracksuit top (which the man-boy pulled tightly around him now, as if he'd been suddenly invaded by ice).

I tried again.

"Did you see? Did you? That...that thing?"

The youth gaped at me, goggle-eyed. And then two thin trickles of blood began to stream from his lovely Roman nose. They cascaded down his mouth and chin in vaguely parallel trajectories, before dribbling loudly onto the tiled floor, where they instantly began to flow towards me. To make my confusion worse, now I could hear the mewling voice of Robbie Williams there in the toilet with us, shrieking out its tired old 'Angels' clichés. The man-boy lingered just a fraction of a second longer, wiped some of the blood from his face with the back of his hand, started to say something but instead emitted a kind of rasping, growling squeak, then, leaping over the blood-pools that he himself had created, scuttled past me and dashed like a mad thing through the swinging toilet doors.

I ran immediately after him. But he was never going to stop for me, not even a backwards glance. I watched him disappear down the escalator, doubtless on the tail of the violent jumbee that had preceded him just minutes earlier.

And as I hauled my exhausted body back onto its bench, my heart thudding more painfully even than it had in East Wing corridor that afternoon after Marianne

Kollek's insult, I felt, for the first time since I'd been coming here to the Damascus Centre toilets, that it was I, not any of the men I'd 'caught out' that day, who was perhaps beginning to lose it. For as hard as I tried, throughout that lonely Friday evening, and all through Saturday and Sunday and Monday, I couldn't shake the very real conviction (and, on this, Judd would simply have to take my deadly earnest word) that the dark-haired, wide-eyed man-boy who'd scrambled past me in the toilets that afternoon was no human—no living one in any case. All I could say of him for certain was that he was a creature, a kindly creature to be sure, but close to dead, and already sporting a shabby, crumpled pair of custard-cream wings.

*I* don't know how long I'd been sitting in the Opoponax Gardens, but as a skeletal whippet sniffed at my foot I suddenly realised that both my legs had given up the ghost.

"Sorry, duck!" said the young shell-suited girl, pulling the mournful grey animal away from me, and leading it up towards the wooded section of the Gardens where they'd recently installed the medieval bestiary.

Was I losing my mind? Had I really just seen a demon and an angel fly out of the men's toilets at the Damascus Shopping Centre? That was certainly what it had looked like at the time. But to cling to the belief that one has had a brush with the occult several hours after the alleged experience is over—surely that is to give in to lunacy. In all likelihood, what I had seen was the aftermath of some sort of tedious punch-up between two repulsive cottagers. I'd read about this kind of thing in *Last Exit to Brooklyn*. The 'demon' had treated the 'angel' too roughly in the course of their toilet-stall fellatio; a face had been slapped, some hair had been pulled, and I had merely witnessed the banal postscript to the whole sordid altercation. I was forever turning the blandest of realities into gothico-romantic mysteries! I'd been doing it ever since I was a little girl. Could I even be sure that my disgusting encounters today with the Master and Marianne Kollek had been real? For all I knew I really *was* just drifting through one long, bad dream, a paranoid-schizophrenic nightmare that had lasted precisely twenty days, seven months and thirty-nine years.

I had to go home. My belly was churning. Beelzebub had just been granted asylum in there, and he'd invited all his friends round to celebrate the good news. At least six different pains stalked around in effervescent rivalry now, each one refusing to be identified with the others, each one jostling for first place. I wanted to cry. And I could only do that at home. I wanted to scream. And I could only do that at home.

As I let myself into the building I kicked over a pile of envelopes lying on the mat. So the post had finally been delivered, after months of fruitless struggles and strikes. I dropped down listlessly to my knees, which crackled and snapped in protest. Everything was for Richard and Judy upstairs (nice kids, if vacant: nurses at the pet centre up in Piperville). No, wait... There *was* something for me. A big, pink envelope, stinking of cheap perfume, and addressed to one "Ms Pinky Smithkin, M.A x 2.". Even without the Viking stamp and Icelandic postmark, even without looking at those insane swirls of green ink, I knew it was from Hélène. She *always* used pink paper for me.

I hauled myself up the stairs, let myself into my hole, and boiled myself a cup of strong, sugary Tetleys.

And then I sat down at the kitchen table to rip the thing open. It was a card, as I'd anticipated by the texture. She'd made it herself. On the front she'd glued a postcard of a curtseying, dog-headed man with a bare torso. Had they honeymooned in Egypt, then? A single red candle was balanced on each of the creature's powerful shoulders, while on its monstrous head and ears sat a crown of sickly-looking yellow flowers. Above the absurd Anubis she'd stuck a string of individually ripped-out letters culled from a variety of newspapers and magazines. The letters spelled out, with Hélène's characteristic blend of simultaneously tacky and terrifying insouciance, the old lie:

*THINKING OF YOU!*

I flipped the card open, trembling with rage and nostalgia. The crazy green ink was splattered like hieroglyphic vomit all over both sides, the script so tiny as to be practically illegible.

*Dearest Pinky*

*Just a quick one to tell you that we're <u>thinking of you</u>. :)*

*All is well with us. Jón has shown me every nook and cranny of this incredible volcanic island. And I'm in love with his village of Höfn in a way I've never loved a really tiny place. Not unless you count the early days of Mameluke Bath. And why would you want to do a thing like that? LOL*

*The local people (or Hornafjarðarbær, to give them their proper name) are earthly gods of hospitality. I am treated like a queen here, and feast daily on the local delicacies (herring, capelin, bacaloa) until I can take no more. In the first week of July we had the annual Humarhátíð, or lobster festival. I thought my mouth would melt from the ecstasies taking place inside it!*

*We live by the ocean, you see. Sometimes, during the night, I creep out of bed, as quiet as a mouse. (It would be unfair to wake Jón, who has to get up very early to fish.) I tiptoe down on my own to the beach. I sit on the sand and cock my head at the crashing waves, trying to take in the vast force that roars at me. Sometimes I find I'm simply unable to process the fact of all this perfection, and I laugh out loud for pure joy.*

*Puffins and skuas circle just above my head, cawing, while the guillemots and fulmars perch on the rocks at my side, staring at me uncertainly.*

*My spoken Icelandic is getting impressive. My mother-in-law Júlíana sings ancient Norse sea shanties with me every day. She's a patient woman. She's terribly pretty too, and she loves me like a daughter, even though we're almost exactly the same age. Every day she asks me when I think I'll fall pregnant. I smile, take her hands in mine, and say: "When our lady Freyja wills it, mother!" and Júlíana laughs and laughs.*

*Oh, Pinky, I know you'll think this is silly, but I feel so much more in touch with myself here! In the North, I mean: the Septentrion. It's so much closer to where I'm really from—in my heart, I mean, in my Helen-soul. This is where I'm staying. This is my home. You can't just write off your strong half! I can't change the fact that half of me—the strong half!—is Danish. No more than you can change the truth that half of you— the strong half!—is Black. Things like this rule us more than we can know.*

*I thought of you yesterday. That's why I decided to send you this card. We were day-tripping at the Great Geysir, which is also in the south of the island. And I was really FEELING that Björk line, you know the one from Bachelorette? The sun was in my mouth, and I really was a fountain of blood.*

*Anyhow, there we were, me and Jón, breathless and trembling at every steaming eruption (don't worry, we kept a safe distance). Then who do you think I notice jumping up and down and singing on the black rocks behind us? You'll never guess. It was the Divine*

*Agnetha! The Divine Agnetha, en vacances in Iceland's Golden Circle, and at the same flipping time as us!*

*She ran like a startled fawn when I screamed, but we finally managed to grab a-hold of her and get her to keep still. And then I told her everything. How Dancing Queen split my soul in two that summer night in '76. All about that hare-brained Marseille-Glasgow weekender I forced us on in '81, just because I was haunted by Super Trouper's opening verse. She listened to me, Pinky. She gave me her ear. And you know what happens when someone gives me their ear? When they open the hole up fully, I mean? Well, you of all people know it's true: that ear is mine for life. I told Agnetha the story of my own Peak District Waterloo. Me and your daddy: the passion, the racism, the struggle. She just couldn't stop crying. I showed her the photos. He'd've made a remarkable Duke of Wellington when he was young, you know, your daddy Mickle. With a black-face, quoi. :)*

*When it was over I rolled us each a nice little clope, and what do you know but Jón had taken this most amazing Polaroid.*

*Ég ást Þú!*

*Mamma and Jón*

On the back of the revolting pink card she'd stapled the photograph of a blonde woman perched on a crumbling black rock. She certainly seemed to resemble an aging Agnetha Fältskog, yellow-grey Swedish mane elegantly swept back over her shoulders, black blouse and zebra-striped shorts looking good on her, despite her advancing years. My mother stood behind her, somewhat leather-skinned, in Posh Spice sunglasses, a curious Breton vest and short white pleated skirt, long arms draped around Agnetha's delicate frame. Hélène's own artificial blonde locks flew in the Icelandic wind.

In the top-left corner of the photo was scrawled in the same green ink:

*To Pinky: Here's to knowing both of us! Love and hugs——Agnetha.*

I don't know how much time had passed, but when I was finally able to unclench all the veins and muscles in my face and neck, my tea was stone cold. I'd been rigid for a good while, then—taut and tight and stringy, trapped in a fixed, open-mouthed cringe of old-school, Edvard Munch horror. My two empty eyes gazed blackly out of their smeary first-floor window and down into Old Saul's graveyard below.

I closed my eyes.

But instead of the warm, reassuring darkness I expected, I found myself adrift in a sickening milky dazzle. I flicked my eyes open again, terrified. Why had it gone so bright inside? I stared back out of the window. But it was exactly the same out on the street as it was behind my lactified eyelids. The dazzling, creamy emulsion was still there, unchanged, as sparkling and thick as it had been a few seconds earlier, like endless shrouds of snow. I closed my eyes—opened them—heard a fly buzz—closed them again. And that was when I realised, when it finally struck. The world around me, behind my eyelids and in front of them too, had become enveloped in a thick wax fog of blinding, choking whiteness.

# III

*I* left my flat on Old Saul Street on Tuesday evening at exactly five p.m. and headed south along the left-hand side of the noisy tram-track, away from Piperville towards the Damascus Centre bus station. The twenty-minute, chatter-tooth, stand-up wait at the overcrowded shelter could have been worse, I suppose. I might not have had an 'iMu' for distraction (I wasn't even sure what one was, exactly), but at least I'd remembered my latest charity shop acquisition: a barely-touched, New Virago edition of *Quicksand*, which helped the purgatorial minutes under the shelter slip away somewhat less distastefully despite the general gloominess of Helga Crane's Deep South travails.

All the same, I was shattered. From Friday to Monday I'd been plagued by dreams of Marianne Kollek. Each time the sleepy visions were identical, and each time they started up in the third part of the night. In the dream I would step out from the photocopying room and into the corridor (less eerie now, almost good), my heart singing, self-esteem growing fresh autumnal shoots of hope. I'd saunter down the hallway, skipping a little, safe in the knowledge that, whatever happened, I would always prove stronger than my tormentors. And that was when Marianne Kollek would creep up behind me like a tiny female bluecap, touch me on the shoulder, and gaze into my terrified, tear-filled eyes, a look of genuine amusement breaking out across her wrinkled, sagging face.

I eventually managed to board the number 82 headed east out of St Pauly centre. The bus was full to bursting, of course, and for the entire fifteen-minute duration of the city-to-Elysian Fields stretch I found myself squashed against the front luggage rack like one of those literally one-dimensional cartoon animals that has somehow survived its own violent death by flattening. Other passengers seemed to enjoy more space than me, somehow. On my right, nearest the driver, towered an ancient, tree-like woman dressed in a long, shiny, khaki-coloured mackintosh, who stood avidly reading the October issue of *Attitude*. Yet again, Prince Harry, wearing only a swastika medallion and what had by then already become his trademark black rubber swimming trunks, posed spread-eagled on its lurid cover. To my left wriggled a tiny, malnourished youth, dirty blond and clad in a purple Nike shell-suit and predictable gold chain. He wasn't reading anything, of course, but instead bopped absurdly to the sound of his purple iMu. I recognised snatches of the worst kind of commercialized hip-hop. Every few seconds the scurvy teenage bugul-noz stared impertinently up at me, each time the same mocking, toothless grin spreading out over his acne-scarred face. He stank of chicken.

We three were the only ones to descend at Elysian Fields Estates. But although we'd staggered off the vehicle in superficially equal states of separation, it became quickly apparent that the old woman and the young boy were in fact 'together'. The boo-hag tore the ridiculous novelty iMu from the tiny bugbear's ears, tossed it (still tweeting the irritating refrain of Jay-Z's 'Girls, Girls, Girls') into her khaki-coloured handbag and enveloped his minuscule head under her left arm in a rugby-style embrace which I struggled to interpret as either affectionate or hostile. And as the strange couple stumbled together along the dirt track in front of me, engrossed in the exchange of irate, melodramatic whispers about the nature and communication of 'respect', it suddenly occurred to me that they might be well placed to advise me as to the precise location of the Lionheart Complex.

The building was so new that it couldn't as yet be found in any existing A-Z of St Pauly. And the mumbling pastry at the council had been terribly vague. I had naively assumed that perhaps the Complex towers would be visible from a cursory glance around, upon alighting at the Elysian Fields Estates bus stop. So much had been made in the local press of their ivory gleam. But about me I saw only a wasteland of murk and gloom. I looked at my watch. It was already twenty past six. Mukelenge would think that I'd forgotten him. I lunged at the tree-woman.

"Excuse me—"

"What do you want?" she shouted, swinging around to face me with such enmity that I literally shrank backwards in fear. The bugbear tittered. The boo-hag harrumphed, turned around and continued on her way.

"Come *on!*" she yelled at the imp, who was still staring at me in amused wonder.

"I'm sorry," I called after her rapidly disappearing silhouette. "I'm really very sorry, but I'm lost. I'm looking for the Lionheart Complex."

"You're right under it!" I thought I heard her mutter.

"What did she say?" I begged the little lutin, who remained still, sitting on the muddy ground before me now, spotty moon-face upturned and laughing hysterically.

"She *said,*" screamed the old banshee, who had miraculously returned and now stood less than an inch to my right (pale, veiny lips spewing out hot, yellow bile at me as if I were the assassin of the oldest and most beloved of her seven tortoiseshell cats) "you're standing right

UNDER it. There! LOOK! That's what *she* said."

The tiny bugbear, literally yowling with mirth now, sprang up, turned on his purple Nike heel, and gambolled off into the darkness. The boo-hag snorted, glared, spat, and chased after her mischievous charge, muttering gruesome threats to the rising wind.

And as I turned to appraise the skies above my head I discovered, with an embarrassed giggle, that the tree-witch was right. Towering above me, so close that I'd failed to notice it in my initial survey, stood an edifice resembling a sort of high-tech lighthouse, from the top of which shone, every thirty seconds or so, a bright pink light. Was this the asylum that launched a thousand rafts, precarious resting place of the totality of Category III Seekers in the whole of Great Britain? It seemed improbable. I nevertheless approached the base of the column, which, as I got nearer, revealed itself to be far wider than I'd anticipated, constructed entirely of one huge, circular, glass panel, which slid open obligingly as soon as I stood within five metres.

I stepped through the opening.

I found myself in a space resembling a ghostly hotel lobby. Its various surfaces and furnishings and attachments gleamed with unwholesome cocaine whiteness. I felt as if I'd tiptoed into the monochrome antechamber of some glamorously post-modern death-camp.

A tiny, middle-aged, bird-like woman, wearing thick white horn-rimmed glasses and a spotless nurse's uniform, rose from the reception desk to greet me with a bright white Stepford smile.

"Visitor or relative?" she asked in dulcet Caribbean tones, not unlike those of Judd.

"Sorry?" My voice was sharp and anxious. "Oh, visitor. For Mukelenge Mambackou?"

"Organic friend or council-recruited mentor?" she inquired in the same bland, purring drone.

"Oh, council-recruited mentor. We were finally paired

last week. They wrote me a letter. Here."

I fumbled in my handbag for the appropriate validation of my apparently unexpected presence.

"How odd!" exclaimed the nurse now, whipping a clipboard from under her arm and scrutinising the list in front of her. "How very curious!"

"Oh?" I said, fighting the panic that now started to come bounding back out of my bowels. "Why is that curious?"

"Well, because...hmm. Be-*cause*..." She tailed off, her mind clearly elsewhere.

She murmured at me distractedly now, stretching the words out in an absurdly slow manner, like a 45 record slowed down to 33 rpm, still peering in optimistic bewilderment at the list, as if sudden revelation might perhaps leap out at her at any moment.

"Because," (her voice sped up again to normal speed now as she returned to post-automaton life) "Mr Mambackou already *has* a council-recruited mentor!"

"Oh?"

My heart sank. I felt as if I might sink abruptly to my knees in front of this idiotic Jamaican nursemaid; weep hot tears of disappointment and rage into her obliging, hygienic crotch.

"Yes! Nice young lad just arrived to see Mukelenge not one hour ago. White boy from Islands in the Sun, you know, the West Indian old folks' home up Piperville way?"

Before I could gather the words together to formulate the obvious next question, she was already blathering on.

"But that don't mean he can't have two! Yes, yes, why *not* two? Most likely doublin' up's goin' to be the norm soon anyways. Everyone wants a piece of the mentor-pie in St Pauly City these days! More mentors than seekers! That's what they've been sayin'! Madness!"

The nurse removed her glasses, wiped them absent-mindedly with her sleeve, and shook her head, eyes glazed over completely now as she gazed, chortling, into the middle distance. I wondered if she might perhaps have forgotten my presence entirely. I waited thirty seconds, just to be polite, then loudly cleared my throat. The nurse continued to wipe her glasses and chuckle, still conversing with ghosts I couldn't see, still shaking her head in disbelief at nothing in particular.

At the thirty-ninth second I put my face next to hers, and bellowed with impatient rage: "So where should I *go?*"

"Where should I *go?*"

"Where should I *go?*"

My shrill voice reverberated hysterically around the snow-lobby, shrieking out the tedious question of a rootless Echo in perennial shit-brown flight.

The interior of the lift was as shiny and new as the lobby, but instead of the bright white surfaces of the base, here in the silent cylindrical box of speedy ascent could be found only pure mirror. Catching sight of my reflection, I saw my face unfeasibly anxious and drawn.

"Drawn Dawn!" I muttered at the mirror with a strange, mechanical giggle.

But I cut my laughter short as I noticed how the lines themselves tore into my vulnerable cheeks and eyeballs. What would Hélène say if she ever returned to behold the sour old maid that pretty Pinky was so rapidly turning into?

I stopped the lift at every other floor for a rapid peep through the doors. Each landing looked identical: a tube-shaped white hall (white stone walls, white tiled floor), around which were lined seven heavy-duty metal doors. The Lionheart Complex seemed stillborn, a twisted abortionist's changeling. Who else could have conceived of such a perfect Spartan synthesis of health spa and lunatic asylum? I wondered how they managed to keep it so pristine. But then I remembered the plaudits the government had quickly won for the only briefly controversial Category III Self-Sanitizing Plan. Of course the seekers would go along with the daily exfoliating scrub! Given how difficult it was to be admitted to Category III without being shipped back home to certain death (or disappearing without a trace in one of the Category II camps on the coast), they were hardly going to spoil their chances of making it to the end once they had come this far, were they?

But where on earth were these self-sufficient guests? Not a soul seemed to be roaming the floors of the Lionheart Complex. I couldn't glean the faintest tinkle. I supposed that it was feasible that most of the current crop of seekers were out exploring St Pauly and its environs. They couldn't have been here very long after all, and it must have felt sort of thrilling to finally have relative freedom of movement after all those months, maybe years, of immobility and restriction. Who knows: perhaps I too would have jumped at the chance of visiting St Pauly centre on a weeknight, or even making the hike to the horrendous medieval Castle, if I'd been through half of what they had?

At Level 14 my eyes filled with tears. I stiffened with excitement. Could it really be? Was this pity? Sympathy for the plight of Mukelenge Mambackou? They'd come! The hot tears for somebody else had finally come! I didn't even bother looking out to see if there was anyone on the sixteenth floor, and instead zoomed to floor seventeen, willing the glass box to fly the final three levels upwards with a cosmic surge of urgency. To hell with the nice white boy from 'the Islands'! She *would* think him simply adorable, wouldn't she, that pathetic, self-hating drudge downstairs? Mukelenge needed me, Christie. He needed my authentic, intimate, dark-skinned knowledge of *this* wretched island—not a patronising crap-act from some white liberal do-gooder from Piperville.

I darted through the lift doors and onto the seventeenth floor, striding purposefully across the circular hall, even though I hadn't the faintest idea which of the doors that lined the radius might be number seven. I stopped dead in the centre. There it was again. A piteous mewling sound, like a wounded kitten caught in a trap. I rapidly scanned the sinister circle. The noise seemed to be coming from behind a small wooden door set into the stretch of wall that lay directly behind me, next to the lift doors from which I'd emerged. As I edged closer to this wooden door—I was now certain that it was indeed the source of the outlandish mewling—I realised that it was quite unlike the doors to any of the apartments, all of which were painted black (and did in fact carry a small number). The shabby brown door outside which I now lingered looked more like the entrance to a broom-cupboard.

I pushed it open.

A tiny girl sat hunched in the minuscule space, surrounded by brooms, mops and various other cleaning materials. She couldn't have been more than nine. She hugged her little knees for dear life, her head buried in the wet, pink, raggedy dress that barely covered them. Every few seconds the girl lifted her head and wailed. Her black shining eyes seemed to stare right through me, utterly consumed in what looked like a grief beyond the telling.

I hovered at the doorway, awkwardly.

And that was when I became aware of the stench. It was like nothing I'd ever encountered, a repellent mixture of repulsive substances masquerading as food. The nightmarish olfactory cocktail was overlaid with the unmistakeable odour of fresh vomit. I felt various sections of my gut beginning to heave in a series of violent, shifting contractions. I stumbled backwards out of the cupboard in panic.

"Please!" whimpered the child.

"What is it?" I mumbled suspiciously, covering my mouth with my sleeve. "What are you doing down there?"

"Please!" she whimpered again.

I started to feel impatient. She wasn't speaking

properly. The words were somehow muffled.

"What's the matter with you? What's that terrible smell?"

The girl slid backwards on her bottom to reveal two steaming bowls that lay on the floor in front of her. One contained a mountain of white-yellow clumps; the other was full to the brim with a bright green, bubbling, viscous material. Lying around the two bowls were several tiny puddles of what my horrified nostrils had already correctly identified as puke.

"What *is* all this?" I gasped in sympathetic horror now, suddenly filled with what felt distinctly like pity for the poor little creature. "What are you doing in here?"

"My father says if I haven't eaten everything in these two bowls (as well as anything I may vomit up) by the time he and my mother get back from cleaning the sixteenth floor, then he'll give me thirty-nine strokes of the belt on my bare bottom," sobbed the child, her tiny head back in her filthy hands again. "I don't know what to do! I'm trying to eat it, but I just can't keep it down!"

"What is it?" I asked, intrigued. "I've never seen anything like it. The smell is just awful."

"It's only boiled semolina and okra," replied the girl, suddenly matter-of-fact, the words still oddly blocked, though. "But I just can't stomach it. My father says it's because I'm ashamed of where we're really from, that I'm trying to deny my true origins. But it's not true! I just don't like the food! We lived for the whole of last year in a Category II camp, and I hated having to wear the bit and the harness, it's true, we all did, but at least I got to eat sausages there! I love sausages. But now we're Category III, and living in this place semi-independently and all, my father can force my mother to cook this...this..."

She began to weep again.

"I can't eat it," she sobbed, pushing listlessly at the plate of okra. "I just can't eat it."

"So where are you from?" I asked eventually. "You talk

like you're from Cornwall or something."

"I learned English off the television last year," said the girl, wiping at her puffy eyes with a tattered sleeve, and gulping. She suddenly smiled, shivering with a frisson of evident pride in my observation. "But the camp was in Devon , you're almost  right. I paid close attention to the warders there. And there were two local children who'd come and talk to me through the hole in the camp fence. I just copied their voices, really."

"Oh, I see," I said.

Then, hating myself, but unable to resist: "But where are you from...originally?"

"My parents are from the Democratic Republic of Congo," answered the girl. "We were the only family they let in after the volcano. I won the contest, when the white lady singer picked me."

"Of *course*!" I exclaimed, suddenly peering more closely at her. "You're Stone-Face Ronette! The Nyiragongo lava-doll. I knew I recognised you from the television."

And I gazed, fascinated, at the left side of her face, so famously converted to black, glittering marble. No wonder she was talking out of the side of her mouth. I tried to carry on speaking as I drank in the freakish spectacle.

"But your parents should be thanking you! You're the reason they were able to escape."

"They don't like it here," said Ronette glumly. "They don't like having to wear their 'A' badges. They don't like being forced to speak English all the time. We haven't been assigned a mentor yet, and you know they can't go out for longer than an hour without one. Oh, and they *hate* having to clean the building. We're the only ones here, and I suppose it's a lot of work. They're always complaining about it. Well, they would be if only they could find the words!"

"But I thought the Lionheart Complex  was full to the rafters with new seekers," I said, surprised.

Ronette shrugged. She looked as if she might start

weeping again at any moment. What was I supposed to do with this peevish fairy? The situation was totally beyond my control.

"I think I should be going now," I said eventually. "I'm supposed to be visiting—"

Ronette began to shriek hysterically.

"Please! Please, Mrs, please! Don't let them whip me again. They've already given me nine strokes. Look!"

She pulled up her ragged dress to reveal a bright red cluster of seeping welts on her left buttock. She wasn't wearing any panties. I looked away in embarrassment.

Ronette was sobbing again now, hugging her knees and rocking backwards and forwards over the two disgusting dishes, tears of loneliness and terror streaming down her poor little face.

"I'll come back for you!" I whispered, checking quickly behind me as I spoke. "I've just got to visit this other person. He's from the Congo too, I think. Do you know him? Mr Mambackou ? Listen, Ronette, listen to me! I'll come back for you later, I won't forget!"

But Ronette wasn't listening. She'd turned her back completely on me now and scrabbled around furiously among the mops and clattering brooms, like a mad thing, searching for a magical nook in which to hide her terrible, stinking bowls, perhaps, or a fantastical mouse-hole down which she might be small enough to vanish for good.

$A$s the door marked 17:7 swung slowly open the unmistakeably inane chorus of Michael Jackson's 'Earth Song' wafted out lazily to greet me, as if in a dull display of mockery.

> *Ah ah aah...ah ah ah ah aah!*
> *Ooh ooh oooh...ooh ooh ooh ooh oooh!*

The late King of Pop had certainly had more inspired moments. More to the point, there didn't seem to be anybody at the door to accompany M.J. in his banal welcome.

I pushed hard at the cold metal all the same, and tiptoed tentatively inside, my heart wild with fear and embarrassment, my hands continuing their wretched drip-drip-drip in anticipation of a certain pair of imminent male hand-shakes. The short corridor was in darkness, but at the end of it I could see a half-open door, from which trickled gentle laughter and a yellow-pink glow.

I heaved a sigh of relief. The warmth of the light drew me closer, assuring me that I had nothing to fear: I'd be welcome here.

I pushed the second door wide open, and instantly spluttered at the sharp stench of cannabis.

The two men stared up at me as if they'd been interrupted in the middle of unexpectedly emotional first confidences. The 'black' one, the man I presumed was Mukelenge Mambackou, didn't look friendly. He looked outraged, in fact, as if the very sight of me constituted some terrible kind of affront. A handsome, well-built, dark-skinned fellow clad in dark blue, baggy Carhartt jeans and stylish, silver Puma hoodie, he reclined regally on a colossal purple beanbag surveying my bedraggled figure with palpable disappointment. I'd worn my best slate-grey skirt-suit for the occasion, but it had become horribly crumpled during the bus journey, I realised now with a tiny grunt of dismay.

"*You're* not Christie Smithkin, are you?" he said at last, getting up from his beanbag, extending his hand (so warm and dry!) and breathing out a cloud of acrid-smelling pot-smoke.

I coughed again, trying hard not to overdo it. Then: "I am, yes!" I cried at last with overstated relief. "So you *were* expecting a second mentor? They never told me!"

"Yes, yes," Mukelenge interrupted, taking a sharp, irritated suck at his crackling joint as he snatched back his sloshed hand in revulsion. "They told me. A second mentor was always in the cards."

I'd thought I'd heard it in the first sentence. Now I was sure. Mukelenge Mambackou, this ebony-skinned African, this recently-arrived asylum seeker, this *true* foreigner, spoke with the unmistakeable air of the Peak District. The accent of my childhood, the accent of the Mickle-Beast, the accent I'd always resisted: the accent of Mameluke Bath. I'd always feared that catching it (or indeed its St Pauly variant, in which I'd been soaked, still remaining fantastically immune, from the age of ten) would distance me even further from Hélène. Instead I'd clung all those idiotic years to the absurd belief that an impossible-to-place, Jane Birkin-esque blend of unknown Paris-Londres *mélange* would better serve to bond us. By the time she finally left me behind for good it was too late to start again. I was stuck with an idiotic, artificial voice, worse than Charlotte Gainsbourg, even more irritating and pitifully incongruous.

At that instant, the envy I felt for Mukelenge Mambackou threatened to knock me off my feet. I stared at him in disbelief. He had stolen my rightful regional accent, the accent I had forfeited through my own childhood stupidity.

Mukelenge indicated with a bored wave of his hand that I should sit. I perched on a bar stool that lurked at the frontier of the sickly yellow living room and the dark cave at the back that presumably functioned as a kitchen. Mukelenge sat back down on a dirty-cream sofa next to the awkward, beaming white boy.

"Christie," said Mukelenge, smiling. "That's an unusual name."

"Yes!" I agreed.

"In honour of the original English darling, Miss Julie Frances C.? Or perhaps the delightful John Reginald?"

"What?"

"John Reginald Christie. Now *there* was one of the legendary Englishmen of times past!"

"What? Surely you don't mean the—"

I faltered, appalled at such a gross—and obscure—allusion to a British serial-killer so early in our acquaintanceship. How could a newly arrived African even have *heard* of John Reginald Christie? Presumably he'd somehow seen the film with Sir Richard Attenborough, *10 Rillington Place*. Perhaps he was old enough.

But now the other, the white boy, the one he preferred, was piping up, something about John Hurt's impressive Welsh accent. I turned my head stiffly, eager to set an initial appraisal in motion. And as my ears took in the barrage of quiet, over-friendly platitudes, delivered in an accent nightmarishly close to Mukelenge's, my stomach started to feel quite sick. I tried to be reasonable: at least the boy's local accent was to be expected; at least this green-eyed youth was a known citizen of the East Midlands. But by the end of the eighth or ninth second I was no longer paying any attention to the details of his try-hard, working-class chatter. I was staring instead at those filthy stumps of wings of his, trying to work out how they could possibly have followed me to the Lionheart Complex all the way from the Damascus Shopping Centre toilets, and praying that they didn't recognise me here and now as I so surely recognised them.

"I'm *glad* there's two of us in the end, aren't you?" whispered Damon, as Mukelenge clattered noisily around the tiny dark kitchen in search of his only box of English Breakfast. "I'd've been dead nervous doing this kind of thing on me own!"

Damon's smile was full of effort. He lowered his eyes. I wanted so badly to be kind to him.

"Well, yes, I suppose it might make certain things easier," I conceded, whispering too, despite myself. "I mean, we probably have different fortés in the mentoring arena. All the same," —Damon's green eyes flashed up at me nervously now, but I delivered the already conceived zygote of resentment, undeterred—"I am just so sick of not being *told* things!"

"What do you mean?" asked Damon, speaking normally now as the kettle started to boil and whistle behind us, and Mukelenge continued his theatrical racket more noisily than ever.

"Well, what do you mean 'what do I mean'? I just mean they could have informed us there'd be someone else working with us, that's all."

"Oh," said Damon, lowering his eyes again. "They told me."

"What?" I heard myself squawk. "I don't believe it!"

I was dumbfounded.

"Yes," he continued, unsolicited. "As soon as they notified me that I'd been given a place on the scheme. They warned me there'd be doubling up. In view of the uneven seeker-to-mentor ratio."

"And when was that?" I asked very deliberately, unbearably tense, not least because Mukelenge was returning, bearing a large white plastic tray laden with teatime goodies.

"Oh, what was it? Six weeks ago? Just before the council held the training day."

But before I had a chance to explode with the surge of fury I felt flooding my entire body, Mukelenge was pouring the tea.

"And so begins," he said with a little laugh, "my great English odyssey. I'm relieved to have made it this far, I must say."

"I suppose it must have been pretty rough up to this point, though," I said, trying to make my voice as warm and sympathetic as I could. "From what I can glean, the conditions they put you through before you even *get* to Category III are kind of insane. Those holding camps on the coast? God, it's like something out of Kafka. Just...I mean, well—maybe you can tell us, no? And even *this*! I mean, okay, it's a roof, it's semi-secure, but I mean, it's all just so bizarre, this place, out in the sticks, and you're still not allowed to work, and there are those terrible tales of compulsory lice-feeding, and——"

"It is exactly as it should be," said Mukelenge, raising the butter knife he'd just covered in raspberry jam, holding it in the air, and gazing at me with the solemn black eyes of a judge of Hades.

Damon smiled nervously at us both, before taking another gulp of tea.

"Oh?" I said. "Have I spoken out of turn?"

Mukelenge ignored me, finished spreading the plate of scones then rose to his feet. He switched on the light in the kitchen for the first time now (why had he chosen to toil on the preparation of the tea and scones in the dark?), and, above the cooker, a huge film poster became visible, framed in one of those expensive black pine things that 'cinephiles' buy to impress their idiotic house-guests. Though I adored cinema with a passion more ardent and real than anyone else I'd ever met, my own numerous posters still hung on my Old Saul Street walls with perfectly adequate blue tack.

"*Intolerance*," declaimed Mukelenge, pointing up at the lurid poster, his butter knife still smeared red, yellow and cream, "was D.W. Griffith's finest film. Made nearly a hundred years ago, its noble wager was to set out various scenes of intolerance across the Ages. And so we see the Fall of Babylon in the sixth century before Christ; we also have the story of the Crucifixion of Christ himself. Then we move to sixteenth-century France for——"

"The Saint Bartholomew's Day Massacre. Yes. We know," I interrupted, more than a little irked at this point by this anglicised African's seemingly inexhaustible capacity for bullshit.

His professorial airs seemed more than a little ludicrous too, especially operating from those Carhartt jeans and that awful silver 'hoodie'. I noticed his hair for the first time now. He seemed to be growing it into a kind of punk Afro (though he must have been in his mid-fifties at least): the central section stood up like a black cockerel's crest, while the sides of his head were clipped practically to a zero.

"But why exactly are you telling us all this?"

Mukelenge laughed a long, patronising, patriarchal chuckle of faux-disbelief, and looked over at Damon with pitying, avuncular eyes. Damon grinned back blankly. He clearly didn't have a clue what was really going on here: his cloak of angelic whiteness protected him from access to such ugliness.

"My point is quite simple, Miss Smithkin," resumed Mukelenge. "I am merely indicating the importance of celebrating the great gestures of *tolerance* that have been enacted throughout Western history. Mr Griffith was far from the Ku Klux Klan apologist that certain hysterical critics (many of whom haven't even seen the great *Birth of a Nation*) have been so desperate to paint him as. And *Intolerance*, this wonderful follow-up movie, is filmed proof of that. The British people are an exemplarily tolerant race. I suppose what I'm trying to say is that I find it unhelpful to focus (but you seem quite determined, Miss Smithkin), on the purely negative aspects of the British Seeker Integration process. There have been passages of difficulty, of course. Yes. Is that what you want me to say? There. I've said it. But I'm beyond all that now. My case has been found credible. I have arrived in St Pauly. And now I don't want favours or handouts. I want simply to be allowed to begin my own process of integration."

I couldn't refrain from rolling my eyes.

"And as for your horror stories of 'lice-feeding'," Mukelenge continued, "I can assure you that they are pure, hysterical inventions of the socialist and communist press. The Lice Act was a deterrent, that's all, precisely what was needed to stem the ceaseless flood of applicants."

Mukelenge chuckled again now, more kindly this time, and came back into the living room. He put his hand on my tense shoulder and squeezed it. I felt suddenly jejune, and struggled to fight the prickling shame that was flooding my child-face and Pinky-limbs. The wise man sat down on the sofa next to Damon, and began to fill his pipe. Smiling like a pubescent, Damon immediately began to fumble in his own pockets, and was soon rolling his own little replacement teat of tobacco and hash. Silence fell over all three of us, as I watched the two men settle down to their contented puffing and sucking. The tiny room quickly filled with more thick clouds of purplish grey smoke.

At last I spoke again.

"So where are you from, Mukelenge? And why did you have to leave?"

"Ah!" tittered Mukelenge. "The inevitable question of exodus and origins. And one to which you yourself are no doubt extremely accustomed, I'm sure! *I had a farm in Africa!* Do you like my Hollywood-Danish accent? Quite accurate, don't you think?"

It was true: his cringe-worthy impersonation of Meryl Streep's Karen Blixen was near flawless. My cheeks burned, but I said nothing. Damon continued to suck vacuously at his joint as Mukelenge spoke again:

"I've prepared some sketches. Since I was so certain you'd ask. Would you mind? They're in the top drawer. That's right. That chest in the corner."

I pulled out a large A3 silver folder that resembled a travelling artist's portfolio of work. Damon's infantile eyes widened now with curious fascination. He looked up at Mukelenge admiringly.

"That's right," said Mukelenge again, his pipe in his mouth. "If you'd just lay it on the table, please, and open it at the first page. I'll talk you both through."

He cleared his throat.

"There are just four acts so far. Raphael has promised to let me rework them as giant murals on the bottom of his swimming pool in Mameluke Bath. Once the fifth act has been conceived, that is."

At the mention of Mameluke Bath my heart skipped a beat. So he *had* picked up his voice from there! The accent is so very nuanced and particular. How had he managed it, I wondered? He must have been so utterly determined to put every tiny scrap of post-camp liberty to good use. But perhaps all would be revealed in the drawings.

"Eden!" barked Mukelenge as I dutifully snapped open the Book at the first page as instructed. "Before the Fall."

The picture resembled an Egyptian tomb painting, all in brown, black, gold, and heavy eye makeup. In the foreground stood what looked like an ancient palace, in front of which danced and cavorted approximately twelve laughing, clapping men. Many wore what looked like leather trousers; many were bare-chested. In keeping with the colour scheme of the illustration as a whole, their skins were brown, black and gold, often all three on a single figure. Two or three of the men wore what looked like Native American feather headdresses. A glittering golden ball hung down from the sky above, and the men's multi-coloured faces were upturned to this disco sun in perfect boogie-nights worship.

"Is that supposed to be a nightclub in Brazzaville?" I asked uncertainly. "Or Kinshasa? Are you from big Congo or little Congo, in fact? It didn't say on the letter."

"Why ask if you already know?" sighed Mukelenge.

"What kind of club is it?" asked Damon in wonder. "The people look so happy."

"They were, Damon. They were. We all were. *Papa Don't Preach* was the happiest thing that ever happened in my capital. For one short year men came from miles around. They came even from neighbouring countries. White men too. It was one place in central Africa where everyone could get clean and have a good time. You know?"

Damon nodded.

"I was the proud owner of *Papa Don't Preach*, as you'll have probably guessed. There I am."

He pointed to a cottage in the background, in front of which stood Mukelenge (recognisable only by his crest of black hair), arms folded in a no-nonsense manner, a smiling, gold-faced woman by his side, wiping her hands on an ABBA apron.

"My young wife," said Mukelenge by way of explanation. "The discotheque wasn't for *me*, you understand. I just enjoyed the good vibrations. Shall we take a look at Chapter Two?"

The second picture was identical to the first in terms of setting—same palace in the foreground, same cottage in the background, similar colour scheme—but instead of musical festivity the people here had been caught up in a bloodbath. Heads lay strewn on the ground; some (all three of the pseudo-Red Indians, I noticed with amusement) were on pikes carried by sinister looking black-brown gorillas clad in golden khaki. Huge yellow flames poured out of the upstairs windows of *Papa Don't Preach*. The cottage in the background had been repainted pink-and-black, and the figure of Mukelenge stood alone in front of it now, cradling his wife's severed head in his arms. Crimson tears streamed down his cheeks.

"Well, congratulations on getting our wretched government to accept that you needed asylum!" I exclaimed. "They let most gay men and lesbians around the world just get lynched. Almost none of them gets into the UK these days, for all our new-found homophilia."

"I am *not* a homosexual!" shouted Mukelenge. "I was offering music and hospitality to a group of stigmatised people."

"Nobody's saying you are!" cried Damon, leaping up to put a red-white-and-blue track-suited arm around Mukelenge.

Mukelenge pushed away Damon's Adidas embrace, but not unkindly.

"It all happened over fifteen years ago, Damon," he said calmly now. "I've had time to make sense of it."

"So what happened next?" I asked, slightly sickened by the show of filial tenderness. "Can't we see?"

Mukelenge complied, but not before giving me a withering stare.

The next page was almost entirely black except for odd sparks of silver, white and gold in each of the four corners.

I picked up the book and held it under the red lamp-bulb dangling over the kitchen table. I thought I could see the word *TÉNÈBRES* spelling itself out across the page in a slightly lighter shade of black.

"There is little to say about this phase of my life," said Mukelenge. "The tiny sparks represent Raphael, my Advocate, and the hope he's brought to me and my case over the years. But the rest...no I can't really talk about it. And, that of which one cannot speak, one should keep shrouded in silence. Isn't that right, Christie?"

I was struggling to prevent the imminent flow of a giant teardrop that had been building in my right eye. It wasn't Mukelenge's story that had got the better of me. On the contrary, I was finding that particular narrative frankly absurd. But M.J.'s Greatest Hits had thankfully come to an end, and now George Michael's 'Jesus to a Child' was arriving at its excruciatingly nostalgic climax of poignancy.

"Let's have a look and see what the last act's all about!" interrupted Damon brightly.

I wiped the tacky tear from my flint-eye, not without a certain violence.

"I drew this one just today," said Mukelenge, looking at me expectantly.

I turned the page.

The final picture was quite unlike the stylised exotica of the others. It looked more like a line drawing from one of Enid Blyton's *Malory Towers* series. It was a room, a simple room, an English room. On the left: an old-fashioned 1950s-style chest of drawers, on top of which stood a vase of vulva-shaped flowers; on the right: a small table laden with hot-dog buns, again slit and filled and garnished in an

obscenely gynaecological manner. Between the two
pornographic pieces of furniture, though, sat the actors.
Primly perched on sturdy wooden chairs, three friends
clinked small china teacups. The man in the middle was
clearly supposed to be Mukelenge, although the figure's
features were now disquietingly woggish. A broad grin of
contentment was painted in thick strokes across his simple
face. On his left was a young man that seemed like a rather
impressive likeness of Damon: frail, pretty, dark-haired,
pale-skinned. He even wore a sports top and baggy jeans.
On his right sat a young woman clad in a simple schoolgirl
pinafore, who looked rather like a Blytonian vision of the
Danish pop star Whigfield. Her long blonde pigtails hung
down daintily from an impeccably scrubbed porcelain
visage. Like the Damon-figure, this woman's calm
expression exuded friendly, dignified tolerance.

Damon looked away in embarrassment.

I felt my cheeks tingle in instant mortified flame.

"Didn't they tell you I was going to be...mixed-race?" I
managed to cough out, despite the tight furball that had
formed at the back of my throat.

"Yes, they did!" smiled Mukelenge. "They did indeed.
But I'd formed the impression that the mixed-race people
of the North resemble *this* girl far more than they resemble
somebody like you. And it said on your application form
that you had Danish blood. Was that a lie?"

I couldn't speak.

"I mean, even Michael Jackson's children all have fair
hair, do they not?"

"They're clearly not his *real* children!" I spat out before
his sentence was even finished.

"And then there was your divine Jade Goody."

I threw up my hands in despair and looked across at
Damon for support. I wanted to shake him. He continued
to look down at his crotch, of course, though, terrified.

"And of course the lovely little Martin Gore of
Depeche Mode fame," continued Mukelenge smiling,

implacable, relentless. He suddenly sang now, in a rich, treacly, synth-pop baritone: "People are people!"

He tittered, suddenly camp.

"Blond as a Hitler Youth, our Martin! Master of the Milk-Skinned Metics! But what does it matter? The important thing is that you came. All the way out to the Lionheart Complex. You're here. You're both here. Thank you."

There was a short pause as we both digested our new father's benediction, Damon with somewhat less colic than me.

"And now I think I must be letting you go," said Mukelenge briskly. "I need a nice hot bath, it's getting late, and you both have a bit of a trek back home to Piperville, haven't you?"

"My flat's on the *edges* of Piperville," I snapped. "Old Saul Street. It's northeast city centre, really."

"Of course," said Mukelenge, smiling at me, not unkindly. "I still need my bath, though."

The bus appeared to be waiting for us as we approached the deserted stop. Dropping my three-pound coin into the slot, I noticed that the driver was the same toothy dog-youth from the 39 that had taken me to and from the university campus for my interview with the Master on Friday afternoon. I didn't know they could just switch routes like that. He didn't call me 'duck' this time, though. He didn't even look at me, and I felt a tiny chest-bubble of regret.

"Nice guy, Mikey," said Damon, burrowing down into the aisle seat next to me.

There was nobody else on the bus, and I was glad.

"What?"

"Mikey. Mukelenge. Seemed all right," clarified Damon.

"Well, if you say so."

Damon reddened, and tried again.

"I think he was just a bit awkward, you know what I

mean? A bit stiff, like. Nervous. I don't think he meant anything by it."

As Damon spoke I felt my chin begin to quiver, and almost instantly two streams of boiling tears begin to flow down my face and onto my neck. They were the usual kind this time, of course, not the new, magical empathy-fluids I had managed to spurt in the lift. These bus-tears were just seepage for my lonely, wretched self.

I wanted to scream out loud from the shame of it.

And then I felt Damon's arms around me. My head was pressed against his frail chest now, and I sobbed and shuddered and heaved like a stupid little canaima.

"Hey! What's the matter? Hey!"

I couldn't answer, I couldn't stop shivering, I carried on.

He began to pat me gently on the back of my head. I don't know how long he must have done that for, or what he was murmuring as he did it. I'm fairly sure he was murmuring something. But when I lifted my head from his chest and blinked my wet eyes open, the bus had stopped, and the dog-youth driver was robotically flashing the lights. We were back at the Damascus Centre bus station.

"Where do you live?" asked Damon, smiling at me gently.

"Old Saul Street. Opposite Opoponax Gardens."

"On my way," said Damon.

The city centre was deserted too, and again I felt glad that I had Damon there to protect me. St Pauly wasn't safe.

"I thought you were really great back there," said Damon at last.

We had gone through the pedestrian stretch of chain-store blandness and were crossing the Old Market Square now, where a few beggars lay strewn out in sleeping bags. Some sat slumped in wheelchairs. One tattered figure had risen to its knees as we approached, hands clasped and outstretched, a professional supplicant.

"When?" I said, my voice tiny, pathetic.

"Back at Mikey's," smiled Damon. "I thought you were great."

"Oh. Thanks."

We crossed in silence from the Square toward the tram-track leading us both north, away from the centre.

"I'm kind of mixed too, you know," he volunteered at last.

"Oh?"

"Me dad."

"Oh. What's he, then?"

"Don't know. Never knew him. But he wasn't from round here."

"Where was he from?"

"East, me mam says. Won't say anything else. And I always say back to her: 'But we're already *in* east, Mam! East Midlands!' Then she gets riled up and says he was from east proper. Turk-east, Jew-east, maybe both of 'em at once. Maybe." Damon smiled and paused, as if on the verge of announcing something of great import. But instead he just said: "All I know is that my name is Damon Bosniak."

We'd long passed the Theatre Royal, and were at last on the stretch of tram-track leading up to Piperville. The turning for Old Saul Street was coming up any second. I grabbed my chance, and tugged at Damon's sleeve. We stopped.

"What's up, duck?"

"Listen, have you heard of Marianne Kollek?"

"Mary-Ann Coley? *X-Factor*?"

"No. *No!* Marianne Kollek: The 1970s Swiss philosopher. The one behind the 'water-turn' in second-wave French feminism. She did that documentary with Chantal Akerman."

Damon thought for a minute. "No. No. Haven't heard of her. Don't read enough. Why, duck?"

I didn't hesitate for an instant. "I *hate* her," I heard

myself hiss.

And I spat, just once, but with a yowling matagot violence that shocked even me as I felt the rasping black bile briefly skim the roof of my mouth and land, steaming, on the icy tram-track to my left.

Damon shrank back for an instant, horrified. Then, almost immediately, he relaxed back into his old warm milk smile.

# IV

You're trembling with excitement as you punch out on Friday afternoon from Islands in the Sun.

"Punching out early, Bosniak?"

It's your line-manager, Mrs Croft. She hovers at your side, daring you to protest.

"No, I punched in early!" you splutter, grinning nevertheless in a desperate bid for appeasement. And you can prove it too, if push comes to shove.

You pray it won't come to that.

Mrs Croft snorts, moves off toward the swimming pool, where only the redhead muscle-twins, Luke and Nigel, still linger so late in the day. It doesn't seem to matter (not even to Mercy Croft) that they have no clients to look after, the old folk having been rounded up long ago for the secure television room. The twins' freckled muscles, juicier and more tanned than ever, glisten under the mild glare of the autumnal afternoon sun. You watch Mrs Croft sit down heavily next to them, all three launching into instant collegial chatter, as if friendliness-tokens have been thrust into the slits in their mechanical necks. You sigh wistfully, swing your red Adidas rucksack over your shoulder, and move toward the exit.

Today you might just as well have been invisible to your colleagues. For Luke and Nigel finally brought in the DVD of that porno film they've just made for Centaurboy, and Mary-Kate and Kinga, NIGE-LUKE's most enthusiastic cheerleaders (and the Islands' *masseuses extraordinaires*), have spent the day in a wild and unshakable ecstasy. All morning long they take turns rushing off to the little girls' room to watch selected extracts from the movie on their iMu, while the glowing muscle-boys (not you, you're never a player in these naughty daytime games) keep an eye out for a mercifully low-profile Croft. Mary-Kate and Kinga's squeals of delight ring out around the silent pool. Three times in the course of the morning old Mrs Lammoreaux shrilly demands exactly what your damn fool colleagues think they're up to today. Her gleaming cat-eyes, puzzlingly greener even than yours, bore into you with a pleading, desperate fury. You haven't known quite how to answer the imperious Haitian *chabine*. You've simpered, grinned, flitted off to chat with old Mr Salkey from Tobago. He quietly sobs, telling you, as he does every Friday, that he loves you more than he does his own treacherous, black-skinned sons. And you hug him for sheer happiness.

But it's five p.m. now, and you're chirping merrily at the rapidly disappearing backs of Mary-Kate and Kinga who, like you, are eager to escape the white-walled, brown-skinned madness of Islands in the Sun. They're making their way as quickly as they can towards the sights and smells of Friday Night. They've linked arms, and every few seconds they skip for joy along the dark corridor that leads to the revolving door. They're engrossed in a conversation that can apparently only be conducted via mouth-to-ear exchange. You don't really mind. But you find yourself shouting as you trot to keep up with them.

"My seeker's really interesting!"

Mary-Kate and Kinga fail to acknowledge that anyone

has spoken. Instead they cling to one another more tightly still, and make a final lunge for the revolving door, cozying up together into the same compartment. You squeeze on your own into the adjacent section, almost too small for you and your bulky rucksack. You always were a lanky lad, says your mam Dawn, weekly. You tap on the glass, smile at the girls. Mary-Kate half-turns, grins back. There's no malice here. They like you at Islands. They really do like you. And why *wouldn't* they? You're nothing if not likeable. But Mary-Kate's grin lasts only the time of the door's revolution, and by the time the three of you find yourselves out in the dying October sunshine, the women are back in each other's ears and mouths. Kinga's brought her car with her to work today, and she and Mary-Kate are now positively cantering towards emancipation on wheels. When Kinga brings her car in on a Friday, it only means one thing: she and Mary-Kate (sometimes with Luke and Nigel in tow) are going to spend the evening in Manchester.

"I'm going to take my Mikey up to Manchester one day! He's from the Congo!" you bellow. "One of these days we'll go out on the lash with you lot! Good excuse for me to check out the Village! My Mikey's never been north of Mameluke Bath."

But Kinga's already started her engine and switched on the car's mega-iMu. As she rolls down the windows you're sure you can hear the voice of Loretta Lynn, the Coal Miner's Daughter, come sailing through the air towards you. You chuckle. They *are* rather like a couple of Tennessee cowgirls, them two. Why on earth have they stayed in St Pauly? They should be running a ranch together, somewhere over on the other side of Brokeback Mountain. Kinga often confides in you, during fag-breaks, of her long-standing desire to retrain as an inexpensive therapist for the rent-boys up in Laurietown. Even regular gay lads would do: couples in trouble, perhaps? Queer folk feel a connection with her, they tell her so constantly. Your grey-green eyes glisten with emotion, and you affirm her hypothesis: she'd be a lovely, tolerant homo-counsellor.

Mary-Kate dangles her hand lazily from her side of the car, twinkles three fingers in your direction, the approximation of a wave.

"Tarrah then!" you scream after the rapidly disappearing car. "Have a brilliant time!"

When you arrive at Ye Olde Yellow Brick Road To Damascus—the oldest pub in England, or so they say, established during the Crusades, frequented by the proto-anarchist forest bandits of the twelfth century, and recently converted (with added 'yellow brick') into the glitziest gay bar in the East Midlands—you spot Mikey deep in conversation with a hairy, overweight, bearded man who wears a pair of thick black glasses and sports a number of red and green tattoos, not only on his forearms but also all over his fifty-something, bulldog neck.

You feel suddenly self-conscious. It hasn't occurred to you that Mikey might already have made other friends in St Pauly. And such unlikely ones!

"Damon!" says Mikey, exhaling a puff of pipe smoke through his smile. "Do you know Brer Gabe?"

Brer Gabe looks up at you, takes off his glasses, doesn't smile. You extend your hand, grin. He accepts you with a cold, rough squeeze.

Mikey chortles.

"Mind yourself, Damon. Brer Gabe's what Grammy Hall would call a real *bear*."

The two men collapse into sudden helpless giggles as they lie gasping in each other's muscular arms. You never noticed Mikey's muscles at the Lionheart Complex on Tuesday. Now you see that they're bloody enormous, lightly covered tonight in a tight-fitting Ben Sherman checked shirt. You squint at what looks like a huge black fishtail jutting down beneath the short sleeve, spreading out across an only slightly less charcoal bicep.

"Who's Grammy Hall?" you ask, climbing up delicately onto the third chair, which isn't really a chair as such, more a bar-stool on walkabout, obliging you to perch an awkward foot above your smoking companions.

But Mikey and Brer Gabe have slipped into a cabaret routine that seems to verge on spirit-possession. And you're excluded from the merry game of trance.

"Cute little moon-face your baby boyfriend manchild has! I think somewhere Nabokov's smiling," remarks a swollen, fantastically Manhattanite Brer Gabe.

"Oh, he's older than he looks!" cackles a magnified, Californian Mikey.

"That's right: sixteen years old, no possible threat at all!" retorts another Brer Gabe altogether: an educated young wasp-woman this time, mock-piqued and horny.

"Your view is so Scandinavian; you're *bleak*, my God!" emits a strangled form of Mikey, all but asphyxiated by the flood of ironies flowing so thickly through his system, and babbling something droll about Kierkegaard.

By the sentence's end, he's clawing at his own throat. Whatever the identities of this panoply of parodic demon-riders, they seem to have turned their two supplicant horses so hysterical that the words, already distorted by a bizarre American-intellectual twang, come out as a series of indecipherable squeaks.

"Everyone good for drinks?" you grin, embarrassed.

You're determined to pay for Mikey all evening. You've arrived to look after him. They lectured you the previous week at the second mentor-training day (and why hadn't Christie been invited to that either?), on the strict illegality of seekers handling currency themselves. Presumably it was Brer Gabe that had bought Mikey that last pint? But where on earth had he gotten hold of that gorgeous fitted Ben Sherman shirt? For one terrible, guilty moment you feel annoyed at Mikey, and at the casually super-cool Englishness he seems to be plugging into with such rapid and perplexing ease.

As you make your way to the crowded bar, you look back at your two new friends, who now sit nursing their almost empty pint glasses in glum silence. Mikey's punkish, Afro crest of the other night has gone, replaced with smooth, straight, oily locks that are combed back simply over his large head. They glow a coppery red. The redness of the ironed strands is impressively organic, somehow, you think, brow furrowed, silently pondering the sudden metamorphosis as you recite the unexpectedly complicated order to the black-vested, dead-eyed barman.

$\int$oon you begin to enjoy the sensation of the ice-cold, pear-flavoured Magners confidently trickling its way through your underfed system. You begin to feel relaxed around Mikey and Brer Gabe. They've only just met this afternoon, in fact, here in Ye Olde Road. They struck up an instant rapport upon Brer Gabe's early discovery of the fact that Mikey's original name was Mukelenge. Brer Gabe likes people who dare to change their name. Brer Gabe used to be called Mike. That was a boring-arse name if ever there was one. They have bonded in the course of the afternoon, playing an endless series of games, all of which have involved the listing and imitation of film characters and stars that have famously changed their names.

For it turns out that both Mikey and Brer Gabe are fans of Hollywood.

You wonder if Mikey's told Brer Gabe he's Category III. He doesn't seem to be wearing his bright grey 'A'. It doesn't really matter either way, though: Brer Gabe seems like an accepting person. You're a bit confused again, though: from your understanding of what they told you at the last mentor training, seekers are only allowed out of their centres one evening a month, and even that evening is supposed to be under the strict supervision of the mentor. It somehow feels as though Mikey's been going out more frequently than that. He seems so...integrated.

Yes, that's the word: integrated. You blow five Marlboro Menthol smoke rings and wave the thoughts away. No doubt, it all must have an explanation. You've probably got the details wrong. Maybe the rules don't apply to all seekers. Maybe Mikey's a special case. You wave the thoughts away.

Mikey suddenly prods you in the chest.

"So you haven't brought along our little friend with you tonight, then? You haven't brought 'Christie'?"

"Who's Christie?" shouts Brer Gabe, back from the toilets already.

The place has filled up substantially in the last couple of hours.

"Bloody queens!" spits Brer Gabe, as twink after skinny twink simpers in, for the most part alone and slightly furtive, but occasionally in huge, blond, shrieking gaggles. "We'd have been better off drinking at Pig People."

"Who's Christie, Damon?" demands Mikey, his voice dripping with cruelty now, nasty, sarcastic, mean. "Your personal Jesus? Who is she? Really? And where does that vile brown chip on her shoulder come from?"

"Oh," you mutter, suddenly self-conscious as four muscular, black-and-blue inquisitor eyes drill into you. "No. I don't really know. I mean..."

You sigh heavily then look helplessly at Brer Gabe, desperate for the kindness you know in your soul would most likely be more forthcoming from the floating ghost of Michael Jackson than from this hard-hearted stranger. It's not that Brer Gabe's a bad person or anything. He simply seems bored out of his skull by the boring question about some random bitch's identity, a question he himself was gay enough to bring up. His blue eyes glaze over with a skin of impatient indifference.

You want to finish, though. You need to: Mikey's still waiting. You don't want to wind up the weakest link.

The right answer finds its way to your lips at last.

You take a deep breath.

You speak: "Christie's just a girl."
Mikey nods his approval.

An enormous queue has already formed outside the club Supernature. The men are desperate to be let in, especially on a night as cold as this. They titter and prance in mental and physical self-preservation. Brer Gabe was right when he promised you that the crowd here would be less skinny, less made-up, less like a bunch of bloody women. As you gaze in excitement before and behind you, you see men of principally three kinds: (i) big, twittering, bare-bottomed men who look remarkably like Brer Gabe, snug in leather and rubber, (ii) strawberry-blond, blue-eyed Prince Harry lookalikes, swastika medallions hanging from their freckled necks, and (iii) swarms of pale youths in tracksuits, trainers and baseball caps, silent, moody, somehow serious, their scowls full of wronged attitude. There are three floors in the club, one for each species, Brer Gabe helpfully explains to you and (you note with a degree of relief) to an equally awe-struck Mikey. Anyone's free to wander onto any floor, though. It isn't a segregated building! You and Mikey both laugh loudly at this last observation, and Brer Gabe grins, pleased at this final demonstration of wit, before bounding up to a group of bear-friends he's spotted about fifty metres ahead of you in the queue.

"Kylie's *Breastdance* came out today!" Brer Gabe shouts back to you and Mikey by way of explanation. "I have to rip it off Kevin...*NOW*!"

And he waves his tiny silver iMu cheekily at the ursine confederation, which, as one, dramatically folds huge, hairy, tattooed arms, awaiting their brother's breathless arrival with a smirking, sarcastic, collective tut of "you're-just-too-much-Brer-Gabe!" censure.

You and Mikey laugh and laugh.

"Do you think they'll let us in?" you ask your mentee after a few minutes' silence.

The wind's really beginning to nip now, and a fine sleet

65

has begun to fall on the shivering queue of hopefuls.

"Why wouldn't they?" says Mikey, his eyes suddenly filling with an anxiety you've never seen in them before. "Why wouldn't they?"

"Oh, no reason. It's just that we're not really dressed like anyone else here. I was just, you know, if there's a code."

"I think we'll be O.K.," says Mikey, relaxing again. "You'd turn heads up in Manchester. Good god, if I was a sculptor!"

He chuckles again, ruffles your hair. Two sailors titter flirtatiously behind you. Mikey ignores them, stays with you, rams his affection gently home with a whispered seriousness which for him clearly signals his delivery of what just might be the ultimate compliment: "You look like a young Dave Gahan."

You blush, even though you're not altogether sure who Dave Gahan is, young or otherwise. It's lucky that the only lighting outside the club Supernature is green.

Mikey slips you one of the little pills that Brer Gabe gave him back at Ye Olde Road, and after a few minutes you start to feel as though perhaps happiness does indeed lurk just around the corner. You light another Marlboro Menthol, start sucking on it with joy. Disco beats begin to pulsate through your heart and brain, stronger, deeper, heavier the closer you both edge towards the front of the queue.

You'll make it, both of you. You've got to.

The door-frisk is positively pleasurable, even if they do take an age inspecting poor Mikey, who, all the way through, maintains a faraway expression you can't quite manage to read. It's all O.K. in the end, of course. Soon the two of you are lounging unproblematically with a gaggle of Prince Harry clones at the crowded bar on the second floor. Such floods of excited delight are now searing all over your body, hot, flushed, contented, that you truly feel as though you may have just been granted asylum in something resembling an earthly paradise.

Everyone's just so friendly!

*(so friendly and accepting!)*

Mikey's just so lovely!

*(so lovely and so warm!)*

Daddy cradling Diamond, and never, never letting go.

"What's this music, Mikey?" you ask, completely and utterly thrilled.

A robotic-sounding humanoid is making a series of frightening declarations. All are sung—no, proclaimed—in a futuristic, angel-interceptor, saviour-machine drone. The electro-chips of heaven against which the statements float and swirl are tiny nuggets of alligator-ecstasy, like a dream, no end, no beginning. The dance floor is starting to fill with all sorts now, not just the three immediate kinds of animal you noticed in the queue, but with various breeds of gayman: enormous hulking Adonises in white vests, hair slicked and oiled like Errol Flynn; tiny little muscular Latin pixies with beaming, come-get-me grins; middle-aged guys in pinstripe suits and loosened pink ties; soldiers in Desert Storm khaki. You can't see any women, though, and, as far as you can make out, Mikey's the only coloured feller on this floor. But so what? You're in St Pauly, not New York, not London.

And St Pauly has never felt so good...

You wonder if you'll run into Luke and Nigel here. This is precisely the sort of place they'd come. But no—they're probably having a whale of a time on Manchester's Canal Street with Mary-Kate and Kinga, celebrating the success of their recent porno film debut.

"*Italo*," says Mikey.

"What?" you trill, confused.

"It's *Italo* music!" shouts Mikey again, pointing the way to a free table near the dance floor.

"What's *Italo*?" you ask as you settle down to yet more pear Magners and ice, eyes wide with anticipation.

"*Italo* was a revolutionary kind of disco dance music

that rose to prominence in the late 1970s and early 1980s," explains Mikey. "When you were just a little boy," he adds with a grin. "Completely electronic in genesis, it was produced by mostly Spanish and Germans and Italians; hence, the name. It was particularly big on the Chicago scene, just before Madonna released The First Album. 'Holiday', 'Physical Attraction'...All that kind of stuff. You can hear the similarity, right?"

You nod furiously.

"But why does it sound so...they sound like they're on...it's like...IT'S LIKE BEING ON MARS!"

"Drums, vocoders, synthesisers, Damon," says Mikey authoritatively, downing his Magners in one.

He burps.

You giggle.

"You know so much, Mikey," you gasp. "How do you know so much? I mean...I'm not being funny..."

Mikey smiles, lays his hot dry hand on yours.

"Integration can't work where there's rage and resentment and resistance, Damon. It just can't."

You gaze at him, mesmerised.

He carries on: "And that's exactly what *Italo* teaches. Simple happiness, acceptance of the situation you're in, acceptance of its fundamental simplicity. It really is the greatest facelift, you know, Damon. Simplicity."

He giggles.

"Oh, Damon. You could be such a beautiful little boy if you'd only do something with your hair. Maybe try it spiky? I can't wait to have a go at you with the gel! We have so much time ahead of us. But come along now, duckie. Let's dance."

All you want is to stay there in your chair, at your table, safe, in your spot, nobody else's, your eyes watching Mikey. You motion that he should go onto the half-empty dance floor without you, if he likes. Mikey springs into action, ruffling your hair again as he gets up. A crowd of smiling, vacant admirers soon forms around him, clapping,

as Mikey jiggles his hips and beats his chest. Together they
chant the chorus of the wondrously grandiose disco tune
that's started up.

*Super-na-ture!*
*Super-na-ture!*
*Super-na-ture!*
*Super-na-ture!*

"That's the theme tune of this place," explains a young
cowboy who's settled quietly down next to you in Mikey's
vacated seat. "Kind of tacky, isn't it?"

You peer at the cowboy. He's coloured, in fact, but he
has much lighter skin than Mikey. He looks more like Mrs
Lammoreaux, your old French West Indian 'auntie' (how
she dotes on you, even though she's sharp!) at Islands in
the Sun. Kind of the same skin as that Christie girl, too. Or
maybe between Christie and Mrs Lammoreaux... The
cowboy has neat little dreadlocks, though. Like little black
worms. And he talks in what sounds, incredibly, like a
Glaswegian accent.

"It's *Italo*," you say curtly.

The brown-skinned Scottish cowboy doesn't appear to
give a flying fuck.

"Is that your friend?" he asks, gesturing at Mikey, who's
whooping now as three blond young surfer dudes touch
his hair in wonder.

"Yes," you reply. "He's my mate."

"Well, if he's your mate, you've got some fucked-up
mates, *mate*," snarls the cowboy.

"What do you mean?" you cry, outraged.

The cowboy laughs.

"Well, if you don't know," he says, preparing to get up,
"not my place to tell you what he's been up to on the scene
all week."

He whistles.

"No siree, nigger Jim, that shit is most definitely not my

joyride. I'm no fucking immigrant."

You snort and splutter a drunken protest in defence of all seekers. But the Glaswegian cowboy shouts you down.

"Hey, little sister, don't get your panties in a wad. I don't give a shit how anybody scores. No judgment, see? I'm just not into the whole lice-feeding scene."

You feel yourself beginning to crumble, and reach out your hands like a dying man towards the diabolical Scot. But he's already disappeared.

You're halfway to your knees now, a crystal of panic piercing your chest, polluting the beauty that had taken root inside you tonight. The flower of your born-again *Italo* soul is wilting.

It isn't fair. You can't let it die. You won't.

You find the strength and leap up, bound toward Mikey, who's still gyrating on the dance floor. You push your way through his still-hysterical fan club with a rage you never knew you possessed. The skinny, clapping boys fall away from you, terrified, like skittles, or zombies.

"What is it, little one?" chortles Mikey, grabbing your cheeks with his hard, warm hands.

He's removed his silver Blondie T-shirt, and you stare at a perfectly formed set of pectoral muscles, glistening with sweat. He wears a pair of dark sunglasses now. On the huge screens surrounding you they're flashing weird images of a man who looks like a young David Bowie, flanked by a glamorous blonde lady in a black hat. David and the blonde lady look like the coolest, most stylish people on the planet: apart from Mikey, of course. The blonde lady is wearing dark sunglasses too. She and David perch on a nightclub balcony, predator-like, gazing down on an enormous dance floor full of joyful, grooving youth, full of anxious, grooving you.

"I'm going upstairs for a minute!" you shout.

You race up the stairs with all the zeal of a born-again Christian after a thirty-something river-baptism in the Mameluke.

"Hey, watch it, scarecrow!" you hear someone bellow after you. "Olympics are so 2012!"

But you don't care. Something stronger than you is propelling you forward.

The upstairs room is a good deal smaller. Nobody dances here (you can't even see a dance floor). Instead, a small number of the track-suited, angry-looking characters from outside loll on black leather sofas, eyes riveted on the huge screens around them. Here and there they've coupled up, greedy hands going down an alternative pair of trackie bottoms for a change. Every now and then, one of the newly-formed twins emits a soft growl or a muttered threat, like a dreaming trauma-dog, eternally distressed, perhaps, but sedated, for now, in a mildly buzzy cloud of anaesthetic. But mostly each one sits alone, hands down only his own pair of trackie bottoms, choleric eyes glued to the plasma screen in front of him, clinging for dear life to the busy, shimmering membrane. Duran Duran's 'Hungry Like the Wolf' plays quietly in the background (how this song terrified you when you were little!), softly enough for the little grunts and groans coming from the screens and sofas to be clearly, embarrassingly audible.

The brown cowboy from downstairs is easy to spot. Apart from the obvious epidermal singularity, he's the only one up here not wearing a baseball cap. He's ordering a pint of Red Stripe at the bar when you march up to him.

"Hey!" you shout.

"Hey," says the Scottish devil, taking his beer from a wan, gold-toothed youth. "That was quick."

You ignore his false bonhomie.

"About my friend," you say.

"Ah, your *mate*, yes," replies the nasty little worm-haired dog, smirking. "So he didn't come up to paradise level with you?"

You're not going to take this kind of shit.

No.

That psycho in the Damascus loo last Friday was the

last time. The last time you let yourself get twatted by cunts. Got to look out for yourself now; got to look out for your friends...

"Mikey's my friend," you say firmly.

You're shocked at this strange hardness that seems to have taken you over. Is it the drugs talking? Are you back in the asylum? But you left that place two years ago, your mam picked you up, took you home, said you were all better—and you were!

Perhaps it's Christie that's come inside you? Maybe some of her angry black bile got splashed on your brain?

*(tu n'as rien vu à Mamlouk-les-Bains!)*

WHAT THE FUCK?

You take a massive breath, afraid you're going to pass out any second, afraid you've been properly taken over now, possessed by something that's not even speaking English.

Then there's a pause. The cowboy seems to lose all interest in the conversation and begins to gaze listlessly over at the porno screen above your head.

"Mikey's my friend," you repeat, determined to ignore that last creepy foreign head-voice. "And he's the most perfect person I've ever met."

The cowboy doesn't appear to be paying any attention whatsoever to you now. You reluctantly decide to give up on your inexplicable mission of conversion, and instead follow the unbeliever's mesmerised gaze up to the screen. You have to turn around completely in order to see what's so captivating if you don't want to twist your neck.

You give a little start of astonishment as you recognise your colleagues, the redhead muscle-twins Luke and Nigel, huger, pinker, and even more freckled than they were this afternoon when you spied them in the pool, chirping, doll-like, to Mrs Croft at Islands in the Sun.

They look beautiful. Luke is partially lying in a luxurious, half-filled, Ottoman-style bath, his mouth wrapped enthusiastically around an enormous pink-and-brown penis that dangles from between the strong legs of a proper Rastaman who swaggers over the rim of the tub. Luke's own powerful swimmer's legs remain high in the air as he sucks away, though, and all the while his kneeling brother Nigel buries a very red tongue deep within, up to the hilt, ecstatic inside his moaning twin's wet, surprisingly hairy, sticky ginger anus.

# V

You turn thirty-five on the seventeenth of November. The weather has turned definitively disgusting; the ceiling is made of glass. All day long you sit by the overheated poolside, your pale birthday moon-face upturned to vicious-looking storm clouds that whisper veiled threats to the slavish grey skies over which they slide and crawl. Even after all these years you haven't quite given up on the hope that maybe, just once, the sun will shine for you on the seventeenth. It never does. And, so long as you stay in St Pauly, it never will.

You sigh, depressed. Even the couple of Tramadol you swallowed from the store cupboard after lunch don't seem to be working properly. They buzz faintly in your temples and calves, pushing you off into a mild daze of toddler-drift and nostalgia. But it's nothing on the scale of that zommed-out time you did Tram with Mary-Kate and Kinga, the day Luke and Nigel pulled a sickie to do their *EnglishLads* shoot in London. That was like being on Mercury. Today it's pretty crappy. You won't bother with it again. Then you remember, sit up with a small jolt of excitement. Things *will* be different this year! Tonight, for the first time in decades, you and your mam Dawn are going to have a third body with you for your birthday tea. Christie's coming to Piperville.

You and Christie have seen a lot of each other these last few weeks. It's difficult to say when it finally crystallised, whatever it is you have together. Perhaps during the first hour of the first outing after the Lionheart Complex, that Sunday you went to the castle together after her distraught dawn call. Or perhaps that moment the following week, sitting at the edge of the freezing moat, when almost simultaneously you began the same pathetic confession: that despite spending practically your entire lives in St Pauly, neither of you has a clue about how anything in this peculiar city actually works. Whatever the case, it all seemed somehow easy with her after that. And today, on your birthday, as you skip home along the side of the tram track, relieved to have survived a particularly nasty day at work (they're ignoring you more or less entirely now), the fact is that it's the thought of Christie's unlikely arrival in a couple of hours that's responsible for whatever pleasure you may be feeling.

It's not only happiness; it's an unlikely amusement too. It'll be *funny* watching Christie interact with Dawn. It'd be funny watching Christie interact with anyone. She's not like other people. She's what Dawn would call a queer fish. Think for a minute: How would Christie handle Luke and Nigel if they started going on about their guest spot at the Acephali Cock Ball next spring in Soho? She wouldn't care that they were the redhead muscle-twins! She'd be perfectly capable of slapping their freckled pink faces. What would she say to Mrs Croft if Mercy accused her of leaving Mrs Lammoreaux soaking too long in the hot tub? She'd—

You chuckle at the various violent possibilities, but the passing tram drowns out your reedy whistle. And again you note the warm buzzing feeling that spreads throughout your chest when you think of Christie, how clever and angry and queer she is. You *do* want her there for your birthday tea tonight. Dawn will just have to deal with it. You'd have liked Mikey to be there too, but Mikey's vanished into thin air. Mikey has proven inaccessible. You've called him a number of times since that wonderful night at the club Supernature, but each time you're simply greeted by the melody of 'Everything Counts (In Large Amounts)' before being coolly invited by an authoritatively upper-class male voice to leave a brief message for Mr Mambackou , making sure to say what your call's concerning.

At the tenth attempt you give up, depressed.

"I don't think Mukelenge needs *either* of us as mentors," Christie chuckles mirthlessly on the telephone when you tell her of the silence. "He's not a real human. He's like The Man Who Fell To Earth or something. He's going to integrate into St Pauly life far more easily than either of us seems to have managed in our thirty odd years."

And you smile weakly as you down that final warm trickle of Newkie Brown, trying hard to focus as Christie chatters on about her ambivalent feelings vis-à-vis the facial mannerisms of an important French actress called Isabel Oopair. But in your heart you cringe like a dog at what it might mean if Christie's actually right about Mikey. What if Mikey really is going to end up better settled in St Pauly than either you or Christie? Wouldn't that be somehow horrendous? Unnatural? Why are you and Christie such freaks? Why haven't you been integrated? Why do you have nobody to turn to but each other? That's not strictly true, of course. You, Damon, have Dawn. It's only Christie who's truly alone. But still, it's as if Mikey's known from the very start that it's not by hanging out with the likes of either one of you two misfits that he'll ever become properly English.

As you turn the key in the front door you feel something scuttle away from the other side and scamper down the hallway. It sounds too large, too human, somehow, to be Irena the cat.

"Mam?" you call, giving the door a violent shove, and stepping inside, a little bit afraid.

"I'll be down in a *mo*," shouts Dawn from upstairs. She sounds muffled, somehow out of breath, red-faced. "Just gettin' me glad rags on. Go to your room, love! Have a look at your prezzies! I left them on the bed."

The back door slams.

"Who's there?" you shout down the dark corridor, terrified.

But nobody answers. And when you creep into the warm kitchen (you note the predictable bowls of potatoes, dozens of them, washed and peeled all over the work surface), you find only Irena there, standing, back arched, on Dawn's chair, and staring pityingly at you.


"So you're from Liverpool originally, Mrs Bosniak?" asks Christie brightly, before taking a first, delicate mouthful of shepherd's pie. "I thought I recognised the accent. Oh, this is delicious!"

You beam. She's making a real effort. They both are.

Christie's brought yellow flowers for Dawn; nothing for you. Dawn takes them with that sharp little smile she puts on when she's trying her best to be civil to someone whose every tooth she would ordinarily love to smash.

"Birkenhead," says your mam, not looking up, tucking into her own plateful.

"No way!" laughs Christie. "Good old Birkenau!"

"What?" Dawn is staring intensely at her now, her blue eyes narrowed.

"Oh, just my own pet name for *de one-eyed city*."

"So *you* know the Wirral?" says Dawn incredulously. "You didn't tell me this, Damon."

"He didn't know," chirrups Christie. "I don't talk about it very much. I went to university in Liverpool—1991 to 1994. I was there for the birth of Britpop."

Dawn smiles, reassured.

Christie adds: "I stayed till 2000. I was a university secretary. God only knows why! I already loathed the place."

"Oh!" cries Dawn.

Your heart sinks: you feel it drop, very suddenly, like an unreliable stone, down, down, down into your guts. You push your plate away.

Dawn tosses back her head of lank, shoulder-length, grey-and-white hair and resumes eating her pie in hurt silence. She looks as if she might start blubbering at any moment.

Christie stares at her now, black eyes open wide. "I hope I haven't offended either of you."

You mumble, grin, but Dawn cuts you off. Maintaining a steady downward gaze, her voice trembling, she begins to explain things of which the likes of Christie are so evidently ignorant.

"Birkenhead, young lady, is one of the finest towns in this land."

Christie is silent.

"The fact that we had to leave it forever when Damon was just a little lad is one of the saddest things I've ever had to live through."

Christie reins in a smirk.

"And Damon knows it."

You nod at Christie imploringly.

"I'm sorry," says Christie, not looking sorry at all. "It's just that my experience of Merseyside as a whole was negative, very negative indeed, and for reasons I'm sure you can both appreciate."

You and your mam stare dumbly at her now.

"It's a very racist place."

The kitchen falls silent, sound switched down at both speakers.

"*Racist?*" Dawn finally repeats in bewildered, offended confusion, as if Christie has just uttered an obscenity, something like "lemon incest", or "cat-porn".

"Well, yes, racist. Of course racist!" laughs Christie. "I mean, that word has become banal through overuse. Misuse. But it'll do the job."

"*What* job?"

Christie sighs, peers at Dawn with theatrical pity.

"The job of evoking a grain of the systematised contempt that's been set in stone in that city. Set in the very stone the black people and the brown people were forced to lay down themselves. Isn't that the ultimate irony?"

Dawn shakes her head heavily, begins to clear away her empty plate.

"So, did you and Damon move straight to St Pauly when you left Birkenhead? When was that?" continues Christie, oblivious to Dawn's evident chagrin.

"Damon, you haven't touched your shepherd's pie," whines Dawn. "I spent two hours on the meat sauce."

"So, did you move straight to St Pauly from Birkenhead?" persists Christie. "Or have you lived in other places too?"

A rumble of thunder struts boldly into the kitchen now. You all listen, briefly united in the elemental melodrama. It's like a horror film, you think. Any second now somebody's going to start spewing in green, groaning "it burns!", or clawing at her gouged and bloody vagina while her head spins round and round.

Dawn slams her plate on the sideboard.

"Mameluke Bath," she replies quietly.

"What?"

Christie stares at your mam as if she's just heard God speaking, or perhaps the Devil.

"Mameluke Bath," says Dawn again impatiently. "A village in the Peaks. You wouldn't know it."

Irena begins to whimper under the table now. Christie reaches down to touch her, the cat turns its tiny dark head, gives a short, sharp hiss and dashes out of the room.

"Will you be wanting afters, then?" shouts Dawn from the dishwasher.

"Please!" calls back Christie brightly, as though suddenly pretending to be Kate Winslet, or Keira Knightley.

She's gone all weird since your mam mentioned Mameluke Bath. Can't stop staring at her. And her voice has gone false and controlled, as if she's trying to keep herself from exploding or something.

"I don't think your cat likes me," says Christie in the same classy, strangled tone.

"No. Well!" responds Dawn, returning to the table with another steaming pie, laying it on the table, though neither you nor Christie have finished the shepherd's. "Apple pie. Damon's favourite."

"Aw, Mam!" you pip. "Gives me terrible zits."

"You *know* what that's about," says Dawn tartly, sitting back down and cutting herself a skinny slice.

"What makes you think I wouldn't know Mameluke Bath?" Christie suddenly whispers at Dawn aggressively. "I mean, why would you assume a thing like that?"

Dawn comes bounding back from her crouching position now, pushes away the apple-pie plate with a sudden terrible violence. She practically shouts her inevitable question (for Christie has pushed her too far, and everybody knows it). "Well, where are *you* from originally, anyway?"

The kitchen is plunged into darkness.

"Oh!" cries Dawn.

"Christ, that's always happening these—"

But before Dawn can tell Christie off for taking her own name in vain, a sudden din, louder even than the torrential rain that's still beating against the door and windows, suddenly invades the pitch-black house. A choir of yobbish voices is outside, singing, screaming in frenzied excitement at the sudden eruption of darkest nature within the artificial molecule that is St Pauly.

"What's that?" whispers Christie, theatrical.

"The anarchists," you helpfully explain. "They'll be stripping off in the garden. They always do that when there's a rainstorm."

"What, in your garden?"

"No, theirs. Next door. They're—"

"Not theirs, Damon, no," corrects Dawn's harsh voice through the dark. "They're squatters. They're there illegally. I've contacted the council, but—"

"Sshh!" whispers Christie excitedly.

(Dawn must be livid in the blackness.)

"What's that they're singing? Hang on. It is! It's—"

And indeed it is. The anarchists are exhorting old Maggie to wake up: they think they have something to say to her. Christie claps her hands in delight.

"That's it!" snaps Dawn. "I'm calling the police. Not in me own home. Not on me lad's birthday."

"No!" cries Christie now, sending you into a paroxysm of panic. "Whatever for? It's a beautiful song."

"It is a *disgusting* song," bellows Dawn. "And those Pussy Rioters or whatever they're called are a *disgusting* group. Should've stayed in Russia. It's illegal, what they're doing, those lies they sing about our country, that filth. Nobody should be allowed to—"

"Oh, please!" snorts Christie. "Are you really saying that you *don't* believe Thatcher and Jimmy Saville were in cahoots when he raped those children? So many people have come forward! The government's not even denying it any more."

"Those girls are nothing but street-walkers. *Urchins*! In balaclavas!" screeches Dawn. "How *dare* they try to drag a great lady like Mrs Thatcher through their muck? Why can't they show some respect? Let the dead rest in peace; that's what I say! What have they ever done for our country, eh? The little sluts sell their own bodies on breakfast television. Do you even know the meaning of the word prostitution?"

"Yes!" screams back Christie's silhouette. "Yes, I do! AND SO DO YOU!"

The lights come back on as suddenly as they disappeared.

You note with slight surprise that Christie's face has turned bright pink-and-brown. You didn't realise that coloured people could blush.

"I'm going to bed," mumbles Dawn.

Your poor mam stumbles out of the kitchen like a disaster victim, wiping the tears that stream from her reddened eyes with the ragged sleeve of her grey cardigan. You look over at Christie with a stare of pleading panic. She isn't looking at you, though. She's staring at the empty space through which Dawn has just passed. She's no longer pink in the face, seems more composed than you've ever seen her, in fact, a faint smile of what looks like it might be triumph trickling across her bitter brown face.

"Where's your music?" asks Christie, her dark eyes darting around your bedroom in critical curiosity.

"I've only got a few CDs," you say apologetically. "Under the bed. I'll get 'em," you add, after a second's thought. You don't want Christie rooting around under there.

"Most of my music's on me iMu," you explain, now on all fours. "But I've left it in me work locker."

You wonder if Christie is staring at your bum.

Christie seizes the shoebox from you, sits down on your bed and begins to root through the twenty-odd compact discs with a careful kind of fury.

"You've got some good stuff," she finally concludes. "Put this one on, will you? I haven't heard it since I was in Liverpool."

You take the CD gently from her.

"*The Lion and the Cobra*," you laugh. "I never really got into this. Always thought she was kinda scary. With the bald head and all."

"She was," says Christie, smiling at you. "That's why I like her."

She begins to sing along softly to the deranged banshee-dirge, something about someone leaving her alone on a cold, dark night so that they could sail the seas, someone leaving her dead for hundreds of years, with her ghosts and her sadness and tears.

"Fucking genius!" she chuckles, taking a breath. Then, adding thoughtfully: "So utterly alive."

You laugh, embarrassed.

"Yeah, it's all right."

"Will she be all right, though?" asks Christie, suddenly stopping her Irish chant and staring at you intently.

"Who?"

"Dawn. Your mother, Dawn."

"Oh...probably. She's just not used to other women."

"Oh, is that it?"

"Yes," you say weakly, uncomfortable with the line of questioning.

"Well, I suppose a boy's best friend is his mother," says Christie, chuckling grimly. "Isn't that what Norman says?"

"Who?"

"Never mind. I'm the Norman Bates around here anyway. I'm sure you prefer baths to showers."

"I don't know what you mean, Christie," you confess, suddenly desperate to cry. It's been such a difficult day. "I don't understand it when you keep mentioning people I've never heard of."

"I'm sorry," says Christie. "I thought you knew about film. You mentioned John Hurt once."

"And what were you talking about when you said that thing about Jimmy Saville and the government paedos? That's what pushed her over the edge."

"Oh, she's been over the edge for decades, Damon," says Christie brusquely. "Listen...I didn't mean anything. I'm sorry. It's just—"

"What?"

"Oh, I don't know. I just hate to see her shoving you around like that. It's like she wants you to be her, I don't know, her...her *thing*."

"She just loves me."

"Yeah, right," snorts Christie again. "People like her don't know what love is."

"How would you know?" you cry as indignantly as you dare. "You only just met her."

"Oh, I know her kind," says Christie mysteriously. "I just think it would be better if some women were spayed in girlhood. But perhaps I'm just talking about my own mother."

"*Your* mam? Where *is* your mam? You never said."

Christie giggles mirthlessly.

"Hélène Jónsdóttir, née Larsen, is livin' la vida loca in the far-off kingdom of Iceland," she said. "Where, like the snow-witch Gunnhildr, she continues to wreak her Nordic havoc. I always thought she'd end up on Crete. Bull-fucking always seemed so much more like her kind of thing."

"Don't you love your mam, then?" you ask, sitting down on the bed next to Christie.

She looks so broken in her rage. You wonder if she feels like crying too.

"My mother is an embarrassment," she goes on, not looking at you. "A pathetic, aging pseudo-siren. A fucking Maenad of the Arctic banal. No, no! There's a word for my mother, from the Middle Ages: I looked it up. My mother is a callitrix. That's a special kind of ape."

"What do you mean?" you ask, meekly.

"What do I mean? What do I mean? Let me think."

She sighs, looks up for the sky but doesn't find it. She starts to speak again. You try hard to concentrate.

"So many women trap themselves in some demented stereotype. And it turns them into fascists, in the end. It's like nothing's actually moved on since Simone de

Beauvoir. No, it's actually gotten *worse*. And what passes for feminism these days...I've told you about that cunt Marianne Kollek, right? The Swiss philosopher they're hosting in my department? At the university?"

"Yes," you assure her, though in truth you've not fully grasped what the problem is exactly.

"Built an entire academic career on reinforcing age-old lies. Claiming women are supernatural *völvas*. Claiming women speak through their vulvas. Saying menstrual blood is cosmic and that women come from rock-pools; that vaginal fluids are actually seawater. Or some such bollocks... I could fucking kill her."

"So, is that what she writes about then? Women's...liquids? Is she a gynaecologist? "

Christie laughs bitterly. "She should be. She should re-train. Look, all I'm saying is that this person is obsessed with trying to use 'philosophy' to prove something she thinks will legitimate her own neurotic sense of being 'different'. Which is fine. But it's dangerous when she turns it into this...fucking...reactionary statement. And then everyone laps it up like it's 'Radical Thought'. We need to get away from these insane notions of what specific types of people 'are' or 'are not', not reinforcing them. And then we need to get organised."

"To do what?" you ask, more confused than ever.

"I don't know. Blow the whole system apart? Start again, and learn to love ourselves so we can finally start loving each other? That kind of shit... It's never really been done, not properly. The proponents of so-called revolution have always been fascists at heart, never seeing further than the end of their own hierarchical noses. They never look at the oppression that they themselves keep going. Never!"

"And what kinds of oppression is this Mrs Coley character keeping going?"

"Oh, what kinds of oppression isn't she keeping going? She's an everyday fascist! Take her name, even. It's made up! From a film! She *stole* that name so she'd sound like she's Jewish! She's not Jewish! And even if she were Jewish, so what? It's not enough to be Jewish..."

"That's true," you agree.

"Take Auschwitz," continues Christie, breathless with excitement.

"What about it?"

"Well, haven't you noticed how it's used as a kind of shorthand for suffering? *The ultimate space of suffering!* The gas-showers, the soap made from Jew skin, the gold fillings, the hair? We latch onto them in such a pornographic way! So we won't have to think too much about the suffering we're part of in the everyday world. Suffering that'll lead straight back to another Auschwitz, of course! In some form or another. Isn't that the ultimate irony?"

"Right."

You grin. You feel more wide-awake than you've felt in weeks, more alive than any night since the club Supernature. Are you somehow enjoying this time with Christie, despite the confusion, despite the steady stream of barked commands? You don't fully grasp the things she's banging on about. But they're strong somehow, they seal you in, they're soothing. She's talking to you, caressing your ears, your soul, stroking your tiny self to sleep. She doesn't expect you to give anything back, doesn't expect you to respond. If she did (but she doesn't), you seriously don't know how you would. If she did (but she doesn't), it would ruin everything. You'd be put on trial, found wanting, and then that would be the end of everything.

"I mean, why isn't Haiti part of the international consciousness, for example?" she's yelling now. "In many ways it's so much more compelling. The slave revolution; the fantastic energy of *vodun*; the endless series of curses and afflictions?"

She raises her eyebrows at you earnestly. It's happening. She wants a response. You could say: "I don't know. Why isn't it?" And, eyes wild with the zeal of the gospel, she'd reply: "Because it would require too much effort! It would require actually having to think and act beyond cliché and cheap nostalgia! Don't you see? It would require actually having to think! And most people would rather do anything than have to think." Or you, yourself, Damon, could try to think. Because if you really thought...Well, then, maybe, just maybe, you could make this Christie lass like you. Love you, even. *Fall in love with you.* That's what she wants; that's what she needs; it's obvious. Maybe if you could just give her *One Original Thought.*

You wrinkle up your forehead and try to think. What was the question again?

Haiti.

Haiti.

You're sure you've heard someone talk about Haiti. Someone who knows it, knows all sorts of things about it, is constantly telling you stories about the crazy things that go on there. You feel your brain stretching, straining, practically to the breaking point. It hurts, you're going to do yourself damage, burst a blood vessel, it's not worth it, it hurts, it——

The spirit of old Mrs Lammoreaux comes bounding into your tiny bedroom, and you brightly speak her thoughts: "Haiti will never be free till the *lwa* and the people in concert will it to be so."

Christie stares at you incredulously. "What did you say?"

"The *lwa* have taken the people to a certain point, but now the people have to give themselves up more fully to their divine horsemen. Forget the spells of the *False West.* Just let the horsemen ride them. The horsemen of the *Real West.*"

"Where did you hear that?" says Christie, laughing.

You blush.

"So it's not true?"

"I think a small part of it's true," answers Christie,

smoothing her black corduroy skirt down with her hands and shaking her head in delighted disbelief. "But it has to be combined with a radical militant programme that forces the world to see what it's done to the place," she adds, still shaking her head. "What it's still doing... Otherwise it's just folkloric mysticism. But still! It's amazing that you've even thought about it. I don't know anybody else who thinks about Haiti. Not in St Pauly."

"Thanks!" you say, aglow with pride.

You can't hear anything else now, and you don't want to speak again for a while. You've made her love you. You've reeled her in. You light a Marlboro Menthol, inhale deeply, and grin.

"Anyway," Christie resumes, "my point is simply that it's not enough to be a victim. Dawn, Mukelenge, Marianne Kollek: all three of them spend their lives claiming 'ultimate-victim' status. But all the while they're participating in the destruction of people way more stigmatised than they are! And because they can't love or protect themselves, not truly, they can't ever love or protect the people who desperately need their love and protection. And all the while the Man is fucking *laughing*."

You're trying hard to digest this last mouthful. You still don't see how old Mrs Coley and your mam are linked. And as for Mikey...

You decide to risk another thought: "But isn't Mikey...I mean, who could be more harmless than Mikey? I mean: he's a seeker, isn't he? What's he ever done to anyone? What *could* he do to anyone?"

Christie laughs. "Oh, Damon. You're so naïve! Mukelenge's one of the strong ones. That much is pretty fucking obvious. Most of the others will have died on the way. He's working for the Man, I'm sure of it."

Christie pauses, frowns, as though considering whether or not to let you into an inconceivably important secret.

"Damon?"

"Yes?"

"Would you help me to do something? Something important?"

"Depends what it is, love. I'm not much cop at anything practical."

Christie looks long and hard at you now, and she suddenly looks as if she might be about to cry.

"Oh, Damon! I wasn't sure before: I didn't dare believe. But back there, in the kitchen, with Dawn...it was like some kind of fucking time-travel. I just can't believe we've actually found each other again. After all these years! Like Orestes and Electra."

You say nothing; hope she'll come quickly to the point.

"We've got so much work to do together!" she suddenly cries.

She kicks off her pink Nike trainers, carefully places her bare feet on the patch of bed behind you and rests her head on your pillow, curled up, snug, Irena-like. You wonder, for a moment, if Christie is mad. Crazy, wacko, bananas; just like *you* were all those years ago when you believed that Leo and BOB were your long-lost uncles, your eastern daddy's bearded little brothers, just because they told you they were, when all the while they were just using you, just playing with your mind and your arsehole, pushing you over the edge, pushing you into another nightmare you'd never escape from. But you *did* escape. Mam was there for you all those years; she came and visited you in the hospital in Laurietown, brought you chocolate, brought you your Fighting Fantasy and Marlboro Menthols, came to collect you when your time was up. Mam's always been there for you; she's told you a million——

"Marianne Kollek and Mukelenge!" bellows Christie. "They need to become better people. They need to be taught a lesson in respect."

And she suddenly leaps up, grabs you by the neck, and whispers into your ear: a plan of corrective action in two short sentences of irrefutable conviction. You nod, relieved that she's not asking you for anything important, eager to return to memories of Mam, Marlboro Menthols and *The Warlock of Firetop Mountain*.

Christie closes her eyes.

"Don't you think, Damon," she muses almost nostalgically, settling back down onto your bed, "that we must have been brought together again for a reason? Like providence... First the Damascus Centre toilets; then at Mukelenge's; and tonight Dawn revealed the Whole Story. Something wants us to find each other again. Something's trying to help us to put the past right through the present."

You smile happily, calmly, but she can't see you, and in any case you prefer it that way. You ignore what she's just said about the Damascus Centre loos, don't want to talk about that now, don't want to think about it. So it *was* her who was in there with you right after the psycho flew out, right after he kicked you in the bollocks and pushed your head down the toilet—you recognise her pink-brown face now, her mad sparkle, that thing in her voice—but it doesn't matter, just a coincidence, no need to dwell on it now.

You wonder if she'll fall asleep here in your bedroom.

"It's never too late for that kind of reunion," she whispers now. "And who knows? This might just be my last stab at the real thing."

She starts to weep, ever so softly.

How will breakfast with Dawn be in the morning if she stays, you wonder? Will the three of you discuss the news headlines together, like a mini-panel on *Question Time*? You giggle to yourself at the very idea.

Her weeping has become louder; now it's a kind of unhinged, animal-like yowling, which causes her entire body to shudder and shake. You hope Dawn's got her earplugs in.

And then the thought occurs to you, as you watch Christie's wailing, trembling, feline form writhing around on your bed, that never in your life have you seen anyone so desperately in need of being stroked. You wish you could show her the friendly, naked men who live in your computer, share them with her, and enjoy them with her. Maybe they'd be just what she needs to stop hurting. You'd give anything to stop her from crying; it's unbearable, you're going to have to switch the computer on, or else run to the bathroom, or, God forbid, to Mam's room; you'll have to, if she doesn't stop it soon; it's more than you can take, beyond your capacities, not fair; why's she doing this to you, and on your fucking birthday too; please, please, just stop your fucking blub—

But Christie's sitting bolt upright now. She's bawling along with Sinéad again, something about burning Troy, her eyes still tightly closed, but her pink-brown face soaked with sweat and dribble and tears. It's like something out of *The Exorcist*.

"A fucking m-m-m-miracle, Diamond," she stammers, both eyes suddenly open, still streaming with tears, and serious as fuck. They stare straight at you, those eyes of hers, so wide you could scream, the blackest lights you've ever seen.

"It often runs in families," she remarked, "just as a love for pastry does."

——**Lewis Carroll,** *Sylvie and Bruno*

# PART TWO
# MAMELUKE BATH

# CHIQUITITA

$P$inky lived with her mother and father and little brother Bruno in an upside-down house high in the hills of Mameluke Bath.

Hélène (for this was the name of Pinky's mother) said that all the houses in Mameluke Bath were upside-down. That was just the way things went here. It was an unconventional place. That was why they belonged there. There was no godly reason why people should have to sleep upstairs and have breakfast downstairs: that was just ideology talking. And did Pinky know the wonderful thing about ideology? It could simply be ignored.

One morning Pinky woke to the familiar feeling of Hélène tickling her nose and chin with the feathers of a long pink boa. In truth, she'd already been awake for some time. She'd heard her father leaving the house (for she and Bruno slept in the room next to the front door), and had also been dimly aware of her mother creeping softly in to take Bruno out of his tiny bed. Hélène usually muttered the lyrics of obscure European pop hits under her breath to wake the infant. This morning Pinky recognised the terrifying strains of Plastic Bertrand being invoked for the matinal anti-lullaby. She heard Hélène getting Bruno quickly up and dressed, then the two of them calling BoyBoy from his resting-place upstairs to come down for his morning walk. Pinky had no desire to join in the canine outing, and kept her eyes tightly shut.

"Come on, chiquitita, rise and shine! We're going out!"

Pinky opened her eyes to see Hélène fully dressed and immaculately made up. She carried a belligerent and extremely wide-awake looking Bruno in her arms. Both of them stared at Pinky aggressively.

"Well, come on!" said Hélène again. "It's a beautiful morning! I'll give you five minutes to get dressed."

"But what about breakfast?" yawned Pinky theatrically, putting her head back under the covers.

"There's plenty to eat where we're going," said Hélène.

Pinky pulled her head out again.

"Are we going to find a school?"

"Not today!"

"Then when?"

"Soon!"

"But term will have *started* already! We'll fall so far behind!"

"Do you see Bruno complaining?" said Hélène. "He's just happy to be back in Mameluke Bath. To be having fun-days every day."

"He's only four," said Pinky, thoroughly annoyed by her mother's blitheness. "He doesn't understand anything."

Bruno glared at his sister, and Hélène quickly twisted his tiny head back so that it was facing its mother again. She gave him a reassuring kiss on the nose.

"Don't mind grumpy old Pinky, little one," she whispered.

Bruno said nothing. Hélène put him down with the familiar groan *("T'es lourd, toi!")* and perched lightly on Pinky's bed.

"What is it, Pinky?" she said. "Aren't you happy we

came back to Mameluke Bath? I thought you didn't like Ollioules."

"I just want to start school," said Pinky.

"And you will! What's the hurry? We've been through so much lately. I would have thought you'd want a little rest."

Pinky said nothing.

"Most chiquititas your age would be delighted to have a *maman* that bought them ice cream every day, and ribbons and dresses and...what about that new Debbie Harry LP?" she suddenly added sharply. "*Koo Koo*? Have you even listened to it yet? You know how expensive it was."

Pinky shook her head. She'd only insisted on having it in order to make a point. Hélène had always considered Debbie overrated, even in her Blondie days, and was accordingly most sceptical about the viability of a solo career. Pinky wanted to prove her mother wrong. Though she'd been fascinated too by that crazy picture on the album cover. It was even better than Queen Bush on the front cover of *The Dreaming*: a vampire-monarch in sepia, tiny golden key sparkling on her tongue, about to French-kiss a drowned man in chains. *Koo Koo*'s cover was more than just weird: it was utterly miraculous. For on it Debbie had black hair, scraped back, and she looked absolutely ravishing. Behind her swirled night and fog and what looked like platinum wisps of lightning. Four sharp metal skewers penetrated her face from left to right: one at the level of her temple, one at the top of her Italian cheekbones, one through the hollow of her cheek, and one through the neck. Pinky didn't know which part of the picture she loved most: the night-and-fog background, the knives, how calm and pretty Debbie looked through it all, or the supernatural fact that she—*she* of all people!—had changed from blonde to black.

Hélène jumped up, rapidly smoothed down her red-and-white Chinese dress with both hands, and gave a little "tsk!" of irritation.

"Come *on*. We're going to the Heights of Rocamadour."

*T*hey'd decided to leave BoyBoy behind in the end. He'd only hold them back. Let him shit in the kitchen if he wanted to protest.

"*Mmm, your hair is bee-yoo-tiful!*" sang Hélène mockingly as the three of them stumbled down the hill road that took them onto the high street.

"What a shameful trivialisation of nuclear war that song is! Bloody Americans. Give me ABBA any day. Oh, do come *on*! You're such a humourless little thing. And vain as hell to boot."

Pinky scowled. She loved Blondie's 'Atomic', and hated the fact that Hélène was always using its chorus to poke fun at her hairstyle. They hadn't had time to take out her nocturnal plaits, which stuck out of her head now like four stiff black devil-horns. Well, that's what Hélène said. She'd been promising ever since their return to Mameluke Bath that first day of August that they'd have to have a proper think about what to do with Pinky's hair. There'd initially been talk of taking her down on the train to St Pauly, finding a proper 'ethnic' salon for her. There was bound to be one there, Mickle had grunted. But the right moment had never come. Instead, the month had rushed by in a simultaneously grey and multicoloured blur of job-hunting, television acquisitions and weekly rows. There'd been that trip last week to nearby Alton Towers, for Pinky's birthday, of course, an excursion of relative pleasure, marred only by Hélène's allegedly flirtatious remark to the twinkly bus driver on the way home. Mickle had ended up almost punching his slobbering Irish lights out, but had contented himself with merely spitting on the ground.

And there was no denying that Mameluke Bath itself was full of pleasant things to see and do. The people were friendly enough (not like those Provençal devils in Ollioules), and if some of the children (and old people, of course) did occasionally feel the need to stare for the longest time, especially at Mickle, well, it wasn't meant badly. But Pinky's new hairstyle would have to wait. In the meantime, said Hélène, she could just carry on making sure she plaited it every night, and maybe that would make the wild frizzy tangles and knots a bit less hellish to manipulate. As for poor Bruno, his tiny head looked clumpier with every passing minute. He'd recently begun to wail when Hélène listlessly tried putting a comb through it, so she'd simply given up, snapping, "Well, *be* a little Rasta, then!" before immediately cooing, "At least your nose is still Nordic."

Mameluke Bath was bustling that morning with its usual mix of tattooed bikers, French tourists (Hélène pointed them out to the children with a shudder of speechless contempt) and chattering mums, careening along the riverbank that ran parallel to the high street with their army of screeching, voluminous prams. Nobody seemed to give a second glance to the little family of three today, and as she waited outside the fish and chip shop for her mother and brother to buy the jumbo sausage and cherry-flavoured Fanta she'd requested for brunch, Pinky breathed a heavy sigh of relief. It was true that things were always worse in that way when Mickle was with them. The sun was already high in the sky, appearing to have taken up a comfortable resting position directly above the residential mountain they'd just descended. And as Pinky gazed up from the bench outside the fish and chip shop at the tiny dot on the mountain that she knew was now their upside-down home, it suddenly seemed to her that, despite all the worries and unpleasantness they'd brought with them from that unspeakable year in Ollioules, perhaps everything really *was* going to be all right now that they were back for good in Mameluke Bath.

"That was their last sausage, chiquitita," said Hélène, emerging from the shop with Bruno in her arms again.

The plastic bag of greasy provisions dangled around his tiny neck.

"You're a very lucky little girl."

"Can I have it, then?" said Pinky, suddenly ravenous.

"No, I think we should wait till we get to the Heights of Rocamadour," said Hélène. "There might be an enormous queue, for all we know."

Pinky couldn't be bothered protesting. She sprang up from the bench and began to march down the high street toward the train station.

"Wait for us, little miss premature!" shouted Hélène, laughing. "Anyone would think you *wanted* to get raped by one of these English Mameluke inbreds!"

The station was just three minutes away. But everything was just three minutes away in Mameluke Bath, once you'd made it down from the hill and into the valley. It was a truly tiny railway station, nervously sandwiched between the gigantic car park at its front and the mad green forest that rose up behind it. Pinky had trouble believing that this silly little village could ever have been as important an interchange in the nineteenth century as Mickle constantly insisted. And as for the legend about the medieval Mamelukes from the East, well, that was strictly for the birds. Either way, the only people who came to Mameluke Bath now were the tourists. Glutted on their quaint afternoon of fish and chips and beer and ice cream in this strange little seaside resort without the seaside (they didn't even bother checking out the hot springs at The Bottom, cried Hélène in disgust), at the coming of dusk they'd pile onto the hourly train that would take them south to St Pauly. From there they would catch another train, a high speed intercity one this time, that would convey them further south still, all the way back to London.

The ticket office was closed as usual.

"Can't we catch a train somewhere?" said Pinky. "We wouldn't have to pay. Look."

"No," said Hélène. "Where would we go? Mameluke? Darley Dale? Whatstandwell? There's nowhere."

And it was true. The villages around Mameluke Bath

were truly dreadful.

One day, when they'd lived here last, before the Ollioules experiment—Pinky couldn't have been more than seven, and Bruno was still just a toddler—they'd made the mistake of catching the train without Mickle to Whatstandwell. The name had just sounded so funny! Hélène swore she remembered D.H. Lawrence mentioning it in some obscure passage of *Sons and Lovers*. They'd been there but an hour when one of the market butchers alighted his attention on Pinky and Bruno. And as Pinky watched the red-faced market-man chuckle and gesture and grin, never taking his eye off them for a second, she felt suddenly relieved. At least they were welcome here! She wondered if he'd offer them liquorice. She didn't fancy any meat, not really, and certainly not raw. But the butcher was already dribbling his merry gaze back over to Hélène, who was goth-like and vaguely Siouxsie that day, in long black velvet skirt, heavy black cashmere sweater and large Norse cross of silver. The butcher slapped his mate gently in the chest with the back of his right hand and waggled a fat, jovial index finger at the paralysed trio: "One o' them niggercock girls!"

He smiled at the children with two rows of yellow teeth, his face purple and open and friendly, before turning definitively back to Hélène now, suddenly hostile: "How much you charge for English prick, duck?"

And the two butchers had held onto one another, collapsed together in hysterical, bloodstained mirth.

They'd fled Whatstandwell. Pinky's eyes had streamed for a minute or so: she was terrified that they wouldn't get out of the market before the butchers caught up with them. But were they even being chased? She soon calmed down on the train. Hélène's chagrin, when it came, was, of course, inconsolable. So violent and voluminous were her sobs as they sped back to Mameluke Bath that the conductor didn't dare ask them to show their tickets. Pinky thanked him with moist brown eyes (nothing like those

Whatstandwell butchers, this one: young and friendly, and on their side, for sure), desperately grateful for his welcome absence of hostility. All three of them had leapt in joyful relief when the inexplicably painted μ squiggle underneath the railway sign for Mameluke Bath finally came into view—even Bruno.

"But I'm so bored with the Heights of Rocamadour," Pinky whined now, back in the safer feeling present, the dangers of overly ambitious exploration quite forgotten. "We've already done it twice since we've been back."

They were on the platform now, preparing to cross the track. Once across (Pinky always felt terrified for the few seconds of the crossing, even though there was clearly no way a train could just surge up out of nowhere and smash them to pieces), they'd follow the path through the forest for ten minutes before emerging at the little clearing from which the cable cars began their mid-air, inter-mountain traversal.

"Look," said Hélène, pointing at the British Rail sign on the platform. "Look at that sign, Pinky. *Mameluke Bath*. And what does it say underneath? No, I don't mean the funny Greek squiggle. Christ, you're obsessed with that thing! I'm talking about the words between parentheses. What do they say? *For the Heights of Rocamadour*. Do you see that? People come a long way for this. This town is world famous for the Heights of Rocamadour. Otherwise they wouldn't bother writing it between parentheses on the station sign."

"But you said yourself that the tourists only come for the fish and chips, not the hot springs. Or the Heights," protested Pinky weakly, knowing the answer that was on its way.

And come it did, straightaway, as if an emergency door buzzer had been pressed in her mother's brain. "We're not tourists," said Hélène. "Come on."

She reached out a heavily bejewelled hand for her petulant daughter to take. Pinky was just about to accept this unusual maternal offer, despite the cold, sticky sweat-rivers that were now beginning their usual streaming across the plains of her own small hands, but was suddenly distracted by the sight of what looked like a woman and a tiny boy sitting on a bench on their side of the otherwise deserted platform, some twenty metres away. She hadn't noticed them before.

"That lady's in trouble."

Hélène peered in the direction Pinky was indicating. "What a hideous coat," she said. "It's like something from my childhood."

But Pinky was already skipping down the platform towards the odd, cringing bench-couple. "Hello!" she said in the friendliest tone she could muster. "Are you tourists? We can take you to the Heights of Rocamadour if you like. We're going there anyway."

The woman gazed up at her uncomprehendingly. Pinky noticed that the whites of her eyes were quite red, redder than she'd ever seen Hélène's. The small boy (if that's what he was) simply buried his face in his mother's repulsive brown mac.

"How old is he?" said Pinky, trying to smile.

But Hélène and Bruno had caught up with her now, and they would ruin everything.

"Is everything all right?" asked Hélène in the same tone of slightly forced amiability that Pinky had just deployed. "Do you know where you're going?"

"Yes, thank you," stammered the woman, her voice trembling piteously. "I mean, no, no, I don't know where to go. I don't even know where we are."

It was Hélène's turn to stare in dull incomprehension.

"You don't know where we are? We're in Mameluke Bath! Look!" And she pointed at the sign on the opposite platform with a long pink fingernail.

"Where is that exactly?" asked the woman. "I don't really...I mean, we just got off here coz the lad was upset."

"Are you running away?" asked Pinky suddenly. It came

out in a sharper, more accusatory manner than she'd intended.

"Pinky!" said Hélène. "You must excuse my daughter," she purred at the stranger. "She's quite forgotten her manners of late."

The red-eyed woman said nothing. The boy continued to hide his face and cling to his mother (if that's what she was) somewhat awkwardly, since she seemed unable to put her own hands on him, and instead held them stiffly in the air, as though performing a petrified number in an unhappy musical.

"We were just on our way to the Heights of Rocamadour," said Hélène. "If you would like to join us, perhaps...?"

She didn't bother waiting for the cow-gaze of non-understanding, and immediately expanded, pointing at the station sign again.

"Heights of Rocamadour. See? One of our main tourist attractions in these parts. It's just behind the station. Just a little way into the forest."

At the word 'forest', the little creature sitting in the red-eyed woman's lap suddenly turned his face towards them and smiled uncertainly. But when it looked at Bruno, who had taken up an authoritative position behind the bench, little arms angrily folded, it shrank back, hiding its face once again in its tiny, tear-stained hands.

*H*élène put the newcomers on the Smithkin family ticket. It made little difference to the price, she said, and it was a pleasure, to be sure.

As the warm glass bubble in which the five of them now sat snugly ensconced began its gliding journey along the thick black snaky cable that stretched so high over the hills and dales of Mameluke Bath, the new child began to leap and hop about the capsule like a hysterical rodent. Pinky had never in her life laid eyes on such a pale, excitable, nervous little thing.

"Mammie! Mammie! Look!" it cried. "We're up in heaven!"

Dawn (for this was the name of the strange lady) smiled weakly.

"Careful, Damon!" she said. "I don't know how safe it is to rush around in this thing."

"Diamond!" screamed the child.

"Diamond," conceded Dawn.

"Diamond?" queried Pinky.

"Diamond," repeated Dawn, refusing to meet Pinky's steady gaze. "It's what he wants to be called now. Name of a boy in some old market book he's been reading. Won't talk about nothing else."

"Diamond the little stable boy," said Hélène admiringly. "*The Back of the North Wind*, no?"

Diamond stared at Hélène now with a look of utter, worshipful amazement. She gave a pleased little laugh, and tossed her mane of long, dark hair. It seemed to glow red in the sun.

"What a delightful book," she said. "I loved all those Victorian children's stories when I was little girl too. Though I had to read them in French, of course," she added thoughtfully.

Woman and boy stared at their hostess now as if she were truly a creature descended from the heavens. Pinky and Bruno said nothing, and instead gazed through the glass down to the valley hundreds of feet below.

"I've been trying for years to get Pinky to read those charming children's classics," Hélène went on. "She won't, of course. Prefers old Auntie Enid, with her clichés and gollies and fascistic ginger-beer morals. Which one are you on now, Pinky?"

"*The Put-'em-Rights*," mumbled the irate little half-caste, her face as black as thunder.

Pinky took another nibble of her jumbo sausage, but shoved it back in the grease-spotted bag with a tiny motion of rage. It was cold. And the Fanta was warm. She was trying desperately to contain her furious disappointment when the capsule suddenly gave a little lurch, and stopped in mid-air. They hovered six hundred and sixty-six feet above the valley, completely and utterly powerless to intervene in whatever dreadful, plummeting fate awaited them.

"Oh!" whimpered Dawn and Diamond in unison.

Pinky smiled, and rested her head against the glass. She wondered (as she always did at this point in the fantastical crossing, when the bubble-car deliberately halted for two minutes, suspended in gaffa, allowing the passengers to properly take in the glorious views) what it would be like if they all came crashing down together now. How long would the fall last? Would it begin to slow down as they got used to the non-stop descent, or would they go faster and faster? Would they all die instantly upon contact with the ground, or would some of them survive, and have to go foraging in the valley for provisions? How long would it take before she'd give in to cannibalism?

But this time there was nobody available with whom to share her morbid thoughts. Bruno sat next to her, but was miles away, his forehead wrinkled up in anxious-looking rage, while on the opposite seat Hélène, Dawn and Diamond seemed caught up in something together which Pinky didn't feel willing or able to understand. She wondered, for one tiny second, if the reason the three of them seemed so bonded now, her mother and these two perfect strangers, was because they all had white skin. Such psychic glue as she felt she was now witnessing between the three of them, sealing them all together, never seemed to trickle between her (Pinky) and Hélène. But then again, it didn't really gel between Pinky and her beastly daddy Mickle either. And Mickle's skin was quite, quite black. When Mickle looked at Pinky, when Mickle alighted his flickering snake-gaze on Pinky's awkward, little-girl brownness, she felt only circles and circles of spite.

Perhaps she was just intrinsically alone. For the umpteenth time that summer, Pinky found herself wondering, with a terrible, shameful curiosity, if Bruno felt that loneliness yet. She hoped and prayed that he did.

"I see no reason whatsoever why you can't both come and stay with us for a short while," Hélène was saying excitedly. "There's plenty of room in the kitchen."

"Oh, Mrs Smithkin!" said Dawn, her already bloodshot eyes filling again with tears.

"Hélène," said Hélène.

"Elaine," said Dawn.

"*Hé-lène*," repeated Hélène, making no concessions to the English woman's mortified reserve. "It's a French word. Like...I don't know...you just...I don't know, just *say* it!"

Dawn's face grew terribly pale.

She looked, thought Pinky (suddenly pleased, giggling inside), as if she might be about to be violently ill.

"I'm not sure I *can* say it," Dawn eventually muttered.

"Try," said Hélène.

And the silence seemed to Pinky as painful and prolix as one of the more recent tracks of the appalling Pink Floyd. But she couldn't help staring fixedly at Dawn for its entire duration. The woman's bug-like discomfort was fascinating. It was as if she was squirming under a pin. Dawn was repulsive.

Diamond gazed from his mother to Hélène and back to his mother again in bewildered little-boy horror.

The car began its gentle glide again.

"Don't worry," said Hélène, clearing her throat and giving an angry little laugh as she gazed through the glass down to the valley.

"Don't worry about it, Dawn," she said again. "You can call me Karin. That's my middle name. It's Danish. No, NO—" (she brightened, grew suddenly excitable again) "actually, 'Dawn', why don't you call me 'Aurora'? We'll be the same...but *different!*" Hélène clapped her hands in delight at the brilliance of her own onomastic inventiveness.

Dawn's blotchy face remained confused, uncomprehending.

"Forget it," snapped Hélène, offended. "Just forget it. You can call me Anni-Frid. Frida, for short."

The Heights of Rocamadour were like a cross between an adventure playground (with the usual mix of climbing frames, sandpits, and plenty of swings and slides) and a space of sheer exception, at once part of the known world and somehow really, inexplicably not. Pinky didn't understand how the Heights could possibly have been reached by humans before the construction of the cable cars, and it was this mystery that made them so peculiar. For how could they be said to have really existed in the past if it wasn't until now that they were actually being lived on? They weren't like a civilised part of the Earth at all, then, but more like some African jungle, a piece of something truly savage and wild, here in the heart of the English Peak District. A little bit like her perhaps? A little bit like Pinky? Except Pinky wasn't really savage and wild. It was only Hélène who told her she was, when they were quarrelling, when Hélène wanted to silence her once and for all with that ultimate charge of an inescapable atavism. It always worked. Pinky didn't like being called a beast. In any case, it couldn't be true about no one having lived here before the cable cars. For hadn't there been a silver mine here in the seventeenth century? That's what the lady in the rock shop had told them last time. But it had been too late to visit the mine that day.

"Maman, let's go to the silver mine this time!" shouted Pinky once they'd all clambered out of the capsule.

"Pinky! Diamond and Dawn are traumatised," said Hélène crossly. "They've just escaped from a violent and terrifying situation in...where was it you said you were from, Dawn?"

"Birkenhead," said Dawn. "On the Wirral," she added weakly.

"Did he beat you, Dawn?" asked Hélène.

Pinky and Bruno stared at Dawn inquisitively, while Hélène attempted to gather her blood-brown mane into a ponytail. The wind gave a sudden hard blow. Diamond looked at his feet. Dawn began to stammer.

"Erm, just once. At the end, like. When I told him I wasn't moving to Yugo-bloody-slavia. That's why I left. I wasn't about to leave England! Not for him!"

"But he never touched the boy?" pursued Hélène, suddenly deciding against the ponytail and ripping off the red band she'd just proudly forced her hair through.

"No."

Diamond continued to study his tiny feet.

Hélène gave Dawn a long, hard stare.

Dawn suddenly stopped in the middle of the patch of grass they were crossing and began to babble loudly. She seemed to be addressing her speech to Diamond now, who pawed at the ground like a tiny, embarrassed mule.

"It was *not* my fault," she said, her voice suddenly more solid and cold than it had sounded to Pinky in all the time they'd been together. "I tried with that man, God knows I tried. Me mam warned me, she told me to watch how I went with a man like that. But would I listen? No. No." She shook her head wearily. "But you never do, do you, Frida?" she added, gazing imploringly at Hélène now.

Hélène smiled reassuringly, taking her by the hand. "No, Dawn, I suppose you don't. But we're all foreigners really, you know," she added. "This is a land of mongrels. Look at my two! I'm sure that your husband's foreignness wasn't really the issue in the break-up of your marriage."

Dawn flushed and said nothing.

"Let's go and get some rock from the café," said Hélène brightly. "Pinky, we'll see about the silver mine after that."

In the café Hélène chattered to Dawn and Diamond

about the Smithkin family's own recent adventures.

"...For we truly felt that if we went to live in France for just a while, you know, that our marriage would...I don't know, regenerate somehow, get that spark back, you know?"

Dawn nodded fervently, gulping her tea like a recently rescued orphan.

"It was all an illusion, of course. Pie in the sky! Mickle never stopped complaining, my sister threw us out before we had a chance to find jobs—it's terrible in south-east France, where I'm from, they're so—well, you know what I mean, I'm sure. We had no choice but to return to Mameluke Bath. My husband grew up in an orphanage in this region. Just outside the city of St Pauly. You've heard of St Pauly, perhaps?"

"Of course," said Dawn, finishing her tea. "I thought that maybe Diamond and me would go to St Pauly to live. I heard it was a pleasant town. I still don't really understand why we got off...here. *Mameluke Bath*. I've never even heard of the place. It just sort of...happened."

Hélène nodded sagely. Dawn seemed to be gaining in confidence and carried on speaking. She never looked at Pinky or Bruno, though, not even to flash a condescending smile at them, the way most grownups tried to whenever there were children around. Pinky hated her.

"So your husband's English then?" asked Dawn, curiously.

"Yes."

"I just thought...when I saw these two..."

Hélène stared at her, puzzled.

"My husband comes from this region," Hélène repeated slowly, as if speaking to a retarded person. "Come on. Let's visit this famous silver mine."

"Yay!" cried Pinky, Bruno and Diamond, in unison for the first time.

*T*he mine was dark and cold and trickled with a scary drip-drip-drip. Pinky wished she'd never made them all come down here. Bruno looked bored to death, and kept yawning every ten seconds. Diamond looked terrorised by every flickering shadow. And Hélène kept asking the stupid-looking teenage girl tour-guide absurd questions about the history of the mine, questions the poor little thick-accented fool was clearly in no position to answer.

They were the only group doing the visit. Everyone else on the Heights of Rocamadour that afternoon (and there was a veritable crowd, since the new school year had not yet quite resumed) seemed to be busy enjoying the more light-hearted, less subterranean pursuits the cliff had to offer. Dawn hadn't wanted to descend into the mine when the guide had warned that there were two hundred and ninety-seven steps, but Hélène had insisted that something like this was exactly what was needed to snap them out of the trauma. And now Dawn hovered at Hélène's side like a slavish shadow-ghoul, nodding at her protector's pretentious inquiries with the occasional, supportive "Oh, I'd been wondering that too!"

The tour guide's name was Trudy. She was shameless. She used every trick in the book.

"What do you think, kids?" she called out to Pinky, Bruno and Diamond, who hovered behind their mothers in the gloom. "Why do *you* think that it was always the smaller children who were sent down here to work?"

"Because they were the only ones who could get into all the nooks and crannies?" asked Pinky, not bothering to hide her contempt.

"That's right!" exclaimed Trudy. "And how old are you?"

"Nine," answered Pinky reluctantly.

"If we were living in 1682 instead of 1982 *you'd* have been headed here to work just after your tenth birthday," said the girl with a silly, faux-sinister cackle. "What do you think about that?"

Pinky shrugged.

"That's not strictly true," interjected Hélène.

"Oh?" said Trudy nervously.

"Well, I know it's dark down here," said Hélène, "but in case you hadn't noticed, my daughter's got brown skin. In 1682 she'd probably have been slaving away somewhere far hotter than Mameluke Bath!"

Trudy's already pale face turned a deathly shade of white. Pinky thought she could almost feel it shining like the spectral skin of an embarrassed English ghost through the darkness of the cave.

"And how old are the little boys?" called out Trudy, only slightly recovered.

"They're four," said Hélène. "Now what about the various deposits in this mine? Surely it wasn't principally silver?"

"I'm not sure," said Trudy. "I'm pretty certain it was a silver mine. I mean, it's famous for that."

"I imagine lead and fluoride were far more habitually extracted than silver," said Hélène firmly. "Even if silver sounds more glamorous."

"Fluoride!" cried Trudy with relief, ignoring Hélène's reproving undertone. "What's that used for?" she called out to Pinky.

"Teeth," said Pinky coldly.

"Well I can see why you have such white ones," twinkled Trudy.

Hélène laughed sarcastically.

"Have you any other pearls of wisdom for us before we go back up into the light?" she asked.

"Well, I haven't told you the story of the Mameluke Bluecap yet!" said Trudy. "I'm sure the little ones would like to hear that."

"Oh, I'm not sure..." began Dawn.

"Go on, then," said Hélène, smirking.

"Well," began Trudy enthusiastically, "legend has it that every year, on the last day of springtime, precisely *nine* little

111

girls and exactly *seven* little boys would mysteriously disappear while they were down here working in the mines."

Pinky was just about to cry out with indignation at the blatant unfairness of the way in which this child-vanishing scheme was conducted when she felt a little hand suddenly thrust itself into her own dripping palm. She looked down to see Diamond's scared little moon-face staring up at her in desperation. Bruno stood a little way back, near a monstrous-looking rock formation, his arms folded, staring coldly at his older sister and her pathetic new elfin charge.

"Nobody knew why it was always the same number of children that went missing every year, or why it was that only seven boys were needed for every nine girls," continued Trudy. "Until a wise old dactyl who lived up in the hills of Mameluke Bath told them the story of the Mameluke Bluecap..."

*MY! MY!!*

Diamond screamed. It was a terrible sound, thin and reedy, yet at the same time truly blood-curdling. Pinky had let go of his hand and now looked down to see Hélène's own big hands tightly wrapped around the child's scrawny neck.

Hélène cackled hysterically in the hapless tour guide's face.

*MY! MY!!*

she shouted again.

And then she sang, or rather shamanically chanted (perhaps inhabited by the voice of the Bluecap itself) the Swedish quartet's inane musical analogy between Napoleon's defeat at Waterloo and a lover's emotional surrender. After the second chorus she stopped chanting and instead began to bellow:

"Wake up and smell the radioactive coffee, people! Prepare for Madame Thatcher's Napoleonic Wars! See your neighbour's upturned eyeballs as they start to shrivel and melt! Smell your mother's rancid body as it crackles and burns in the yard! Behold the cataracts and cancers in their sickening one-year bloom! That's if you're *serious* about scary stories."

Diamond began to whimper.

Trudy stared at Hélène in angry, red-faced confusion.

"Come on," said Hélène. "Let's go back up. This is utterly ridiculous. And as for you," she whispered to the quivering Trudy, "I hope there's a baby inside you when the mushroom cloud appears on the horizon. And I hope you piss your cheap Woolworths pants for the fear."

They were all exhausted by the time they limped into the upside-down house at 111 Mastema Drive.

"Pinky! Take BoyBoy for a walk!" commanded Hélène.

"But I'm tired!" yelled Pinky.

"So are we all!" retorted Hélène. "But BoyBoy needs to pee, I need to feed Bruno, Dawn and Diamond need to be shown around the area, and I don't see your father here to help with any of it, do you?"

At just that moment the front door opened and Mickle strode in, his overalls spattered with blood.

"Hello!" he said, smiling at the assembled company. "Who have we got here?"

Dawn stared at the floor in embarrassment.

"Dawn," said Hélène. "My husband, Mickle Smithkin."

"Pleased to meet you," murmured Dawn, still not looking at Mickle. She looked closer to vomiting than she had all day.

But Diamond stared at Mickle, fascinated, wide-eyed.

"Mickle is from this region, as I was telling you earlier, Dawn," said Hélène triumphantly. "Even if he's what Grammy Hall would call a real *nee-gra*."

Mickle snorted, and began to march purposefully up the stairs to the living room.

"Diamond and Dawn will be depending on the kindness of strangers for a few days," Hélène shouted at her husband's rapidly disappearing bulk. "They've come from trauma! How was the first day at the abattoir, pumpkin?"

There was no answer. The living room door could be heard being kicked roughly open. BoyBoy came bounding down the stairs, closely followed by a disdainful-looking Sula. The living room door slammed shut again, and the familiar, crazy, muffled strains of Fela Kuti and his Magic Band came floating down to the English day-trippers.

*Zombie-o, zombie!*
*Zombie-o, zombie!*
*Zombie-o, zombie!*
*Zombie-o, zombie!*

Hélène sighed, and stared petulantly at the two arriving pets.

"Oh, I'd forgotten all about Sula," said Hélène. "I suppose she'll want feeding too. Oh, I can't do everything!"

"I'll feed the cat if you tell me where you keep the food," said Dawn quickly. "I like cats."

"Oh, Dawn, you're an angel," said Hélène. "Pinky, show Dawn where we keep the cat food. And now I simply must feed Bruno. He's been very patient. Where is he?"

But Bruno had already rushed into the bedroom he shared with Pinky, where he was doubtless sitting up perkily on Pinky's bed, waiting for Hélène to come to him with her own special brand of royal jelly.

"Are you feeding him in there?" asked Dawn uncertainly.

"Well, where else am I going to feed him?" said Hélène,

unzipping the back of her beautiful Chinese dress to reveal an exquisite pair of lacy white bra straps.

# II

*M*y eyes opened early on Saturday morning. The first few lines of John Lennon's 'Number 9 Dream' still swirled around my brain, their strange blend of silliness and beauty so savage it split me in two. My bedroom was flooded with a strange glow. It seemed to have bulldozed its way past the curtain border (underneath them, around them, straight through them, who knew?) in a way I'd never seen before. I thought of *Threads*, and panicked. But was this particular golden light necessarily atomic? I resolved to meet the situation. There was no earthly reason why it should be linked to nuclear holocaust.

As I pulled back the thick yellow flaps, and heaved open the guillotine window, I felt a rush of unusually warm, first-of-December air and St Pauly birdsong float across Old Saul Street from the Opoponax Gardens on the other side of the tram tracks. The eerie feeling melted at once. The snark wasn't a boojum, the glow was only light, the cigar *was* just a cigar, after all. I laughed, relieved at reality's revelation, and congratulated myself out loud on my own small act of bravery.

I jumped back onto my bed (still bathed in light, but no

longer uncanny) and tried to remember my dream. Judd would be pleased. For once it hadn't been a nightmare. For once it hadn't involved Hélène and the Mickle-Beast locked in wondrous, nauseating reunion, as I kicked, clawed, screamed in the background, desperately trying to get them to stop necking and look at the drowned and rotting mess that was Bruno, splayed across the kitchen table with his guts hanging out. For once I'd been spared that. Last night's sleep had offered me something new. And while I wasn't sure if the new dreaming was attached to any kind of coherent narrative, after several minutes of intense concentration my fingernails finally started to remember: in the third part of the night, and into the early morning, I'd experienced myself as a strong and peaceful matagot.

I leaped off the bed and laughed out loud again. My Friday session up in Mameluke Bath with Judd had gone so wonderfully well! I'd been completely correct to renew my therapy at the end of November, correct too to sell another egg on the internet, the week after Damon's birthday dinner. The money from the clinic would pay for Judd till spring. And God knows, I didn't need the eggs. Therapy was what I needed: wise counsel and care! I felt a thousand times closer to myself.

How much less sinister the events of the autumn now seemed. And how much less demonic Mukelenge! I'd projected so much onto that poor creature. I'd conflated him with the Mickle-Beast, and in such a shamefully racial way! *Wouldn't be the first time you turned a dark-skinned man into the dusky revenant of your devil-father, eh, Christie*, Judd had chuckled, not without a tinge of reproof. So I'd been immersed in repeating my own childhood trauma (not remembering, not working through!) via the hologram of a poor African tin-man. I'd forgotten just how unhinged an experience of the world Mukelenge himself must be undergoing at the moment——the horrors he'd fled, the humiliations he was probably experiencing now. And as I struggled to communicate clearly to Judd that this was precisely what I'd wanted Mukelenge to admit—that it was precisely the African's misplaced, downright bizarre stance of Uncle Tom-ish gratitude towards St Pauly that had riled me so back in September—I couldn't help but concur with his overall judgment that I was expecting far too much from someone like Mukelenge at such an early stage in the mentorship.

I'd skipped out of Judd's consulting room and down his hallway, past his demented painting of a grinning Freud and Fanon shaking hands like the hallucinatory Martin and Malcolm of *Psychotherapy: The Musical*, my heart singing with hope. The one thing I hadn't managed to get off my chest was the way Mukelenge's accent had made him sound like he came from Mameluke Bath. Had I perhaps imagined that too? Either way, Judd would never have believed me. *He'd* lived in Mameluke Bath since the early nineties, and he still spoke like he was fresh off the boat from Jamaica. I thought maybe that was affected too, Judd's accent, I mean, some pretentious form of old-school *négritude*.

Still, everything felt cleaner and more possible now. And Judd had facilitated that. I would let go of my Mukelenge vendetta. It was only Marianne Kollek that needed punishing now. I'd already decided on the method; and I was sure that Damon would help me. He owed me that much. I didn't care anymore, not even if the Master terminated our deal and suspended me from the university. This was something that couldn't just be waved away. I was gaining a better sense of the relative importance of things now.

As I filled my scaly, furry kettle right to the top (fuck the 'environment': I wanted several coffees), I thought about Damon. I wondered what he was doing now, this very minute, while I sat alone, sipping bitter Nescafé at my kitchen table, a friendly framed image (my only one!) of Roy Orbison's bespectacled ghost hovering just above my head. Would he and Dawn stay in all weekend to play

Cluedo, Radio 5 Live chirruping a reactionary background hum to their own trivial chatter? What was Dawn like, really? It had always been so difficult to penetrate her terrified exterior, I thought, soaping my body, post-coffee, post-shit, in my tiny shower room. The questions and memories were pouring from my brain now, swirling crazily around my wet, caffeine-addled head in a positively unending stream. Was she, deep down, as sweet and bright and gay as her innocent, beautiful son?

One thing was certain: September had been a kind of Revelation. Meeting Damon again, first on that Friday afternoon in the Damascus Centre toilets, then that Tuesday night at Mukelenge's flat—it had been written in the stars. There was something gentle and clean about little Damon, something that cried out for protection. Something inside him was damaged, but it was sacred too, and essentially intact. As I stood under the last hot blast of water, I screamed Cat Stevens' 'Wild World' (a pop song of person-centred jihad if ever there was one) as ferociously as my lungs could manage. I still felt strong. I pulled on white socks, pants, bra, then reached inside my wardrobe for my baggiest blue jeans and my biggest black corduroy shirt. After a moment's hesitation I buttoned the shirt right up to my neck. Judd could fuck off with his "let your inner woman out" nonsense. He wasn't the one who had to carry those jugs around. That glorious, sunny morning was for being uncluttered and free and just *beyond* all that divisive, dichotomous gender malarkey. I still had to sort out my hair, though. I began to root underneath the sofa for the adversarial twin relics: 'Adam Lives in Theory'—the opening track on Lauryn Hill's *Unplugged* CD—and my hot straightening Braun comb. The two of them had to be used together. Lauryn's holy, judging voice reversed the damage the comb's heat was doing to my insides. But that was probably just self-flagellating bullshit too. Lauryn Hill: the hippest superego in town. I switched on the comb defiantly, as the dreadlocked Fury began to sing.

As soon as I was done conking, I bounded down the stairs and out of the building. I hadn't eaten breakfast, but there'd be plenty of time for that. It was only ten o'clock. I wanted to meet St Pauly, go to him happy for a change, in a state of ecstasy, with none of the usual stupid anger and wild-eyed *ressentiment* I usually lugged about the place. Today St Pauly was friendly. He whispered suggestions, helpful ones, compliments and encomia, a multitude of promises and revelations he had in store for me as soon as I finished my PhD. His tram-tracks whistled cheerfully at my every passing step, and I thanked them too for being there for me, dependable, ever-present. They'd carry me out of here if ever I needed them to, or at least convey me post-haste to the train station. And if the place I was fleeing to turned out to be even worse, they'd bring me back home to Old Saul Street. It was for me to decide. Ruby-slipper engineers of a magic mobility no boo-hag could ever take from me, St Pauly's tram tracks were pure, benevolent facilitation.

As I passed the Theatre Royal and began to head down the hill towards the city centre, the Saturday morning crowds began to thicken and congeal. Resentment filled my limbs. I struggled, fought the negativity. These people had as much right to enjoy the Saturday streets of St Pauly as I did. I just wished there weren't quite so many of them. They flooded in at the weekend, from the villages. I know I should have felt sorry for them. But I hated them so much! They were inbreds, essentially, cretins, something straight out of an East Midlands *Deliverance*. During the week, St Pauly centre felt almost properly multi-cultural (depending on street, shop and time of day, of course). But on a Saturday the city was awash in a tsunami of white-pink Emmeline Thomson necks and faces, in proletarian form, of course. Their howling *Brood*-babies were even worse.

Something peculiar was going on in the Old Market Square. Were they doing Christmas shows already? The entire northwest corner of the square was jam-packed with noise and confusion, and the squawks and excited chirrups of the moronic villagers—combined with the bizarre animal noises of some semi-human assembly around which the same villagers were solidifying—could be heard all the way over at the McDonald's on Meek Street. It looked and sounded as if some infernal carnival had come to town. I found myself strangely propelled toward the crazy site of distraction, as if the not altogether delicate hands of a stronger, superior being were pushing me. It was as much as I could do to keep my baggy jeans from being yanked clean off my hips. Like the mysterious incubus afflicting poor Barbara Hershey in that terrible *Entity* flick, something just kept *shoving* me. And when finally I emerged on the other side of this ocean of grasping, frolicking kids (but the mothers, as one, were turning their heads away from the horizon, flushed, embarrassed, overwhelmed) I wasn't altogether shocked to find that on the stage of pandemonium danced none other than the spectacular figure of Mukelenge Mambackou.

Mukelenge took one look at my disbelieving face and broke into an enormous grin of amusement. But he quickly flicked his gaze elsewhere, still grinning like a madman, and continued the deafening drumming of which he appeared to be in charge with a redoubled frenzy. Clad in a brightly coloured African-style robe (impossible to say what colour: turquoise, indigo, crimson and cobalt swirled into one another like so many ice-cream shards of holy light), Mukelenge seemed to be the bandleader of an outlandish troupe of performing apes. No, *not* apes: men— they *were* men—but these men were decked out in such bestial, demeaning garb that for several minutes their human status quite escaped me.

Although all the creatures wore the bright grey 'A' pinned somewhere about their person, they definitely weren't all alike. They appeared to be divided into several sub-groups of aberration. One group was stripped nearly naked, only a tiny yellow rubber loincloth masking its collective genitalia. Painted red, white and blue, it danced and jigged to the rhythm of Mukelenge's drum, chanting again and again the same refrain, one that seemed oddly familiar to me but which I couldn't for the life of me manage to place within its overwhelmingly foreign arrangement. The African accents (if that's what they were) were a distraction too. A second group of the creatures under Mukelenge's charge appeared to be wearing old women's dresses, the sort of outfits you would expect your great aunt Betty to have worn in her middle years (around the time she turned lesbian). Their black, mannish arms protruded helplessly from the sleeves of these 1950s-style, polka-dotted, tightly fitted ensembles, twitching and trembling like electrified branches, shrieking out their desperate wish to break free from this bizarre encasement. They wiggled their hips suggestively, the transvestite clowns, mouthing the words of the strangely familiar song, but failing to produce any sound. A last, lone dancer was simply dressed as a lion. Fairly convincing, this final animal-man blew on a bugle and pawed the retarded village-children, causing some to squeal in delight, but making others wrinkle up their tiny pink faces in terror. At one point, the lion, red ribbons tied prettily in his golden mane, bounded up to me to offer a playful tap on my shoulder. I leaped back, stunned by the impertinence of it. The lion laughed, and danced his way to the back of the group.

And that was when I noticed the true bandleader. It wasn't Mukelenge in charge of this motley crew of dancing freaks, no: standing tall on a box behind his various gyrating performers was an enormous, square-shouldered man (white, almost deathly), square black glasses pushed back firmly on long thin nose. The man looked not unlike Fred Gwynne in his legendary Herman Munster role. But this was definitely Herman after an Oprah Winfrey makeover. The jeans, far too trendy for someone of his age (he was fifty if he was a day), were the low-hanging, zigzag kind that all the St Pauly students were insisting on that winter. His top was a black-and-silver Benetton hoodie, which clung to his colossal frame with an inappropriate intimacy, and on the left breast side of which was prominently pinned a bright red ribbon of Awareness. As black-and-silver as the hoodie, though, were the long hairs that protruded from Herman's nose, which was a pity for him, and all the more noticeable to me since my recent, long-delayed acquisition of special hybrid glasses (I am, maddeningly, at once long-sighted *and* short-sighted). And as the Thing conducted its monstrous orchestra, nostrils flared and enthusing, I finally latched onto the song that was being sung over and over again. For he was singing it too, more loudly and clearly (his Etonian tones easier to understand than the various African efforts around him) than anybody else: Kate Bush's eye-wateringly jingoistic hymn to Albion, 'Oh England, My Lionheart'. I've always loved it, despite myself, but at that moment wished that the Bushes had been sterile.

Suddenly Mukelenge stopped his drumming. The loincloth savages stopped their chanting, the polka-dotted man-ladies stopped their swivelling, the cowardly lion stopped his prancing. And the monstrous upper-class leader clapped his hands and whipped out a microphone, from which, gargantuan and sickeningly erect on his box, he addressed the fascinated crowd. Parents had rejoined their hysterical children now, eager to find out what this bizarre spectacle was all in aid of. And, as the giant began to speak, and I felt myself hemmed in more and more tightly by the sickening, foul-smelling, Puma-clad throng, I began to swoon at the multitude of squeaks and twitterings I could hear all around me, before me, behind, the words on the stage and within the crowd running and melting into one another, an endless snake of indiscriminate culture, unconscious thoughts and implied subtexts as clear and true to my raped and prodded eardrums as the words that were actually riding the market square airwaves.

The people of St Pauly were no different from the rest of England's faceless masses, began the plum-toned Herman-creature, even if their merry-men past of medieval banditry was rooted in a rather more exciting mythology than that to which most of so-called Little Britain could lay claim. What was its identity now? A nothing-identity, that was what, a mush of senseless combinations and intermingling that had been forced upon the people without their consent by the same old oligarchs ruling us from Whitehall. And nobody trusted a word Davina McCall said about immigration these days anyway. But the British people weren't to feel guilty: they *were* being exploited, they *had* been short-changed, they had, in a word, been bamboozled. Why should they feel happy about the strange smells and noises they came home to find, after a long day's honest work, in their council-block corridors? He understood their chagrin, everybody did, whether they said so or not, whether they faced up to the unpleasant truth or not, and it was time they started to let themselves off the hook. What precious energy was consumed in feeling guilty all the time! It was well out of order, what that Paki cunt had said to Joanne's niece! Why should they welcome the prospect of Koran-quoting grandchildren with that ever-ready, masochistic grin of English tolerance? How tired it made you feel when people told you that you had no right to the simple emotion of rage! But there was a way to channel all that legitimate negative energy. And it didn't involve turning to the likes of Marina de Kant's neo-nazi nationalists. No one liked having to eat humble pie. That way led to holocaust and madness. But they'd *never* employed men with beards where Ceri worked, so where exactly was the conspiracy? Did the good people gathered here, with their healthy, rosebud lambs, in the Old Market Square of St Pauly the Converted, *really* think that British values meant sending the poor, underprivileged brown creatures who'd scrambled for dear life onto this island's white-cliffed shores back to certain death in the killing fields of their own ravaged, backward continents? Their youngest had Down's; they didn't like taking him out in public, and it was all just so fucking depressing. Did the good people gathered here really want to see a barren Britain, emptied of the singing, dancing wretched of the earth, the gay-hearted minstrels who had brought the land so much colour and joy these last few decades (and, in some parts of the country, centuries)? What a terrible pity that would be! What a pity and a loss! He wasn't being funny, but that arrogant twat had better shut the fuck up and apologise. That, to coin a phrase, would be akin to throwing the baby out with bathwater. But that was all the likes of Jessica understood: take, take, take. That, to put it clearly, would be giving up a valuable source of happiness and pleasure. Cutting off one's nose to spite one's proverbial face. It wasn't an option. No one liked a faker. And Abdel wasn't being his real self: he had a game plan. Baby and nose: these were things to cling onto! The answer lay in seeing things clearly. But you *couldn't* tell John Barnes and Ashley Cole apart, not in that light! And it wasn't racist to say so. The answer lay in learning to cut out the static. It was so hard to do, he knew, cutting out that crackle, focusing on the clear message of truth that potentially rang out so loud and so clear. His mate had just been to a village where the people actually wore hats made of raw meat! He'd put the photos from his stag do on Facebook. And it wasn't about burying our heads in the sand either, pretending we were all the same. No: that way too lay apocalypse. Almost everyone in London was foreign; it was totally surreal. She was like a genie in a bottle: you just had to rub her the right way. But what was a life based on pretence? People *weren't* all the same! This was precisely the kind of thing that Fiona had always feared: finally meeting her real mother after all these years, then realising the old bitch was one of those lezzers she'd let finger her while passed out

blind drunk in *The Mule*. The French had imposed their
iron rhetoric of sameness throughout the Republic from
the start of their barbaric Revolution, then whinged and
complained when the Islamists organised themselves into
tighter and tighter sub-groups of difference and darkness,
driven underground and gaining in strength every day.
Jacqueline's ghost had just wanted to tell Little Jackie that
everything was going to be all right. As for the Americans,
there was no point even going there. What-*ever*! Talk to the
hand. Tiger Woods had actually been one of her clients.
But social workers were absolute fucking mentalists,
especially in the East Midlands. There was no happy
ending possible for the sick individuals who called
themselves the Irachnids, and the African-American
President's bewildering protection of their perversions at
the very heart of the nation, in the very beds of his
daughters, brought sorrow to Herman's inner soul. The
yoghurt her boyfriend insisted on eating actually had the
live eggs of germs breeding in it, but it was his human right
to choose that. In America another civil war was brewing.
She'd actually *dumped* him for making her come too loudly!
It was beyond comprehension. Harmony was so easy, so
feasible, so perfectly within reach. But the answer lay in
calling a spade a spade. Look at these men! These singing,
dancing animal-men! Were they dangerous? Were they
evil? Did they pose the slightest problem to national
security or identity? Of course they didn't. Wilko's was just
a poor man's Woollies. The reason was simple. They were
grateful to be here, they were delighted to have an
audience to perform for and—this was the clincher—*they
knew who they were*. Beaming, white-toothed guests in this
country, they hoped to stay for the full innings, for sure,
but they were under no illusions. And what exactly had she
expected to see out of the first-floor window of a
Lowestoft boarding house? The Hanging Gardens of
Babylon? What wouldn't they do to earn the right of an
extension? A single bout of N.L.P. would sort out Diane's

negativity forever. What songs and ditties wouldn't they trill to be allowed to linger just a little longer in England's green and pleasant land? There were none! These frolicking creatures belonged to a simple time, a time past, a time outside History, properly speaking, and that was precisely the time when things like true peace and harmony were possible. But wasn't Carrie ultimately just looking for Mr Goodbar? That was clearly the moral of last week's episode. These men knew who they were. Did the poor, lost tribe of England gathered here today realise the joy to be found in being able to make such a statement? *They knew who they were!* Not Britons, no! For what would have been the sense in such a masquerade? He felt sorry for his girlfriend's nephew, the retarded one, and encouraged him to sing at any opportunity. No, no, they were just themselves, simple, smiling African boys and men, Azrad, Cary, Djibril, Dumah, Godlove, Mohammed, Mukelenge and Sufjan: no more, no less, here to serve St Pauly in any way the people deemed fit. They would feed the lice: they were glad to do it! They'd feed 'em till the little suckers burst with black blood. There were no limits to these dusky angels' willingness to work hard for this country, to give something back, even if it was only their long-suffering, third-world flesh. It had been obvious that it was never going to work—the girl just had no sense of irony. They weren't about to claim to *be* the people of St Pauly! What kind of fuckery would that be? They were just themselves: visiting, sunburnt friends, no more, no less. They wouldn't pretend to be anything else, no more than a lion would pretend to be a tiger, or a tiger would pretend to be a bear. Big Issue? Big Issue? Ke$ha's aunt had often warned her that animals were instinctively attracted to glitter. You couldn't escape from the facts: no one liked a pretender. But to be allowed to be themselves, and to be allowed to entertain us, to serve us, to give us the kinds of pleasure we'd been lucky enough to experience today, they had to be allowed to stay in the country, not shipped off to some terrible place in the desert, not left to languish and rot in one of those terrible camps on the coast! It was in our hands, the English people's hands. His Polish secretary had finally confessed to him that she'd learned all her English from listening obsessively to a single Lady Gaga interview on repeat. We had only to make our voices heard.

Concluding thus, the beastly orator gave a stiff little bow and jumped off the box. At once a flock of interested listeners gathered around him and the leaflet-crammed stall that stood behind his stage.

I was shoved violently aside in the rush; my glasses went flying off my face. I heard the inevitable snap, and groaned.

The aristocratic Munster snapped his fingers at the seated lion.

"Hello? Cary! Come and lend a hand here!"

The lion cleared his throat and obediently sprang to his disgruntled master's service.

Mukelenge slowly lifted his drum off his chest, placed it carefully on the floor of the stage and strode towards me, hands outstretched in welcome.

"Miss Christie!" he cried. "What a lovely surprise! Oh, your hair is beautiful! Did you see the ad in the Piper?"

His accent had changed. Gone was the Mameluke Bath drawl of Tuesday evening. Today, Mukelenge spoke like a bona fide African.

"No."

I didn't know what else to say. Spectacle and cacophony combined had left me reeling.

"Raphael's great, isn't he?" Mukelenge gushed, oblivious. "He's from East Anglia, originally."

"Who?"

"The speaker, over there? That's my Advocate: Raphael E. Dubois."

He pronounced it *doo boyz*, and I grimaced.

"His people came to Felixstowe with the Huguenots."

He pointed over to the wan, middle-aged colossus at his stall that was now surrounded by a cluster of laughing, anaemic children, the dancing lion, and a whole harem of semi-naked or transvestite assistants.

"My friend. My Advocate. My friend. My friend. Raphael does asylum. He *gets* it. He's completely transforming the way the British could conceive of that crazy word 'asylum'. Do you understand?"

Mukelenge's eyes rolled in bugul-noz excitement. His shouting voice went up and down, rolling and undulating in a bizarre cocktail of non-specific Africanity.

"He's changing everything. What can be thought, what can't. It's a shift, a revolution. *IT'S IN THE TREES. IT'S COMING!*"

He began to laugh manically, like some sort of demented cross between Vincent Price and Frank Bruno. I felt my cheeks burn, and looked around anxiously. What if somebody from the University saw us together? The Master and Marianne Kollek, out, arm-in-arm, for a sick city centre stroll?

"I think you mentioned the Advocate when we last met," I muttered blankly. "Doesn't he live in Mameluke Bath?"

"That's right, Miss Christie!" exclaimed Mukelenge. "Good golly, you do have a good memory."

He began to grasp for something that was apparently lurking underneath the folds of his multicoloured robe. After a few seconds of overstated huffing and puffing, he managed to extricate two slim magazines. Motioning me over to a vacant bench some twenty metres from the stall, he sat down and spread out the flimsy volumes on the space between us. I looked down at the images that Mukelenge's fingers were now flattening meticulously against the brown wood, and felt myself beginning to choke. On the four pages before my widened eyes lay hundreds of tiny, stamp-sized photographs of boys and men in various states of undress and indecency. Some lolled on black leather stools in tiny Calvin Kleins; others preened, fully naked, their oversized (most probably airbrushed) penises jutting out for the world to see. These minuscule males were flesh for rent.

"What are you *doing?*" I shrieked at the delighted Mukelenge.

I snatched the magazines from off the bench, and raised their covers to my half-myopic, half-hyeropic eyes. I wanted the names of these shameless publications. Eventually I managed to spell out the messages of the garish red letters.

*MANDINGO*, boasted one.

*EUROBOYZ!* screamed the other.

A naked, black-skinned teenager in iron collar and chains grinned out at me inanely from the first publication. On the front of the second simpered a topless pair of muscular, redheaded twins. These were pornographic revues. Gay ones. I threw them back down onto the bench, shuddering with rage and confusion.

"Not there!" giggled Mukelenge, re-opening the magazines to the pages he'd already rammed down my throat, the commercial pages at the back. "There!"

He pointed with both his indexes to small blue ads in the top right-hand corners of each magazine:

### RAPHAEL DUBOIS
#### Shaking up asylum
#### Specialist in unusual ebony males

Next to each ad I noticed identical throbbing green panels, both advertising cut-price organic Viagra.

"Amazing, isn't it, the publicity he's getting?"

Before I could even think about an appropriately scornful answer, I felt a dark shadow fall across the loathsome sunlit pages. I raised my head, terrified. What kind of bogeyman was looming over Mukelenge and me now, as we snuggled up together on our scandalous bench? What if it was Emmeline Thomson, out enjoying the bright Saturday sunshine with her philosopher husband and precocious teenage son? *(I didn't realise your father was still alive, Christie!)* How sickened and embarrassed she'd be to see me here, with Mukelenge, poring over this collection of filthy images!

I slowly turned my head.

But it was only Raphael Dubois. He looked even more like a Boris Karloff horror-show when you saw him up close.

"What are you doing, Mikey?" demanded Dubois. "I need you over there. At the stall. Do you really think Cary's capable of conversing with these people? He's floating in some kind of depressive dream today."

I stared past Dubois over to the stand he'd left in the apparently unsatisfactory care of Cary. Most of the other men appeared to be sleeping. They lay scattered around the stall. The bigger children giggled, and began to kick gently at their snoring heads. But the poor pseudo-lion was wide-awake and hard at work. He'd removed his head, which he carried under his arm like a motorcycle helmet, and was trying to talk to a concerned-looking elderly couple about his plight. I could see that they weren't really listening to his words. And it wasn't even his white-pink, freckled albino flesh, or his crown of white-blond curly Afro hair, that was causing them the most intrigue. No: they were straining to hear something *behind* the words (bemused, horrified, fascinated wonder written all over their wrinkled faces), focusing all their geriatric concentration on the reedy, whistling quality of the lion's voice, whose silvery, fragile notes escaped from the stall area, borne on the winter breeze, to land in my own eardrums with an eerily robotic insistency.

"What have you done to him?" I squawked up at Dubois from my cringing position on the bench, my own vocal chords cracking with uncontrollable pity for the pathetic, trilling beast. "What have you done to his voice?"

"Castrated," replied the Advocate matter-of-factly, not bothering to look down at me. His gaze was fixed on a sheepish Mukelenge, who was busily stashing the magazines back between the folds of his robe.

"When he was thirteen. Uganda. Charlatans!" Dubois added, as if this final exclamation of reproof should be enough to satisfy my tediously feminine curiosity.

"We can show you the scar. If you want. I mean, if you don't believe us," stammered Mukelenge, gazing up at Dubois, anxious, child-like, grasping for official validation of his spontaneously kind offer.

My mouth fell open.

"*What?* This is...I mean...you're..."

My outrage tailed off feebly.

Dubois had turned his back to us both now, and was straining his own ears back towards Cary at the stall, trying to eavesdrop on whatever words the lion might be offering the old people on the subject of asylum. Dubois bobbed his head gently up and down and from side to side, drawing in whatever frequencies he might be picking up. He looked like some kind of supersonic cockroach. Any second now he was going to go back to his business, I could tell.

I couldn't let him.

I rose from the bench, tapped the giant's bulky shoulder, and began to shout: "You're sick! You're abusing that Ugandan albino boy just as badly as his castrators did! You're humiliating him! You're turning him into an animal, a clown!"

"Don't be ridiculous, Christie!" exclaimed Mukelenge, leaping away from our bench to stand by his master, his accent mysteriously back to Mameluke Bath again.

Dubois seemed barely aware of his winged monkey. He was still straining the stalks of his disgusting insect-ears towards the stall he'd left behind.

Mukelenge carried on gently scolding me, thick arms folded over his bulging, multicoloured robes, eyes wide open in platitudinous censure: "How can you even think those things you just said, Christie? This is the first time Cary's ever been safe in his entire miserable life. Do you see anyone trying to hack off his penis here in St Pauly? Do you see anyone burning down his house here in St Pauly? Do you see an entire gang of East Midlands men raping his sister so as to stop her from ever turning witch like her brother? How can you even *begin* to compare England to Uganda and all its horrors, real horrors? Your over-privileged, mixed-up, liberal brain can't even begin to imagine it!"

I felt myself starting to blush: Mukelenge was right. I didn't know the first thing about Africa and the atrocities that went on there. But I began to shout back at him regardless.

"Wouldn't they begin the crucifixions here in England too, if things were set up for them to get away with it? Wouldn't——

But Dubois had listened to enough of our internecine squabbling for one day.

"Come *on*, Mikey!" he barked, tugging crossly at Mukelenge's robes now, bearing him brusquely away from our debating bench as if Mukelenge were the errant youngest son he'd finally tracked down at a disreputable local amusement arcade with a gang of feral, council-estate hoodlums. "We haven't got all day!"

"But Raphael, hang on a minute, you haven't been properly introduced. This is Christie Smithkin. She's my——"

"We don't *do* women, Mikey," interrupted Dubois. "We've been through this. They've got their own channels."

The Advocate stopped, turned, gave me a quick, hard stare of appraisal. His grey eyes lingered an instant on the open buttons of my corduroy blouse (how had they come undone?). He quickly looked away again, smirked at Mukelenge.

"Tell her to call that heavy-duty dyke...Anjelica what's her face. Oh, or what about..." (he cackled obscenely now) "...Tamara Jessel and her lascivious *sensuchi*? I'm sure this girl would have plenty to offer those two legal eagles. They'd be game. What stage is she at?"

"No, Raphael, no! She's from around here! She doesn't need a lawyer! She was born in Mameluke Bath!" I heard Mukelenge twittering breathlessly as he scurried after Dubois's rapidly disappearing back.

But I was already striding away in the opposite direction, a frozen hiss of broken ego-glass bubbling through my cauterised gut.

# III

$A$s I heard myself mutter the words "Follow that van!" I realised that I'd finally crossed over into the tackiest of bad dreams. The bright-eyed, black-bearded taxi-driver seemed amused at the campness of it too.

"Charlie's fourth Angel, are you, duck?" he laughed as we sped out of the city, his dark eyes meeting mine in the rear-view mirror. "They could do with another remake."

He wasn't being malevolent.

"Once upon a time there were four little girls..."

I felt myself starting to grin.

"Well, you might say that," I said. "I just need to check something out here, or...well, I might never be able to forgive myself."

And the merry young Turk's twinkling visage turned suddenly serious in the mirror, respectful, before focusing intently on the traffic-filled road ahead of us.

We were on the motorway now, and I already knew where we were headed. It was all so terribly predictable. Dusk was falling as we drew into Mameluke Bath. My taxi followed Raphael Dubois's van down the main village street, passing the railway station on our right. I rolled down the window in back. I wanted to hear the murmur of the Mameluke as it flowed past us. It might be able to tell me something. But all I could hear was the noise of Saturday night's family cars, returning, like us, to Mameluke Bath, in all its sleepy safety, after a hard day's shopping in St Pauly.

"Don't lose them!" I squealed, as the white van suddenly took a sharp left.

It was climbing the hill of Clairwil. Many a time I'd climbed that hill as a child, running for dear life from Hélène or from the Mickle-Beast, sometimes in the middle of the night, sometimes carrying Bruno and his little scrap of blue velvet, once with BoyBoy and Sula in tow. I couldn't refrain from giggling at that particular cat-and-dog memory. But almost immediately afterward I wanted to weep. Poor BoyBoy; poor Sula; poor us!

"Don't worry, duck, I've got it," smiled my driver through his black beard, swerving smoothly up into Clairwil. "Creepy little village it is, though!"

"It's where I grew up," I snapped through my tears.

"Oh, no offence, duck, not being funny, just meant—"

"Shit, they're stopping!" I whispered. "Reverse down the hill!"

We parked outside a tiny cottage halfway up Clairwil. I looked and saw that it was *Seven Swans*. Back in the day, *Seven Swans* was the home of our stone-deaf piano teacher, Mrs Derbyshire. How I'd loved that name as a child! We were just plain old #111. I'd tried to get Hélène to let us christen ourselves *Chimera*, but she just laughed, and called me pretentious. Mrs Derbyshire was always so sweet to me, though, and it didn't matter if I hadn't done a stroke of practice. Even on the weeks when I produced no music for her whatsoever, not one note of Satie or Grieg, just vast, shimmering pools of silent perspiration dripped from my hands all over her spotless keyboard, she wouldn't ever dream of being mean. I'd cringe with shame, holding my breath as I waited for the short, sharp cry of revulsion. But it never came. She'd simply squeeze my shoulders between her hot, gnarly fingers, and bellow: "A little bit o' hand-

liquid never scared me, lass! You're no sea monster, for all
your watery palms." She had a very strong Mameluke
accent. A terrible piano teacher, though. She must be long
dead now.

"Can you hear me, duck? How long do you want me to
wait with you?" asked the driver.

I suddenly remembered that I didn't have any money,
and groaned. I must owe him at least forty pounds.

"Don't worry about the fare, duck."

He looked at me in the rear-view mirror again, a stare
of utter kindness shining from his black and serious eyes.
"You're in a dark place."

*I* crept like a shadow into the front garden of the tall grey
house called *The Shallows*. If they caught me here tonight it
was all over for Christie Smithkin. That much I knew for
certain.

Half an hour had elapsed since the departure of my
Turkish carriage. I'd hovered at the crossroads of
Delamarche and Littlejohn; just beyond lay the house I
knew I was heading for. I'd told the taxi driver to leave me
after just five minutes, reassuring him that I knew what I
was doing, and that maybe we'd run into each other again
one of these days in St Pauly. I wouldn't give him my
number, though. Even if I have nothing against secular
Muslims, you can never be too careful.

The upstairs front window of Raphael Dubois's house
was lit up and slightly open, like a sleepy giant's yellow eye.
The ground floor bedrooms were swathed in darkness, of
course: this was Mameluke Bath, after all, and everything
remained inverted, even after all these years. I could hear
the sound of Saturday night television trickling down to
where I crouched beneath the colossal leylandii as a theme
tune started up. So this was it: they were watching *Friends*. I
swallowed a violent impulse to retch. They really *were* there
for each other. They had a Saturday night companion such
as I'd never sniffed at. I had to see them: just one tiny

glimpse, just for a minute. How was I going to scale the wall? Suddenly I noticed a fire-ladder leaning invitingly against the house. I uttered a tiny whoop of triumph. I slithered up the ladder in a matter of seconds, and put my hands on the windowsill. There was a small gap where the curtains were not quite fully drawn. I pressed my face to the gap and gazed into the window: a brown-skinned Glenn Close (minus blonde, shaggy, *Fatal Attraction*-perm), my wide and sickened pupil taking in the scene of first-floor domestic bliss like an injection of pure hemlock.

Raphael Dubois lay splayed across a huge black leather sofa, smoking a large joint, laughing at the American gags that spurted thick and fast from the television. He was wearing only his underwear: a tiny pair of green-and-yellow 'Aussie Bum' briefs. His long, grey, muscular body was repulsive, like the malevolent creation of a particularly perverse scientist-god. Mukelenge sat cross-legged on the floor at Raphael's feet, still wearing his African robes from that afternoon. He too seemed like he might be lost in *Friends*, but there was no real way of telling. He didn't laugh like Raphael, and his eyes stared dully into the space ahead of him.

What had they done with the men? What had they done with the seekers? They hadn't returned them to the Lionheart Complex. They hadn't had time. They had to be here, languishing somewhere in this terrible house in Mameluke Bath. But there was no way I could get into *The Shallows* to snoop around its mysterious chambers. Even to attempt such a thing would amount to pure folly. I slid back down the ladder and decided to climb over the fence that marked the entrance to the back garden. Something told me it might be worth a shot. And anyway, I wanted to see that damned painted swimming pool that Mukelenge had kept going on about.

Scaling the fence was easy: I was wearing my baggiest jeans. I crept as silently as I could manage through the gigantic empty yard, occasionally stifling a cry of pain as I tripped over a can or a bottle. They were certainly no gardeners, Tweedledum and Tweedledee; that much was for sure. Even in the pitch-black of the early evening, I could sense the desert-like nature of the terrain across which I was crawling. In this bleak and barren wasteland was a complete and utter absence of life. I could make out the faint glow of some kind of construction in the distance, though, and I let out another tiny whoop of excitement. So there *was* something to discover chez Raphael Dubois after all! I jogged the last fifty metres, not caring if I tripped. It was halfway between a garden-shed and a full-blown log cabin. The weak light emanating from the edifice—the glow that had guided me so far through the gloomy backyard, perhaps from the very start of my journey—was, in fact, trickling from a single window on the left side of the wooden hut. For the second time that afternoon I took my courage in my hands and tip-toed around the cabin to peer into an open flap.

But how different the spectacle that now greeted my eyes from the gently nauseating banality of just a few moments ago, when I'd drunk in Raphael, Mukelenge and the dubious comforts of *Friends*! It was just as I'd guessed: the seven men I'd watched 'performing' earlier that day in the Old Market Square were lying flat out in this cabin of horror. They stretched out, apparently unconscious, on various shelves that jutted out from all four walls of the building. They were chained to the shelves with heavy silver bonds that looked like something out of *Roots*. All were naked, and appeared to be deep in slumber, for they breathed in and out with heavy, grunting snores, their clouds of breath lit up in the yellow air of the shed. How cold they must have been!

But there was something far more shocking than their freezing exposure. I hadn't noticed at first, so fixated was I on the strangely muscular bodies of the men themselves. Strapped up and down the length of their bulging limbs were what appeared to be a series of small, glass flasks.

And, as I strained to catch a glimpse of what these strange accoutrements might be, for the second time that afternoon I fought back the urge to puke my guts out. The tiny, transparent containers teemed with armies of swarming lice.

"What are you doing here?" suddenly trilled a weak and reedy voice. "Don't you know it's dangerous?"

The tiny warning was coming from the shelf directly underneath the window. I hadn't looked down there. I'd been drawn to gaze at every shelf except the one on my side. And now, as I gazed down at the cramped space below, I saw the pinky-blue, blond-lashed eyes of the lion-boy Cary blinking up at me from his shelf. His tangled mop of white-yellow African hair stood out from his pale, freckled moon-face like some kind of crazy halo. He looked like a cross between Angela Davis and William Katt. And, of all of them, he was the only one who could be described as skeletal.

"Cary!" I cried, strangely overcome with emotion.

"Shh!" He put a long, thin finger to his full, pink lips. "You'll wake them."

He motioned for me to climb through the window quietly, which I managed without much difficulty. My agility today was proving remarkably cat-like.

"We met earlier this afternoon," I whispered. "In the Old Market Square."

"I remember!" said Cary, in his sweet castrato voice. "I recall thinking at the time that you seemed rather lost."

I looked around us now at the slumbering men. Their snores were louder than ever.

"They're actually not in much danger of waking up," said Cary. "Once the lice-nests get strapped on they're usually out for the night. I just wanted to be on the safe side. I haven't been here long, and I don't know whom I can trust. Personalities don't seem very stable."

I looked now at his strapped-on appendages. I concentrated on the flask closest to me: it was fixed to the young man's left shoulder. Inside writhed a multitude of the most disgusting little white worms I'd ever seen. Many times before I'd tried to imagine what lice-feeding might be like, whether I'd ever be up to the repulsive job, if it ever came to that. But the lice had always remained abstract, little lines of abjection, symbols of a state-of-emergency wretchedness to which I might need to submit briefly, Cinderella-like, so as to triumph over my enemies at the end of the ghastly fairy tale. My blood had remained abstract too. But here and now I saw Cary's blood seeping with a true and tragic foulness, from a bruised and puckered wound on his pale shoulder. The lice swarmed around the wound, dancing and squirming across it, under it, inside it, entering Cary's body, coming back out of it again, engorged and swollen, drunk and pink on the blood of a gentle man in chains. The same scene played itself out over seven different parts of his frail and milky body.

"We need to get you out of here," I gasped, ready to weep with rage and pity.

"There's nowhere for me to go," laughed Cary. "And this really isn't as bad as it looks."

"How can you say it's not as bad as it looks?" I screamed. "It's fucking disgusting!"

Cary looked pained, letting his head fall back onto the dirty rag that appeared to serve as a pillow.

"Listen..."

"Christie."

"Listen, Christie. I'm not sure who you are, or what exactly you're doing in this place of suffering, but if you want to help us, you must listen to me and then leave immediately. Take my story to the outside world. But only speak it to people you can trust! There must be people out there you can trust? People who can advise you what to do?"

I said nothing.

"The police are no good. They helped Mr Dubois to transport us here from the Lionheart Complex. They laughed and joked when I begged them to save me. You can't trust the doctors either. They're the ones who bring the lice. It helps them in their work."

"Can't you begin at the beginning, Cary? Tell me how you came here, what the fuck is going on?"

Cary winced at my second utterance of the 'fuck' word. I grimaced a reluctant apology. Cary nodded, taking my sweaty hand in his. And then he sat up on his shelf.

"Don't worry. It's not your fault you've been defiled. That's one thing that's never your fault."

I smiled at him gratefully.

"Very well. I was born nineteen years ago, in the village of Jufureh, on the northern bank of the river Gambia."

"Oh, but I thought they said you were Ugandan!"

"Those two white devils don't know the first thing about Africa," replied Cary tartly. "Especially the one who calls himself Mukelenge. Shall I go on?"

"Please do."

"Very well. I am one of the Mandinka people—"

"Oh, I know a few words of Mandinka!"

"Look, do you want to hear my story or not?" snapped Cary crossly.

"I'm sorry," I said, mortified at my own puerile boasting. "Please, carry on. No, really, Cary, please! I won't interrupt you again."

"I am one of the Mandinka people," he slowly repeated, settling back on the shelf and propping himself up on two sharp elbows. "And, in many ways, I am proud of the Mandinka people's up-and-down past. It's not many cultures that found vast medieval empires yet still managed to turn into the iconic slaves of modernity.

## CARY'S CURSE

"When I was a still a small boy, my mother, Margaret-Aba, told me I must suffer the punishment Allah had seen fit to deal me, and I must suffer it without gripe. If I was pink and white and yellow like this, then it must be for a reason, and that reason would become clear enough in the course of my life and death. It was necessary only to wait. Denaturation didn't happen by accident. Needless to say, my father hadn't the time to speculate with me thus regarding my unfortunate ghostly hue: the minute he saw me, aged three and a half months (he'd been in the capital, on business, at my birth, and nobody had dared tell him how I'd turned out) he gave a roar of such outrage and revulsion that the entire village had assumed that my mother's end, and mine, were nigh. But he let us both live. He wasn't a cruel man, Daddy, and he had other wives and children.

"I was left to my own devices. Or rather, I was left to Margaret-Aba's. They didn't want me to attend the village school, since persecution seemed inevitable, and they wished to spare me the cruelty of common strangers. And so, for the first few years of my life, my mother educated me. Since she herself had received no education to speak of, you can imagine that her instruction was pretty substandard. I was forced to learn a mish-mash of Qur'anic dogmas and traditional Mandinka legends, all of which invariably combined to convince me that I was in fact the living, breathing embodiment of Darkness. My pale appearance was the ultimate ironic joke. Sometimes, when she'd been visiting her friend the marabout for the afternoon, Margaret-Aba would return to our tiny home consumed with the desire to correct me by magical incantation: she'd grab my hands and pray with me on the floor, forcing me to repeat mantras about the sins of ghost-people, and would urge me to confess my ongoing transactions with Shaitan. As I invariably refused, she'd drag me kicking and screaming to my cabinet, where I'd be shut in, sometimes for days, without food, to reflect upon the horror of my ghostly denaturement. In the cabinet was a large catalogue of photographs, obtained by my mother from god-only-knows where. These photos were full colour snapshots of an endless series of tiny ebony genitalia: the miniature reproductive organs of hundreds of healthy black children——natural, normal infant body-parts, the like of which something as pink and sickly as me could never dream of possessing.

"Needless to say, my other family members didn't bother to intervene. My father had fallen madly in love with his fourth wife, an overweight English teacher named Lynne, from Penistone, South Yorkshire, who had provided him with two healthy sons. Their pallor was a blessing, apparently. My father seemed to have no problem brushing off the taunts of our neighbours as far as my little hybrid half-brothers were concerned. He trusted in a higher authority, to which he seemed to have been exposed either in the capital or on his various trips abroad, which asserted their ultimate superiority over us all. As for the other two wives and their children, they kept themselves firmly to themselves. These two ladies lived together with their seven offspring in a slightly larger house of the compound and, now that I have had time to reflect on it, I imagine that they were probably lovers.

## CARY AT HIGH-SCHOOL

"When I turned nine my parents decided it was time for my circumcision and that, following the glorious cutting, I would be sufficiently manly to start attending the village school. The three years that followed were the most intensely painful of my entire existence. Daily life among the village boys was torture, the likes of which not even Margaret-Aba's maltreatment could have prepared me for. The boys seemed hell-bent on breaking me. Each day promised a new cruel surprise, a fresh act of perversity. One afternoon they'd push my head inside the latrine; on another they'd poke sticks in my anus. And every morning during registration I'd be greeted with the same abusive chant: *Cary White bleeds from a pig-cunt!* They'd even carved it into my desk. The teachers were no better. Not only did they turn a blind eye to my various injuries, they positively joined in, sometimes *en masse*, shrieking with delight at my predictable torrents of tears.

"To make matters worse, I began to realise that I'd fallen deeply in love with my most malevolent tormentor, Omar Ceesay, second-in-command of the most powerful clique in school. This clique was a triumvirate of well-built, handsome jocks, all of whom went by the first name 'Omar'. Omar Ceesay was two years my senior, the son of the most respected man in the village. Mr Ceesay was a noble griot, whose renown had spread even to the capital, where he'd been based for the past five years, claiming to be hard at work on an album with Dame Annie Lennox. It was clear that Omar was in great distress over what he clearly perceived as abandonment by his glamorous griot father. The young jock's rancour and spite grew daily, and it found a perfect outlet in me. Omar would wait for me at the school gates every morning. Eyes wide with excitement, he would whisper all the things he and the other Omars intended to do to me that afternoon, before hopping swiftly away, bent double with furious mirth. God, I loved him. I loved his dark, glittering eyes; I loved his strong, bulging biceps; I loved his vast collection of Eurythmics T-shirts, one for each phase of Dame Annie's metamorphosing identity. But most of all I loved the pain he carried around with him, a pain I knew only I could soothe and make slip away, if only he would give me the chance. We were alike in so many ways, you see, if only Omar could have realised it.

"Sometimes I wondered if my attraction to males (for my nightly horn extended not only to Omar: I would dream about some of the wickedest teachers too and, in one particularly shameful nocturnal reverie, I even seeped for my mother's old friend the marabout) might not in fact be directly related to my pallid, spectral hue. It was impossible to put into words, but the more I thought about it, the more it seemed feasible that the one difference perhaps proceeded, ineluctably, from the other. It wasn't that I thought all ghost-skinned Africans were biologically disposed towards those of their own sex. (After hours of diligent library research I'd finally discovered I wasn't the only ghost-skin, learning on YouTube of the international renown of our great Albino musician Salif Keita.) Such a conflation of stigmata would be scientifically absurd. But my desire to touch the flesh of men sometimes felt like a genuine choice I had made in accordance with myself, a choice over which, paradoxically, I had some kind of limited control. As I pumped my freshly cut penis, thinking all the while of the insults I'd received that day from Mr Sanyang the football coach, my spurting semen felt somehow like a belligerent response to my skin-difference and to the daily chagrin this caused me, all of it directed by some psychic offshoot of me that was more deeply rooted in 'me' than 'I' was 'myself'. But of the two forms of difference—the one I'd had foisted on me at birth, and this new one that I was myself cultivating post-circumcision, it seemed to me that the second one was preferable, a genuine act of creative rebellion, something that might one day set this stupid, joyless village on fire. And—who knew?—maybe it would help me to enjoy being a ghost-man a bit more too.

"I'll never know how it happened, but just after my eleventh birthday it became apparent that the other boys had guessed what I was turning into. Their morning chant subtly shifted from one day to the next. Now, when I crept into class for registration, I was greeted by the chorus: *Cary White likes cock in his pig-cunt!* The teachers laughed louder than ever before, and now took advantage of the palpable change in atmosphere in order to stick long, eager fingers into my rear-end, as well as the usual sticks and pens. The only one who seemed suddenly better-disposed towards me was, of all people, my Omar. He no longer tormented me at the school gates, but instead offered me advice on how I might best make it through the taunts of the day. He barely seemed to associate with the other Omars anymore, inaugurating a semi-official clique-severance, which, as you can imagine, caused endless whisperings in the school corridors. (Omar Condé was said to be livid with rage.)

"Sometimes Omar even walked me home. He carried my books, and drove off potential assailants with loud declarations about the non-negotiable injunction of universal fraternity. I didn't know what to make of it. One evening, as we hovered awkwardly at my threshold, I invited him into my house to meet Margaret-Aba. She was in the middle of swaying, as usual, to the marabout's holy recordings, but quickly straightened upon our entrance, and offered to make Omar some tea. And as the three of us chatted and laughed about Dame Annie's new album of Christmas songs (containing, Omar assured us excitedly, backing vocals by both Omar's own father and the ghost-skinned superstar Salif Keita himself), I felt more joy flood through my veins than I'd thought possible for a young boy to experience.

"The next few weeks were the happiest of my entire existence on this sad blue planet. Margaret-Aba seemed to have changed entirely in her attitude towards me, now that I had been endorsed by such a powerful and popular ally. Needless to say, she had heard nothing of the 'pig-cunt' stories at school, and so had no cause to suspect anything untoward in my new and unlikely friendship. Her discovery of Salif Keita's international approbation-despite-albinism also seemed to have shifted something in her attitude towards my unfortunate singularity. 'If it's good enough for YouTube!' she'd smile, patting me on the head, before adding: 'Maybe one day *you* will be a tunesmith entertainer, like the famous ghost-man Keita!' Even the harassment at school seemed to be dying down, thanks to Omar's protection.

"And then, one day, just before the break for Christmas vacation, it came: the thing I'd been dreaming of for weeks now. Omar sat me down after school in the empty classroom, and asked me if I would be prepared to accompany him to the January Ball. He wanted me to be his Best and Most Special Friend (BMSF). I couldn't believe my ears! I, Cary, the most abject boy in school, to accompany Omar Ceesay to the January Ball, as his BMSF? The whole thing beggared belief.

"I have re-played the minutes that followed Omar's invitation a million times in my mind, over and over and over again. In the course of the dreadful months and years that have passed since that warm December afternoon in the deserted schoolroom, the memories give me something good to hold onto. I remember Omar's face coming closer and closer to me, closer than I thought bearable, his mouth descending on my mouth, his arms wrapped incredibly around my shoulders. I remember letting myself go limp, closing my eyes tightly, losing my accursed body altogether, and floating, sprite-like, on the wings of the most wonderful dream.

"I opened my eyes to the terrible racket of screaming laughter. Something warm and yellow like urine was dripping onto my head from above. I really was being pissed on. Omar had let me go, and the entire classroom was full to bursting. At every desk there now sat an open-mouthed, baying schoolboy, and all around the room stood the teachers, shaking their heads in uniform disgust. The other two Omars held onto each other, their eyes pouring out tears of mirth. My parents were at the classroom door, with Lynne, all three heads bowed in shame. Omar was standing with the headmaster, his hand gripped tightly in the older man's embrace, and being warmly congratulated on having performed such a difficult role to perfection. Before I knew what was happening, I'd been tied up and was being carried high in the air by a troupe of the smallest boys. I knew where they were taking me. If I'm truthful with myself, I think I'd known forever that it was there I'd end up.

"The village square was reserved for annual celebration and for animal sacrifice. As they lay me at the feet of the statue of our Mandinka ancestor, the thirteenth-century founder of the village, I wondered what form my sacrifice would take. I prayed that it would be speedy, and that the elders would allow me to talk to my mother before the very end came. When the knife blade finally tore into my scrotal sac, I marvelled at how accurately I'd anticipated the precise nature of the pain. Not that it wasn't excruciating beyond the telling—it was—but it also felt somehow like *déjà vu*, like an operation I'd suffered already, even if only in dreams. I sometimes think, when I look back at that moment now, that one of the reasons the physical pain wasn't that overwhelming was because I was so distracted by the pain in my heart. The sadness I felt at my mother's complicity in all this sickness was more than I could bear. It made me want the world to explode from grief. True, Margaret-Aba had *always* been disappointing, had *always* made me feel bad about myself when she might instead have tried to make me feel good. But we'd had real moments of togetherness too, you know? We'd spent my entire life together, laughing about the ways of the village, talking about her hopes and fears. How could she be standing back and letting these monsters carve me up like this? Me, her little Cary! Did she approve of what they were doing? Did she even care? I remembered her telling me once about the death of an older brother of hers, Modibo, also sacrificed, also castrated, when he was twelve. There'd been no particular reason (or none admitted) for the killing of Modibo: they'd just found him the next day, floating down the canal: dead, wrapped in plastic, and missing a penis. 'But he never should have been hanging around the canal after dark! What did he think he would find there if not witches and necromancers?' Margaret-Aba would always add angrily at the end of the terrifying story. 'My father warned us never to go down there! And what did Modibo do? *He went down there!* And she'd wander into the kitchen to peel the potatoes for supper. She would tell the same kind of dismissive story about me when I was gone, perhaps to my future nephews and nieces, I suddenly realised, and I began to weep bitterly. Suffering in our family seemed so terribly banal.

"But the shouts and the drumming had stopped. The entire square had gone silent. I couldn't see anything—my eyes were bandaged—but it sounded as if all life had suddenly come to a halt. Had I died already, and gone straight to hell? I wondered what Shaitan would look like. Wouldn't he in fact be pleased with me, given that I'd been dutifully performing his Evil Will on a number of fronts since birth? And that was when I felt a pair of gentle hands pulling off my eye-bandage and wrapping it tightly around my groin. The angel began to cut at my ropes with a knife. I opened my eyes to find myself staring into the kindly face of Omar's prodigal father, Mr Ceesay. He was back from the capital, he sang, and was accompanied by two British musician friends, Dame Annie and Sir Sting, who had wanted to see exactly where their lovely Mandinka friend came from. At that very moment they were waiting for him, in a tour bus parked just outside the village square. I don't know what happened next—I think I must have passed out.

"Over the next few weeks I was taken care of better than I could ever have dreamed. Mr Ceesay had arranged for me to be conveyed as quickly as possible to the capital, where, thanks to the influence of Sting and Annie, I was treated in a big hospital, my castration-wounds sutured as best they could be. Annie and Sting were horrified by my story, which I told them in broken English from my hospital bed. Mr Ceesay merely shook his head in embarrassment, vowing never to return to the small-minded pettiness of the provinces. Annie and Sting would publicise my plight, they said, would make sure the African persecution of homosexuals and albinos was properly spoken about in the United Kingdom. Mr Ceesay, who'd now obtained a British work visa, thanks to his ongoing collaboration with Annie (a follow-up album, *An African Easter*, was already in the pipeline), added that he would participate in the public awareness campaign: he had already enjoyed a fruitful Skype chat with Salif Keita about potential bridge-building projects. At last my three noble guardians spread a hundred and one pounds across my duvet, wished me all the luck in the world, and softly sang goodbye.

## CARY AND THE CITY

"When I stumbled out of the hospital two days later, I hadn't the slightest idea where to go next. The money my powerful friends had left me would see me through the next ten days, assuming I wasn't robbed before then, but my most urgent mission was clearly to find myself a job, and fast. As I hobbled along the dusty road that led away from the hospital towards the city centre, ignoring the various horns that loudly beeped their outrage at my singularity, a large car drew up beside me, and the voice inside asked me where a pretty boy like me could be heading all alone at dusk. Alain Souleymane was a French-Senegalese businessman, and was heading home to Dakar after six days spent closing a deal in our dreary capital. Would I be interested in travelling back to Senegal with him? I needed no time to reflect. I clambered into the back of Alain's vehicle without hesitation, my heart pounding, but my mind made up. What was the worst he could do to me? Kill me? There was every chance of this unexpected free ride offering me the chance of a new career in an exciting new town, and the slim possibility of my own murder wasn't going to put me off seizing this chance with both hands.

"Alain Souleymane wasn't a killer, as it turned out. He was, however, a kidnapper and a pimp, and he liked to steal things. He set me up in a special house for fetish-clients, on the outskirts of Dakar's nineteenth arrondissement. Very soon I became the house's main attraction. Men came from all over Senegal, and some from even further away, to sample my ghostly delights. The other six boys in the house didn't seem to mind. On the contrary: they stated their relief that, foreigner and interloper though I was, I was helping to generate new business (for money was shared equally among the boys, even though Alain took the lion's share). Their own particularities—extremities of tallness, shortness, blackness, depth of voice, garrulousness and foot size respectively—were increasingly old hat in the bustling, cosmopolitan environment of Dakar, and Alain had been worried, until my arrival, that the house of games might finally be forced to close.

"The clients were, unfortunately, another story altogether. While some were very kind, treating me as the spectral, sexual son they'd never had (or already had but dared not use), the vast majority were brutal, no matter their caste or education, using their time with me as an opportunity to act out all manner of violent complexes. Their fantasies seemed, invariably, to revolve around their fathers, their mothers, or, in the case of some of the older ones, colonial administrators from their boyhood. It ended up being no great comfort to me that I had generally friendly colleagues, or that I'd been afforded the chance to learn to speak both French and English flawlessly: at the end of six months in the brothel, I was as sick of my life in Dakar as I'd ever been of it back in my Mandinka village. I longed to see the sea, to sample Dakar's famous music scene, to at last taste French cuisine—in short, to discover a life not entirely shaped by the dreams and desires of others. I began to hatch my plan for escape.

"Raphael Dubois wasn't the first white man (nor indeed the first Englishman) to enter through my bedroom doors, but he was certainly the most amusing. From the very first time he came he had me in stitches with his endless tales of England, of boarding schools, toasted crumpets and loyal fags. England was a place where anybody could be what they wanted to be, as long as they were willing to muck in, to work hard and play hard, to earn their keep with a good humour and an absence of rancour. England was a place where every difference could be accommodated and absorbed, as long as it was reasonable, rational and fair-minded. My father's white wife Lynne had always said much the same on the few occasions we'd talked.

"On his third visit, Raphael, whom I'd already started to look upon as a kind of benevolent uncle, supplemented his charming, autobiographical stories of England with carefully selected extracts from Enid Blyton's incredible high-school novel, *First Term at Malory Towers*. And that was when I started to become a little hysterical. I begged him to tell me how I might be permitted to enter his magical island, a place of such evident wonder, so suffused in an atmosphere of all-pervasive tolerance and magnanimity, that I couldn't believe that until that month I had believed that English was a language invented in the United States of America. It was simple, said Raphael. Just as all Britons were committed to caring for their neighbours on the island itself, they also set very great store by the offering of golden opportunities to the right kind of foreigner. Was I prepared to work hard for my place in the sun? At my yelping, agonized flurry of nods, Raphael took my head in his hands and promised that he would help me.

"The Winston Churchill Technique was a tried and tested one, Raphael assured me. In the dark days of the Second World War, its constant (if underground) practice had saved literally millions of English men, women and children from dying of typhus and the deadly Black Country Spotted Fever. Essentially an exercise in the most innovative form of disease prevention, it involved acting boldly on the revolutionary discovery by Charles Nicolle, in 1909, that lice were the vector of most infectious illnesses. Genius and renaissance man that he was, Churchill came up with the idea of developing Nicolle's observation by crushing infected lice into a magical vaccine paste which could then be used to protect the poor and most vulnerable from disease. All that was needed to produce vast amounts of this enchanted substance was a million lice—and the human blood needed for them to grow, of course. In the boroughs of Haringey, Bromley, Enfield and St Pauly, enormous, secret medical centres were developed, in which students and gypsies, convicts and homosexuals, deserters and freshly arrived Jews were all able to give something back to the society that so generously hosted them, by themselves hosting the sacrificial lice, offering the creatures their blood, all with the noble aim of fighting universal sickness. After the war, of course, the practice fell into disuse, becoming an almost-taboo topic of conversation. (For this is the downside of English gentility, Raphael added with a rueful laugh: we are never very comfortable in the accommodation of any discourse involving seepage.)

"Raphael, however, was accustomed to keeping his ear close to the ground, and had become aware that over the last five years certain British scientists and doctors at the forefronts of their fields were developing a fresh interest in the possibilities of lice-farming, possibly with a view to tackling more contemporary British illnesses such as swine flu, gristles, chicken breath and AIDS. While it was clearly out of the question for underprivileged members of the British public to strap themselves anew to armies of ravenous lice, might not this be the perfect opportunity for so-called asylum seekers to prove their loyalty to the Motherland? After all, any third-world trickster could swear his allegiance to the Queen, or learn the names of the rivers flowing through Oxford, but surely only a truly born-again Brit would develop six-month intimacies with hordes of lice for the right to dwell among the people of

Albion?

"An asylum seekers' advocate of the highest order, Raphael put his burgeoning ideas to the medical establishment and to the fledgling coalition government, and the rest, as you know, is history. Since the 'Asylum and Lice Act' passed this summer, immigration applicants from the developing world who sign a statement professing their total willingness to lice-feed have a three thousand times higher success rate in gaining entry to the Islands than those who turn their noses up at the mission, no matter what their reasons for claiming asylum in Britain may be. Needless to say, I agreed to Raphael's proposal immediately; he settled my ransom with Alain Souleymane in full and, before the week was out, Mr Dubois and I were on a plane out of Dakar bound for St Pauly, England.

## DO YOU KNOW WHERE YOU'RE GOING TO?

"*I* arrived at the Lionheart Complex precisely six weeks ago. The grounds were already deep in snow. Thanks to Raphael's influence, I was spared much of the interrogation that I believe accompanies the vast majority of African entrants to this island, and I was advanced, as promised, to the status of a Category 3 seeker.

"The Lionheart Complex is a miserable place, although in comparison to this appalling outhouse we now find ourselves in, it seems like some kind of luxury hotel. Mukelenge rules the Towers with three co-generals (*sonder-sultans*, they call themselves, each one of the four from a different corner of the African continent, or so they say; as far as I'm concerned, Mukelenge is like no African I've ever encountered or imagined), and they rule it with a rod of velvet and cream. On my first day there I was given my bright grey 'A' badge and shown to my room, which I shared with four other men, each from countries whose languages I don't speak. Mukelenge explained the system. For the first week, a sort of observational period, I was free to wander the twelfth floor as I pleased, and to spend my time in whatever manner I desired, as long as I made sure to (a) keep the lice-flasks strapped to me at all times and (b) drink every drop of my three daily milk-shakes in full and without fail. Cameras (the footage from which was being beamed live on constant stream to Channel 4) would be on me at all times, in any case, and everyone would know if I was up to anything untoward. And then he inserted the first batch of lice. I say 'inserted' because before strapping the glass containers of disgusting, writhing creatures onto my external body, he also insisted on the need to place a small number of the animals into the various orifices of my body. These internal lice, Mukelenge assured me, were no different from the others, and would do me no harm, but it was possible that they might grow far more quickly than the others, owing to the warmth and nourishment of my internal organs. If that were the case (and I should say if and when I felt excessive itches or bulging), they would be duly extracted by pipette and sent on to the pasting-wing at the hospital near St Pauly University campus. I closed my eyes and said nothing. As for the shakes, Mukelenge went on, these were a simple mixture of bananas, ice-cream, chocolate, creatine and a special medicine called Viagra. The attendants would carefully monitor the effects of these nutrients on me and the other carefully chosen African male inmates—women, young children and Asian males were offered a less interesting diet—and the manner in which my body responded to them would largely determine what was done with me next.

"I grew very quickly, and began to feel almost constantly aroused. Mukelenge seemed pleased, and within a week I was taken, along with just one of my roommates to the place we find ourselves in now, a dismal shed in the back-garden of a tall, grey house called *The Shallows*, high in the hills of the village Raphael calls 'Mameluke Bath'. And here, my progress has been somewhat less dazzling. For some reason, my body has stopped responding to the treatments. Not only are the shakes having no effect on the growth of either my muscles or my libido, but according to Mukelenge the lice have stopped feeding on me too. They've given up putting in the internal ones altogether. You may say it's normal, that perhaps my organism is resisting the extreme cold, or the fact that I'm being kept all day immobile and in chains—yet the others in here seem to be responding quite differently. Every day I see my colleagues getting bigger and bigger, and the lice appear to be in heaven. When Mukelenge removes the flasks at the end of each night I sometimes hear him gasping in amazement at how engorged the little beasts have become.

"Meanwhile, my colleagues' behaviour is changing drastically too. While I seem to be getting wider and wider awake, on some nights barely managing even a couple of hours' sleep, the other men appear to be entering into a state of almost constant sleepiness. I say 'sleepiness', but what I really mean to say, I think, is SOMNAMBULISM. For if you look closely, you'll see that they're not exactly asleep—nor are they anything close to awake! They seem to drift forever somewhere in between, their eyes half-open in a perennial glaze of depression. During our walking breaks, which take place every day from noon until two (although today's show in St Pauly town square was in lieu of our usual exercise), and always on leads, they wander about as if they were zombies or automata, muttering stories about terrible, faraway childhoods, under their breath, as if in the grip of a supernatural trance. Sometimes Raphael and Mukelenge hold iMu microphones under the golems' chins, apparently desperate to catch whatever intense drops of magic and trauma are there to be caught, regardless of the culture that has produced it, or the twisted suffering of the mouth spewing it out. Our masters seem particularly excited by any tales they can find relating to myth or folk culture, or anything that seems to smack of 'authenticity', especially if the stories have the slightest connection to something they call RECONFIGURATION. Sometimes Mukelenge sketches the men's mumbled *récits* in pencil, shouting over to Raphael that this one or that one will look particularly fantastic in the swimming pool. I myself pretended to enter an autobiographical reverie just this week, spouting garbled tales of my telekinetic infancy, possibly similar to the self-portrait I've just now spun for you this evening, possibly not: I make up so many stories depending on the desires and fantasies of my interlocutor that sometimes it's hard to know what's real and what's a total dream. But Mukelenge seemed unimpressed. A Haitian metal sculptor who washed up here two weeks ago was the object of his almost constant hysterical scrutiny, though, and, given the fact that he also seemed to grow like the wind, it was perhaps unsurprising that after only four days Frankétienne (for this was the Haitian's name), was rushed forward to the next stage.

"For there *is* one more stage after this one. I'm not sure exactly what the nature of that final stage is, but I am fairly certain that making it there is, once again, dependent on how well one's body responds to this one. They're building something deeper into the forest, beyond the empty swimming pool, and they're calling it the *GollHouse*. Every day Polish workmen arrive to carry on with the construction. They march past our shed, smoking and singing, occasionally peering in through the window to laugh at us. Nobody notices them but me, of course. I don't know why these Polish workers feel they're so much better than us. Is it just because their skin glows so white? Such a detail means nothing these days. Mukelenge says that an Albanian, a Turk and a Lithuanian Jew are all on their way from the Lionheart Complex next week, and that these new breeds promise to open up an entire new market. And besides, does my own skin not glow just as snow-white as a Pole's or a Jew's?

"Sometimes I think that perhaps Raphael and Mukelenge may actually be sorcerers. Once, during the third part of the night—"

$B$ut my body had entered into a cycle of choking, hysterical spasms, and Cary was obliged to cut short his grisly storytelling. He pursed his lips and held onto me tightly, all the while whispering gentle reassurances in the attempt to stop me from twitching with quite so much violence.

I just couldn't take in any more of the horrors, you see. It was selfish and weak of me, I know, but I just *couldn't* be expected to imbibe more and more disgusting visions of misery and humiliation, all of them related by this unfeasibly damaged, white-haloed youth, all of them enounced in the same self-effacing, don't-pity-me drone.

And as he struggled to hold onto me, I began to babble and scream, great gobs of drool hanging off my chin. It would all have been all right (for he carried on comforting, his sweet nothings appropriate and fraternal), had I not suddenly noticed his face. It was totally spattered. Long streaks of blackish, stringy sickness glistened and drew on Cary's white-pink cheeks under the grey light of dawn. From his chin dangled a gluey blackish bile-ribbon so elongated that it nearly reached the surface of his shelf, suspended in the air, rising occasionally back up to his face before falling again, though never quite arriving at the bottom or breaking away altogether. His thick blond Afro curls were thick and treacly with the stuff. The worst of it was the expression on his face: Cary was totally indifferent to his unexpected drenching. Bitter absence of surprise silently screamed in his wide-open, unblinking blue eyes, as my putrid bile-globules hung from their fair lashes.

Exhausted, I brushed listlessly with my sleeve at the last gobs that still hung from my own lips. It was all right. It was over. Cary had yet again managed to stay calm in the face of assault. And now he began the self-cleaning motions necessary to wipe away of the worst of my filth.

"Don't cry, Christie," he muttered gently, as he reached up from his ablutions to stroke my own hot-combed Saturday-hair. "Everything's going to be all right, you'll see."

But I wasn't even listening. I was staring across the shed, my blackened mouth wide open in terror. It wasn't any of the gaggle of half-awake, half-asleep, loudly snoring muscle-men that was causing me to convulse so with fear. In the early morning gloom they were all much of a muchness, and I'd grown used to their vacant half-stare. Nor was it the same men's vibrating exo-wombs of guzzling lice. Really, it's true what they say: you can get used to anything in a few hours. No, the horror that was gnawing its way into me like a forest-shark was coming from the face I had suddenly glimpsed hovering at the window.It was a ghastly apparition, a face I knew of old. It floated there, the horrible head, at the pane on the shed's far wall, peering in at us with a look of care and concern. Mukelenge smiled. He gazed at Cary, then back at me, shaking his head with a strange mixture of excitement and relief. Was the sight of Cary and me, entangled together there on the shelf, in a pool of our own exchanged fluids, somehow turning him on? I sincerely hope not. The very idea of such an arousal still makes me shudder. I like to think that maybe he was just genuinely happy to see me— at last!—in the arms of a suitable boy.

# IV

You're prodded awake, as you are every morning of this life, by the menacing rumble of Irena, who stands on tiptoe, back fully arched, on the edge of a dirty pillow next to your head. Today her ghoulish purring is accompanied by a series of paw-blows, which she administers at three-second intervals to your left temple.

"Fuck off!" you whimper peevishly. "It's Saturday!"

Irena doesn't care what day it is; she just wants you up.

Why doesn't she ever leave the house? You and Dawn spent *months* planning that Filt-a-Cat Portal for her. You hemmed and hawed about the microchip implant. Cats without the right chip (or, as is generally the case around Piperville, without any chip at all) are left out in the cold: only Irena is free to come and go through the frontier as she pleases. The vet's security arguments eventually won you and Dawn over. Then you both wracked your brains as to whom you could beg to install it. You finally persuaded Dawn to let you ask Raj, the fit Asian handyman from Islands. He looks kind of like Mowgli from *The Jungle Book*, only with bigger muscles. He did a good job.

But does Irena use her open-sesame kitty-gate? Does she take the initiative to step, even momentarily, out of self-imposed captivity? Does she take advantage of her natural freedom to go for even a short wander in the back garden, or through the alleyways of Piperville, safe in the smug-cat knowledge that no stray can follow her back into the warmth?

Does she, fuck!

You pull the covers tightly over your head, groaning with self-pity, knowing, as you lie there cringing, that Irena won't give up. You suddenly remember what's coming next, and try desperately to yank your feet under the covers, but it's too late: you feel the toothy nip on the third toe of your right foot, and scream into your pillow.

"*Please*, Irena! I need me sleep. I'm so tired."

But she's implacable. She begins to jump up and down on your covered head, making angry little cat-cries as she bounces. You surrender, groggy, and begin to climb out of bed. Irena jumps off at once and stares up at you triumphantly from the floor.

"Fucking bitch," you whisper.

At that moment your bedroom door is thrown wide open, and Dawn comes striding in.

"Mam!" you shout, scrambling back into bed. You've got a massive boner, and are clad only in your baggy white Kangols.

"Damon, come downstairs, *now*!" cries your mother, manifestly uninterested in your erection. She looks simultaneously furious and mad with upset, and paces up and down your tiny bedroom.

Irena dashes, mewling, out the open door.

"What is it, mam?" you ask, as impatiently as you dare. (Why can't she ever just be *calm* of a weekend?)

"I don't know, lad," says Dawn, going to the window, staring down into the street with a series of exaggeratedly suspicious head and neck movements. "I don't know."

She picks up the battered burgundy passport that lies

on your windowsill, leafs through the madly torn and bitten pages in disgusted amazement.

"What have you been *doing* to this, lad?" she breathes incredulously. "You haven't been abroad since we went to Mykonos."

"Wasn't me," you mutter glumly.

*"It's time the tale were told...*" you read out loud, in faltering, vaguely embarrassed tones.

You scrutinise the envelope again. There's no return address on the back. You stare again at the DVD.

"Is that the name of a film?"

"No film I've heard of," says Dawn. "Go on, then, put it on!"

"Have you already watched it?"

"Yes!" shouts Dawn.

"Then why do you want to watch it again?"

"I want *you* to see it, soft lad!"

"But what is it?"

"I don't *know!*" she shrieks into your splintering eardrum. "Just put it *on.*"

You obey your mother.

Sliding the disc through the player's narrow slot, you shiver, even though you've managed to slip on your thickest dressing gown before being bundled wordlessly down the stairs. It isn't even that cold, not really, not when you remember (shit, forgot the rabbits) today's the first of December and they've predicted snow for the end of the weekend. The central heating is jacked up to full blast. But shivering is never linked to coldness, not with you. You're not Charles the First. No: you just tremble whenever you know something beyond your capacity for coping is about to take place, and it *always* feels like decapitation.

"Stop shaking," says Dawn, crouching down next to you in front of the television. "You're making me nervous. Just watch."

You start to glide down the busy main street of what

feels like a seaside town in early winter. Mothers pushing their babies in oversized prams stream towards you, occasionally stopping to peer into the lens and smile. Huge, tattooed men in black bikers' leathers stride past, again stopping to peer and occasionally leer at the person or entity holding the camera. Although the sky looks grey and overcast, at least half the passing, seething population seems to be licking at enormous ice cream cones, or nibbling at some seaside rock. And then you notice: there's not even any sea. It's a wide, grey-green river that flows past you and the ghostly cameraman. On the other side of the river lies an enchanted black forest. But you're turning away from all that now, away from the street too, you're veering right into a deathly quiet side street, a side street that seems so aggressively steep that you think for a moment you're perhaps going to tumble backwards from sheer fatigue. But no: you carry on, climbing and climbing (can you hear the occasional tiny huff and puff?), up the winding, punishing hill, past innumerable red Saint George's crosses painted on white, billowing flags (they've been impaled every ten metres on both sides of the road), until it all begins to flatten out, and clusters of funny-looking redbrick houses begin to appear randomly, houses that are apparently unattached to any particular street or conglomeration. And at last you stop outside one house. This one isn't red like the others; it's painted entirely black. On the ebony front door you read a shiny grey number: 111. The coal-black knocker is moulded in the shape of a bulbous, smiling face. This face is the face of the Devil.

"What the—" you start to say, blandly, but Dawn silences you with an urgent shush.

The screen's gone black now, and you wonder whether you might perhaps be allowed to speak. You're about to take the chance and open your mouth again, when suddenly the momentary blackness ends and you find yourself floating, high in the sky, looking down over a sea of treetops.

"What's this?" you say, despite yourself. "How did we get so high?"

"It's the same place," says Dawn grimly. "Look: there's the river. There are the houses on the cliff. It's the same town."

"From God's point of view," you laugh. "That's funny."

And then the film really does end, and this time the screen turns not black but a misty kind of red.

"So, what was that?" you ask, getting up from your crouching position in front of the screen. Your left leg's croaked on you, and you try to shake it back to half-life, groaning with the effort.

"That's precisely what I wanted to ask you," says Dawn, flopping onto the sofa, folding her arms.

"Well, how would I know?" you squawk.

Your mother's really beginning to get on your nerves now.

"You're the one bringing strange people in here," says Dawn. "We never got anything like this before."

"What are you talking about?" you say, genuinely puzzled. "Do you even think this thing is meant for us? It's probably just some tourist—"

"Of course it's meant for us!" shouts Dawn, leaping up from the sofa. "Who else would it be meant for?"

You say nothing. You feel your face start to grow hot. You tap your foot nervously.

"Stop that!" shouts Dawn, aggrieved.

You stop.

"So, you don't recognise it?" she asks, fixing her stare on you now.

You feel yourself getting smaller.

"What?"

"The place in the film! Do you or don't you recognise it?"

"No," you say, frowning. "I don't think so. I mean, I—"

The doorbell rings.

"Who's that?" hisses Dawn, jumping back onto the sofa. "We're not expecting anyone!"

She clasps a protective cushion to her chest.

You run to the window, squint through the sparkling net curtains. Two burly men stand chatting on the doorstep, too engrossed in their conversation to notice the shape hunched behind the glass.

"Oh, shit!" you cry.

"What?" whispers Dawn.

She looks terrified.

"I'd completely forgotten! Mikey and Raphael are driving me up to Manchester today!"

Dawn drops instantaneously to the floor; then, a second later, tears up the stairs like a woman-child possessed.

*I*t doesn't take you long to jump into the shower (you're a big boy now, and baths are for babies) and pull on some acceptable clothes: twisty Bench jeans, blue-and-white K-Swiss trainers, red Puma T-shirt, and—your pride and joy—the blue-and-silver Adidas track top that Mary-Kate and Kinga unexpectedly brought in for you the week after your birthday. Mikey and Raphael wait patiently for you in the car. You've explained, apologised, your mam's feeling quite poorly today, isn't up to having strangers in the house.

As you skip merrily out the front door, shouting up to a silent Dawn that you'll definitely be back by midnight, and prance towards Raphael's waiting silver Volvo, you feel as if you're lucky enough to be riding to the Senior Prom with not just one divine jock, but two—one of each colour! You pray you won't mess things up. It's so kind of Mikey to be giving you a second chance.

"Hello, Damon!" smiles Raphael as you approach the car. "Why don't you sit here in the front with me? Mikey doesn't mind bringing up the rear, do you, Mikey?"

Mikey merely grins in reply, indicating with his hand

that you should be his guest. He's transformed again since the last time. Today his dark skin is glowing a ruddy aura, as if some expensive new facial cream, blended and combined with actual fire, has been rubbed into his flesh every night for a hundred years. His eyes twinkle an electric blue, while his hair, or what remains of it, shines with a fantastical white-on-blond hardness.

Mikey is tremendous.

"It's really nice of you to be taking me out like this," you gush anxiously, yanking at your seatbelt.

"What kind of music would you like to hear, Damon?" asks Raphael.

"Oh, whatever you fellers want," you answer, flattered that he should even consult you.

"You are one *compliant* little chap, aren't you?" grins Raphael, fiddling with the car's sophisticated looking iMu. "You weren't telling me porkies, Mikey."

Mikey laughs again, throwing his head back this time, chuckling in a forced, throttled monotone, a friendly, demonic, wind-up wax doll, blond and adrift in a carnival of sorts.

$T$he first half of the two-hour drive to Manchester passes without you fully realising you've left St Pauly behind. You're simply enjoying the ride, the dramatic, mountainous, scenery, quietly listening to Raphael's music, first a comprehensive selection of *Italo* (you chirrup along to some of the tracks you heard that night at the club Supernature, much to Mikey and Raphael's loudly-proclaimed amusement), then a compilation of Madonna tracks you've never heard in your life.

"*Milk of Madonna* I call this mix," says Raphael proudly. "It's completely mad the way nobody ever listens to this stuff. Madonna covering Marvin Gaye? Like, total genius."

And you have to nod your agreement. It *is* really excellent.

When *Milk of Madonna* finally comes to an end with the

one track you do in fact know (a girl-power three-way with Hillary Clinton and the Pussycat Dolls), you three bucks begin a more masculine interaction.

You try, politely, to find out more about Raphael's legal work and Mikey's progress. Where does Raphael find his seekers? How is Mikey dealing with the mountains of St Pauly bureaucracy? But neither of them seems very keen on going into details.

"Mikey's doing just fine here, aren't you, Mikey?" says Raphael. "I mean, isn't that obvious? He's more at home in England than the bloody English, for goodness sake!"

Mikey titters his agreement.

"And don't you have other clients?" you pursue nervously. "Christie mentioned—"

"Just *what* did Christie mention?" barks Mikey from the back.

These are the first human words that have passed your old friend's lips the entire journey. You look out of the window awkwardly. You notice with pleasure that you're driving through Chesterfield. Chesterfield is the furthest away from St Pauly you've ever been—a school trip when you were fifteen, about which you can remember almost nothing except that someone said Chesterfield was near Manchester. This person had said that he or she once knew someone in St Pauly whose cousin had lived in Chesterfield but who actually lived in Manchester and drove between the two places every day. And now you yourself, Damon, are passing through Chesterfield in order to get to that place on the other side, over the rainbow, at the back of the North Wind: Manchester. As far away from St Pauly as you'll ever have been. Except for Birkenhead. And Mykonos, and Mameluke Bath. But you can't remember any of those, so they don't really count, do they?

"Mikey asked you a question," says Raphael harshly, turning his head from the road to stare at you.

"Oh, sorry!" you say, flushing. "I was miles away. What

did you ask, Mikey?"

"He asked about what the girl, Christie, had mentioned to you regarding my clients," says Raphael in the same aggrieved tone, still staring at you rather than at the road.

"Oh, nothing, really," you stammer. "Just last week, on me birthday. That you probably had lots."

You grin awkwardly.

"What else, Damon?"

You feel four red-hot metal eye-skewers burning into your cheeks, into the back of your neck

"I don't know. Nothing! She only ever met Mikey once, anyway, and that was way back in September. And she's never met you."

"What else, Damon?"

You rack your brain. Why's it so hard to remember what people say to you? It sometimes feels as if your head's filled with straw, or treacle, or lube.

Then it comes.

"'Not like Mikey.' That's what she said. I remember now. That the others are probably nothing like Mikey. 'Mukelenge's one of the strong ones,' she said."

The two men laugh in unison.

"She's Ms Dynami-tee-hee!" cackles Mikey.

"The original Student of Prague! She'll say he's stolen her reflection next," adds Raphael.

You laugh too, even though you don't understand what either of them means.

"She was talking rubbish anyway; just drunk, I think. We'd both had quite a bit. It was me birthday."

"Well, she's right. Old Mukker Mikey here *is* pretty bloody strong," says Raphael, looking back at the road now, to your immense relief. "I'm thinking of shipping him over to my Minneapolis branch, test out his muscles in the States!"

And then it becomes easy with them both again, and you find yourself chattering, like a silly little woodland creature, answering the barrage of low-voiced inquiries coming at you from your back and right:

Did you realise that 'Minneapolis' is a blend of the Greek and the Red Indian for 'city of water'?

Have you really never heard of the Twin Cities of Minnesota, and of the other St Pauly?

Who else works at Islands in the Sun?

How many years did they keep you locked up in that loony bin in Laurietown?

What finally drove you over the edge? Drugs? A man? A cult?

What's your mam like?

Did she come and visit you when you were wacko?

What kind of guys do you both tend to go for?

Do you find the goblin gang-rape scene at the end of Centaurboy's *Skrikercock* convincing?

At first you feel tense when Raphael starts his cross-examination. You never discuss that kind of thing with anyone, not even Christie, much as you wanted to that night of your birthday when she was curled up like a cat on your bed and you wanted her to love you. But Raphael seems safe. He isn't judging you. He doesn't hate you for being different. Maybe he's even different himself? And who knows what Mikey is? But that doesn't matter. Mikey's your mate.

"I actually *know* two porn stars," you volunteer, quietly giggling at them both, like a little boy attempting to impress his hippie mother's cool, bearded, pagan younger brothers.

"My, my!" screams Raphael, honking on the horn in excitement. "Who?"

"Well, um, have you heard of Luke and Nigel Bendemann?" you venture, encouraged.

"*Duh!*" shout Mikey and Raphael at the same time, and then, in the same impressed whisper: "*NIGE-LUKE!* Well, la-di-da!"

"I actually *work* with them," you proudly confess. "They're my colleagues at Islands in the Sun. Though rumour has it they're about to, er, move to Vauxhall. In London."

"You are one mysterious little boy," says Raphael, putting a big, hairy hand on your thigh, rubbing vigorously through the twisted denim. "You're like some kind of doll or something. The queers are going to die for you up on Canal Street."

*I*t's late in the afternoon when you and your friends arrive. The Village is deep in snow. You've been expecting the yellow brick street to be full of friendly-looking characters dancing in the colours of a tribe of Indian chiefs at Mardi Gras, or muscle-bound policemen, bulging out of their blue uniforms as they chat loudly with quiff-bearing intellectuals in black-rimmed spectacles about the sexual politics of the musical comedy. Even if the temperature *has* dropped substantially since you set off from St Pauly, you've heard it repeatedly said by Mary-Kate and Kinga that café culture thrives in Manchester like nowhere else in the United Kingdom, and have therefore assumed that even in inclement weather such as this the locals will probably prefer to sip their pints out on the terraces and rooftops. But instead you see only an exceptionally small, thickset old man in leather trousers smoking a cigarette outside the entrance to a pub called Via Recta.

"Sex Dwarf!" calls out Raphael to the man.

"Isn't it fine?" sings back the bouncer in a gravelly Lancashire tremolo, smiling reverentially at Raphael, and giving a little bow.

"Nobody's out," says Mikey to Raphael, peering gloomily into yet another deserted bar.

"Normal," replies Raphael, marching on in front. "They're running scared since the Pope's latest exorcism decree. There are a lot of Catholics up here in Manchester."

He sighs.

"Northern fairies really are a bunch of big girl's blouses,

171

though. So frightened all the time. And so thin!"

"Where shall we go?" says Mikey, his voice dull and empty.

"Minotaurs," says Raphael. "It's too bloody cold to be anywhere else."

And as if he's uttered a magical command, the three of you find yourselves at the corner of Canal Street, outside a dimly lit building on which you read the rainbow-lettered words: MINOTAURS, MAGICAL BATHS. Underneath the sign they've painted a golden bull, and some funny kind of foreign-looking squiggle in pink.

$$\mu$$

You've seen it before, that squiggle, in maths lessons maybe, somewhere long before that too. And carved onto your iMu too, of course; it's the logo, but then you put that zig-zag zebra cover on. It makes you feel like you're going to throw up. No wonder you've always hated maths.

"What is it?" you ask in wonder.

"Can't you read?" says Mikey. "It's a sauna."

Raphael pushes open the heavy glass double doors and ushers you two inside ahead of him.

"Hi there!" says the tanned, blond youth at the reception. "Three?"

"Three," says Raphael, reaching into his pocket for his wallet.

"How much is it?" you ask the boy, suddenly embarrassed.

"Don't you worry," says Raphael. "I pay for you. And for Mikey, obviously."

The receptionist suddenly peers at Mikey more closely, then gives a strangled little yelp. He's forgotten to tell you something crucially important. Not making eye contact with any of you, he begins to speak in an embarrassed, robotic drone, staring blankly to a space beyond the entrance.

"Can I just ask, gentlemen... You *have* seen the notice. Right?"

You follow Raphael's irritated gaze to a prominent sign in pink-and-black felt tip, a scrappy A4 sheet stuck hastily onto the front of the reception desk with a single pin.

You read slowly, as though your frozen thumb is moving across each scribbled word:

*IDENTITY NIGHTMARE!!*

*MINOTAURS is legally required (by law) to ask any patron we suspect of being ILLEGAL to supply us with the necessary proof of his British identity. It's a real nightmare, but we're legally obliged by the Law!!*

*Thanx*

*xxx*

Nobody speaks.

You read the notice again, silently this time, not fully grasping what this has to do with any of you.

The receptionist carries on staring into the middle distance.

Mikey's sitting down on the bench by the entrance now, and seems to be inspecting his own trainers for traces of dog shit.

"Are you alluding to him?" snaps Raphael at the hapless boy, waving impatiently at Mikey's hunched, seated shape.

"Yes," says the boy, flushing.

"He's legal," says Raphael coldly.

"Can I see his ID? It's just that we've had our windows smashed three times already this year, and if they thought we had illegals in here too, I just don't—"

"I said he's legal," shouts Raphael.

"I'm sure he is, I am, but it's the law, sir. I'm really

sorry, it's just—"

Raphael suddenly lunges for the young twink's head. You cringe, begin to back towards the door.

"Stay right there!" shouts Raphael, not looking at you.

Bringing the receptionist's scarlet ear towards his mouth now, Raphael begins to whisper into the pink hole, which nods and twitches in terror and abasement.

Raphael lets go.

"That man is as British as you are," he growls at the humiliated pastry. "And don't you forget it."

The receptionist straightens again behind his counter, smiling with false brilliance.

"You fellas have a good time," he bleats, handing Raphael three keys.

Mikey springs up from his bench, places a warm hand on the back of your neck.

You grin, take your bull-key from a smiling Raphael. You think again how lucky Mikey is to have a friend such as this, a friend who's willing to treat him to luxuries like a sauna in Manchester's legendary Village, when all the other asylum seekers and refugees you've heard about or talked to back at that training day in August seem to be living on a pittance that barely allows them to eat twice a day. But isn't it Mikey's due, in a way, if he's so likeable and strong? If he's managed to make Raphael care for him so deeply that Raphael wants to offer him presents—well, then, isn't that a tribute to Mikey's goodwill and success at integration? And all these good qualities will surely lead Mikey to many more offers of friendship and hospitality in England.

You take your white, bull-themed towels (and is that a packet of bull-condoms and bull-lube buried at the centre of the thick white folds?) and push your way through the doors leading to the changing rooms. When you enter the sweaty chamber, clap wide-open eyes on the scores of semi-clad men chatting, preening, or simply standing, stark-naked in front of their lockers, staring out every new immigrant who arrives into this steamy land of plenty, you almost turn tail to run back into the snowy streets of Manchester.

"Not expecting so much flesh?" says Raphael with a little laugh, chucking you lightly under the chin. "You'll get used to it, little one."

Raphael and Mikey begin to disrobe, and you reluctantly follow suit. When you reach your boxers you look around nervously. Mikey and Raphael are sitting, arms folded, on the bench across from you, already changed and tucked safely into their towels. Their bull-keys dangle idly from their wrists. You turn your back to them, take a deep breath, and pull down your plain white shorts.

"Nice," breathes Raphael. "Put on that towel really tight, little one. Every bull in this maze is going to want to get his hands on a piece of *that* arse."

"They've got a new snack bar upstairs," says Mikey. "*Obake.* Japanese. Brer Gabe told me about it. Shall we go for a bite before...?"

"Of course, Mikey," says Raphael. "I could do with the calories. Have you already eaten lunch with your mother, little one?"

"No," you mumble.

"Well, isn't that something?" says Raphael, leading the way through the changing room, away from the area where most of the men seem to be clustered (the entrance to the steam rooms, you assume), towards a large wooden door in the corner, on which the word 'SUSTENANCE' is marked in bright blue paint.

*Obake* (Jap-Bites of Happiness and Health) seems to be doing a roaring trade. At least a dozen men clad only in their bull-towels and blue rubber wristbands sit around the bar or at the little booths that are arranged all around the room, tucking greedily into mouth-watering sushi rolls or little tubs of delicious-looking frozen yoghurt.

"I'll take a Blue Velvet, please," says Mikey to the

barman.

The boy looks oddly blank, offers a nod of reluctant acknowledgment.

It's your turn next.

"Could I have a Hippogriff's's Dream?" you ask shyly.

You *love* the sound of honey nuts mixed in with frozen caramel yoghurt!

"Hippogriff's Dream, coming right up," smiles the barman. "And for you, Mr Dubois?"

Raphael frowns at the menu. "Blueberries and lovedean granola," he says eventually, licking his lips. "By golly, that sounds *good*. I'll take your Blue Moon Breakfast."

"Of course," says the barman, bowing.

You notice now that the boy's pointy nipples and skinny torso are held tight within a leather harness. How wonderful it would be if Raphael were to offer to buy *you* one of these for Christmas.

"Wait a minute," says Raphael.

"Yes, Mr Dubois?" says the boy in the harness.

"I'm hungry. I need more than yoghurt. Get me a spicy crab, avocado and sesame sushi roll."

"Sure thing," smiles the boy, bowing again.

"Open Sesame!" shouts Raphael, grinning.

The boy smirks, protected, and swings on his heel, doubtless gliding off—apart from the harness he wears only a studded leather jockstrap—to take the order to an invisible chef.

You don't really want to get into the hot tub quite so soon, but Raphael insists.

"A good hot jacuzzi will loosen you up, little one," he says. "Steam you up, too."

Mikey nods his agreement.

And by the time you've made it through the surprisingly convoluted mirror-maze, at the centre of which the tubs are situated, you're more than ready for a nice hot soak. You're positively gasping.

You watch as your friends slip off their towels and hang them on gilded bulls' heads above the tub. You're simultaneously pleased and disappointed to notice that their knobs are both significantly smaller than yours. Raphael really isn't very attractive: his enormous, outlandishly tall body (like a giant or an ogre) is muscular, broad, but in a singularly artificial manner, the result of years in the gym, or maybe a few months' worth of steroids. The flesh bulges so painfully that angry, red-and-grey stretch marks are visible all over his dead white skin, especially around the torso. You wonder for a moment if it's possible that Raphael's ever been taken apart and sewn back together. You could believe it. Mikey, unsurprisingly, is straightforwardly hunky. His physique is masculine and alluring in that generally lean and uncomplicated black-man way (even skinny old Obama looks like that since he's started working out properly), and you find yourself wondering, as you so often do these days, why it is that black people seem to think they have such rotten luck when nine times out of ten they're so much more attractive than pasty old Caucasians—especially the mixed ones, the ones with the lighter skin and the crazy hair. Christie, for example: she's a lovely-looking girl, if only she knew it. You're sure old Mrs Lammoreaux was a stunner in her youth too.

You take a breath and slip off your own towel, jumping into the tub near the source of the copious, friendly spurt of bubbles.

"Oh, it's hot!"

Raphael and Mikey smile at each other, gaze over at you affectionately, like a pair of doll-uncles.

You giggle, duck your head down beneath the surface of the water. And as you crouch down there, safe within the folds of the lovely, swirling fluid, eyes clamped tightly shut, listening to the soothing, bubbling sound of the machine, you realise that what you long for most in the world is the certain prospect of finding four, warm, electric-blue uncle-eyes riveted to your beaming pink face as it slowly emerges out of the steaming liquid.

You squeal to yourself in delight, begin slowly to rise to the surface.

When you open your eyes you notice with annoyance that another boy is with you in the tub now. The boy looks kind of crazy. He keeps grabbing hold of Mikey's biceps in a series of violent, jerking motions, while Mikey struggles, laughing, to envelope the child's pale, skinny frame within those same, strong arms. Raphael is laughing hysterically. They seem to have forgotten all about you.

"Fuck me! FUCK me!" mewls the scrawny lad, a tiny creature possessed.

"I'm Paul D., the pig-boy! So fuck me now!"

His voice is desperate, demented, like the cry of a pubescent wood-creature that's been fatally wounded, and now shrieks its last worldly desires to the other beasts of the forest, as it lies dying in its steel-jawed trap.

The adolescent's pornographic command reverberates around the otherwise empty steam room.

"Don't you worry, Paul D., the pig-boy," says Raphael, "he will. Just as soon as you stop writhing around like you're some kind of bloody *eel*."

Paul D. suddenly freezes then turns round in the tub to stare at Raphael. For a moment, he looks terrified. Then he shouts again, in the same disquietingly feline, Mancunian wail:

"Really?"

"Well, yes!" chuckles Raphael. "Just climb up out of the tub now, and get going to the first empty booth in the room next door. My boy here will join you in five. And if you're very lucky, I shall be right there by his side."

Turning to Mikey, Raphael says: "This one would be perfect. We really need to start branching out. And the under-classes *are* like seekers, in a way."

The boy scrambles out of the jacuzzi as if his life depends on it. But instead of making his way obediently to the room next door, he squats on the edge of the tub, pointing his tiny, bony arse towards the three of you.

He grunts softly.

His back still facing you, he grasps the edges of his bum-cheeks, opens up his anus for view.

You stare in fascination at the sore-looking red aperture.

Mikey and Raphael are roaring with mirth now.

But Paul D. merely whimpers: "Now! Put your tar-boy fist inside me guts. Now, now, I want it there now! Shove it in, up to the elbow, right up to the tail of yer fuckin' fishy tats."

And, to your fascinated horror (what if there are cameras?), after fumbling briefly in a strange, small flask that Raphael has been carrying around under his arm ever since you left the changing-room, this is precisely what Mikey proceeds to do.

"Goodness me!" squeals Raphael. "This one *is* excited!"

But Mikey doesn't appear to be listening. He's fished what he wanted out of the flask, and is now utterly immersed in the procedure, jabbing at Paul D.'s puckered pink anus, first with one probing finger, then two, then three. He looks like a kind of lunatic magician. You half-expect him to pull out his hand now, give a quick clap, and summon three fluttering white doves from out of the twitching orifice. But he doesn't. His entire fist is in there now, and the boy begins to writhe and moan and utter his now familiar whingeing imprecations.

"Yeah, man, keep it comin'; yeah, that's it, all the fuckin' way!"

He bobs up and down on Mikey's forearm like a manic demon puppet.

"Gosh, that crystallised miaow-miaow really is quite something," sighs Raphael, sensually, to nobody in particular.

Mikey turns to face you now, his thick arm still buried deep inside the boy's frenzied arse. "Something's wrong!"

he whispers, his usually serene dark face suddenly contorted in panic.

"You can say that again! This little pig-zombie is completely bizarre!" Raphael retorts nonchalantly, as the boy continues to yowl and hiss.

Mikey's gazing imploringly at you now, and you stare back at him reluctantly, embarrassed, petrified, stuck.

"Damon, help me!" whispers Mikey, tears beginning to flow from his big brown eyes. "I didn't mean to do it here!"

You eventually manage to move your head to look around you, behind you, to your side.

But there's nobody there.

Nobody else can help.

You look up to the dark dripping ceiling.

"Oh Jesus, God no!" screams Mikey now, and yanks out his stinking arm with a sudden, electric desperation, falling heavily backwards into the tub as he does so. He collapses in the bubbling water with a massive cartoon splash, causing Raphael to roar more loudly than he has all day.

But you're still watching Paul D.'s quivering white buttocks, out of which now gushes an alarming mixture of red-and-brown substances. They trickle steadily for a few seconds, then out of the anus spurts a powerful jet of pinkish intestinal fluid. The boy bends lower, jutting his bottom higher into the air, causing the arc of foul-smelling rosewater to gush up into the air like an out-of-control hosepipe, before it uncouthly penetrates the aqueous membrane of the innocent, effervescent jacuzzi like a shitty liquid-barbarian.

"Northern fairies!" laughs Raphael, wiping the tears from his eyes as he clambers past the three dazed bodies that lie, shocked, in the water. "You're *already* dead!"

He continues to giggle and to mutter to himself as he reaches for his towel, which hangs just where he'd left it, mercifully white, dry and unsullied.

# V

*E*ven in my saddest moments of anger and despair, the opoponax usually had something reassuring to tell me. The star of wormwood didn't need to be out. I would sit in the Gardens on my favourite bench and wait for the panic to subside, as it always did, even if just for a short while. After Hélène took off with Jón for the magical kingdom of Iceland, I'd hike up to the Opoponax Gardens every day, even though I still lived in the awful environs of the university campus. It was worth the bus journey, just to be allowed to sit still amid the wisdom of their whisperings, just to be calm and to listen to the only true thing anyone on this sick planet has ever been able to tell me: *Christie, you'll always have yourself.*

But after everything that had happened during those warm, then suddenly freezing, first few days in December (the snow had reached St Pauly at last), as I hurtled towards the final challenges of the year, I was no longer sure that I *did* 'have myself'. What did it mean to 'have myself' after witnessing the horrors that were being visited upon Cary and the other seekers, not just in the public square of St Pauly, but in the abusive privacy of a garden shed in Mameluke Bath? I'd started re-reading Gogol's *Dead Souls* for advice on the matter, but it didn't seem to be telling me anything I didn't already know.

What, for that matter, had it ever meant for me to 'have myself'? What good had that stupid mantra ever done me, really? How had it saved me from the ongoing humiliation of those disgusting years of living with Hélène again in my thirties, after my brief, failed attempt at an independent life in Liverpool? Getting married to my own mother, even after everything I already knew about her, had turned out—true to the horrors of Greek tragedy—to be the only way I'd ever get the woman to even *think* about showing me the seedlings of her love. I accepted sharing her with the Master. He was a damn sight less hateful than the Mickle-Beast. But even that betrayal of myself hadn't worked! I'd tried so hard those nine and a half years to maintain the insanity of domestic interaction that I knew made my mother feel really alive. But I'd never managed to play my own father (or, perhaps, the phantasm of *her* own father) quite convincingly enough for Hélène's post-oedipal tastes. What purpose could I serve, in the long run, with no Icelandic cock, and fewer and fewer prospects of developing fetish-pleasing Nordic tentacles? And after one lovers' tiff too many, she'd left her tiresome Calabar-cat of a daughter for good. When all was said and done, Gunnhildr, Harald Bluetooth, and Iceland's unending stream of other Arctic perversions—none of them bleeding, none of them real—were simply more fun for Hélène to fuck with.

After gazing upon all these obscene dents in the fabric of what the sane conceive as the thinkable, I was no longer sure that I *could* still be said to 'have myself'. I felt more like someone's blood-dripping statue. Not even Yoko's *Yes, I'm A Witch* on constant loop with Madame Simone's 'Ain't Got No/I Got Life' carol was able to lift me from my supernaturally doleful ennui. And, significantly, that December morning, the opoponax too remained silent.

Only the humming and mewing of my head-ghosts continued, my own personal Furies, screaming interminable variations of a repulsive childhood curse: the godforsaken µ.

*Mu!*
*Mu!*
*Mu!*

They howled the Greek letter at me like demonic whales, shrieking with such demented, fork-tongued choler you'd think it painfully trapped underneath their collective divine fingernail.

"We may hurt like mad, but our name is the Kindly Ones," they insisted: "here to guide you, gash you, and goad you towards the terrible duty it is ineluctably yours to perform."

I looked at my watch. It was ten past ten. Damon would already be at work with his old folk. My seminar paper, 'Saint Paul According to the Matagots', to which I'd hurriedly put the finishing touches late last night, was due to start at the campus at two. It was my only chance of catching Marianne Kollek before Christmas. I was sure she'd come to the trap. But I had to see Damon first. I had to tell him what I'd seen over the weekend in Mameluke Bath. I had to warn him about Mukelenge and Raphael Dubois. I had to convince him not only that he was in danger, but also to help me stop the evil from spreading.

The redheaded *candileja* stared at me like I was something the cat had puked up.

"Visiting day's Sunday," she said.

"I'm not a visitor," I replied.

She carried on staring, not even bothering to try to hide the contempt in her steely blue eyes.

"I'd like to see Mr Damon Bosniak," I said, with as much brisk authority as I could muster. "I believe he works as a nurse here?"

"He does," she smirked. "He's working."

"It's an emergency," I said, refusing to deviate my statue's gaze. "His mother's been taken ill."

She eyed me suspiciously.

"And who are you to them?"

I didn't hesitate for a second. "Family," I said.

And then I saw Damon, hovering nervously behind the flame-haired cunt. He flashed me a terrified grin.

"Mrs Croft, this is an, er, friend of mine. If you could just give us a few moments? I'm sure it's very—"

"She said she was family," snapped the *soucouyant*.

"She is," said Damon quickly. "She's a friend and she's family."

At that moment I felt a rush of warmth in my heart so utterly reassuring that I thought I might fall down dead with happiness. I loved Diamond like he was a part of me. *More* than if he was a part of me. For what was I? I defied the very capacities of human language. But I knew what *he* was, and it was simple and good.

"Well, this is most irregular," said the lilin-shaped tumour. "But if it's an 'emergency', like she says, go to the swimming-pool courtyard, and don't let *any* of the patients see her. They'll only get confused."

"Thank you, Mrs Croft," said Damon, smiling at the foul-tempered empusa with a pukey, eager-to-please gratitude that made me sick to my stomach.

He led me through the sterile hallway, pushing through a pair of double doors that opened onto a snow-covered courtyard. The place seemed utterly deserted; a portrait of Sethe's *Sweet Home* plantation after the flight of the enslaved.

"They're all in the pool," explained Damon, pointing vaguely towards a shed-like glass structure that stood at the other end of the yard.

And as I cocked my head to listen, I *did* think I could hear the echoed cries and whispers of a gaggle of old brown zombies: ghastly, low-frequency, gassy-sounding noises, that seemed to be reverberating around a deathly chamber of poisonous water.

"They're like babies," he said, as if reading my thoughts. "It's the only place they're ever truly happy."

I nodded, wiped the snow off one of the white plastic garden chairs with a black leather-gloved hand, and perched on the edge of the seat, looking up at Damon expectantly.

Damon stared down at me in confusion. I motioned for him to have a seat too.

"What is it, Christie?" he asked softly, gently lowering himself into the chair opposite me, wrinkling up his unusually spotty-looking forehead with that pained but still good-humoured expression he used so well. "Why have you come here?"

I took a deep breath before speaking.

And then I said: "Damon, listen to me: Mukelenge and his Advocate Raphael Dubois are evil, and we have to stop them before they destroy all goodness in the world."

Damon laughed, almost as if such a response came as a relief, so patently ridiculous (and what else was to be expected from someone as crazy as Christie?) that it could safely be ignored.

"I'm not joking, Damon. I saw something last weekend. Something truly..."

I put my head in my hands and groaned; hoping against hope that he would scratch my chin, fondle my ears, anything to try to make a connection. But he didn't. I carried on speaking, muffled now, through my hands, spewing out my long semi-sob of post-traumatic horror.

"I followed their van from the Old Market Square all the way up to Mameluke Bath. I took a taxi, I...oh, I'm not sure this is the best place to discuss it!"

"Was it you who sent us that DVD?" asked Damon, as if I hadn't actually spoken, as if I hadn't just said what I'd said (and I was absolutely sure I'd said it).

"What?"

"That madman DVD. The seaside town, or whatever it was. The cliffs. It arrived at our house on Saturday morning. Gave me mam a proper fright."

"Really?"

I grinned. This was good news.

"So you did send it?"

"Of course I sent it," I said impatiently. "The truth has to come out somehow. Might as well be in homage to Haneke. And this whole thing: us, our reunion. You've got to admit it's nothing short of a miracle."

"I don't follow," said Damon, fumbling in his tracksuit for tobacco.

"Oh, I'll talk to you about it some other time, Damon," I sighed. "It's been eclipsed by something else now. Something even bigger. Listen— "

"I don't know why you sent it," he interrupted, taking a puff of a Marlboro menthol, "but I really think you shouldn't of. It's upset Mam, big-time."

"Good!" I shouted, causing Damon to cringe and look about the courtyard warily. "It was supposed to! People don't *like* ghosts suddenly confronting them with their past, do they? It *does* make them upset. It does. Big-time! But that's no reason why—"

"Christie, love, you can't just—"

"Yes, I can!" I yelled. "Yes, I can! And I must! It is my moral fucking *duty* to look out for you now that I've found you again. And that *woman*, she's..."

"What?" he demanded aggressively. "What is she?"

"She's a cunt," I said simply, staring into his watery green eyes without flinching. "Dawn's a weak, selfish, self-pitying boo-hag who has never met your needs, not ever. Christ, she even makes *my* mother look almost...well, honest in her evil."

"I don't know your mother," said Damon sullenly.

I ignored him and carried on.

"It's her fault that you're thirty-five and have no self-confidence whatsoever, her fault your sexuality's completely fucked, her fault you're prowling the toilets of the bloody Damascus Centre like some ghoulish...adolescent...leopard!"

Damon hung his head, and I think it was at this point that he began to quietly weep.

"Damon, please!" I whispered, trying to make my voice as soft as I could possibly manage. "You're in danger! I just want to help you. I just want to wake you up. I just want you to come out of that bloody alabaster chamber you're sealed up in with her. I know it feels safe in there, but it's not, it's not, it's...don't you see? If they hate me, they'll hate *you*!"

"I don't understand anything you're talking about!" cried Damon, suddenly furious and shaking and red. "I don't understand you when you speak."

"I know you don't, Damon," I said kindly, touching his quivering arm. "I know. Just try to listen. The other stuff can wait. It's none of my business anyway, your relationship with Dawn—just forget it. I'm sorry I sent that DVD. But this other thing I'm trying to tell you about: well, it's huge. We can't just ignore it and hope it'll go away."

He began to smoke another cigarette, his hands shaking.

"It's like you're trying to programme what I should think," he said crossly. "What I should be."

I said nothing.

"We're not in some kind of Stieg Larsson thriller, you know. You're not the girl with the dragon tattoo."

My mouth dropped open with outrage. I could have smacked him.

"What are you trying to say?" I growled. I was trembling with rage. "Is that supposed to be some kind of joke?"

"Mrs Croft will be back any minute, Christie," Damon continued, ignoring me, staring straight past my blushing, tearful face. "We should talk about all this later."

I couldn't let him just brush me away like this, as if I were some annoying insect. I seized his skinny shoulders with both my hands.

"I need to tell you this now, Damon. Listen carefully. This is what I think. I think Mukelenge's what they call a grine."

"A what?" He struggled to pull free.

"A grine. Or maybe just a gwyllion, I'm not sure. Oh, I don't know, call him Frankie Lee or Judas fucking Priest if you like: the point is that he's Pure Evil. It's like he changes, or shifts, like he, it's crazy, I don't know, like every time he takes a hot bath he somehow manages to come out of it with a new layer of skin."

"Well, isn't that what everyone wants to do?" tweeted Damon lamely.

He'd managed somehow to yank himself free from my grip, but he was red-eyed now, tragic, failing miserably to light the ring under his warm milk smile, no matter how hard he clawed and scraped at the knob.

I ignored his flim-flammery, and carried on talking.

"And Raphael Dubois is some kind of powerful demon. I think he's in league with the government. I think they may even have hired him. It's a supernatural shock doctrine he's devised, no more, no less. The idea was already inherent in the culture; he's just taken it to a new level. Like Madonna, in a way. The difference is that Dubois is actually, fully demonic."

Damon shook his head, obstinate.

"They're preying on the weak, and transforming them, Damon! Together. The weak, Damon! People who haven't got anyone to protect them. People being chopped up in Africa for being witches, then rounded up here for being foreign, or illegal, for swamping us. The seekers, Damon, the real seekers: they are totally helpless. And your friends are changing them into terrible things, such terrible things..."

I tailed off, seriously in danger of starting to weep now, or vomit.

"What do you mean, the 'real' seekers?" cried Damon. "Mikey *is* a real seeker!"

"I don't know what Mukelenge is, Damon; I truly don't. I'm sure you know more than I do. You've been spending so much time with them."

"I haven't," said Damon. "Christie, I think you should try to see that doctor of yours more often. The one you see in the Peaks, in that Mameluke Bath place, isn't it? What's his name? Dr Judd? When's your next appointment? I think you're—"

I could have lunged at him with a red-hot poker. Instead, I said: "I'll go now." I was desperate for him not to say any more, not to say so much that I'd end up hating him too. "I'll go. But I just want to read you something first."

I rummaged in my bag for the book, pulled it out, and opened it at the marked page. Damon stared at me, nonplussed.

I began to read from Goffmann, out loud. I've always had a lovely reading voice. My old Latin teacher, Miss "Baby Jane" Hudson, used to ask me in front of the whole class when it was that I'd first taken elocution lessons, when it was that I'd first learned to speak so nicely, never believing me when I said it came naturally, the racist baba-yaga.

*"I also learned that the cripple must be careful not to act differently from what people expect. Above all they expect the cripple to be crippled, to be disabled and helpless: to be inferior to themselves, and they will become suspicious and insecure if the cripple falls short of these expectations. It is rather strange, but the cripple has to play the part of the cripple, just as many women have to be what the men expect them to be, just women; and the Negroes often have to act like clowns*

*in front of the 'superior' white race so that the white
man shall not be frightened by his black brother."*

"Damon. Damon! Don't you see? A golem programme
would take care of all that! The lice-feeding's just the first
stage!"

"What?" stammered Damon. "Sorry?"

He looked at me pleadingly, his eyes filling with tears.
Why was I trying to frighten him? Was I speaking in the
tongues of Beelzebub? Perhaps he'd simply drifted off,
bored, and all the rest was my own paranoid projection.

I pressed on, returned to the text.

"Think about it, Damon! Think about the cripple's
observation! That's precisely what they're up to! That's
exactly what they peddle. They know that's what people in
this country really want; they know that's the only way
they'll ever accept foreigners here: as malleable, coonish
zombies!"

I grabbed at his frail shoulders again, suddenly
desperate. I had to wake him up from his enchanted
slumber. It was breaking my heart. I'd do anything: learn to
speak backwards, guide his trembling hand across the
Ouija board; I'd do anything—ANYTHING!—just to
spell out our ghostly names and make him hear me.

"We broke out of that old house, Damon! You and me!
We didn't die, we're not *in* there any more, we don't *have* to
be, we can..."

Damon suddenly stiffened.

"Shite!"

He spat his cigarette out into the steaming snow as if it
had burned his tongue. He crushed it into the ground with
his trainer. A small, dark figure of a woman was making its
way towards us from the end of the courtyard.

Damon screamed at the withered brown shadow: "Mrs
Lammoreaux! What are you doing out here in your
swimming costume? Get back in the pool! You'll catch
your...death—"

But the old woman pushed past him as if he were no more than an ineffectual scarecrow. It was me she wanted to see. And as she bent her wrinkled brown face over mine to scrutinise whatever it was she wanted to scrutinise, and as I felt, smelled, saw her rancid breath spreading out into the air above my nose, I knew with certainty that it wasn't just white women I hated with a vengeance, it was all women! No, all people (for what were men if not the filthy bluecap-sorcerers pulling on the garters of their various wretched whore-wraiths?), all *people* who dared to look at me in that way, dared to examine my hair and face and body as if these were things being sold on meat-hooks in the Old Market Square.

The old brown boo-hag stroked my left cheek. She appeared to find me to her liking.

"*Bonjour, ma sœur,*" she said.

"*Allez vous faire enculer?*" I snapped back. "You platitudinous cunt."

I picked up my bag, knocked over my chair, and ran back towards the house. I would doubtless have to struggle to elude the redheaded *gargouille* still keeping her monstrous watch inside.

*I*t was, as I think I've already mentioned, the last day of term. 18 Frimaire, Year 220. Lierre: Day of Robespierre's Revolutionary Ivy! But the girls and boys of this particular Ivy League (counterrevolutionary, needless to say) were drugged and sequestered in their nearby digs, preparing hysterically for predictable festive frolics (a school-uniform Xmas 'bop', at which The Ordinary Boys were, according to the anthology of excitable posters, to make a 'surprise' appearance). The campus lake was frozen over, and I thus mercifully had the space to ponder my predicament undisturbed, no longer having to contend with a herd of pubescent South African teen-goats gambolling on the icy banks around me.

The hour of my seminar was approaching, but I felt

strangely calm. So what if Emmeline and the other academic hambones didn't appreciate my line of argument? The important thing was that Marianne Kollek would be there—and, at last, I would have my revenge. Although I'd seen neither hide nor hair of the beastly boo-hag since that dreadful day in September, I knew that she was definitely crawling in from her Lace Market cave to listen to this, the last School of Humanities seminar of the term. I'd checked it first with Emmeline.

"Marianne can be a little funny with everyone!" my spineless supervisor had stage-whispered at me as soon as I'd mentioned Kollek's name. "It wasn't just you, Christie. It wasn't personal. And it wasn't...I mean, I'd hate you to think it was a...I mean, I don't want you to think it's because you're..."

She tailed off wretchedly.

It was pointless trying to discuss a thing like this with Emmeline. She was hysterical with embarrassment and bad faith. It didn't matter anyway. It was enough to know I'd been granted my second chance with Marianne Kollek. And if it didn't come today, there was always tomorrow, figuratively speaking. For Kollek was due on campus later in the week, for her own special jamboree: yet more posters, plastered all over the place, even floating in the grass by the lake, announced the annual day-long *gynécée philosophique*, a "feminine workshop", modelled on Kollek's Geneva practice, to which twenty female doctoral candidates (and up to five male students who identified intensely with women) were invited to swim with Professor Kollek in a "salty, supportive ocean of sisterhood". Idiotic felt-tip seascapes decorated the posters announcing the horrendous event, against which shimmered silhouettes of joyful, dancing mermaids. I had to swallow down the puke.

But I was ready for the Kollek-creature, or anyone who wanted to defend her. I'd given up on getting Damon to help me with this particular project. He and I had bigger fish to fry with Mukelenge and Raphael Dubois. But really: how was I ever going to toughen Damon up? What a wretched little milk-rat he'd turned out to be! What a sad-faced piece of dead, grey gristle! He was practically an automaton. A terrible thought suddenly gripped me: What if they'd already turned him? *What if Damon was already dead?*

But then I remembered his eyes. They still had life in them, just. That look of awkward, fearful pity he'd had as I'd run from the courtyard of Islands in the Sun, and that embarrassed grin at the two blonde bitches who'd run in to catch Mrs Lammoreaux (who'd hollered and shrieked after my necessary retort like the mad creole sister of the first Mrs Rochester). And what the fuck had he been trying to insinuate with that Stieg Larsson reference? "*You're no girl with the dragon tattoo.*" Was that supposed to be some kind of racial dig? Was he implying that I wasn't as Scandinavian as I thought I was? I never should have told him about my mother. He'd been so surprised, so incredulous, just like a stupid, ignorant, uneducated white racist. But why was I so surprised, knowing that mother of his? None of it mattered. The point was simple: Damon would *never* be free. He'd sooner die than wake up to the truth, no matter what I showed him, no matter what incontrovertible evidence I piled up like a vast and bloody motorway disaster. He wanted to stay fast asleep in Piperville, and that was his privilege and right.

Let him see where sleep would get him. Auschwitz, or its twenty-first-century English equivalent, that's where! And he'd deserve it. It was as if he'd failed to learn *anything* from all that life had dealt him, from all the abuse I knew he'd endured, all the daily humiliations he'd learned to lick right up like a stupid little zom—

"Christie?"

I looked up to see Emmeline Thomson's teenage son bending over me, a look of profoundly inappropriate concern in his helplessly bourgeois, pale blue eyes.

"Yes?" I said, mildly frosty.

"They're all waiting for you in the seminar room. It's packed."

"But it isn't supposed to begin till two!" I muttered, gathering my things together, and getting up slowly.

"It's nearly two," apologised the well-spoken youth.

As we scurried towards East Wing, Emmeline's boy explained that he was looking forward to hearing me speak. His name was Brewster, he explained, but his mates mostly called him Bruce, or even 'La Bruce', he giggled, half-attempting to catch my eye now, his ears suddenly turning hot pink.

I glared, pushing my way ahead of him, bristling at the very idea of his awful, pretentious 'mates'. His 'urban' look was absurd. How false and misplaced the baseball cap, the diamond studs, the dangling silver chain! I would call him Brewster, and he would take it.

"I'm applying to Cambridge next year, to read philosophy?" gushed Brewster at my back. "We're just biting the bullet. There's no price on education, Dad says. I'm really into all that kind of, you know, the new ethical stuff? So when Mum mentioned you were giving a paper on animal rights interpretations of Saint Paul—"

"It's really not about Saint Paul, and it's certainly not about animal rights," I quickly countered. "My name's not Brigitte bloody Badiou. I'm simply using Paul's *Letter to the Romans* as a kind of perverse springboard. What I really want to talk about are different forms of silenced precariousness today, articulated through biblical animals, especially cats. They offer the potential basis for a radical new form of universalism."

"Right," Brewster agreed, his voice tiny and broken behind me.

I glanced over my shoulder, an unexpected current of pity suddenly trickling through my irritated veins, and saw that his entire face now flushed hot pink. I tried to smile, but it was useless: he'd pulled his baseball cap right over his eyes now, and any new connection we might have begun to forge was severed.

As we climbed the stairs in silence, and I began to picture the seminar room filled with false, awkward, ashen academics—from Ethics, from French, perhaps even an emissary from Theology!—I felt my bloodstream split into its habitual opposing currents of terror and contempt, and my hands begin their usual grisly flow. I hadn't even checked who was chairing, so consumed had I been by the various soap-operatics Damon and Mukelenge had set in motion these last few weeks. Whoever it was, I prayed they wouldn't try to shake my rotting zombie hand. Let them offer me a friendly kiss instead.

Brewster and I were jogging down the long *Shining* corridor now. It was (as usual) empty, but might just as well (as usual) have been cascading with rivers of blood. The two Julies were standing at the door of their administrative slave-quarters, and waved at our approach.

"They're all in there, Christie!" beamed Julie One. "Break a leg!"

Why were they all making such a big deal of my paper? It was just the School of Humanities seminar, for Christ's sake! I nodded at them politely, didn't even begin to slow down.

"Christie!" shouted Julie Two as I passed them. "Have you seen your mum?"

I stopped dead.

"What?"

"Your mum, duck! Up there!"

They pointed as one, a pair of crazy, empty dream-dolls, at the enormous green notice board that hung on the wall to the left of the admin office entrance. Exam results, posters announcing The Ordinary Boys and the end-of-term bop, scribbled adverts for second-hand set texts: all were pinned up and spread out higgledy-piggledy as usual. But in the top left-hand corner of the green, I saw a poster-size image of my mother. She was sitting, cross-legged, with Agnetha Fältskog, among the black rocks and hot springs of Iceland. This time, she and Agnetha were holding onto one other tightly, like long-lost, long-haired sisters from the Norse afterlife, finally reunited in their icy heaven of Valhalla.

"We blew it up at the Print Unit," explained Julie One. "Doesn't she look happy? Like a classier version of Paula Yates. Mrs Helen Jónsdóttir. With the original Dancing Queen of Euro Pop."

"Old Hel deserves a bit of glamour after all she's been through," added Julie Two.

And Julie One nodded sadly.

Where had Brewster gone during the whole appalling encounter? Had he even noticed me being assaulted by my mother and her three disgusting sisters? It was as if he'd simply been erased from the universe, as if the moment he'd yanked down his baseball cap he'd simply fallen off the edge of my world, left me to deal with those four ghostly boo-hags all on my own. I wished there was some way of getting him to pull it back up—forgive me—come back to me—ask me a thousand more questions about St Paul's animal rights.

He led the way now, wordless, with never a backward glance.

I was on the verge of screaming his name, I was ready to plead with La Bruce to stop in his tracks, to forgive me, to tell me I wasn't going mad, to reassure me that somebody *was* singing, that I wasn't imagining it, that the sickening song of the sirens was really, undeniably there. But he was out of my reach now. He'd arrived without me, his bulky teenage boy frame already bathed in the light shining from the other side of the glass seminar door. I was alone with the music, alone with the poisoned ditty the maenads were singing to drive me insane: the saccharine chorus of 'Dancing Queen'. The nauseating refrain was being blown down the *Shining* hallway of East Wing by one, or both, or all four of the shallow, demented, well-meaning she-moths.

*M*arianne Kollek wasn't there yet. I didn't care: let her play the aging rock star. Let her arrive late. She'd get hers. I'd break into her *gynécée* with Freddy-gloves if I had to. I was ready for a slashing.

Daisy Temple from Theology was chairing. She was an allegedly brilliant young Deleuzian Quaker: long, blonde, becoming-Rasta dreadlocks; jagged, uncut, becoming-vampire fingernails. She'd just joined St Pauly from Johns Hopkins in Baltimore, but her vibe, the dreads notwithstanding, was altogether more Mary Vivian Pearce than the black streets of *The Wire*. Daisy gave me a hypocritical and condescending thirty-second introduction, without even looking me in the eye. I began to read my paper. And as my opening words rang out over the hushed, expectant confederation of intellectual ghosts, I remembered with a sigh of inner contentment why it was that I found academic work so rewarding. The thing was this: I simply loved explaining to others how exactly it was that my mind worked. I loved demonstrating to a captive audience how *simple* apparently complicated things really were once you allowed yourself to strip away the bullshit, once you were able to see what it was that was really important in a given essay, in a given film, in any given enunciation. How, if you had the courage to combine that insight with what was truly going on in your heart (an organ whose existence academics seemed to forget with all too lamentable frequency), you were halfway to producing something that could potentially rock the world to its very foundations.

I kicked off with my favourite quotation from Agamben's *Coming Community*:

> *"If human beings were or had to be this or that substance, this or that destiny, no ethical experience would be possible. This does not mean, however, that humans are not, and do not have to be, something,*

*that they are simply consigned to nothingness and
therefore can freely decide whether to be or not to be, to
adopt or not to adopt this or that destiny (nihilism and
decisionism coincide at this point). There is in effect
something that humans are and have to be, but this is
not an essence, nor properly a thing: It is the simple
fact of one's own existence as possibility or
potentiality."*

Just reading those gorgeous words of truth out loud,
forcing the others in the room to hear them, was, for me,
the pleasure of a communion beyond Christ. And so it was
with enormous irritation that, just one and a half pages
into my paper, I noticed the two Julies hovering like
distracted ostriches at the open door of the (indeed
bulging) seminar room. Daisy Temple pressed me lightly
on the arm.

I stopped speaking, furious. At that moment I noticed
a copy of the *Kollek Reader* poking ostentatiously out of
Daisy Temple's khaki handbag, and inwardly marvelled at
the woman's absence of scruples. At least her long, cultish
fingernails were a good cover for my own secret weapons:
I'd been growing veritable talons these last few weeks.

"Yes, Julie? Is something the matter?" whispered the
ridiculous Temple, in that kindly tone the more radical
academics reserved for the secretaries.

"Oh, yes! Yes! It's terrible!" gasped Julie One, bursting
into tears.

Daisy Temple leapt to her feet in panic.

Julie Two crept into the academic chamber, now more
animated than I'd ever seen her in all the years I'd known
her as my mother's friend and colleague.

"It's Professor Kollek!" she shrieked at the embarrassed
throng, her pronounced St Pauly accent grating the
delicate surface of the bourgeois sonic regime even more
rudely than the unexpectedness of her brainless intrusion
into a space reserved for Thought.

"What is it, Julie?" said Emmeline Thomson, all the pink draining suddenly and alarmingly out of her fat face and neck.

Brewster put his arm protectively around his trembling mother's shoulder.

"She's dead!" wailed Julie One from the doorway.

"In her bath!" clarified Julie Two, beside herself with palpable grief.

Absurd really, I couldn't help thinking, since Kollek had been nothing but the biggest of bitches to both these Julies. Just that week she had stamped on poor Julie Two's foot in rage and frustration (a horrified student had tweeted as it happened), after a particularly poorly attended city-centre workshop (on the possibilities of water-feminism for the women of the global South) that Julie Two had completely forgotten to advertise in the Piper.

But none of this mattered: the wicked witch was dead. And on the same day as Lennon, it suddenly struck me. I remembered that December morning of 1980 in Mameluke Bath like it was yesterday. Hélène had been inconsolable all the way from the 8th up until Christmas, when she had tearfully announced that the tragedy outside the Dakota Buildings had been a sign from the spirits that we were all to move in with *Tante* Colette and *Oncle* Georges in Ollioules. I never did grasp what John Lennon had to do with any of it. Then again, I'd never fully grasped how a fictitious narrator named Holden Caulfield had instructed Chapman to shoot Lennon in the first place. Was I a new Mark Chapman, perhaps? In brown, feminine form? It was true that I'd pictured Kollek's death by flying hatchet so many, many times! But which novel had unconsciously served as my grimoire? I'd never even read *The Catcher in the Rye*.

But really, none of this mattered: the academics had begun their wild moth-fluttering. And I didn't really register any more than that. I remained at the speaker's desk, immobile; perhaps, for a time, paralysed. Even if someone had violently shaken my frozen head (and it is perfectly possible that one of the do-gooders there did just that), I don't think I'd have snapped out of my catatonia. My head was filled with a swirling, red-and-black blood-vision of Marianne Kollek's recent, still-warm death. Even though it would never be admitted that this was the way it happened, in my caladrius soul I saw the true representation of things. And I knew, with equal certainty, that it was my indefatigable will that had made things unfold so blackly for the false feminist prophet. In my reverie I saw Marianne Kollek in an enormous Ottoman-style bathtub, her wrinkled, butchered, open-veined arms dangling over the sides of the overflowing vessel like a used pair of pipe cleaners. Her tiny, grey eyes were as wide open as they had ever been in life, the death-mask diamonds of an emptiness and a panic without limits. Her gore-filled bathwater trickled steadily over the rim of the tub, and a small white cat licked patiently at the ever-expanding floor puddle.

I'd only intended to scratch her face!

But I couldn't stop myself from letting out an enormous purr of joy. And I felt the desk literally shudder beneath the supernatural vibration. I looked down to see a gigantic, lightning-shaped gash emerge in the surface of the painted wood. But I really don't think anyone else would have noticed.

# WATERLOO

*111* was bitter. Black with a white woman's bile.

That's what Hélène would say, nearly every morning, usually after breakfast, before bursting into a loud cackle of hysterical laughter. She'd say it again today. Pinky would glare, and stare out of the window, Mickle would push away his half-finished bowl of cornflakes with an exasperated sigh, maybe leave the kitchen altogether, Bruno would giggle softly to himself, and Dawn would smile nervously, all the while glancing anxiously down at Diamond to do the same. But Diamond didn't understand what was meant by this cryptic daily saw, nor why its by now predictable matinal utterance should elicit such astonishingly diverse reactions from the various members of the upside-down household on Mastema Drive of which he and his mother were now a provisional part. And so he would merely stare back at his mother blankly. And as he snuggled deeper and deeper into his tiny sleeping bag on the kitchen floor, hugging his tiny body for warmth, wondering if anyone would have remembered to buy a new selection of mini Kellogg's variety packets, listening to Dawn still snoring heavily (even though the first rays of the November morning light were already peeping through the windows), he remembered with a little thrill of excitement that today was his fifth birthday. He wondered if Hélène would make the funny bile comment at breakfast anyway. Suddenly he felt Sula walking boldly across his head. He cringed, quickly stiffened. The rotting meat-smell was back again. It always seemed to float in around this time of the morning. He wasn't sure if it existed in tandem with Sula, or if it lived independently, attached to the house in some bafflingly autonomous fashion. It didn't really matter, though: if he held his breath and pretended to be dead, both of them usually went away.

It was always at this moment in the day, before Dawn was awake, before Hélène and the others came traipsing into the kitchen to eat, before BoyBoy began his terrifying, sinister howling for morning release, that Diamond opened his eyes very wide in the depths of his tiny sack, and tried to make out what the various speechless creatures who lived in the dark blue fabric of the bag were trying to show him. It was most often just his father, who always looked the same: ashen-faced, demented, and baring a perfect set of huge, brown teeth. He was usually dressed, somewhat bewilderingly (and with so terrifying an effect that Diamond sometimes thought he might soil himself from the sheer horror of it all) in a suit of dried-out, dark-brown leaves, which covered his entire body, including his enormous, waggling hands. Today he was dressed in the pair of blue jeans and the red check shirt he'd always worn when they'd all still lived together in Birkenhead. He was advancing out of the sleeping bag, arm in arm with a beautiful, dark-haired woman clad only in a pale pink nightgown, a woman who looked remarkably like Hélène. Together they laughed and crept and skipped towards Diamond, arms outstretched, teasing and cajoling, imploring Diamond to let go, to take his hands away, to stop being such a silly, frightened, girly little mouse-boy. And then the wind would begin to rattle against the kitchen window, just as it started to do now, even though it was his birthday, and Diamond realised, as he always did at this point in the morning, that the woman coming towards him with his father out of the sleeping bag fabric wasn't Hélène, even if she looked just like her, but the North Wind, coming with his father to take him far away, to a country where it was impossible to tell men from wolves or trees. And the moment when the wind began to rattle the window was precisely the moment that Hélène herself, the real Hélène this time, not the woman living in his sack, would come bounding into the kitchen with BoyBoy on a lead, to prod the snoring Dawn roughly awake.

"Happy Birthday, Chicken Little!" she shouted, giving Diamond's tensed, curled-up body an unexpected, gentle kick. "Come on, Dawn, it's your only boy's special day! Let's get this party started!"

Diamond felt Dawn spring out of her own white sleeping bag like an obedient, terrified jack-in-the-box, and begin to shake her little boy with frenzied robotic determination.

"Diamond! Diamond! You must wake up! Frida wants to wish you a happy birthday!"

Diamond rapidly emerged from his sack, poked his head out of the hole like a tiny woodland coon, and opened his eyes, rubbing them to feign an only recent awakening. Hélène was standing over him and his supine, equally bag-bound mother, smiling broadly and utterly naked. She held tightly onto the lead of a quite demented BoyBoy, who was rushing to and fro, bounding as close to the kitchen sink as his lead would allow, then rushing back to sniff and snap at Dawn and Diamond, who recoiled in terror, as they always did when BoyBoy acted mad like this.

"Don't *do* that!" shouted Hélène angrily. "I've told you how much it hurts his feelings. I've told you how BoyBoy's a trauma-dog, just like you and your mother, haven't I?

You two wouldn't like it if we pulled back from *you* like that when we saw you in need, would you?"

Dawn eagerly reached out her hands to caress the slavering, rolling-eyed BoyBoy. Hélène nodded approvingly. Pinky appeared at her mother's side.

"Happy Birthday, Diamond," said Pinky.

Diamond smiled at her, and began to scramble out of the bag. BoyBoy seemed interested only in Dawn now, who clasped the dog to her skinny chest, laughing falsely as she attempted to use her sleeping bag to wipe off the copious swirls of drool without Hélène noticing.

"Take BoyBoy for his walk, Pinky," said Hélène impatiently. "He's absolutely desperate. I'm going to have my bath with Bruno. And today Diamond is going to join us!"

Diamond shot a look of panic at his mother. But Dawn seemed completely distracted by an invisible insect that was apparently crawling on her arm.

"Mammie!" he whispered, looking anxiously at Hélène and Pinky as if they were a pair of predatory leopards.

"Mammie!" he whispered again, tugging at Dawn's T-shirt.

"He doesn't want to bathe with you and Bruno," said Pinky coldly. "And can't you put some clothes on? It's freezing! And we don't want to—"

"Shut up, Pinky," said Hélène. "Diamond is just shy, that's all. It's his fifth birthday, and I think he should—"

"He doesn't *want* to!" shouted Pinky furiously.

"How do you know?" shouted back Hélène equally furiously. "You are getting far too big for your boots, chiquitita! I want to have *both* the jumblies in with me today! They would enjoy it so much. Why must you *always* try to spoil the pleasure of others? Why? Your father—"

"What *about* your father?" boomed a voice from the doorway.

Diamond breathed a sigh of relief. Even if Mickle could be ever so scary himself (those lip noises he made, then the laugh, or that vinyl recording of execution sounds), he could perhaps be relied upon, together with Pinky—perhaps—to serve as some kind of buffer against Hélène in this moment of dire emergency. When Diamond had seen the strange husband and wife have their first row, the very evening he and his mother had arrived at 111 Mastema Drive, Mickle so gruff and so black, Hélène so trilling and pretty and pale, his little-boy instinct had been to side in his heart immediately, and with all his soul, with the woman. For wasn't it always the daddy that raged and prodded and brandished and mocked, while the mammie sat still in the corner and simply wept? But as time had gone on in this peculiar new upside-down home, Diamond had begun to notice that the true violence in this house didn't actually emanate from Mickle. He growled and shouted and broke things; that much was true. And that was more, much more than Dawn had ever been able to do back in the sick little yellow house in Birkenhead from which they'd fled at the end of the summer. But somehow it was Hélène that was truly the king. It was Hélène, and now Dawn, that the old ladies in the alleys and cafés of Mameluke Bath spoke to and smiled at, just as they looked through, or away from, or too hard at Mickle; and it was Hélène (with Dawn's fulsome, nodding support) that ultimately decided how the household was to be run, whether it was a question of what time the central heating would be switched on, or where they would go to—up to the Heights or down to the Bottom—to see the fireworks on Bonfire Night.

"What about him? The father?" said Mickle again, coming into the kitchen now and staring at Hélène's exposed body in amazed disgust.

He knelt down beside Diamond's sleeping bag and gently ruffled the little boy's dark tousled hair.

"Happy birthday, little Diamond," he whispered.

Diamond noticed Pinky slip quietly from the room.

"What about the father, I said," repeated Mickle,

suddenly rising from the ground like a bullet, his voice as vicious now as it had been tender just an instant before.

There was something different about the way Mickle was talking to Hélène today that made Diamond wonder if he'd perhaps been drinking early in the morning with his friends, the blue-and-green tattooed biker-men who came round to the upside-down house one evening a week, men for whom Hélène made no attempt to cover up her contempt, mysteriously referring to them in her secret language now as *voowayoo*, then as *payday*.

"NOTHING!" shouted Hélène, throwing down BoyBoy's lead onto Dawn's lap and stomping out of the kitchen, pausing just once, halfway to the door, to turn her thwarted, beautiful head.

"You people will be the death of me."

Diamond watched in fascination as her white, fleshy bottom moved angrily away. He hadn't seen his own mammie without her clothes since he was three, the year his own daddy had banned him from going to perch on the toilet to prattle away about Danger Mouse as Dawn sat sighing and soaking and sobbing in her bath. But he didn't remember her bottom looking like that, or her dondees, for that matter. They had all seemed much smaller and thinner somehow. The strange thought struck him, as soon as Hélène was out of the kitchen, that he couldn't for the life of him, the whole time she'd been standing there naked over him and his mother, recall actually seeing her wangoo.

They sat in the kitchen all morning. Dawn appeared to have lapsed into some kind of mild catatonia, remaining slumped at the breakfast table even when Pinky had cleared away all the bowls, and Hélène and Bruno had disappeared into the living room to watch the new Betamax video of *Moominland in November*. Diamond sat by his mother's side, saying nothing. Pinky came in and out periodically, apparently very busy with some crucial project that seemed to relate to copper sulphate crystals and the tending of watercress. Mickle was nowhere to be seen.

By noon it had become clear to Diamond that nobody was going to arrive for his birthday party, despite his carefully placed invitations of the previous morning. He began to weep. From the kitchen door, Bruno stared at him, his eyes wide open with spite. Hélène's tall, slender shape, clad now in what looked like a kind of wrinkled, custard-cream spacesuit, appeared almost instantaneously by her frightening dark son's side.

"What's the matter, Diamond?" she cried. "It's your birthday!"

"It's because nobody's come!" shouted Bruno at his mother in delight.

Hélène started to laugh uncontrollably.

"Oh, Diamond!" she said in disbelief. "You didn't really believe me when I told you to put the invitations in the hollow of the tree, did you?"

Diamond nodded, looking up at his mother for encouragement. But Dawn was still staring vacantly into space.

"You really thought the woodland creatures of Mameluke Bath would get the message and come to celebrate your birthday with you!" continued Hélène, wiping tears of mirth from her eyes, and holding onto Bruno, who held his sides, a mask of exaggerated hilarity covering his tiny brown face. "Oh, silly little Diamond!"

"Silly Diamond!" repeated Bruno over and over again.

But Hélène was marching over to Dawn's seated figure now. She shook her friend violently by the shoulders. Dawn failed to respond. Hélène clapped her hands loudly several times in front of the dead woman's face. And at last they all saw Dawn give a sickened little jump back to her life.

"Come on, Dawn!" said Hélène. "Today we're going to celebrate Diamond."

Dawn and Diamond were bundled into the back of the car in no time. BoyBoy sat in the back with them, drooling quietly onto Dawn's increasingly sticky lap. Pinky sat in the front with her mother.

They'd had to leave Bruno behind at the last minute. Mickle had appeared out of nowhere, face pressed menacingly next to Hélène's window, insisting that he wanted to spend his only day off the abattoir with his only son.

"No!" Hélène had spluttered. "Absolutely not! Bruno's coming out with us."

"Yes," Pinky had agreed, glaring at Mickle. "He's coming out with us."

Mickle ignored Hélène, and instead walked all the way around the car to the passenger side. He crouched down to stare in at Pinky. His entire head poked in through her open window now, and Diamond felt quite scared, even though he was relatively safe in the back with his mother.

"What did you say?" asked Mickle incredulously.

Pinky said nothing and looked down at her hands.

Mickle gave a brief, dry little chortle of disdain. He looked over the entire assembled company now, huddled in the car in their various positions of exasperation, fear and avoidance. Eventually he cast his mocking eye on his daughter once again.

"Come on, we're going," said Hélène, starting the engine.

Mickle slammed his hand on the bonnet of the car. Everybody jumped. Hélène stopped the engine.

Mickle walked round to Pinky's window and began, giggling, to sing his song. And as he crooned to his only daughter, who squirmed and shifted on the soft leather seat, her only father's calypso curse getting louder and louder, Diamond felt sure that the sky behind Mickle was changing colour, that the grey sky was turning somehow pink and red, that the clouds, so boring and ordinary up till now, were actually, horrifically aglow. Mickle's face grew larger and larger as his funny island-song went on, his smile broader and broader, his off-white teeth larger and larger, and it felt to Diamond as though they (he and his mammie, Bruno and Hélène) had all magically disappeared, leaving Pinky and Mickle all alone, together, the two of them, trapped in this strange musical world which had suddenly sprung up to encase them, bonded in a bubble of hateful, inexplicable accusation, the obscure details of which Diamond would never fully comprehend.

> *Your cheeks may blush in rose and rouge*
> *But Pinky, Daddy knows your heart-wish!*
> *And the Negro blood in those coalition veins*
> *Will never fade to grey!*
> *Never fade to grey!*

Mickle grinned, seeming to change colour like an Ibong Adarna bird after it has tweeted its magical song, and gave a deferential bow.

"The West Indian demi-god, Lord Lewton of the Islands," he explained.

Nobody said anything. Tears rolled down Pinky's face. Hélène sighed.

Once again Dawn looked as if she were perhaps going to be sick. Diamond clung to his mother's trembling goose-flesh arm and prayed.

"You women take your trip," Mickle said eventually, his upper lip curled in the same sneering contempt. "Let this be a day for the European Female. But I'm telling you: give me my son now, or as God is my witness, I will chop each and every one of you people into a thousand tiny pieces."

Hélène hadn't bothered arguing further (even though Bruno had loudly mewled his chagrin), merely pushing her solicited son out of the car and onto the gravel with a suddenly extended arm that shot into the back and flailed there briefly like the murderous limb of a despotic zombie.

"Take the boy," she said sarcastically, turning the ignition key and pulling out of the driveway with a snort. "Show him dirty pictures if you want. Compare dick sizes, like last time. I wash my hands of it. We girls are going to have some real fun for a change."

And now they were heading for the swimming baths on the other side of the station. As they drove down the hill, Hélène laughed derisively about Mickle's silly little performance.

"Good grief, it's sad. He was listening to the same self-pitying Blackman bullshit when we first met," she sighed, shaking her head in a gesture of pity. "That whole Last Poets Black Power shebang. Really adolescent, you know: fashionable pessimism. I mean, I liked it back in the seventies, but, I mean, alright, you outgrow it. You absolutely outgrow it. Oh, well... You know what the wise ones say: *L'émotion est nègre comme la raison hellène*. And some people just can't change."

Pinky stared out the window.

At the swimming pool they watched Hélène swim her usual twenty lengths from the little café behind the glass. Nobody had thought to bring swimming costumes for Diamond or Dawn, and Pinky hated swimming. But it was pleasant enough watching Hélène thrash around among the other swimmers, and Diamond enjoyed sipping on the endless cherry cokes that the pound note Hélène had left them seemed capable of buying from the booth. There was a juke box too, in the little café, and Pinky squealed at her discovery of the swimming pool café's latest acquisition: a record called *Too-Rye-Aye*, by a band called Dexy's Midnight Runners. Again and again she spun the same track, an already interminable song that Pinky insisted was called 'I Believe in my Soul'. She mouthed the lyrics breathlessly and with such black-eyed intensity that Diamond began to feel quite afraid. Dawn sighed with obvious irritation. But she quickly returned her attention to Hélène's performance in the pool, for Hélène was keeping a close watch on her audience.

They weren't allowed to stay in the little café once Hélène had finished her lengths. Hélène had insisted

Dawn accompany her to the changing rooms for "little girl talk", and Pinky and Diamond were to wait on the benches near the exit. It wasn't going to be for long. Who knew what kind of weirdoes hung around the café, waiting for precisely this kind of situation to prey on unprotected children? Through the glass doors of the exit Diamond and Pinky could see BoyBoy thrashing madly at the windows of the car. A group of teenage boys had ambled past, casually knocking on the bonnet, driving BoyBoy wilder than ever with righteous indignation.

And now the youths swaggered into the leisure centre. Diamond tensed in terror; Pinky took him by the hand. He noticed that her hand was strangely cold and wet, but he didn't mind: he knew she'd look after him.

"Heeeeere's...PINKY!" shouted one of the boys mockingly.

Pinky glared and said nothing.

"Who's your little friend, Pinky?" asked another one. "Little Bruno turned white, is it? Where's his microphone hair?"

"*Ebony...and i-vory!*" sang the third, joyful executioner of the inevitable musical *coup de grâce*, as he rotated and gyrated his head grotesquely, keeping his eyes shut improbably tight in a ludicrous charade of blindness. Diamond (and even Dawn) had picked up on it now: the sarcastic bellowing of a line by Stevie Wonder or Michael Jackson whenever Pinky, Bruno, or (especially) Mickle was in sight, was any sniggering, have-a-go impressionist's guarantee of loudly-proclaimed hilarity for miles around.

And then Diamond felt the warm, slimy, lumpy yock running down his forehead in a steady stream, before it dripped onto his nose and into his mouth. Looking up at Pinky he saw that she only had it on her jumper.

The three boys burst into peals of convulsive laughter, moving off as one through the swinging doors that led to the changing rooms.

"Cunts," said Pinky.

Diamond said nothing, but clung tightly to Pinky's still clammy, freezing hand.

By the time Hélène and Dawn emerged from the swinging doors—Hélène emanating a rosy, healthy glow, Dawn paler and more cadaverous-looking than ever—it had begun to snow.

Diamond stared at the falling flakes through the glass entrance in dumbstruck fascination.

"Haven't you ever seen snow, Diamond?" asked Hélène incredulously.

"It never snows in Birkenhead," answered Dawn, morose. "Too much water."

"Well," said Hélène with conviction, "that settles it. I was going to take you all to the squash club, but I've changed my mind. Let's go down to the Bottom."

The Bottom's hot springs bubbled and gurgled and steamed. The snow seemed to have no effect on them, except to make them assert their essential, indefatigable heat more spectacularly and aggressively than ever.

Even though it was half-term in Mameluke Bath, the Bottom was deserted. According to Hélène, this was due to a recent spate of scare-mongering amongst the local parent population, who had become convinced that if Peter Sutcliffe ever escaped (which he was bound to, sooner or later, modern, liberal prisons being what they were), the Bottom was *precisely* the kind of place he would probably hide out.

"Let them stay away!" she cried in exasperation. "Little Englander hysterics! It just leaves all the more room for BoyBoy and us to play. Those people wouldn't know true enjoyment if it spunked in their whining, whingeing faces!"

And to be sure, the fun to be had down at the Bottom was out of this world. Diamond and Pinky raced around among the fallen leaves, hurling snowballs at one another and even at Hélène, who laughed approvingly, occasionally bending down to hurl one back at them. The springs spurted up on the slope to their right, while on their left the Mameluke glided elegantly by.

"I wish we could live on the Mameluke!" whispered Pinky to Diamond as she helped him rise from the icy ground to which he'd just come crashing, despatched by a particularly powerful flying snowball issued from a cackling Hélène. "On a barge, floating downriver to London, just you and me, and maybe Bruno, if he could be forced never to speak."

Diamond smiled shyly at Pinky as he rose out of the muddy snow. Meanwhile, BoyBoy tore from person to person like a thing possessed, yapping and leaping at the fluttering leaves as if they were canine candy. For the first time since they'd arrived in Mameluke Bath, Diamond didn't feel afraid of the dog. BoyBoy meant no harm. Even when he snapped his teeth at them in that terrifying way (as when he'd woken them up that morning), he wasn't actually trying to *bite* Diamond or his mother: it was just his way. Diamond gazed over at Dawn now. She was sitting on a rock by the springs, her head in her hands, her short mousy hair entirely covered by snow. And as he looked from his mother to the frolicking, wild-haired Hélène, he found himself wishing for the first time that he could stay with this beautiful witch-mother of Pinky and Bruno, that *she* could be his mammie (she looked more like *him* than she looked like Pinky and Bruno!), and that they could play games and be happy and carefree together forever and ever in the hills and valleys of Mameluke Bath.

"Get back down!" shouted Hélène suddenly.

Diamond was confused. Was she talking to him? She loomed above him like a giantess, almost blocking out the grey sky.

"Get back down, Diamond!" shouted Hélène again. "Get back in the mud!"

"Hélène!" yelled Pinky from behind her excited mother. "It's freezing!"

"You get down too!" screamed Hélène, beside herself

with what seemed to be an enormous joke she had just conceived. "We're going to re-create ABBA's Battle of Waterloo! Defeat at last for the arrogant French!"

"What?" snapped Pinky in irritated disbelief. "No fucking way. Dawn, stop her!"

But Dawn was still on her rock, miles away in some faraway place whose identity Diamond could but guess at. Wherever it was, he was sure it was still in England.

"Come on, Pinky," pleaded Hélène now. "Don't spoil everything. Not on Diamond's birthday. I deliberately brought my camera along in case a good opportunity like this came up."

She yanked out a hefty Polaroid from one of the many zips in her custard-cream spacesuit, and brandished it before the children triumphantly.

"Dawn! Get over here!"

Dawn leapt to attention like a fresh zombie being summoned to work by her new *houngan*. With a coy, respectful smile, she took the camera that Hélène was thrusting impatiently into her hands. And before he really knew what was happening, Diamond found himself back in the mud and snow, not just lying in it this time, but actually buried, his entire head and body submerged, with only his mouth free to breathe in the fresh air of the Bottom. He vaguely thought he could recall his mother helping Hélène to get him there, the two women eagerly digging and scooping in the earth about them, pushing him back and covering him up as if he were being tucked in by two over-zealous mammies in a bed of icy filth. Could it really have happened to Pinky too? It seemed improbable, and yet he was dimly aware of something that felt like the little girl's presence, buried in the patch of ground to his left, muttering and cursing at the playful gravediggers, and yet, for all her protestations, apparently allowing herself to be similarly entombed.

And then Hélène began to sing. Except it wasn't really singing. It was more like a terrifying, satanic yelping, just like it had been that day they'd first met, that day she'd shrieked "*MY! MY!*" down in the old silver mine. But this afternoon the chanting sounded even more powerful, as if Hélène herself had been magically transformed into a nineteenth-century army general, lashing her doomed French pop troops through their cheerfully musical extermination.

"SING!" he thought he heard her howling above them.

He also thought he could hear his mother snapping away on the camera, and wondered what BoyBoy must be doing now, all on his own, with nobody to pay attention to him.

He felt a hand roughly brush the snow away from his ears.

"SING!" Hélène yelled again, amid what sounded like a cacophony of baas and oinks and brays. "You're finally facing it! Finally facing your Waterloo!"

"*W*hat a wonderful little pair of Napoleonic foot-soldiers!" said Hélène approvingly as they headed back in the tiny car to Mastema Drive. "Especially you, Diamond!" she added. "I'd always had Bruno in mind for that particular show, but you did just as well. Show them the photos, Dawn."

Diamond's mother obediently got out the batch of Polaroid snaps she'd managed to get before BoyBoy had gone mad and bitten Diamond's exposed ear, thinking perhaps that it was a tasty morsel left by some obliging serial killer after a hard day's night in Mameluke Bath. It had only bled for a short while. It was only an ear, after all. Van Gogh cut his off, and he was a genius, laughed Hélène! Diamond looked in fascination as his mother showed him the bizarre images she'd captured. Hélène danced like a Hindu goddess, or just some kind of otherworldly pop star, crouching and flailing behind the two lumps in the snow, pulling a series of increasingly demented faces. The trees and skies of the Bottom framed her like a dream.

"I should send those into *Razzmatazz*," said Hélène proudly. "I bet ABBA would do a live interview with me and everything. I bet nobody's *ever* done anything like that for them. A serious historical tribute."

Nobody answered.

Pinky was staring out the car window again, shivering.

"The mighty Anni-Frid and friends!" chuckled Hélène happily as they pulled into the driveway. "So much more political than Blondie!"

Diamond and Pinky tramped their muddy, sodden selves through the front door and along the corridor to the bathroom, not bothering to look round to see if their mothers were following to help them. Diamond wondered if Pinky would allow him to take his bath first. What if she expected them to share? What would he say then?

But no sooner had they reached the end of the corridor than they heard a terrible shriek from upstairs. It was Hélène.

"Pinky! Get up here now!"

The two freezing children rushed up the stairs to the kitchen, where Hélène, Dawn, Sula and BoyBoy stood in horror-struck paralysis around the table, like characters from some creepy old illustration of the living statues of Narnia. And the animals really did look as if at any moment one of them would begin to speak. But of course it was Hélène who spoke. She shook the letter in Pinky's face.

"There! That's what's left of your lovely blackamoor Daddy!"

"What?" said Pinky, her teeth chattering.

"Gone! They're both gone!"

She began to wail now, lifting up an invisible skirt to her waist, holding its hem with a pair of white, clenched fists, and dancing on the spot like a demented bear.

"Give me that!" said Pinky, ignoring her mother's spectacle. She began to read in a voice oddly resembling that of the young Hayley Mills:

**M.B.**
**PROVED TOO MUCH FOR *THIS* MAN!**
**HEADING TO GEORGIA;**
**TAKING THE MIDNIGHT TRAIN.**

**GONNA FIND US A BLACKGIRL,**
**SHORT TIGHT NEGRESS CURLS**
**(NOT FOR ME BUT FOR BRUNO).**

**IT'S TOO LATE FOR PINKY:**
**DE-NATURED FROM BIRTH.**

**WE GOTTA BE BLACKMEN.**
**WE GOTTA BE PROUD.**
**(COS NIGGERS ARE <u>SCARED</u> OF**
**REVOLUTION.)**

**RESPECT**
**MICKLE X**

At several points in her reading of the letter, Pinky looked as if she was going to have to sit down and have a good, long, spiteful guffaw. But by its end, she too had begun to sob.

Diamond watched as the strange mother and daughter stood there moaning, both their faces (their features for once oddly similar) red and streaming with tears, each alone in her distress, untouched by any other human or animal in the huge cold room.

And then Pinky rushed at Hélène, arms outstretched in murderous, matricidal fury.

"You fucking witch!" she screamed, beating her icy fists against Hélène's breast. "It's your fault! Why did you do it? You're completely mad!"

"Ow!" shrieked Hélène, leaping away. "You nasty little

217

matagot! Ow! Stop that!"

She gripped the little girl's wrists tightly between blue-nailed hands, and immediately Pinky went limp, falling to the floor, sighing and trembling as if she'd just suffered a fit.

"Yes, that's right," Hélène was saying calmly now, standing over Pinky's still shivering body. "Put the blame on Mame, boys. Put the blame on Mame. Why don't you change my name to Corinne bloody Foxworth? Or maybe just plain old Joan Crawford? Oh, I'm worse than Frances Farmer's mamma, I am! I *knew* I should never let you watch these sordid Hollywood melodramas. I should have insisted we see the Bergman."

"It was *me* who wanted to see the Bergman!" screamed Pinky from the floor, but Hélène wouldn't be stopped.

"You can't separate pictures from reality, that's your trouble, Pinky," she went on. "It's him who's always hated you, you fool: your father! Not me. And now he's taken my only boy. God only knows where they've gone. You don't really believe that nonsense about the midnight train to Georgia, do you?"

She looked at Dawn for support. But Dawn had slumped onto one of the chairs at the kitchen table again, her mouth wide open in a deathless, silent scream.

"He did once tell me he had a cousin in Atlanta," continued Hélène, undeterred. "But I really don't believe he's got any family at all. His parents were from Nigeria— and their name wasn't 'Smithkin', needless to say! I sincerely hope you don't think he was actually christened 'Mickle'."

"What's his real name?" whispered Pinky from the floor.

"I think he said it was 'Mbembe'," said Hélène briskly. "Something like that. Anyway, his parents abandoned him here in England when he was a baby. To go back to Africa...and finish their PhDs! Can you believe it? Their PhDs! Nigerians: completely and utterly bonkers."

She shook her head in a kind of pity, and shuffled towards the kettle while wiping her eyes with the sleeve of her custard-cream spacesuit.

She shouted above the noise of the tap.

"So that's where he's gone: Calabarland. Oh, poor, poor Bruno. Do you even know what goes on in that part of the world, Pinky? The drownings? The metamorphoses? The ritual river-castrations?"

Pinky got up from the floor and went to sit at the table in the chair opposite Dawn. Diamond was still rooted to his spot by the door. BoyBoy came over and licked his hand. Diamond thought he heard Pinky mutter something that sounded like, "I spit on your snatch," before she folded her arms and calmly lay her head on top of them, as if in docile preparation for an enforced kindergarten siesta.

"You need to watch that temper of yours, chiquitita," said Hélène, softly stroking the boiling kettle. "It's diabolical. And I won't put up with such negativity."

The kettle began to whistle, but instead of taking it off the heat Hélène sank into the third chair at the table, next to Dawn. Sula leapt onto her mistress's lap, and Hélène began to stroke her gently.

"It's him you get that from, you know," she said loudly, over the warbling kettle. "It's him. That black rage. That anger. It's from Calabarland."

Pinky half-lifted her head from her folded arms.

"What the fuck are you talking about, Hélène?", she shouted.

"I'm talking about the Ekpe curse, you foul-mouthed little girl, that's what I'm talking about," Hélène bellowed back. "You may think that you're English just because you were born in Mameluke Bath, just because you memorised all of Marianne bloody Faithfull's lyrics by the time you were six, but it's Calabar blood you've got running through those uppity little veins of yours. Leopard blood. That's why you go wild like that. They *slit* people like you when it all gets too much. When the canaima takes you over.

Special sword and everything."

Pinky snorted, laying her head down on the table, her eyes moist and full of hate.

The kettle carried on its infernal scream.

"Oh, Pinky," sighed Hélène, standing up, throwing Sula from her lap and pushing Dawn's slumped form aside.

She tried to reach over the table to touch Pinky's quivering head.

Pinky slapped the hand away.

"Stop it! Stop the kettle making that terrible noise!"

"Oh, Pinky," screeched Hélène, ignoring her, trying to grab at her ears. "Would it kill you to stop being so angry all the time? Would it kill you maybe to thank me?"

Pinky looked as if she was about to choke. She lifted her hot red head entirely now, gripping the table with both hands and glaring into her mother's earnest face, black eyes wide with an incredulous fury. Nobody could hear what she yelled over the whistling, but the two sentences her twisted mouth spat out looked something like:

"THANK YOU? WHAT IN GOD'S NAME DO I HAVE TO THANK YOU FOR?"

"Did you hear that, Dawn?" Hélène chuckled ruefully (or so it seemed), patting Dawn's head lightly as at last she drew back from her daughter and finally made her way to the kettle.

The shrieking duly stopped.

"Did you hear that?" Hélène chuckled again from the sink. "She just asked what she has to thank me for."

Dawn twisted her head around to offer a weak smile of sympathy.

"I'll tell you what you have to thank me for, chiquitita," said Hélène, throwing two teabags into each of the three Moomin mugs she'd lined up along the sideboard. "You have to thank me for giving you life!"

Pinky didn't miss a beat. "I gave *you* life," she said.

"It's a miserable story!" said Bruno. "It begins miserably, and it ends miserablier. I think I shall cry. Sylvie, please lend me your handkerchief."

"I haven't got it with me," Sylvie whispered.

"Then I wo'n't cry," said Bruno manfully.

—**Lewis Carroll,** *Sylvie and Bruno Concluded*

# PART THREE
# THE THIRD PART
# OF THE NIGHT

# I

"Take two," said Mukelenge imperiously, staring straight at me, and proffering the open box with intent.

He'd definitely grown since I'd seen him last in Mameluke Bath. Here, in his domain at the revamped Lionheart Complex, sitting jovially astride his enormous desk, greying hair clipped conservatively short and clad in the most elegant of black-and-white pinstripe suits, he seemed almost genuinely authoritative, quasi-presidential.

They *did* look good. For a split second I considered asking if, before making my selection, I might perhaps be permitted to consult the guide to the different flavours that could usually be found on the inside lid of the second layer. But I came to my senses in a flash. I knocked the box out of his hand and onto the plush carpet at our feet. The chocolates scattered all around us.

Mukelenge looked as if he was considering whether or not to punch me in the face. But instead he hopped merrily off the desk, stepped forward, and smiled like David Dimbleby.

"Oh, Christie," he sighed, returning to the chair behind his desk, sitting down and crossing his legs. "What on earth have you done to your hair?"

I ignored him. It was so predictable that he'd pick on

that as a way to attack me, a way to make me feel ugly. How he must hate women, I shuddered to myself. How he must hate himself...

While he was busy gawking at my fresh scalp from his throne by the window, I snatched a quick look at the newspaper that lay spread out on the desk in front of him. It was the *Daily Mail*. GYPSY MOB EATS CAMERON BABY, the fascist headline shrieked.

"What's your game, Mukelenge?" I whispered from my spot by the door. "Why are you acting like Raphael Dubois's satanic slave?"

"I think you should make up your mind whether I'm Satan or slave, Christie," laughed Mukelenge, suddenly springing to his feet. "It seems difficult to be both things at once."

He reflected for a minute, gazing through the window at the steadily falling snow.

"Though it's true that I've played a lot of different parts in my time. I've had to. And it's also true that Satan was a kind of slave. I'd have thought a post-modern kind of girl like you could appreciate such paradoxes."

"Don't call me a girl," I snapped. "I'm nearly forty years old."

"I know how old you are," said Mukelenge in what sounded now like an oddly strangled Texan accent. "Your birthday isn't for a while yet, though. "Oh, Christie," he sighed again, almost plaintive, "I wish you could realise that I'm just busy surviving."

I glowered. What did this demonic quisling know about survival? It was quite clear to me by now that he certainly hadn't come out of Africa. He might even have received a public school education for all I knew.

My body felt weak with hunger. I'd barely eaten since the eighth of December, the day of my abortive seminar— and of Marianne Kollek's curious death. I'd been feeling too frightened for Damon even to touch a bowl of pasta. He wasn't returning my calls. And today was already the seventeenth. But now all I longed for was to pick up one of the delicious-looking Black Magic chocolates that still lay scattered across the carpet.

"Go on, take two; I said you could," chuckled Mukelenge, as though reading my thoughts. "They're not poisoned or anything."

"I wouldn't eat your chocolates if you were the last man on the planet," I hissed. "That's how much I hate you."

Mukelenge whistled and giggled.

"All right, Saint Joan," he said. "I might have known you'd find a way of bringing sex into it. Listen: would you like a tour of the Lionheart Complex while you're here? What did you want to talk to me about, anyway?"

"There are four wings," he explained, as we crossed the circular corridor from his sumptuous first-floor office to the mirror-pannelled lift I'd first taken back at the beginning of autumn when I'd naively believed Mukelenge to be a simple asylum seeker from the Democratic Republic of Congo. "I'm in charge of the west wing, but we have a different sonder-sultan for each of the other three wings. The others aren't as close to Raphael as I am, of course, not any of them, but they've all done something to set themselves apart from the common or garden seeker."

We entered the lift. And, just like the first time I rode here, that fateful Tuesday evening in late September, I couldn't resist taking a good, long look at my face in the mirror. But this time I rather liked what I saw. I didn't think I looked especially drawn. I thought I looked rejuvenated. I thought I looked beautiful.

"You do look lovely, Christie," said Mukelenge, meeting my eye in the glass. "I feel very proud of you. Even bald-headed as you are, I think you're possibly the prettiest Negress I've ever met."

I glared at him in the glass.

The doors opened at level four.

Immediately we were greeted by the blaring sound and vision of Aqua. The Danish pop group's obscene 'Barbie Girl' hit filled not only our ears, but also our overwhelmed eyes, thanks to the huge, MTV-beaming screens that lined the walls and ceilings of the corridor.

"This is a fairly typical floor," said Mukelenge as we stepped out into the madness. "Seekers from all over the third world and eastern Europe. None of them lined up for transfer to Mameluke Bath, though. They just get on with their business here at the Towers, and everyone's happy."

Wandering around that circular hallway I was greeted with the most sickening array of sights and sounds. They grafted themselves onto Aqua's Lene Nystrøm and her Nordic colleagues like parasitic leeches, fusing perfectly with the robotic moves and pornographic vocals to create a sonic and visual monster of wealth, style and obscene suffering. I could change into a log tomorrow, and those corrupted memories would still be flowing through my resin and bark as I sailed downriver. Women of all ages sat cross-legged all around the circumference of the hall, each of them holding a pair of trainers in her lap, which she variously sewed, washed, painted, or otherwise manipulated. Each woman wore an identical white cotton gown, practically see-through, and filthy with stains of red, brown and yellow. On the arms, legs, shoulders and necks of each of these broken, seeping female workers were strapped the predictable seven flasks of unholy, filthy, writhing lice.

Some of the women sang along to Aqua as they sewed, but mostly they just wailed, a cacophony of different languages and tones streaming from their lips and throats in an endless cry of Babylonian grief. Babies and toddlers wandered and crawled along the way. Incredibly, they too bore lice-flasks, but only one each, and were at least spared the labour of trainer fabrication. These infants cried in one enormous, uniform shriek as they gurgled and lurched from one pool of vomit, urine, blood and excrement to the next. They seemed to be searching in vain for their mothers, or anyone else who might be willing to take care of them.

"It's obviously not footwear on every floor," explained Mukelenge helpfully. "On floor five, for example, they're answering international calls for Barclays. That job requires some modicum of English, though. Each of the different tasks generally requires quite different kinds of talent and skill, so many of these children's parents are either upstairs or downstairs, performing to their various strengths."

"How do you sleep, Mukelenge?" I began. "Do you really think—"

But suddenly I noticed the shape of a child I recognised. It was little Ronette, splayed out next to the wall, at a far edge of the circle. She sat upright, but only just, her head lolling oddly on her neck. She was quietly singing in that funny Cornish accent of hers, singing about how she was a Barbie girl, in a Barbie world. A whirring camera hovered with a little cloud of flies, just above her drooping head. A pair of glittering red Nike trainers filled her tiny crotch; her entire, exposed, stone-faced Barbie-body swarmed with armies of ecstatically dancing lice.

*I* declined Mukelenge's invitation to visit floor nine, where cards for deficient iMus were apparently being cleansed and re-chipped. Instead, I marched down the stairs toward the main lobby, my eyes brimming with tears of impotence and rage. Mukelenge's voice hectored me from behind. I felt his hot, self-justifying breath slithering down my neck, and I wanted to vomit.

"Wait, Christie! Why are you being so sensitive? This is a system just like any other. These people want a roof over their heads: they have to work for it. They want a country to call home: they must honour it. It's all about the rules of hospitality, Christie! Guests are welcome in every house on earth, but nowhere do they do simply suck on the blood of their hosts and expect to be allowed to live! The system depends on everyone being prepared to give something back."

"I don't want to hear any more!" I shrieked, pushing hard against the stairway door in anticipation of my demented rush into the lobby.

But two hands grabbed my waist from behind, dragging me back into the dark stairway.

"Don't lie," whispered Mukelenge directly into my ear. For a second I swear he slipped in his hot tongue. "You want to know about Damon. Come all the way downstairs with me and I'll tell you."

He pushed me gently down the cellar stairs and into the boiler room ahead of him. The room was hot like a sauna, and smelled faintly of gas. It seemed insane that such a huge building as the Lionheart Complex should be heated from its foundations by such a dark and tiny hole. There was barely any room to move. I huddled into a corner next to the wheezing boiler and waited for Mukelenge to come closer. He would have to, if he wanted to enter the room fully, but I wasn't sure I'd be able to handle the intimacy that such proximity would entail. This man was simply the most repellent being I had ever encountered. He made me want to hurt myself.

There was a serious gas leak going on, that was for sure! If I'd had a cigarette lighter I think I would probably have been happy to explode all of us who found ourselves there that day in the Lionheart Complex —me, Mukelenge, Ronette, the lice—then and there, send us flying, sky high and in pieces, up into the grey clouds of St Pauly's Elysian Fields. But I didn't have a cigarette lighter. I was unprepared, as usual: I had no weapon, no rabbit-hole either.

He was there now, practically inside me, still smiling. Our knees practically touched.

"I know what you're up to," I said calmly. "You and Raphael Dubois. I know what you are."

"Oh, you do, do you?" Mukelenge seemed amused.

I said nothing. The truth was that I really had no idea.

"You're concerned about your friend, Damon," he said. "You have no reason to be."

"I care about Damon very much, yes," I answered hotly. "And I'm not about to let you destroy him."

"We have no intention of destroying him, Christie!" laughed Mukelenge. "No more than we want to destroy your other new friend, the little yellow Afro eunuch. Good God, why should we of all people want to destroy anyone? All I, personally, would like for Damon is that he be allowed to have what he has always so manifestly longed for."

"And what's that?" I whispered, dying to stick my fingers in my ears.

"Peace, quiet and cock," answered Mukelenge gravely. "I know these aren't things *you* want, but they're things *he* wants. Your friend...the boy that you love. When you really love someone, you have to give in to *their* desires, not your own. But you don't actually understand desire, do you, Christie? You don't actually know what desire is. Have you ever felt an uncomplicated, straightforward craving, a natural hunger for flesh and gratification that comes from somewhere deep within you, something that doesn't need to be controlled, measured, explained, justified and theorised out of existence? You can't feel your own pleasure, so you have to second-guess everybody else's. And then, when you think you've found out what it might be, you try to stamp it out of existence! You're a prude! You're castrated, Christie, just like your little yellow eunuch friend! You're jealous of Damon, you're jealous of me, you're jealous of *all* men for simply being able to access our own desire. Damon is so beautiful, so simple, so utterly *human* in a way you could never be! He has a lovely way of simply going with the flow, of just relaxing into life, rather than always tensing up to spoil it."

I hissed at Mukelenge through the dark. And for a

second I thought I saw him jump back slightly, as if genuinely afraid. Could he have seen something in my eyes that made him actually fear me?

"I'll kill you before I let you take Damon back to Mameluke Bath," I shrieked, emboldened.

"Ah, Mameluke Bath," sighed Mukelenge, moving in again. "So is *that* what all this is about? Your hatred of a harmless village?"

"It's *not* a harmless village!" I said, shaking my head furiously. "It's a realm of pure evil."

"Oh dear, Christie: 'Frances Farmer Will Have Revenge On Seattle'! You really haven't changed at all, have you? Listen, my girl: there is nothing 'pure' about Mameluke Bath, not now, not ever. Mameluke Bath is a space of radical impurity. Therein lies its greatness."

"What do you mean?" I said, intrigued, despite myself.

"Christie! I thought you were supposed to be a scholar. Well, I'm no academic, but do you really know nothing about the place of your own alleged birth?"

"What do you mean?" I said again, flummoxed at this potentially embarrassing exposure.

Mukelenge grew more and more like the Master of St Pauly with every passing minute. But I really wanted to know what he had to tell me.

Professor Mambackou cleared his throat, and began his inaugural lecture:

"We'll never know whether the Mamelukes actually made it to the Peak District. And it's true that this story, charming though it may be, does, in the final analysis, seem somewhat lacking in *vraisemblance*. But that's not really the point, is it? The legend of Mameluke Bath may be a legend without substance, a fairy tale constructed after the fact in order to explain an otherwise inexplicable moniker. There probably never was a harem there, nor the beginnings of the English sultanate system they sometimes speak of in the tourist guides. After all, how stupid would that have been, really? For Richard the Lionhearted to allow returning Crusaders to transform the name and customs of an old English village to honour the bastard-children they'd fathered with Mameluke slave girls from the East? Not only is it improbable, ludicrous, even; it would have constituted nothing less than an unthinkable act of heresy, punishable by the stake. But none of that changes the fact that the village's identity has been shaped by a name, by words, by fantastical configurations and symbols which may all be pure hokum, yes, but which have ended up providing a clear set of stories for the people there to tell themselves and their children. These stories make people feel *better* about themselves! Why can't you understand that? Why must you deny yourself and everyone else a history? Isn't this great nation just one massive cut-and-paste collage of dubious, saucy stories? Haven't the people of these islands always been a constantly swirling soup of signs, ground up together to produce a patchwork puree of multicoloured mush? But out of this mush can come great myths! What is so wrong with that, Christie? What is so wrong with mixing cultures, yes, but hanging onto the bright colours and even bolder dreams that went into that terrific soup in the first place?"

He was starting to give me a pain in the ass. He was also starting to remind me of my mother. Hadn't Hélène made similarly inane speeches about what she called the *créolité intérieure of the Norden*, first when Björk had dated trip-hopping Tricky and jungle-king Goldie in rapid succession, and, later, on the occasion of Ulrika Jonsson's heady tabloid romance with striker-turned-dogger Stan Collymore? You'd have thought Björk and Ulrika had turned black themselves, the way my mother carried on.

"There's always been a natural pull between Africa and the lands of the North," she'd squealed over her breakfast *Mirror*. "Your father and me were the proof of that. Black and yellow complement each other perfectly. You see it in nature all over the place."

I didn't bother reminding her that she hadn't turned

blonde till *after* the Mickle-Beast's departure. And it was, in any case, pointless trying to engage with any of the shit my mother spouted. Hélène's lines were endlessly adaptable because there was no integrity or substance to them in the first place. Once the string of St Pauly rasta-bus drivers she fucked her way through in the eighties and nineties gave way—first to the Master, and eventually to Jón—all that Afro-Danish honeybee talk morphed into another rhetoric altogether, a rhetoric that, on the eve of her flight to Iceland, was sounding suspiciously like the latest brand of Nordic fundamentalism. Anyone who claimed that 'identity' could determine the way you lived or dreamed or loved was bound to end up talking bollocks, no matter what angle they came at it from.

But Mukelenge and I were still together in the hot, dark boiler room. And he was still trying to devour me.

"Your own approach to mixture, Christie, seems to me to be the greyest, most joyless thing imaginable. Are you not a mixture of the most incredible histories and so-called cultures? So why is this swirling mass of origins and influences so threatening to you? Why have you worked so hard to completely forget and repress this fascinating heritage that is yours? Why have you churned it up and erased it so as to become the simultaneously boring yet psychotic cat-creature we have before us? Christie Smithkin: wild, exotic and irrational both outside and in— yet at the same time saddled with a second exterior, a second interior of the most *remarkable* blandness! Why are all four of her conflicting surfaces and planes so tediously folded, welded and looped together, all of them suffused in the most appalling frigidity? Why can't she salvage anything in the least bit sexy or solid about where she actually comes from?"

"Because she doesn't 'come' from anywhere!" I bellowed into the darkness. "Nobody does! You've just said as much yourself! Remembering the past and tapping into pleasure isn't about bearing the flag (or flags) of some hallucinated fake identity (or set of identities), whether they're 'pure' ones or 'mixed' ones, all so you can explain to stupid, prying people who you 'really' are! That's a recipe for madness and genocide! Why is that so hard for you to understand?"

"I think it's hard for *you* to understand, Christie," said Mukelenge softly, "and that's why you're as dry a creature as ever walked this earth. You have no community. You have no kin. Why is that, Christie? Why do you deny yourself those basic comforts in this cruel and lonely world? Why do you make life so hard for yourself? Listen to me. Listen to me, Christie, and don't cry. I think, in many ways, that we actually agree about the absence of true identity. But Raphael and I are merely trying to put this endlessly adaptable culture to *work*. There is nothing authentic or real about these islands. And if there ever was, it's been lost forever. Now, all that remains for the British is laughter and experiment; capital and pleasure; and the sheer joy of putting on all the lovely costumes available to us! We've got to stop being so afraid of smearing on the face paint! We've got to embrace the flux. And we have to tap into the floating vestiges of true magic that still remain. That's what our *GollHouse* at Mameluke Bath is all about: it's a place for stories, for dreams, for history, for pleasure. All the things you've denied yourself, that is, all the things you'd like to deny others, so that you can focus on the dusty articulations of God-only-knows-what. Emptiness? Abstraction? Theory?"

"All I want is clear sight and justice," I groaned. "Justice for the seekers."

"The seekers are our walking dream material. You can't have them."

"Is Damon your dream material too?" I said, holding my breath.

Mukelenge laughed.

"And we've slid back down to Damon again! That's all right, Christie. That *is* what we said we were here for, after all, isn't it? Well: strictly speaking, Damon's not a seeker. But you're right. He *is* potential dream material. And, in due course, there may well be a place for him at the *GollHouse*."

And that was when I threw myself onto my knees and I began to beg like a dog.

"Please, Mukelenge, please! All Damon needs is someone to protect him. He was never protected, not ever. He deserves to be happy, he deserves a partner, and he deserves to be alive."

"You don't know anything about what Damon desires or deserves, Christie! I've told you that!" said Mukelenge angrily. "You're so arrogant! So horribly pretentious! Damon doesn't want to live with you, no more than he really wants to be alive."

"I'll save Damon. I'll protect him from you. I'll care for him."

"And what loving, selfless care you'd give him, eh, Christie?" cackled Mukelenge now. "What a saintly mulatress you are! I've already told you this, little one: that boy just wants care from a cock."

"I'll kill you."

"You won't be able to kill anyone once you're locked up in here, Christie. And believe me, princess: you are headed straight for these enchanted towers. Your head will stay shaved, and the lice will suck you till you're white. But perhaps that's when you'll stop your whining and start to feel at home! When you're finally languishing in a real house of blood! Wouldn't that be the ultimate irony? There was no blood before, Christie, but there will be, believe me. And in blood you'll find your people."

"You're pure evil."

"We've been through this, Christie. None of us is pure. We're all mongrels."

"I've been sent here to stop you."

"In my long time drifting through this sad planet at least I've learned this much: each man is doing the very best that he can, even us nasty old vampires. You've got to let bygones be bygones. And do you know what? Whatever any of us may end up doing, it usually works out for the best. Every man has his reasons."

"Oh, please stop spouting these appalling misquotations and clichés!" I screamed. "Surely you can't really be that stupid?"

Suddenly Mukelenge looked as if he might at last be about to grow a hand of fingernail-knives to slash me with. But he didn't. He didn't try to strangle me with his regular hands either. Instead, he simply said: "Very well, Christie. I shall give you an accurate quotation. It's a quotation that your sharp little ears know only too well, the one that turned you into the angry, bitter, dried-up woman you are: a string of words which you'll never, ever shake off, in fact, no matter how much Mameluke Bath water you swill around that tiny English head of yours!"

And he began, very softly, to sing the demonic Caribbean ditty that indeed lay buried between the various layers of my flushed and reddening skin:

> *And the Negro blood in those coalition veins*
> *Will never fade to grey!*
> *Never fade to grey!*

"Remember that one, child? Of course you do! And the wonderful thing is: you won't EVER forget it, my tragic little Pinky-mule."

I collapsed onto the steaming, scalding floor, my head buried in my hands, muttering something about God.

"You conjured me, Christie!" whispered the Mickle-Beast. "With your grimoires and anger and Princess-of-Denmark theories. I am your own *Number 9 Dream*."

And, with that, my father gave me an affectionate kick in my left breast, sighed heavily, and began to climb the stairs that led back to his provisional fiefdom.

# II

"Get *out* of there, you silly little niggles!" screams Dawn, an angry blue vein throbbing in her neck.

Irena, once again, has jumped out and scared her half to death with a petulant miaow from the top shelf of the bedroom wardrobe. Dawn feels as if she's going to burst into tears at any moment. Everything's just so stressful.

"Captain Quint will be here any minute now," Dawn clarifies reproachfully.

She's decided to receive him this afternoon against her better judgment. The afternoon before Christmas Eve is normally safe—there isn't a year gone by since Damon's been working at that Black home that he hasn't been tied up there for the pre-Christmas festivities on the twenty-third. And since it's the only day of the year Captain Quint ever comes to visit, this makes for a perfect arrangement.

But this year is different.

This year Damon's gone missing.

He went to work as usual, the day before yesterday, but has simply failed to come home. Dawn's tried his mobile four times, twice last night, twice this morning, but it's going straight to message mode.

He's punishing her, but she isn't going to let him win. He's staying with Christie, isn't he? Perhaps they're even sleeping together now—what does Dawn know? She wouldn't put it past either of them. Dawn feels her stomach heave at the very idea. No, why should that boy stop her from bringing in the biggest sum they make all year by forcing her to cancel Captain Quint? What does he think pays for the turkey, the Quality Street, the Irish bloody cream? Certainly not the pittance he takes home from that disgusting West Indian sanatorium. When Dawn thinks of the sacrifices she's made—and continues to make—for Damon, sacrifices he seems to take as his God-given right...well, she feels as if she'd be capable of killing someone for the rage.

This Christie business is the final straw.

Ever since she started sniffing around, Damon's been acting funny. Critical. Finding fault, making snide little remarks, implying she's been a bad mother; it's no coincidence. It's as if the brown girl's cast some kind of spell, planted some loony tune in his head, made him start to doubt who he is, what he owes her. It's a kind of terrorism, in a way, and yet more proof (as if any were needed) that people like that just shouldn't *be* here. They only stir up trouble and bad feelings where none existed before. Where's she from, anyway? Dawn can't remember her ever having said. Dawn can't really imagine someone like that actually being from anywhere. She seems rootless somehow, anarchic, bent on pure destruction, like the London rucksack bombers, or those terrible Irachnids. Oh, why can't all those kinds of people just be rounded up and taken somewhere, gotten rid of, destroyed? They always make things so ugly, always turn innocent, light-hearted situations so unpleasant ones. Always insinuating unfair treatment, always looking for "discrimination" where there's nothing but British honesty and good humour, always demanding retractions and apologies, never showing the slightest bit of gratitude to just be allowed to live here in the first place—here, England, rather than rotting in some godforsaken warzone somewhere in Afghanistan, or having to hunt for their dinner with the lions and tigers of the African jungle. It's so arrogant, so outrageous, when you start to think about it, that someone like Dawn, who's lived and struggled in this country all her life, like her parents and grandparents before her, who's suffered so much, so much that it's truly beyond telling, should have to start explaining herself to the likes of Black Madam, who turns up in England one fine day and decides to make herself queen. What's Damon *doing* with her? Is it some way of getting back at Dawn? What's she done to him? His whole life she's never done anything that hasn't been so he can have a better chance at happiness than she had. They left Birkenhead for him. They came to St Pauly for him. And before St Pauly? It's like a black hole in her head. When she allows her mind to remember those weeks, that hell, it's as much as she can do not to just break down and die, then and there, on the spot. She suffered so much there, went through so much heartache and humiliation that it's hard to really conceive now, in their lovely home in St Pauly, that she was the same woman. All power sacrificed, given up, sucked away, like she was just, just—well, nothing. But she was desperate then. And it was all for Diamond, always for Diamond, her dear, darling little boy, the only thing she's ever really had in this lonely life. Sometimes she thinks she should write a novel about that time, about everything she suffered there, and everything she learned. Like the diary of Anne Frank, or that *Flowers in the Attic* serial, but for normal English people. Damon should learn something about how that whole terrible time felt from *her* end. Not that he even remembers the first thing about how it felt from his own end; he was far too little. He loved it so much in that strange little village, with the hot, bubbling springs and the old silver-mines and cable cars. If it had been up to her, she'd have stayed in the Wirral, found a decent feller there, an English lad, from West Kirby , perhaps; it wasn't as if there hadn't been offers. But no: she'd wanted to give the boy a fresh start, the possibility of forgetting everything that'd already happened, wipe out the filth of that queer eastern psycho who'd fathered him. But that's just it! Isn't that just it? Damon's *half* the foreign bastard! Things like that don't just evaporate with a bit of goodwill. There's a reason everyone on the whole of the bloody Attica Estate warned her about getting involved with Dragomir: they weren't just trying to interfere. They were actually looking out for her. And still, even now, she's paying the price; still, even now, she's living in a world of regret for what she did to her poor parents, who accepted that scum into their home (at least it wasn't a Black, her mam sobbed, half-laughing), accepted him, because at the end of the day they were honest, tolerant, English people who did believe in giving people a chance, who didn't judge a book by its cover, not even when the cover was as dark and perverted and ugly as that Yugoslavian werewolf she dragged home from an ill-advised night on the town in Liverpool. And Damon's half of that! You can see it in his cat-eyes, in his greasy black hair, in the way he walks, even in that disgusting filth he's involved with in his bedroom every night of the bloody week. It all comes from his father. No wonder he's teamed up with that arrogant little Christie-animal! They're the same. No, that isn't true: Damon's better than the brown girl. At least he has a *chance* of integrating, of fitting in properly, of being liked: he's a white boy, after all. And nobody need ever know anything about those years in the mental place in Laurietown, not unless he tells them about it. But no, even though he's out of there now, he has to carry on being a loner, accumulate strangeness upon strangeness, make things as difficult for them both as he can possibly manage, reject every well-meaning attempt by Dawn to make him normal; and now, to cap it all, get involved with a pretentious lesbian half-caste terrorist slag who actually believes she's better than

English people! It's all too much.

She feels the doorbell buzz through the vibrating wardrobe.

Irena races out of the bedroom with a feline squawk.

"Silly niggles," repeats Dawn crossly, as she slides on the red slippers that Captain Quint always likes so much, then rapidly checks her appearance in the full-length mirror (she's incapable of judging—how would *she* know what men like to paw?), and skips coquettishly down the staircase like a Georgian belle from generations past.

They come straight back upstairs. He doesn't want tea and crumpets. He doesn't even want to talk, as he has done the previous two years, when he's wept hot, salty pig-tears in her lap almost as soon as he's arrived, blubbering at her of the loneliness he has to endure all year with his ugly, terrible wife in Nuneaton, of her moon-faced idiocy, of how often he's prayed that he'd roll her over one morning to find she's simply died in her sleep. But today he just pushes Dawn towards her bedroom as if she's some kind of whore (or one of those doll-slaves they say they can breed in the States now), not even looking at her, just grunting that there's no time, no time, it's going to snow heavily again and he has to be back on the motorway to Birmingham before it starts. And then he's inside her, jabbing away with his little pink turkey-thing, jabbing and crying and sweating and spitting. Would Damon really be capable of this with a woman? Dawn thinks it unlikely. Not that she blames him. It *is* disgusting, and puzzling, and essentially barbaric, this thing that Captain Quint and the five other ex-army officers drive all the way from the West Midlands to St Pauly to do to her once a year (thank God they don't all want to come at Christmas). But she's clearly doing something that makes them come back for more, even if she doesn't fully understand what it is. Can it really be the way she just lies still and lets them do whatever they want? It's not very difficult. What else would she do? What else would any woman do? It doesn't bear thinking about.

That Christie's probably like some kind of monstrous filthy jungle-creature with poor Damon, of course; she's probably pinning Dawn's frightened little boy to the bedpost this very minute, as she flails and shouts and screams in Arabic. That's what those kinds of women are like. But are they even women? Shameless. Something so bitter and spiteful about them. Whenever she looks hard at one in the supermarket it strikes her that she can find absolutely nothing in common with herself marked on the features of that inscrutable, angry, brown little face. Just anger and ingratitude. The ones that are always laughing are the worst. Their laughter covers up the worst kind of horrors. And just so rude! As for the ones with the veils and hoods, it won't be long before all that'll be over. Absolute nonsense.

"Changing at Baker Street," grunts Captain Quint, turning her over, spitting on his fingers, and fiddling impatiently with her bottom.

Dawn tries to relax. She's made sure to empty herself and wash thoroughly down there. There's no excuse for filthiness, not even when this kind of thing is being demanded. She never quite understands that "Baker Street" expression (he isn't the only one to use it with her), but imagines that it's some kind of reference to something they do down in London. But why would Captain Quint refer to London? He's never lived there as far as she's aware. Who would want to live there? It looks utterly nightmarish, out of control, from the reports she watches on the television. Marina de Kant's dead right when she says London isn't really England any more, that spending just one month in the repulsive borough of Haringey (a month of being ogled, chanted at, spat on, every hour of every day, by subhuman, bearded, hook-handed zealots, and all because the lady had the temerity to show her English face on Green Lanes) was enough to show her the light and lead her, Damascus-like, to found what was fast becoming the second largest party in Britain, and the only real provider of concrete moral change. Spot on, Marina, thinks Dawn: it must have been dreadful for you down there, being pawed at every day by those bearded, chattering beasts! Mind you, what is 'really' England these days? Liverpool? Birkenhead? Certainly not St Pauly. For just a moment Dawn's mind alights again on Mameluke Bath. Is *that* still England? It certainly was back then, charming in its old-world quaintness—you'd have thought it was still in the nineteenth century, what with the woods and the tourists and the high road that followed the river. But then she remembers: no, they'd already got to Mameluke Bath, even back then, ripped its true identity away from it. By now it's probably swamped.

It's only been going on a couple of minutes, and isn't hurting a bit this time, when she feels him start to get to the place he's come to get to. He begins to move faster and faster inside her tired bottom, and for an instant the face of Dragomir flashes into her head, the way Dragomir would look at such moments, never behind her, of course, but looming above (disgusting), like some demented Turkish jackal. Does Damon realise what it means to be a mother? Does he have the slightest conception of the sacrifices you have to make just to get through a single day of this exhausting life, exhausting before you even had the child, but utterly unmanageable once it's popped out, demanding to be looked after, played with, loved. Loved! Who ever loved Dawn? Who ever played with Dawn? She doesn't remember anyone coming to ask her what *she* wanted out of life, what dreams *she* needed to pursue! No: she was left to sort things out for herself. And that's exactly what she did. Does she blame her mother for everything that went on in her childhood? Of course not! What would be the point? What would that achieve? Just blame and recrimination, all the way back to Adam and bloody Eve! A waste of time, a demonstration of bad grace, and a totally *unhelpful* way of going about things. Life's about endurance, acceptance, putting up with things, being thankful for what you've got. But Damon will never realise that. He's such a selfish boy, so consumed with his own needs, his own disgusting pleasure, a sort of——

"Who's that?" whispers Captain Quint in alarm, rapidly pulling himself out of Dawn's suddenly sore, long-suffering rear.

The voice comes again, sharper this time, more threatening.

"Mrs Bosniak! I need to talk to you!"

It's in the front garden. It isn't going away. It's never going to go away. Dawn groans, and turns over to lie on her back. Quint kneels on the bed next to her, his little thing still rigid and purple and dripping, looking like it's about to explode. Dawn wishes it would. Just explode here and now, blow them all up, drown them in a sea of bitter, sticky milk, end it all now, bury them in a mountain of white sperm and rubble, anything, anything, anything just to shut up that unforgiving little black shadow-ghoul, still out there, scratching, mewling, accusing them of all sorts in their own front garden.

# MAMMA MIA

*H*élène wept every morning for exactly thirty-three days after Mickle and Bruno's unexpected departure.

Nobody offered Bruno's now empty bed to Diamond, so he continued to sleep on the floor in his bag next to Dawn. He'd gotten used to it in any case. He was no longer woken up by Sula's needle-claws, by BoyBoy's slavering tongue, by the ghostly rotting-meat smell, or even by the North Wind screaming and rattling her rage at the kitchen window. Instead he would become aware, early in the morning, when it was still pitch-black outside on Mastema Drive, of a feminine shape sitting hunched over a cup of strong-smelling coffee, rolling cigarette after cigarette, wailing and singing to itself, sometimes in French, but mostly in English.

One morning, upon opening his eyes and gazing at the shape sitting at the table, he discovered to his amazement that not only was it already light out, sunny and bright, but that a brand new Hélène sat above him, fag in hand. She bounced around excitedly at the table, opposite a yawning, sombre Pinky. She sported a flowing mane of long, blonde, wavy hair.

The brand new Hélène smiled at Diamond, showing her polished teeth, and blowing out a mouthful of grey smoke.

"What do you think, little Diamond?" she laughed. "Do you want to take your bath with me and Bruno now?"

"What happened to your hair?" cried Diamond in wonder. "Is it a wig?"

Hélène chuckled.

"No, it's my real hair!" she replied. "Just coloured it yellow. You know what they say! Gentlemen prefer blondes! And diamonds are a girl's best friend. It was time for a change. The age of Anni-Frid is past."

"Oh, Frida, you look wonderful," said Dawn, who'd woken in her bag now too, and was rubbing her eyes in wonder. She looked at the smart black skirt-suit Hélène was wearing, and gave a theatrical little start of shock. "Wow, Frida! Are you going somewhere special?"

"Didn't you hear what I just said, Dawn? I said that the age of Anni-Frid is over. From now on you can call me Agnetha. As for your question, well, it just so happens that I am indeed going somewhere special. Today I have an interview at the University of St Pauly with a certain Dr Emmeline Thompson. Dumb blonde Hélène may just be about to bag herself a respectable secretarial position!"

Dawn clapped her hands for joy, and leapt out of her sack.

"Oh, Frida!" she cried. "That's wonderful news!"

"Agnetha, I said!" snapped Hélène, stubbing out her cigarette in the gmouth of a demon-shaped ashtray. "And I haven't got it yet. Now stop chattering at me, Dawn, and get the kids some breakfast. I need to get a move on if I'm going to make it at all. The train for St Pauly leaves Mameluke Bath in fifteen minutes."

While Hélène was at the university campus having her interview with Dr Emmeline Thompson, Diamond and his mother walked down to the high street in Mameluke Bath.

There was shopping to be done.

Pinky had stayed in her bedroom to read. She'd made it clear to everyone that she expected to start school in January, no matter what Hélène said or did.

Christmas was only ten days away, and there was no sign as yet that Hélène had any intention of doing anything special. Dawn had decided to take charge of the situation, and was going to spend the last of her savings on a big seasonal thank-you to their fairy-queen benefactress. After the New Year they would see what was to become of them. For the moment, everything was up in the air.

"If they end up moving to St Pauly, we've got to try to go with them," mused Dawn to nobody in particular, as she and Diamond hovered by the rows of frozen geese.

Diamond said nothing.

"Because I just can't cope on me own. Not with you to look after as well. What will you eat? Where will you sleep? We *need* Agnetha to look after us. We need Agnetha to be our hostess."

Diamond wondered what St Pauly would be like, and whether the houses there would be upside-down too.

"And for Agnetha to be willing to do that, to carry on being our hostess, well, we've got to be nice to her, Damon. We've got to make things easy for her. We've got to be good guests, Damon. Lad, listen to me."

Dawn turned from the freezer and looked at Diamond gravely now, as if what she was about to announce was the most important thing she'd ever had to say to her disappointing son. "Damon, lad. We've got to..."

She paused, her eyes half-closed now, as if in deep concentration, or a kind of trance, searching for the word that would suddenly make this terrible night and fog at last come clear for both of them.

"I've got it!" she suddenly whispered. "I've found the word! *Integrate.* That's the word. We've got to integrate."

She lunged triumphantly at a frozen goose near the back of the freezer and tucked it gaily under her arm.

"Come on, lad," she said, smiling vacantly. "Let's get a move on.

*H*élène returned home at half past four. Diamond, Dawn and Pinky were upstairs in the living-room with BoyBoy and Sula, all five of them glued to Hélène's latest charity-shop acquisition, a Finnish Betamax import of *The Exploits of Moominpappa*. Nobody could understand a word the melancholic hippo-creatures were saying, but it didn't really matter. There was something so moving about seeing flashbacks of Moominpappa in his youth. As they heard the key rattling in the lock downstairs, then the mad trip-trap of footsteps streaming up the stairs like an overexcited devil, all five anxious houseguests tensed in anticipation of the door being flung open, and their mistress's announcement of their fate.

"*I GOT IT!*" screamed Hélène, tears of joy running down her tired face.

Pinky ran at her mother and threw her arms around the tiny, successful waist, sobbing with sincere and positive relief. Dawn nudged Diamond (who was curled up in the corner of the sofa, as far away from BoyBoy as he could manage) that he should jump up and do the same. He hesitated: whenever he made sudden movements BoyBoy seemed to come alive and attack. He glided as elegantly as he could toward the new mother-daughter unit, and gently laid his tiny face against Hélène's thigh, turning as he did so to look for his mother's gaze of approval.

But Dawn had leapt from her place on the sofa too, and was standing at a respectful distance behind Hélène, her hands clasped in a new stance of wonder-struck rejoicing.

"Oh, Agnetha!" she said again, wiping the tears away with her grubby dress sleeve. "I'm so happy for you."

"Come here, Dawn!" said Hélène, beckoning over the two children's heads. "Come and be with us."

Dawn edged shyly towards the three figures, inserting

her head within the configuration at a convenient opening above Pinky but below Hélène. Diamond felt his mother's tear-sodden, stale-smelling arm drop, momentarily covering his face. He felt as if he might gag, but resolved with all his might that even if he did, he would hold it in.

"Come on," said Hélène at last, disentangling herself from her gaggle of groupies. "Let's go into the kitchen. I bought some special Yule Log at the market in St Pauly."

As the children tucked into their cake, and Dawn busied herself at the stove boiling milk for the hot chocolate, Hélène told them of her afternoon's adventures at the university. It had been a whole panel that had interviewed her, not just Dr Emmeline Thompson, as she'd been earlier led to believe. Emmeline was merely the young lecturer from the French Department who'd handled her application: Hélène had had to impress a whole host of other formidable characters to ensure that the job would in fact be hers.

"The dong from Human Resources was the worst," she chuckled, taking a deep drag of her cigarette. "He just kept asking me *again* and *again* and *again* what I'd been doing for the last two years, like it was some crime to not have been working or something! And when I said I didn't think my estranged husband's former profession was in any way relevant to my suitability as a university administrator, well, you should have seen his face!"

The children beamed.

"But that all worked in my favour, in the end," explained Hélène gaily. "The fact that I wouldn't let him pull that class bullshit on me. The rest of them were intellectuals, politicised people, anti-Thatcher to the core. They loved me for resisting. Especially this erotic guy from Economics, Bryan Ferry he was called. Crazy! Quite old, but erotic. Bright grey. They threw him in as a wild card. I'll fuck him if it comes to it."

Pinky began to whimper, but Dawn cut her off.

"You were right to stand up for yourself, Agnetha," she

said in her monotonous Wirral drone, pouring the hot, frothy milk into the four mugs. "People try to get away with anything. They'll walk all over you, if you let them!"

"But do you know what the best thing is?" Hélène resumed, looking only at Diamond now.

"What?" asked Dawn and Pinky in unison.

(They glared at one another in annoyance.)

"I don't feel like a wog anymore," Hélène sighed, her eyes shining with lucid, emotional sincerity. "You know, like in the song? The Stranglers, non?"

Dawn looked blank.

Pinky groaned.

"N'importe," Hélène continued. "Like a wog. That's how I've been feeling for years now. It was really starting to get me down."

Nobody responded.

But Hélène was determined to carry on explaining the nuances of her emotional recovery, undeterred by the suddenly sluggish audience.

"You know what I feel like now?"

Dawn shook her head.

Hélène began to sing in a heavy French accent. When she spoke normally, her accent was all but undetectable, a tiny, infinitesimal beauty spot of detail, a sprig of rosemary you wouldn't even notice garnishing an otherwise perfectly English roast. But, as she sang now, her French accent trickled out grotesquely: an obscene, Hercule Poirot joke of an accent, a joke of which she seemed, madly grinning as she was, in complete and utter control.

"A super trouper," she clarified eventually in her normal voice. "By ABBA. I'm Hélène Larsen. I believe in angels. I have a dream. And I finally feel like a human again."

The week leading up to Christmas Eve passed by with lightning speed. All four human members of the household felt as if they'd been offered a new chance, that great things were just around the corner, if only they could simply not mess up this time, if only they could milk the opportunities they'd been offered.

Hélène had spoken a number of times about the need to start house hunting in St Pauly in the New Year, but had remained imprecise as to whether it was a place for four or two that she had in mind. Pinky's school was arranged, in any case: there was a free school right outside the St Pauly University Campus that took pupils from seven to eighteen. Emmeline Thompson had raved to Hélène of its reputation, adding that much of its intake were offspring of the St Pauly academics themselves.

"It sounds so lovely, Pinky!" Hélène squealed, as she excitedly showed her daughter the prospectus pictures of happy-looking, ruddy-cheeked children hard at Latin and woodwork.

And Pinky herself had shivered and gulped with a palpable frisson of delight.

Diamond and Pinky sat watching ATV in the living room. It was late. Hélène and Dawn were presumably in the kitchen, talking, as was their now habitual practice at this time of the evening. BoyBoy and Sula were both fast asleep in their baskets, which had been definitively moved downstairs. *The Monster Club* had finally ended, and Pinky, deeply impressed, was raving.

"What an amazing twist!" she cried again and again. "Giving the old horror writer full membership at the monster club in the end, because 'human beings are the greatest monsters of all!' And that's so true!" she kept repeating. "It's so, so true!"

Diamond hadn't understood the 'twist' at all. Nor was it entirely clear to him why the old author would ever have agreed to accompany the vampire to a nightclub full of monsters in the first place. To be fair, the club itself hadn't been so frightening...but those three stories the vampire had told! Each one more disgusting, more genuinely repugnant than the last, each one crawling into Diamond's

251

delicate brain, slithering into the most private corners of his already ravaged heart like a foul-smelling, incurable disease. The worst of it was that he felt as though this monster-world was a place he already somehow, inexplicably recognised. For hadn't Diamond always felt a little like the sad and lonely Shadmock of the first story? Half-werewolf, half-vampire, the Shadmock lived a wretchedly isolated existence in his castle, unloved by anyone. How happy the Shadmock had been when the human girl had appeared to fall in love with him! And how terrible it had been when he realised it was only a trick, a ruse, a miserable lie for which the girl would have to pay with her ignoble, treacherous life. As for the final segment (the village of ghouls!), Diamond had thought his heart might finally stop beating in repulsion: could they actually be eating *people* in those crates? But, as with the Shadmock story, it had been the intrusion into the scenario of a half-monster (the shy and delicate Humghou: half-human, half-ghoul) that had made Diamond really sit up in wonder. How could the filmmaker possibly know of the existence of such creatures? How could anyone else know about these monstrous incarnations of excess and incompletion, these mythical halflings, oozing the same feelings of confusion and self-disgust that he, Diamond, had always oozed, without ever having had the words or pictures to say so?

"I wish *we* could join the Monster Club," said Pinky, switching off the television with a sigh, and pulling out a vinyl record from the cabinet.

They couldn't have been dancing to *Thriller* for more than a few minutes ('The Girl is Mine' had just begun, and they'd already begun to squabble about who would sing Michael and who would have to be Paul), when Hélène and Dawn came barging into the living room, nightgowns already on.

"Turn that horrible saccharine racket down!" shouted Hélène. "It's nearly midnight!"

"But it's the holidays!" protested Pinky. "And 'Thriller' is the next song!"

"No!" said Hélène. "Not on Christmas! Oh, Pinky. You know that I love you more than I love my own hair colour. But why must you be so perverse, Pinky? Why?"

"Please, Maman!" mewled Pinky, ignoring the last question. "We want to hear the Vincent Price thriller-rap! We were just watching him in *The Monster Club*!"

"All the more reason why you've had your fill of him for one night," laughed Hélène. "Come on, chiquitita. Off to bed. You too, Dawn."

Dawn immediately began to shuffle out of the room. Pinky stared at her mother.

"Well, are *you* going to bed too?" she demanded suddenly.

"Not yet," said Hélène. "I'm taking a bath."

"What, now?" Pinky was incredulous.

"Yes, now," snapped Hélène. "I don't need your permission, chiquitita."

"What about Diamond?" whispered Pinky, her brown skin suddenly strangely pale.

"He's coming in with me," said Hélène firmly.


$A$s Diamond sat shivering in the gradually filling bathtub, watching Hélène pull her nightgown over her head, he suddenly wondered in terror if she would have turned blonde all over. But no: the forest of thick curly hairs between her legs was as black as he'd always thought it would be.

And as he watched her standing there, her head entirely covered, her legs and wangoo utterly bare, there, inescapable, he thought she looked like nothing so much as a female Shadmock. He was definitely seeing it all this time, not like the morning when she'd stood over them in their bags in the kitchen, and it had been (he later reasoned) as if someone or something was shielding his eyes. He felt his heart start to beat painfully hard now, as she began to clamber over the edge of the tub to sit next to him.

He shrank away despite himself.

"Oh, you silly little jumblie," she laughed. "What do you think I'm going to do to you?"

He said nothing, and floated subtly away towards the still trickling taps. The water was warmer and deeper at that end. It was almost, he tried to tell himself, as if he was suddenly in an adventure playground (not that he'd ever been to one, but they'd passed by some swings and slides that day at the Heights of Rocamadour, and he'd often seen adverts for Alton Towers on the television).

Diamond began to splish-splash. This might be fun. It was exciting sharing Hélène's bath, wasn't it? Pinky never got to do that. And now that Bruno was gone, maybe Diamond really *had* become Hélène's special little boy, the one and only jumblie? Would he find his skin turning brown over the next few months, brown like Pinky, brown like Bruno? Maybe he wouldn't stop there: perhaps he would turn darker and darker, until he was as black as Mickle himself? Stranger things, after all, had happened to Young Diamond in the book: expansion; shrinking; flying with the North Wind through the black and starry sky.

But this wasn't a book, he knew that much. Mameluke Bath was real, and everything that had happened to his mammie and him in Mameluke Bath since that day they'd been found at the station was real—even if it sometimes *felt* like a dream. Even the miniature version of his father, quietly living and breathing in the morning-lining of Diamond's sleeping bag, all dressed up in his suit of dead brown leaves, was real; real too the terrible things Daddy said, the things he wanted, the huge silver scissors he jingled and jangled and waved.

Hélène had swum over to sit next to Diamond in his place by the tap now. And as she swung and shimmered and flecked her hair (dark again now, dark and utterly wet), she began to sing. Had she grown a fish's tail? Diamond couldn't quite see, not now that there were big, frothy bubbles in the bath. But it felt, sitting as closely as they now were, as if something might have changed down there, as though it might be scales he could feel pressing next to his own little legs, not human flesh any more.

"Lay all your love on me!" sang Hélène. "What a funny little Fernando you are!"

And that was the moment, Diamond was sure, that he suddenly noticed her dondees, how big and hard they'd suddenly become, pointing straight at him, as if they were a pair of angry missiles.

"Don't be afraid, little blood-diamond jumblie!" laughed Hélène, noticing what he was staring at with such alarm. "They're just my *mamelles*. They're good things! We need them to stay alive when we're small."

Diamond stared hard at the tap.

"Your poor mother hasn't got any, of course," she added thoughtfully.

Hélène continued excitedly explaining something about her friendly mammels and what they were for, and her heart still belonging to daddy, but Diamond couldn't be sure exactly what she was saying now. It all felt too confusing, like a sea of words he didn't understand any more. Was she even speaking English? And Bruno was in there with them too, floating around in the bubbly fluid, an angry, crying, brown water-baby. Bruno stared at him with his hard little black diamond-eyes, drilling into him like they wanted him to die, shouting at him that he should be dead, dead, dead instead of Bruno. But wasn't he really Bruno now, and wasn't Bruno in fact precisely what he, Diamond, had become?

The bathroom windows were wide open now, and the North Wind came rushing in. She whistled through the entire house, making BoyBoy howl, making Hélène's hair (blonde again now, blonde and quite fluffy and dry) whirl around like a wig of poisonous yellow candy-floss, cutting against Diamond's burning cheeks and his hot wet forehead with an icy knife as if she wanted to kill him, kill him or carry him somewhere far away, he couldn't be sure, for she had already killed Mammie, already blown the life quite out of her, and her body was floating here with him and Hélène, and Pinky watching, an empty body, eyes wide open but utterly dead, fishy, white-and-grey, like a mouse in a tank, or like one of the poor people in those terrible church crates that the village ghouls so merrily gobbled and tore at and chewed.

# IV

*I*t's late in the evening when you arrive. The village is deep in snow. The carriage you've been riding in is crammed full of young people and their obligatory Christmas rucksacks, iMus on full blast, expressions blank and unreadable as they make their way home alone for the obligatory three-day festen. They scatter and vanish as soon as the train pulls up in Mameluke Bath, darting off separately and in a multitude of directions. Some float out into the main road in front of the station car park: left, right, and straight across, up into the dark parental homes that are dotted about the hills; others march gloomily back over the train track, streaming haphazardly into the forest that lurks behind the station.

You exit the ticket-office, make your way to the gateway at front of station, and stare about you in wonder. So *this* is where you and Dawn had fled. This was your haven from scary eastern Daddy. You don't remember it. But it's dark tonight.

Raphael left extremely precise directions for you at the hotel reception. His "little grey castle" is located just five minutes from the station: directly across the main road, and up a hill road named Clairwil. It's the last house on the left before the crossroads at Delamarche and Littlejohn.

Raphael and Mikey will be expecting you.

You jog across the quiet high street and, whistling cheerfully, trip straight up into a well-lit path that is indeed clearly marked 'Clairwil'. You begin your steep ascent up the silent hill.

But you stop almost immediately to light the first of a brand-new pack of Marlboro Menthols. Having inhaled deeply, you breathe out the cloud of warm, grey lung-smoke, floating on a feeling of complete and utter relief. There's nobody else about. The snow continues to fall gently, landing on your face like benevolent flakes of cool, crisp sympathy. This feels right. You have to make a break from Dawn at some point, and it may as well be now. You'll call her on Christmas morning, let her know you're okay, you're with friends, just need some space, a bit of time to think. She'll just have to deal. Maybe she can invite Christie round for Christmas dinner? You giggle at the thought. How sad they both are! How sad and bitter and old! When will they see that life's too short for so much anger, so much aggression, and so much bile? You've learned just to get on with things, to put a brave face on it, to give strangers a smile and see if they return it. And, nine times out of ten, they do! You were wrong to quiz Dawn that night about the things Christie told you at Islands—you can see that now. But equally, the way she responded was just so vicious, so angry, and so mean! No, you can't live with that any more. Maybe you owe Christie a thank-you. At least she provoked you to get away, to grow up, to be a man. But it isn't with her that you're going to live your new life, your grown-up life. She'd only ruin it. Christie's incapable of forgiveness, of pleasure, of lightness. She lives in a dark, heavy world of vengeance and pain, and you can't deal with that, no more than you can deal with Dawn's non-stop ignorant prattle about terrorists and lesbians and Pussy bloody Riot. No, these women are incapable of pleasure; they think too much; they'll never, ever be happy. Suddenly your head's filled with Christie's wacko words from that morning at Islands, just before she insulted Mrs Lammoreaux in French, and ran out, shaking like a madwoman. *There's no life without Honour, Diamond, only living death. I'll paint our Dishonour in such bold colours, Diamond, be our wounded Honour's surgeon too.* You shudder and throw your Marlboro Menthol into the snow in front of you with a rueful sigh. Poor, poor Christie; she's completely and utterly nuts.

And there it is, on your left, just as Raphael said it would be: a tall house called *The Shallows.* It really does look like a little grey castle! You feel surprised, somehow, that there's no moat to cross before arriving at the front door, where you stand now, suddenly cold, unbearably cold, and shivering. You hesitate before ringing the bell. For a song's just begun, presumably coming from a stereo, or perhaps a television they're watching in the living room. But where is the living room? All the rooms on the ground floor appear to be dark, and the only light you can see is coming from a room upstairs, the window of which is drawn with a thin pink curtain, blowing gently in the wind.

A man's voice begins to sing. No words, just a gentle kind of animal cry. The words start up, and you begin to weep. You don't know why you're crying, except that the singing man seems to be speaking of a love so pure that it feels intolerable. The love's a supernatural force, he says, taking over his body, cleaning, purging his soul. And it's twisting your body inside out too, until there's nothing of you left, nothing but the love itself, energy pure and simple. You know the song, of course: it's 'The Power of Love' by Frankie Goes to Hollywood. But never has it made you feel so extraordinarily moved and helpless and broken.

You jump, giggle, grin.

Mikey's standing on the threshold in front of you, dressed in what looks like a butler's outfit, a glass of red wine in his hand. He stares at you quizzically.

"Well, are you coming in or not? You're letting all the heat out."

You apologise under your breath and follow Mikey sheepishly into the enormous hall.

"Upstairs," says Mikey, jogging briskly up. "Everything's upside-down in Mameluke Bath. We're just in the middle of watching one of those Christmas *Top of the Pops* retrospective things."

Raphael is splayed out on an enormous black leather sofa that seems to take up most of the room. He's wearing nothing but a pair of thick blue socks and a tiny pair of black Calvin Klein jockey shorts, and his huge, pale, freckled beanpole body seems to have taken on the dimensions of a skinny fairytale giant. The room's sweltering, and you instantly began to feel rivers of sweat running down your thighs.

"Mikey, you missed it!" yells Raphael plaintively.

"I did not," says Mikey. "I was there for the first verse. Anyway, I don't like 'The Power of Love'. It's really cheesy. Give me 'Relax' any day of the week."

"That's true," agrees Raphael. "Gosh, 'Relax'. Now that was a tune."

Mikey sits down primly on the one tiny corner of sofa that's not taken up by Raphael's weird bulk, and motions impatiently to you to take one of the chairs.

"Hello, little one," says Raphael, presumably to you, his eyes, however, tightly fixed on Andrew and George, Pepsi and Shirley, and their various festive antics. "Did you find us all right?"

"Yes, thanks," you say shyly, still standing. "Thanks for inviting me."

"Of course," says Raphael, still unable to take his eyes from the screen.

You remain rooted to the spot for a few more seconds before finally deciding that maybe it is, after all, as simple as that. They're your friends, they've invited you to their home for Christmas since you have nowhere else to go, and now you're all going to watch *Top of the Pops II* on the television together. No worry, no stress.

You make your way to the armchair next to Raphael's head, drop your rucksack by the side of the chair, and sit down gingerly. But no sooner are you seated than Raphael prods your leg.

"You haven't seen the place yet," he says. "Mikey, why don't give our guest a tour? You can start with the pool. We emptied it especially for Damon, didn't we?"

Mikey sighs heavily, and stands up again.

"Come on," he says, holding out his hand as if you're a particularly tiring and troublesome pet monkey. "Let's take a look."

You have no particular desire to go back out into the cold and snow to look at the specially emptied swimming pool, not when it's so warm in here with Raphael and the television, and the central heating on full blast. But you must be polite to your hosts.

"So, are you living here now? At *The Shallows*?" you ask as Mikey leads you through suite after suite, all so thoroughly dark that several times you trip over some unidentifiable object lying on the carpet. Every second you feel as if thousands of gleaming animal-eyes are staring out at you from hidden indoor lairs.

"What do you mean?" snaps Mikey.

You blush through the dark.

"I just wondered if you'd left the Lionheart Complex and moved in here with Raphael?"

"Left the Lionheart Complex?" snorts Mikey. "No one leaves the Lionheart Complex. The whole point of places like the Lionheart Complex is to keep seekers under strict surveillance for their first ten years in Category III. Don't you read the papers?"

"Not as much as I should," you confess, ashamed.

"Well, that's the only reason the government's still in

power, and there hasn't been a nationalist revolution," laughs Mikey. "It's a sign of goodwill to the British people. They needed reassurance. After that last lot of seekers that just went AWOL. It really shook people up."

"Right," you say.

"I mean, they can't risk another Humberside panic-pogrom now, can they?"

You don't reply. You're not altogether sure what a panic-pogrom is, and feel quite dizzy enough for one Christmas Eve, thank you very much.

At last you're moving though the huge kitchen's back doors, and out into the garden. At the bottom, Mikey tells you breathlessly, just beyond the shed, lies the empty swimming pool. It's Raphael's pride and joy, the reason why the relationship between Raphael and Mikey began to be something rather more than seeker/advocate dependency in the first place.

"He fell in love with my murals," explains Mikey, beckoning you toward the sunken space. "And in some strange way, he reminded me of my ex-wife. She managed to turn me for a while too."

"Turn you?" you ask, intrigued. He makes his life sound like *True Blood*.

Mikey hawks, spits into a patch of icy mud.

"Yes, little Damon: turn me."

> *And the law is: that when a free-born woman*
> *Of noble ancestry really chooses a slave to marry,*
> *Then he is free; and his slave chain*
> *Is hung in the church's nave. Forgiven*
> *Is all earlier guilt; the husband*
> *Of the Lady receives equal rights,*
> *The same rank and standing that she*
> *Occupies. He is free! Yes, free!*

You whistle, impressed.
"Have you ever heard of Hans Christian Andersen,

Damon?"

You think for a minute.

"'The Ugly Duckling?' I *loved* that story when I was little!"

Mikey chuckles. He stops for a moment in his tracks, turns to face you. He stares at you for the longest time. For a minute you think he's going to take your face in his hands, but he doesn't, just carries on staring and smiling.

"You haven't changed, Diamond," he suddenly says, tenderly. "You've still got that look you had when you were a child."

You giggle, embarrassed, and carry on walking. The shed isn't all that far away. You can see its dim light in the distance.

But Mikey seems rooted to the spot.

"Hans Christian Andersen didn't just write 'The Ugly Duckling', you know, Damon. He was a very prolific author. Those words I just recited are from his romantic play *Mulatten*."

"Oh, right," you say, not really understanding.

"I've been freed two times, Damon. I've been lucky enough to find my Lady twice. It doesn't matter that Raphael's a man. Who's your Lady, Damon? Have you found her yet? And how do you think she'll turn you?"

You shrug, embarrassed.

"Never mind, Damon," says Mikey now, wiping his mouth and pushing you forcefully through the grass.

You trot along like a young goat, happy to be guided by your kindly, experienced goatherd.

You're going past the shed now. You don't have time to peer through the window; Mikey keeps pushing you forward.

"Don't be so nosey, Damon! You know it's not polite."

You start to apologise, but Mikey's kicking at something on the patch of ground between your feet. Immediately the swimming pool lights up. You breathe in sharply, amazed.

"It's beautiful, Mikey!" you exclaim. "It's..."

"Come on, little duckie," says Mikey, holding out his hand. "Let's take a proper look."

As you watch Mikey jump into the empty swimming pool, the irrational thought strikes you that following him to the bottom will probably mean changing forever. Something will *shift* the moment you hop onto that wonderful black-and-white surface, like a newborn chick jumping out of its broken shell. Perhaps it's already shifted, perhaps the movement has already irreversibly begun, and now it's merely a question of allowing yourself to be gently carried by the machine's ineluctable motions.

You let yourself slide down.

Mikey pretends to swim through the pool's empty air. He's opening his eyes and mouth very wide, then closing them, blowing out his cheeks like a demented sea-monster zig-zagging around the checkered surface in his butler's uniform, his now utterly bald scalp glistens under the neon light. Mikey resembles, you think, nothing so much as a gigantic chess-piece, something like a cross between a knight and a rook. You begin to laugh gaily from your place at the pool's edge.

"You're funny! Keep doing that!"

But the creature has swum up to you now, cheeks still monstrously swelling and contracting. It's bearing you away in its huge arms, like you're a tiny morsel of undigested fish finger.

"Come and see!" babbles the creature, as if it's speaking underwater. "Come and see!"

And you feel yourself being conveyed around this new realm, wrapped tightly among the warm scales of your new friend, the Mikey-creature. And there you are, at the far wall of the empty pool, staring into the face of a painted Damon. This Damon is huge, though, clad in what looks like a golden suit of Trojan armour, muscles bulging uncontained from under shining epaulettes and tunic. He smiles as he fires his arrow, which can be seen flying through the black-and-white sky-wall (you glide along with the Mikey-creature to follow its trajectory), about to penetrate the face of a new, gigantic Christie. But this Christie is revolting, barely human and covered in what looks like a set of dark-brown, slimy scales, naked but for a pair of high-heeled leopard-skin shoes. She totters on them miserably, cowering in the certain knowledge that at any second she'll be split in two by the heroic, Cacus-slaying arrow that sails merrily towards her. Worst of all is her hair: not the tidily scraped-back black bun of iron-straightened strands that you've always known in St Pauly, but instead a disgusting, matted mess of thick, black, uncombed Rasta-snakes.

"Little Lord Christelroy by the rivers of Babylon!" titters a merry voice. "Do you like the swimming pool avatars, Damon?"

You turn with the Mikey-creature (who seems to be controlling your entire body now, gripping it tightly, as if it's no more than the disabled carcass of a dying toddler) to see Raphael standing there, smoking a pipe. He's fully clothed now, thank goodness, in a warm-looking pair of snow-proof khaki combat-trousers and a thick grey-and-white Peruvian-style hoodie, on which two hungry-looking knitted wolves are baying at the moon.

You gurgle what you hope will sound like a positive response from the back of your throat. And it's at that moment that you begin to hear the screams. They're coming from the woods. At first you think it must be cats. Irena often sounds like a human when she makes that terrible noise that indicates she wants to be fed. But as the noises become slightly louder, you start to feel sure that they contain something that sounds unmistakeably like human language. Raphael speaks against them beautifully.

"You haven't seen everything yet, little one."

You concentrate very hard, harder, perhaps, than you've ever concentrated in your life. You wrench yourself out of Mikey's grasp and stand on your feet, facing the two men on the swimming pool floor.

"You're not from the Congo, are you?" you stammer at Mikey.

Mikey and Raphael hold onto one other, tears streaming down their faces. When they finally stop laughing, Mikey begins to speak.

"Oh, Damon," he says. "You kill me. No, I'm not from the Congo. Not from either of them. Not big Congo, not little Congo. They don't let people from the Congos into this country any more. Stone-Face Ronette and her parents were the last ones. The fact that you ever actually believed that I was from 'the Congo' says more about your irredeemable stupidity than anything I would ever have thought possible. You needed me to be more foreign than I actually was. More foreign than *you*."

"What do you want?" you whisper.

The two men rock with mirth again.

"What do I want?" asks Mikey. "*Was will der Schwartz?* It's not about what I want, Damon. I'm just trying to fit in. Adapting to difficult circumstances. That's all I've ever been trying to do. From Whatstandwell to Mameluke Bath, that's all I've ever tried to do, eight days a week, come rain or come shine, a ton of stinking pig-fat on my back. And let me let you into a secret, duck: integration ain't easy when you've got skin as black as mine."

And it's true.

As you stare at Mikey now, the thought occurs to you that never in all your life have you seen skin as black as this. Apart from...

The screams are getting louder. It sounds as if they're coming from the shed *and* the forest now, from behind you as well as ahead.

"Borderline?" says Mikey spitefully, watching your eyes grow wider and wider.

He actually wants to hurt your feelings now.

"Feel like you might be losing your mind?"

"Come on, boys," says Raphael sharply. "Stay friends,

won't you? You're both just poor little Munchkins in this mixed-up valley of the dolls. Damon, do you want to see the mural at the deep end? I think it's Mukker Mikey's triumph."

You hang on to Mikey and Raphael as they march you down the checkered slope. Gliding along, you notice a massive webcam, pinned to the pool wall, just where it dips. Its electronic eye winks at you. And why not, you think? Maybe there are lubed-up blokes glued to all three of you now, as you wander across a computer screen somewhere in the middle of Afghanistan.

At last you reach the mural at the deep end. Facing you this time are five giant figures. Raphael, at the centre of the piece, is the largest of the five. Dressed entirely in leather, a peaked cap perching on his enormous head, he gazes down at the two young men who crouch at his left. These men, you realise with a jolt of comprehension (but what do you comprehend, really?), are your colleagues, the redheaded muscle-twins. Luke and Nigel wear only a simple pair of black leather underpants. Their ginger hair glows white in the monochrome logic of the mural. Looking up at Raphael with lascivious gratitude, they are primed and ready to lick at his knees. On the painted Raphael's right side sits a painted Mikey. Except it isn't just Mikey! It's Mikey and Mukelenge. The one on the left looks not unlike the man you met that first night at the Lionheart Complex. Confident and somehow ageless, he sits cross-legged on a tall, black-and-silver barstool, staring out at you with a cool, steady gaze, looking for all the world as if he has no greater concern than deciding whether or not he should wear the hood of his grey Bench hoodie over his head, or if he should leave it casually dangling. The other Mikey, the one on the right, stares across at his cucumber-twin in what seems like a crystal of wretched devotion. Barely daring to sit on his barstool, he hovers at its edge, a stinking wraith, bloodstained overalls hanging in tatters about his emaciated body. Most curiously, though, you notice that the two Mikeys seem to be connected by a thin, transparent, medical-looking tube. A miraculous conduit, it appears to be carrying a thick, yellowish fluid from the heart of the raggedy ghoul on the right to the temple of the designer-labelled nobleman on the left.

"You've got to love the doubling effect, no?" says Raphael. "This U.K. painter's got talent."

They're both right up next to you now, one on each side, leaning and breathing into you like a pair of affectionate uncles.

"Welcome to the *GollHouse*," says Mikey. "No need for preparatory stages. You'll be its seventh guest. And its first white-skinned, Gentile Goll."

You shiver. It's freezing in this disgusting, painted play-pit. You want to get back inside the house. You picture the stairs snd imagine how long they'll take to climb in your weakened state. You'd give anything to be on the upstairs sofa now, watching the rest of the nostalgic Christmas *Top of the Pops* with your mam. Who's on now? Which Christmas minstrel is playing? Slade? Kate Bush? Paul McCartney and his merry band of lukewarm Wings?

But Mikey and Raphael keep pressing closer and closer, squeezing your frail shoulders with their strong fingers, rubbing and pinching as if you're made entirely out of clay.

The shed-screams from behind and the forest-screams ahead have stopped entirely now. They've been replaced by what can only be described as an ever-growing murmur, a grey, fuzzy rumbling sound that seems to be rising from the pool itself, filling it up, swirling coldly around you on all sides.

"Relax!" croons Mikey, slipping his warm tongue into your wide-open scream.

"The power of love!" serenades Raphael, jabbing a fat finger into your terrified anus.

The lice are swimming inside you now, and you're paler than you've ever been.

They let go.

And as you realise that a dark sea of muscular arms is bearing you away from your two friends, towards the forest that lies beyond the empty swimming pool, lifting you up into the December sky like the conquered white-worm trophy of an army of pumped-up ants, you feel your thickly gelled hair beginning to come unstuck in the sheer force and spiteful new sleet of the gale, and remember, with a tired grin, that at least Hélène, the queen of these pathetic, black snow-creatures, will be on the steps of her beautiful palace in the forest, waiting for you, a handful of delicious Turkish Delight smilingly outstretched, her own mane of blonde, lacquered hair floating excitedly in the rising wind.

# V

*I*'ve often longed for an unreadable body. I sometimes think that the failure to definitively attain this has been my single greatest source of frustration. That familiar rage I've always felt surging through my bloodstream at the realisation that some vapid little bugul-noz genuinely believes that he or she has some kind of insight into me, into who I actually am, based on his or her cursory, misguided, arrogant glance at the flesh-vessel I travel around in. I've spent so many years of my life trying to confound this idiotic watcher, this pseudo-reader, this robotic dolt, just trying to make it *think*. Trying, against all the odds, to reproduce for its blank, dull, uncomprehending gaze the impossible complexity I knew I carried inside. Trying to make it obvious, clear, and on the surface, since I knew that the surface was the only level at which those appalling, cow-eyed creatures could operate. Trying to make my tangled tale apparent and understandable to these automata, these bugbears, these brainless zombies.

It was a tall order. Too tall, really. And kind of paradoxical. For what was it I really wanted? To be understood? Not to be understood? For the impossibility of ever really understanding me to be understood?

And how might that ever be achieved? Divine violence? Electro-shock treatment? Really biting satire?

A tattoo?

An amputation?

A veil?

The novelty of a bald head had worn off almost instantly.

And, as year after angry year rolled by, as I sat shaking in bitter fury under my glittering star of wormwood, it seemed to me a less and less escapable fact that only a lake of fire would do.

*I*'m not altogether sure which of the various Christmas Eve debacles eventually drove me, wild, hungry and in aching need of dialogue, to board that train on the 27th of December, the train to Mameluke Bath. It had certainly been difficult to shake off what had happened with Dawn and that disgusting old naked army captain, what they'd cornered me into having to do. There would almost certainly be consequences. I'm not sure, though, if that was truly the deciding factor for my flight from St Pauly.

But was it really Damon's disappearance? This was certainly what I told myself at the time, the excuse I used. I couldn't bear the fact that he'd abandoned me too. This was even more unendurable than the very real possibility that he might very well have entered death, or something like it, at the hands of Mukelenge and Raphael Dubois. Judd was the only one who could help me now. I didn't care if I was crossing a line. I didn't care if we weren't scheduled to start therapy up again till the 6th of January. I had to see him. I had to talk about everything that had happened.

The 11:59 to Mameluke Bath was almost empty. I imagined that the train going the other way would be the full one, the one that carried hordes of Christmassy children-pilgrims back to their adult lives in St Pauly and beyond, exhausted and depressed after the usual three-day sacrifice of choked familial horror. As we pulled into the station I gazed out at that sign, unchanged after all these years: 'For the Heights of Rocamadour'. The curious μ symbol was still up there too. Would the cable cars be open today? Would it be worth going up to have a look? I shook myself sensible. Now wasn't the moment to give in to hollow, self-indulgent nostalgia.

Judd's house was on the quiet road that led down to the Bottom. I'd always been grateful for that. If he'd lived up in the hills, anywhere near Mastema Drive (or indeed Clairwil), I think it would have been too much. We'd often discussed the benefits of the mysterious fact that Judd actually lived in Mameluke Bath—the myriad associations, transferences and projections (not to mention his constant, unchanging blackness!) that this would undoubtedly provoke in me. But I'd always felt it at the same time to be something of a fine line: just one iota of excess in the treatment, in this unholy place, might be enough to send me tipping, wild-eyed, into a Mameluke Bath psychosis from which I'd never re-emerge.

I scurried down the high street, trying not to slip on the rivers of slush at the same time as keeping my eyes open for Judd. He'd be easy to spot in this pale pink crowd of post-Christmas shopping-pigs. Presumably he *did* leave his house sometimes? Or did the good doctor perhaps have a ceaseless stream of patients, all day, every day, throughout the vacation period and up into New Year's Eve, veritable armies of panic-stricken, tragic British mulattoes, bussed in from Carlisle, Dundee, Humberside, begging and pleading and screaming to be cured?

There was nobody home. Of course he was on holiday. Why wouldn't he be? I sat on the doorstep, and wept. I should have known he'd have taken off for Trinidad or Jamaica, or whatever fucking island in the sun he originally hailed from. Wasn't that, after all, why he was the doctor, and I was the stark, raving patient? Unlike the tragic little Pinky-mule, Judd (together with his serene black wife and their two well-balanced black children, no doubt) actually had somewhere to go. I don't know how long I'd been sitting there, hunched into myself, the freezing wetness of the stone slab seeping into my pants, vaguely terrified that someone would come along, back from the Mameluke sales, and tell me to clear off, arrest me, section me, kill me. They wouldn't care that I was complex, labyrinthine, in distress. Why would they, if someone as clever as Marianne Kollek hadn't? If my own mother, who claimed to love me, didn't? They'd look at my quivering shape, and see only a wet, brown marid.

I decided to hide in the Bottom itself.

It was decades since I'd been down to the Bottom. It never occurred to me to have a wander round there after a session with Judd, or to arrive early, perhaps, and do it beforehand. I was always in a hurry, always rushing to get back to St Pauly as soon as I possibly could. The idea of night falling with me still in Mameluke Bath had always been unthinkable. But what did I have to hurry back to, now more than ever? I could live for years in the Bottom, on wild berries and crisps, and no one would ever miss me. I began to cry again as I pushed my way blindly through the frozen undergrowth, feeling my face scratched by branches and thorns that nobody in this stupid village ever thought to cut away.

I sat down in the mud and snow.

I wept.

I wept for everything that Pinky had suffered here and afterwards—not so much for its harshness (for surely others all over the world had suffered, were suffering, would suffer, even more intensely, even more invasively than poor little Pinky) as for its spectacular bad faith; its shallowness; its dull-eyed, incurious somnambulism. Perverseness in my house had been so bewilderingly vapid! Why couldn't nuanced, analytical Judd have been my father, not the Mickle-Beast, with his simplistic hatreds and smirking, liquidizing contempt? Why couldn't my parents have been people who'd protected me, respected me, people who hadn't needed to treat me as if I was some kind of risible, vaguely shit-spattered doll? Why couldn't I have had human beings for carers, not scarecrows and maniacs? Just one would have done! Just one person who gave a fuck what life might actually be like for me, who asked me, just once, what I might be feeling inside. Why had even the air outside that terrible house been so thoroughly, comprehensively toxic, so green and heavy with persecutory gas? It was as if everywhere Bruno and I turned we found only tongues and faces that confirmed our essential worthlessness, repeated the non-negotiable charge that, at bottom, we were mistakes. We'd had nobody but each other. And for each other we'd had nothing but disgust. At least Damon had escaped that terrible doubling of horror, had managed to 'pass' in some slight way. He wasn't struggling every single minute of every wretched day for recognition as a legitimate subject, as a human being. He didn't know how easy he'd had it. He could have a community if he wanted one; yes, he could. Just like that. It wasn't so straightforward for me. From the moment of my conception, I'd been *no-crowd*.

I collapsed in the mud and snow by the side of the hot spring. I pulled off both shoes, followed by my shapeless jeans. It felt as though the denim, loose-fitting though it was, was nipping and burning the flesh over which it so unglamorously hung. I ripped off my pants, pulled off my glasses, snapped them shut, and, still crying, started to run the end of the whole thing—lens and arms and hinge together—frantically up and down the lips of my suddenly tingling vulva. It was the only option I had. What was the point of weeping and wailing, of bemoaning my terrible lot, as I sat hunched, in tense, misunderstood, mute agony, trapped by campus lakesides for the rest of my life? And as I turned and pushed and wriggled there in the mud and the snow, loving the reassuring, organic insight of this pair of warm, suddenly sexual spectacles (new that week from St Pauly Specsavers), feeling the benevolence of the December rays of sunlight shining down on me here in this deserted *locus amoenus*, my brain was suddenly filled with images of all the white women I'd known and loved and wanted to be and hated, doing exactly the same thing with their cunts. Dawn; Mrs Croft; Marianne Kollek; Emmeline Thom(p)son; 'Baby' Jane Hudson; Hélène fucking Larsen: these women had *hijacked* my sex, so to speak, had filled me with a lifetime of rage over the way they used their own, the simultaneous stupidity and arrogance with which they'd invested their own pretentious vaginas! I'd quite forgotten the fact that I had my own body, my own friendly body, with whom I could have whatever kind of communion I liked. It was up to me. Not up to the Mickle-Beast, with his crass, retarded assumptions about what he'd thought 'black' people were, or could be, or should be (*why'd you marry Hélène, then?* I cackled and screamed at the wind and hot springs). Not up to Marianne Kollek, with her tired, pseudo-feminist stereotypes, which merely sealed women into the idiotic water-theories she wanted their bodies to illustrate. Fascists! No wonder the likes of Damon had gone mad, so completely and utterly dissociated from his own knob, nipples and arsehole that he had to peddle them via webcam (oh yes, I'd pried *that* one out of him on our second date) to horny bluecaps in Lille, in Split, in Istan-bloody-bull! I was fucking myself, now, at this very moment, in the mud and the snow of Mameluke Bath. It felt good, but it didn't mean anything. It wasn't some symbol or epiphany, a metaphor for finding myself or the cosmos or 'monstrous-feminine' subjectivity. It was just the right thing to do at that moment in time. Meaning came from real acts in an ethical context, from taking responsibility, from making decisions, from caring for others weaker than oneself, from—

The wind began to blow, and I finally stopped thinking. Unbelievable, that moment I finally eased into the warm mameluke bath, that moment I finally stopped thinking.

But I did feel different, and there was no getting away from that. My body had changed, something had shifted, no matter how little or how reluctantly I cared to admit it. Would I have been able to enact the atrocities I so effortlessly visited at *The Shallows* upon the perfidious winged monkey Mukelenge and his demon-keeper Raphael Dubois if I hadn't had that special time with myself (but was it still myself?) down in the Bottom? Would their dull eyes have opened so wide with terror as they saw me coming for them with claws (but was it really still me?) if I hadn't physically been a new, vengeful Christie, risen from the mud and snow and ashes? Would their flesh have torn so cleanly, so easily, if I (but what on earth was "I" now?) hadn't been literally transformed? I'd always known that inside myself I contained a roar whose capacity for apocalyptic damage, once released, could not be doubted. But until that afternoon no human had ever heard it.

I barged my way into the shed at the bottom of the garden to find it evacuated, but for Cary, whose pale and emaciated body lay lifeless on his shelf, a handful of lice hanging around it disdainfully, their minds on other matters. I had no time to weep. On leaving the shed, I wandered through the empty swimming pool, gazing at the ridiculous, insulting murals in disgusted disbelief, and happier than ever that I'd finally slain those evil fucking bastards.

The *GollHouse* was situated about a hundred metres into the wood. It was exactly as I'd dreamed it: a glittering, exotic, vaguely Ottoman-styled edifice, an appalling mixture of Black Lodge, Blue Mosque and gingerbread seraglio. The door was unlocked. I released the nine men I found in each of the pleasure-rooms in a matter of minutes. All were in a state of some severe stultification, although many of them were considerably less dopey than

I'd feared. All wore heavy golden chains, animal-masks, and different varieties of rubber and leather fetish underwear. I wished them luck and bon courage in the journey that awaited them, an English odyssey surely more terrifying for them now, in the reduced state to which they'd been brought, than any of the horrors they could possibly have been fleeing in their own lands. They didn't respond, but stared vacantly at me, eyes wide and full of panic, no doubt wondering where the next muscle-shake would be coming from. They'd probably have only a few hours before being captured anew by the government's thuggish army of chanting *tontons macoutes*. But, perhaps, in the space of those few hours, something miraculous could occur, a more definitive salvation than the one I was prepared to offer them. One by one, they lumbered off into the woods.

At last, once that pornographic palace had been emptied of its horde of demeaned and dehumanised inmates, I spied in the final chamber the pale, inert shape of the one remaining inhabitant. I crouched down, laughing, and whispered for Diamond to come to me.

They'll say that I've exaggerated the seriousness of things, the unacceptability. They'll label me insane, hysterical, claim I've milked melodrama and the fantastic in order to labour an already tired series of political points. They'll say that unless (a) my parents actually sodomised me whilst (b) schoolmates repeatedly called me a nigger-ape cooncunt, following which (c) both my arms were wrenched from their sockets and tied behind my back, as a bugul-noz dwarf tap-danced to Roy Orbison's 'In Dreams', then it really doesn't sound as if it was actually as bad as all that. They'll say I need to learn to grow up, to look on the bright side of life, to count my innumerable blessings, and for heaven's sake, to stop crying child abuse and 'racism'. It only puts people's backs up. Things are far less civilised in Africa. And it's not as if anyone ever saw any blood. And yet, what if some of those things really *did* happen (would two out of three be enough?)? And what if I find that it's actually the *other* things, the thousand and one, half-hidden, smiling sicknesses, the quotidian winks and cover-ups and betrayals, the endless moments of inexpressible, madness-inducing malaise—all the fripperies, then—that actually make my life in this country (in any country) so precarious; my relationship to my family (to any family) so unliveable? What if I don't give a shit about putting people's backs up? What if all I care about is truth and retribution? What then? Will you arrest me for posing a threat to peaceful integration?

I tried to integrate. I wasn't allowed. I lacked the secret weapons. I'm not Leona Lewis, or 'Scary' Spice, or dear Dame Kelly Holmes. And I spat out Woolf and Beauvoir. I can't sing, I can't run, and all sense of humour was scooped from my soul by the time I turned six. I take myself too seriously. I don't believe it's the thought that counts. I don't have a *dual heritage*. I have no heritage at all, no *roots*, none but those I've attempted to trace in these hideous, implacable pages. Mameluke Bath will never be mine and, even though it was all I ever wanted, I'm glad it's ultimately been denied to me. For this deprivation has given me the lucidity to hawk in its hog-face, to shit in the mouth of its fascist-liberal principles of genocide and exclusion. I'm not a woman, not a Fury, but a world.

They'll say that the character of Damon Bosniak is my own hysterical boo-hag's fabrication, that his saintly blandness is too caricatural to be believed, and that the alleged masculinity of his perspective is laughably unconvincing and accusatory. They'll say that I never really became a matagot on those two miraculous occasions, when I tore the throats first of Dawn and the naked old army captain, then of Mukelenge and Raphael Dubois. They'll say I'm just a cold-hearted killer; that bastets and matagots no longer exist. They'll say too, perhaps, that I have simply invented the story of Pinky and Diamond, and their time of brief friendship and solidarity in Mameluke Bath. They'll ridicule these flashbacks as saccharine, sentimental, Victorian-era pap. This last denial, dear reader, is one whose sheep-brained announcer I will be ready to *crush* with the sheer force of my righteous ire. This is one indignity to which I will not be prepared to submit. No man, woman or angel has the right to cast doubt on the veracity of Pinky and Diamond's unnameable kinship, or on the miracles to which it gave rise.

*I* bundled Damon into the crowded compartment, and tried hard to ignore the stares. I pushed him as best I could towards our two hastily reserved seats, in the specially-designated Quiet Section. New Year's Day was clearly a popular choice for people leaving St Pauly for London. Were they all running for dear Life as we were? Leaving behind all aspirations to the fetters and chains of 'names' and 'communities' and 'roots'? I laughed softly to myself, as I tucked Diamond safely into his seat, draping the warm blanket over his bony, shivering knees. They should be so lucky.

I'd never in all my life travelled to the English capital, and now seemed as sensible a moment as any to swap the Mameluke for the Thames. Why shouldn't I do my bit for the ethnic cleansing of London? We were leaving the Midlands at last, abandoning the shallow signs and empty significations of Mameluke Bath and its ilk for new sounds, new visions, for seven golden fat-calf years that would match the hours and times of the original Mamelukes themselves. For were we two survivors not akin to the real Mamelukes, their natural, youthful, post-modern inheritors? Soldiers out of slaves; captured as children; a veritable kaleidoscope of origins and facets: were we too not superior to the natives, and always on the move? We are the possessed, and we will swamp you. Europe is our playground: just as once were Delhi, Cairo, Baghdad. All we needed were new names, new identities.

Names and identities we could change each day, after breakfast, along with our shared bra and boxer shorts.

Damon and I sat together in stunned, contented silence. We were fused by our complicity in survival, like Dustin and Katharine, grinning sheepishly at the back of their post-Robinson bus, or Dorothy and Toto, whizzing the holy fuck out of Oz. But we wouldn't *ever* stop grinning. And we weren't ever going back to Kansas. No matter what they'd done to us, no matter what liquidized crap they'd tried to pour down our ears and into our souls, we'd survived, wide awake, our dreams and ruby slippers intact, and we weren't going to stop till we found the land where the Bong Tree grows. Though, at bottom, of course, we were no owl and pussycat, Diamond and I, not opposites at all. We were one and the same beast. Opposites were precisely what the world and its vile ideologies of separation had wanted us to think we were. And we weren't going to play that game anymore; we were through with psychotic extremes. From now on, we would live life in the folds, Diamond and I, and we'd live on in comets and stars. I would shave his head as soon as we found a hotel.

If London didn't wake Diamond up, make him speak again, crack open his half-dead eye, well, then, we'd just have to move on to Haiti. Help it rise from the rubble. Find a *houngan* there who'd show us how to reverse the spell, whirl like fucking dervishes if we had to. I was ready to do anything, make any sacrifice, anything at all to wake my sleeping toddler. What was certain now was that we were leaving Babylon for good. Like a pair of happy minstrel-demons, bearing high our bugles and maracas to celebrate our felicitous expulsion. Out of the dreaming at long last, and headlong into life.

*Que toda la vida es sueño*
*Y los sueños, sueños son!*

Did I even agree with that? It sounded beautiful, at least, profound.

"Diamond! Diamond!" I whispered. "What do you think of that?"

I repeated the Golden Age citation slowly, translated it quickly into English, and repeated my question.

"What do you think? Is life really just one long dreaming? And could a dreaming really be *just* a dreaming, and absolutely no more?"

Diamond stared blankly back at me. I sighed, and slid slowly back down into my clammy, pea-green boat-seat. The two hours trickled by without either of us really noticing them. Did we sleep? Wakefulness seemed to have taken on a permanently sleepy quality ever since Christmas. What was the point of trying to make such facile, dichotomous distinctions, in any case? They meant nothing any more.

The red turrets of Saint Pancras station at last came into view, as wonderful as I'd imagined them when, as a child, I'd first watched Jimmy Somerville and his band of untouchable pals on the ATV *Chart Show* zooming down to London, away from Scottish persecution, on the fastest train they could find, in the video for 'Smalltown Boy'. I shook Diamond by the shoulders, but he seemed to register nothing. I sighed again, my heart lurching and flitting with every second that passed between dull despair and ever-sharpening worry. Surely London would welcome us, me and my pale prince of absence, my moving Adidas rag? Surely Gog and Magog would protect us? Wasn't that the point of London's friendly daemons? To hold and to shelter people like us? I suddenly had my doubts. What would they have called Diamond in Auschwitz? The feeblest of the *Figuren*? New *Muselmann* on the block? I laughed at my own overblown ridiculousness. We *weren't* arriving at Auschwitz-Birkenau. We were arriving in London Town. The sky was glowing, the most beautiful New Year's Day sunset I'd seen in all my life; and the red turrets of Saint Pancras were like something from a fairy tale.

And Damon Bosniak may have been a rag. But at least he was a rag with potential.

You have to have a little faith in people.

"Hey, kid!" I whispered, as the train finally drew to a complete halt. "Hey, kid! You're a rag with potential!"

His eyes glittered blankly back at me. For all they knew, we might just as well have been arriving at the golden gates of a death-camp, or touching down in crumbling, downtown Port-au-Prince!

But those dead-diamond doll-eyes were beautiful, no matter what they mistakenly believed, or simply didn't see. They were sublime, they were mine, the only things that ever had been. And I knew it was true: that it was the singing stars who put it best. Sailing from their holy mouths, the words were transfigured. I'd spent my whole life lapping them up. And I'd carry on regurgitating. Wasn't that the only good milk my ears had ever had? I'd get Diamond's clogged and frozen canals to soak up the sacred songs of Mameluke if it killed me. I'd pierce through his eardrums with the sharpened end of a runcible spoon if I had to. There was no other Troy for me to burn.

"Diamond?"

Silence.

"We've beaten them, Diamond."

Nothing from the eyes...

"I'd kill a monster for you, Diamond."

Just shimmering pools of mad-making blankness...

But the strange thing was, looking into those empty, grey-green diamond-pools made me feel so unspeakably, so improbably alive.

Just like Judd said I would...

God, I wish you could have been there.

21537213R00155

Made in the USA
Charleston, SC
21 August 2013